SKELETON GOD

SKELETON GOD

ELIOT PATTISON

MINOTAUR BOOKS ❦ NEW YORK

SKELETON GOD. Copyright © 2017 by Eliot Pattison. All rights reserved. Printed in the United States of America. For information, address St. Martin's Press, 175 Fifth Avenue, New York, N.Y. 10010.

www.minotaurbooks.com

Designed by Kelly S. Too

Library of Congress Cataloging-in-Publication Data

Names: Pattison, Eliot, author.
Title: Skeleton God / Eliot Pattison.
Description: First Edition. | New York : Minotaur Books, 2017. | Series: Inspector Shan Tao Yun ; [9]
Identifiers: LCCN 2016044898| ISBN 9781250067623 (hardback) | ISBN 9781466876095 (e-book)
Subjects: LCSH: Shan, Tao Yun (Fictitious character)—Fiction. | Ex-police officers—Fiction. | Buddhist monks—Fiction. | Murder—Investigation—Fiction. | Tibet Autonomous Region (China)—Fiction. | BISAC: FICTION / Mystery & Detective / Police Procedural. | GSAFD: Mystery fiction.
Classification: LCC PS3566.A82497 S54 2017 | DDC 813/.54—dc23
LC record available at https://lccn.loc.gov/2016044898

Our books may be purchased in bulk for promotional, educational, or business use. Please contact your local bookseller or the Macmillan Corporate and Premium Sales Department at 1-800-221-7945, extension 5442, or by e-mail at MacmillanSpecialMarkets@macmillan.com.

First Edition: March 2017

10 9 8 7 6 5 4 3 2 1

*This book is dedicated to
the International Campaign for
Tibet and Tibet House.*

SKELETON GOD

CHAPTER ONE

If you would know the age of the human soul, an old lama had once told Shan Tao Yun, look to Tibet. Here at the roof of the world, where humans were so battered, where wind and hail and tyranny had pounded so many for so long, it was a miracle the human spark remained at all. As Shan gazed at the old Tibetan herder beside him, knee-deep in mud, grime covering his grizzled, weathered face, and saw the eyes shining with the joy of life, he knew that he was looking at something ancient and pure. In Tibet souls were tried, and souls were tormented, but always souls endured.

"Put your back into it, Chinese!" the old man gleefully shouted, revealing two missing teeth, then twisted the tail of the yak in front of them.

Shan leaned into the dank hair of the animal's hindquarters. With a loud bellow the huge yak strained at the mud that trapped it, then sank back.

The four Tibetans he was with were called ferals, not because the old couple, their granddaughter, and her son exhibited the wildness of their remote mountain home, but because they numbered among the few Tibetans who refused to register as citizens of the Chinese government. Their precious bull yak had become mired in the soft mud of a river crossing uncomfortably close to the township's main road, and Shan, standing up to his knees in the ooze as he pushed the gentle, massive creature, did not miss the worried glances the old Tibetans began casting down the road.

"Gyok po! Gyok po!" Trinle, the old grandfather, shouted to Lhamo, his wife, who was tying the lead rope to Shan's truck. Desperation now crept into his voice. "Hurry! Hurry!"

The young woman in the battered truck eased it into gear, tightening the rope around the animal's chest, propelling such a shower of mud onto the yak and Shan that the boy in the back of the old pickup burst into laughter. The rope tightened, the yak snorted, and Shan and Trinle strained against the hairy haunches. A single yak, provider of hair for the felt used in tents, blankets, and clothing, milk for nourishment, and dung for fuel, could mean life or death to such impoverished nomads during Tibet's harsh winters.

The yak grunted and leaned forward, the truck's wheels found traction, and with a mighty heave the animal broke free, so abruptly that Shan fell facedown into the muck. He rose to the laughter of Trinle and his great-grandson, who leapt from the truck to give an affectionate hug to the gentle beast. In a moment they were all laughing, the old woman Lhamo pointing to Shan's mud-covered face, the grandfather scooping up a mud ball and playfully throwing it at his wife. Yara, the woman at the steering wheel, leapt out, her beaded braids swinging, relief shining on her face. "Ati," she gleefully called out to her son, "when we clean him you can ride him up to the meadow by the—"

A shadow fell over her and she froze.

An army truck, its cargo bay hooded with canvas, was braking to a stop. A young Chinese officer emerged from a gray sedan behind it and studied the faded insignia on the door of the pickup. "I seek the constable of—" He hesitated, consulting a map in his hand. "—Buzhou," he finished. "We have . . ." his words drifted away as he took in the yak, now docilely grazing; the old woman, who had fearfully grabbed the boy and began pulling him toward the slope above them; then the two mud-covered figures still standing in the river. As Shan moved upstream to wash in the clear water, the officer decided to address Yara, who was still standing by the vehicle and the only one with clothes that were not filthy. "I am Lieutenant Jinhua," he announced. "Constable?"

Sensing disaster, Shan gave up trying to rinse away the mud and threw himself into the frigid water. With a shudder he stumbled across the stream to the side of Trinle, who stood still as a statue, murmuring hasty mantras.

"Yangkar," the young Tibetan woman corrected him. "The town is called Yangkar."

Shan gazed at Yara in disbelief. Had she not recognized the officer's gray uniform? Did she not know she was arguing with a knob, an officer of the dreaded Public Security Bureau, whose own patrols had replaced all the road signs with ones that displayed the new Chinese names given to the remote Tibetan towns?

"No, I am certain it is Buzhou," the officer countered, seeming oddly flustered. He turned the map toward her, then aimed a finger at the Chinese name. "Like I said. Buzhou, Lhadrung County. And my directory says you have a jail."

Yara's eyes flared. "Prisoners?" Her gaze moved toward the frightened Tibetans now visible in the rear of the truck, most wearing the fleece coats of the *dropka*, nomadic shepherds like her own family.

Strangely, the lieutenant took off his hat. "Mere detainees. They are being transported to a facility outside of Lhasa to start a better life. Too far to travel before nightfall. We just need to keep them together, under control. Accused of no crime."

"Accused of living a life too far from Beijing's grasp, you mean," Yara shot back, in the scolding tone of the schoolteacher she had been before tearing up her identification papers.

Shan urgently pushed Trinle's shoulder. The old Tibetan turned and saw that his wife and Ati were now leading the yak up the wide grassy slope, away from the road, and hurried after them. "Yara!" he called in a voice full of fear, then turned and ran up the slope. Shan headed to his truck and grabbed the dark blue tunic lying in its bed.

"I have some tea in a thermos," the Chinese lieutenant offered.

"Good," the young woman replied, gesturing toward the prisoners, who crowded at the back of the truck, looking out with fearful expressions. "They look thirsty."

To Shan's astonishment the officer grinned. "My name is Jinhua," he declared again. Perhaps thirty years of age, he had a slight build and an almost boyish face, except for its restless, calculating eyes.

Shan slipped on the tunic, straightening it over his still-dripping back as he stepped beside Yara. She turned, saw her retreating family, and slowly backed away, the officer's eyes still fixed on her. For the first time, it occurred to Shan that the slender Yara, with her high cheekbones and deep, brilliant eyes, was a strikingly handsome woman. He stepped closer, blocking the officer's gaze.

The lieutenant's disappointment was obvious. "You?" He frowned. "But you were in the mud."

"The mud was where I was needed." Shan, only three months in office, had dreaded contact with Public Security, had even begun to hope that the knobs didn't even know about his remote hamlet high in the mountains. "How may the constable's office serve you?"

"We will never make it to Lhasa by dark. The roads are too dangerous at night, so we would have to make a camp in the wind and the cold. But then I saw Buzhou on the map. When I stopped at the turnoff for the town to ask some farmer where I could find the constable, he said you were working down the road."

As Shan opened the door of his truck, he glanced back at Yara, who was running toward her family now. On the long grassy slope beyond her, a rider on horseback was galloping toward the shepherd family. He pointed to his truck to keep Jinhua's attention away from the ferals, who otherwise might end up with the prisoners.

"I have two cells designed to hold two prisoners each. You have at least a dozen."

The lieutenant shrugged. "Through mutual sacrifice our nation will reign supreme," he replied, reciting the slogan from Beijing's latest propaganda poster.

Shan pulled his truck onto the macadam, and Lieutenant Jinhua tossed his keys to one of the soldiers and climbed into the cab with Shan. As they threaded their way up the long switchbacks that led to Yangkar's high valley, the knob looked out the window with the gaze of the inquisitive tourist. After a few minutes he lifted the little Buddha carved of stone that sat on the dashboard.

"Look at the belly on him!" the young lieutenant cracked. "What a curious thing. If they're going to make an image of their god, why make him so fat and ugly?" he asked as he tossed it from hand to hand. Shan considered snatching it from him. The little figure was a gift from an old hermit, and it was centuries old. "He looks like some lazy old gardener who just woke from a nap."

Shan, not sure if he was being baited, stared straight ahead. "What a curious thing," he repeated. "A solitary Public Security officer with half a dozen army soldiers." Jinhua held the Buddha still and stared at Shan. "A quarter-hour north of here," Shan said, "you passed the road that would have taken you through the pass to the Lhasa highway. If traffic was light you could have made it to Lhasa by dusk. Even if you hadn't, there would have been much larger towns, larger jails, and plenty of guesthouses."

"Blocked by a rockslide," Jinhua explained, then pointed as they crested the ridge and the ragged little town came into sight at the center of the valley, a pocket of run-down structures framed by barley fields and pastures. "A junkyard at the end of the world. Comrade, you must have really pissed someone off."

Shan slowed to pass a donkey cart full of yak dung. "Not the end of the world, the top of the world. A paradise of four hundred thirty-two souls. We are so high and remote we escape the shadow of the rest of the world."

"Four hundred thirty-two Chinese grateful that Beijing is so far away," Jinhua said, as if correcting Shan.

"More precisely," Shan rejoined, "four hundred nine Tibetans and twenty-three Chinese, most of who would gladly leave tomorrow if they could. But they took money from the government to be pioneer settlers, and no one can afford to buy out their contracts." As the knob officer, seemingly not listening, leaned out of the window to watch mounted Tibetans in broad-rimmed hats herding sheep toward the summer pastures, Shan reached under the steering wheel and switched on the flashing light on top of his truck. "Cowboys in China," the young lieutenant mused. "Who knew? What other miracles do you hide in your township, constable?"

"Life here is just one miracle after another," Shan said. "You just need to know how to look for them." He glanced uneasily at Jinhua, who had pulled a map from the dashboard and was studying it. Shan knew from painful experience never to trust a knob who behaved so casually. Even a junior lieutenant had the authority to throw someone in jail for a year on his signature alone.

He slowed as they reached the outskirts of the town, crawling past the large official sign announcing BUZHOU in Chinese characters, with a hand-painted one, in the only language most of the inhabitants could read, fixed below it, declaring BLESSED YANGKAR. Half a dozen Tibetans on bicycles, having seen Shan's warning light, rode hurriedly by in the opposite direction. The mechanic in the town's only garage paused in repairing a tire to stare at their little convoy. Ahead of them in the small town square a young nun halted her work on a little onion-shaped structure with a steeple on it, a small *chorten* shrine, and rushed to the curb, trying to see inside the truck as it slowed.

Passersby stared silently. All activity in the town had stopped. Suddenly a gunshot broke the silence. Frightened onlookers darted into buildings and alleyways. As Shan slammed on his brakes and leapt out, the soldiers erupted from the prison truck, cocking their weapons and aiming them toward the few remaining townspeople before looking toward their sergeant, who had darted twenty feet away from the truck before stopping.

"Someone threw in a device!" he shouted at Shan. "Lit the fuse and ran!" He waved his still-smoking pistol toward the Tibetans on the street. The sergeant was an older career soldier, probably well aware that Tibetans in the remote mountains had once waged a dogged resistance against the Chinese. "Don't go up there, you fool!" he warned as Shan climbed in among the prisoners. He watched as an old woman walked along the two benches, pausing by each of the occupants to touch them with smoke from the bundle of incense sticks she now held in her hand.

"Grandmother," Shan patiently asked, "when you are done may I have that?"

The old woman replied with an uncertain smile. When she handed the bundle to Shan, he cupped the fragrant smoke over his own face before turning. Jinhua stood at the tailgate, studying Shan with an intense curiosity. "Not a device," Shan called out to the nervous soldiers. "Just some incense, to summon protective spirits."

He tossed the bundle to the sergeant, who let it drop to his feet, then angrily stomped it with his boot.

Shan guided the truck to the front of the one-story stucco building facing the center of the town square. A small cordon of residents had already assembled by the station's door. He recognized Mrs. Weng, proprietress of the town's largest store, Mr. Hui, the town dentist, and Mr. Wu, the town clerk. They had anointed themselves as the Committee of Leading Citizens, an adjunct of the township Party apparatus. All were Chinese.

Shan ignored their approving nods as he led Jinhua inside. He passed through a sparse outer office into the darkened room beyond, where two cell doors hung open. Switching on the row of naked light bulbs that ran down the center of the ceiling, he lifted a uniform cap from the table and tossed it at the figure lying on one of the cell cots.

"Customers!" he called out. "We'll need more blankets, more spoons, more bowls. More of everything. Bring some pallets from the guesthouse."

The middle-aged Tibetan on the cot rolled over, rubbing his eyes, then shot up as he saw the soldiers behind Shan. He grabbed the tunic stuffed between bars of the cell and hastily pulled it on.

"My deputy," Shan explained. "Officer Jengtse."

Jengtse straightened and awkwardly saluted as Lieutenant Jinhua approached, followed by the army sergeant, then flushed as the sergeant jeered at him and gestured to the prisoners. "Six to a cell," the sergeant ordered the deputy.

Jengtse, who had served twenty years in the People's Liberation Army, mostly along the Russian border, dutifully hastened to retrieve the keys from the table.

Jinhua lowered himself into the chair at Shan's desk and watched with an amused expression as the office, crowded with prisoners and soldiers, gradually assumed a degree of order, with the frightened Tibetans being herded single file into the cells and the soldiers bringing their packs from the truck into the office.

"There is a government guesthouse behind us," Shan explained to the sergeant as he realized the men were intending to sleep in the station. "More than enough beds." He saw the skepticism on the man's hard face. "The cells will be secured. The prisoners are in our care for the night."

Jengtse locked the cells and turned to Shan with a despairing expression. They had both seen the tags pinned to the clothing of each prisoner, even the two children. *Yi, er, san, si.* One, two, three, four, and on up to twelve. The prisoners had lost their names. They were part of the wave of displaced persons coming off the high plains, where army patrols had been sweeping, scouring away the nomadic families who had lived there for centuries. When they arrived at the internment camp they would be given new, Chinese names. After a few weeks of reeducation focused on the ever-correct ways of the motherland, the adults would be sent to factories in distant provinces and the children to boarding schools, not to see their parents for years, if ever.

The small door at the back of the cell block suddenly opened. "Shan! Constable Shan!" called the woman even before she had stepped inside. "The dead are rising!" It was Yara, whom Shan had last seen escaping toward the mountains. Tears stained her dusty face. "You must—" Her words choked away as she saw the soldiers. She looked at the prisoners and visibly shuddered. Her eyes welled with moisture and she backed away, leaving the door open as she fled. How could she have made it to town so quickly, Shan asked himself, then remembered the rider who had been galloping toward her.

A surprised murmur left Jengtse's throat, and he bent to pick up something Yara had dropped. He studied it for a moment, then looked up at Shan in alarm, glanced at Jinhua, and stuffed it in his pocket.

Shan retrieved a key ring from his desk and tossed it to the army sergeant. "The long stucco building along the wall of the rear compound. Washroom toward the rear, bedding in the closet just before the washroom. Our guesthouse."

The sergeant eyed the keys uncertainly. "The prisoners are in my charge."

"The prisoners became my charge when you put them in my cells," Shan rejoined. "You can see they are going nowhere. If you prefer to take them back to your truck and make a camp in the mountains, feel free to do so. But you'd better hurry; you'll need at least two hours."

"Two hours?" the sergeant asked.

"That's how long it will take you to find enough yak dung to keep a fire going during the night. Not much firewood at these altitudes."

The sergeant gave a discontented grunt, then studied his six weary men. "Bedding in the closet," he repeated. As he hurried his men outside, Shan turned to Jinhua, still sitting at his desk.

The knob stared at Shan for a moment, then shrugged. "Perhaps there's something that resembles a café in your metropolis?" the lieutenant asked.

"A noodle shop. At the east end of the square."

"Fried rice and chicken?"

"Rice comes in once a month, and usually it is gone after the first week. You can cut your noodles into tiny pieces if you are that homesick." Shan knew better than to goad the young knob, but he resented that a Public Security officer was sitting in his chair, resented that the arrogant young knob had just derailed his efforts to build trust with the local Tibetans, and especially resented being forced to help with the resettlement campaign that was bringing torment to so many Tibetan families. "There's a small separate apartment at the back of the guesthouse. If you hurry you might claim it before the sergeant does."

Jinhua's cool grin sent a shiver down Shan's spine. The knob bowed his head as if surrendering, then rose and stepped out to the street. Shan returned to the cell room and found Jengtse staring at the object Yara had dropped. "Old beads," the deputy observed. It was a *mala*, a Buddhist rosary. "Bone. Made of bright white bone," he added pointedly and dropped them on the table in front of Shan.

But the beads weren't white; they were so pink Shan at first thought they were made of coral. As he lifted them from the desk his heart went cold. The bone beads, each intricately carved into the sacred image of the eternal knot, were sticky. They were covered in blood.

"Nyima!" a woman gasped from the nearest cell. She was staring at the beads.

"Nyima?" Shan asked his deputy.

"The old hermit nun who comes to town on market days," Jengtse explained. "She spins an old prayer wheel covered with dancing leopards and promises a thousand turns for you if you drop a coin in her basket."

"Where does she live?" Shan asked.

"I don't know exactly. In the mountains north of here. Some call her a witch because of all the old rituals she performs. The old ones still buy curses and charms from her."

The mountains to the north. She could be anywhere in a hundred square miles.

Shan realized that Jengtse was staring over his shoulder. He turned to see the woman who had spoken the nun's name reaching out through the bars. She was staring at the bloody rosary.

"Where did these prisoners come from?" Shan asked his deputy.

Jengtse shrugged. "The sergeant just said the mountains to the north, from the summer pastures, I guess. Easy to round them up there since they have to go through those high passes. Like funnels, just deploy squads at the mouth of the pass and you've got them."

The woman, in her late thirties, looked up at Shan in silent pleading. Her eyes, welling with tears, were of an unusual green color. "Do you know the nun?" he asked as he approached.

"Nyima," the prisoner said again, and snatched the beads out of his hand.

"Where is she?" Shan asked, but the woman seemed not to hear him. "Nyima," she repeated in an anguished tone, then retreated to one of the cots and sat with the beads stretched between her fingers. When he asked again, more loudly, she sobbed and buried her head in her hands.

"Find that woman who left them," he said over his shoulder to Jengtse. "Her name is Yara."

But his deputy was not there. Jengtse stood at the outer door, trying to push someone away. "He's Chinese, you fool!" Jengtse said in an urgent whisper. "Meet me in the stable."

Shan pushed down his anger and stepped past his deputy. Rikyu, the young nun who maintained the town shrines, was standing outside. She quickly buried her hand in the folds of her robe. Shan just as quickly pulled her arm away. Rikyu was holding a small, once elegant prayer wheel, now smashed nearly flat. Its copper surface was embossed with silver images that appeared to have been dancing leopards.

"Where?" Shan demanded. "Where is Nyima?"

"I don't know," the nun said. "She sleeps in a cave up past the old salt shrines."

"Can you get me there?"

Rikyu gave a nervous nod. "At the end of the road they use when they truck sheep out of the mountains, just before the pass to the Lhasa highway."

"Show me," Shan said, pushing the nun inside and pointing to a map pinned to the wall. Rikyu indicated a circuitous dotted line that ran from the highway north of town and ended at the base of a steep ridge. "She probably just fell. I will go see her. Not for you to worry about," she said, meaning it was Tibetan business, for Tibetans to worry about.

He extended his hand for the ruined prayer wheel, then pointed to a jagged pattern in the soft metal. "A heavy boot did that. Not the shoe of a nun."

Rikyu kept her eyes lowered. Neither the nun nor his deputy trusted him. They knew that if an unfamiliar Chinese constable showed up by himself in the mountains, the few Tibetans who lived there would likely scatter like deer. "Go find Mrs. Weng," he instructed Jengtse. "Tell her the Committee of Leading Citizens has been called to duty."

Jengtse grimaced but obeyed, muttering his disapproval as he left the building. Rikyu hesitated a moment, as if seeing something new in Shan's eyes. During Shan's first weeks in office the nun had kept her Bureau of Religious Affairs registration, her license to wear a robe, pinned conspicuously to her clothing, and behaved like a submissive servant whenever Shan approached. Shan had finally taken her into the office and made a duplicate of the license on their creaky old copier, then told the nun he would just keep it on file so the nun would not need to display her papers. Afterward she had seemed even more skittish, and Shan had realized Rikyu had taken his action as a threat.

Ten minutes later, Mrs. Weng had assembled the officers of the committee in the station. Shan shuddered at their mounting enthusiasm as he described what he had in mind. "A full bowl of noodles to every prisoner, and let each, one at a time, use the washroom before eating." He pointed to the keys hanging on a peg by his desk. "No one else in the building while I am gone. And no, Mr. Hui," he said as he saw the dentist's jealous glance toward the weapons locker. "No firearms. No one in the cells committed an act of violence. A bowl of noodles for each prisoner," he repeated to Mr. Wu, the town clerk, whom he took to be the most dutiful of the three. "And tea for all.

My surveillance cameras will tell me if you fail to comply." The committee members stiffened and nodded their understanding. Mr. Wu cast a furtive glance toward the ceiling as if looking for cameras, then offered a clumsy salute.

"Bring a medical kit," Shan said to Jengtse, "and some blankets."

As they left town, Jengtse carefully arranged the little Buddha on the dashboard so the god was looking ahead of them. "We don't have cameras," he observed.

"So add it to the next requisition list. And fingerprint kits."

"You should be more realistic," his deputy said. "Maybe pencils and paper, but anything more and they will just—" His voice trailed away as he pointed toward the slope above town. Shan pulled over and focused his binoculars on the pass. Figures on horseback were hurrying up the long slope from below, converging on the pass that led into the high ranges. Shan looked through the back window. Rikyu, sitting on a bundle of blankets in the bed of the pickup, was pointedly ignoring Shan as she pressed her *mala* to her lips. She was frightened. *The dead are rising,* Yara had said.

The old truck wheezed and groaned as it climbed the overgrown road indicated by Rikyu. It was a region Shan had not yet explored, the far northwestern tip of Lhadrung County, known for its high, inhospitable ridges that rose up like fortress walls to isolate the lands above. The road faded into grass-lined ruts, then abruptly ended at a broad clearing surrounded by rock outcroppings.

"She lives in a cavern on the first flat, by the ice caves," Rikyu explained as she climbed out. Shan followed her arm toward two flats above them, separated by a steep embankment. He made out the heads of several people who were watching them from the second, higher, flat. Rikyu cinched up her loose robe and began running up the worn trail.

The old nun lay in the narrow gap between two outcroppings near the top of the path to the second flat, a surprisingly broad, level plateau that extended for nearly half a mile. She had been struck on the head with a vicious blow that left a ragged, open cut across one temple. Blood oozed down her jaw and onto her neck. One hand was bloody, with two fingers bent unnaturally, obviously broken. Her robe was spotted with blood. Rikyu already sat beside her, clasping the woman's uninjured hand. *"Om mani padme hum,"* Rikyu murmured, the mantra that invoked the Compassionate Buddha.

Shan knelt at the nun's other side. "Grandmother," he asked in Tibetan, "who would do such a thing?"

Nyima pulled her hand from the young nun and waved it back and forth as if to dismiss him. "It's nothing, a trifle," she said in a cracking voice. "Find my donkey. The *amchi* will have me right," she continued, using the term for a traditional Tibetan doctor. Shan was aware of no doctor in Yangkar, Tibetan or otherwise. "I am not the one who needs help. They need to find their way, to be able to speak with the ghost. So he can take us to his paradise."

Shan followed her gaze toward a small group of Tibetans thirty yards away, gathered around a patch of ground covered with tufts of grass and lichen. *"Hal lei lu jah,"* the old nun murmured, *"hal lei lu jah."* It was not a mantra Shan had ever heard.

He felt conspicuous, out of place, as he approached. The old nun did not want his help. None of the Tibetans wanted his help. Not for the first time Shan silently cursed Colonel Tan, governor of Lhadrung County, for forcing him into the blue tunic. He longed for the tattered work clothes he had worn for years, clothes that would have allowed him to sit beside these simple, reverent Tibetans. A woman retreated behind a sturdy-looking herder as they saw Shan. Two children were quickly sent away toward the sweat-stained horses now grazing at the end of the plateau.

"She found you, constable?" one of the old men asked. To his surprise Shan recognized Trinle, who now glanced with anticipation over his shoulder. "Yara did not join us," Shan replied, considering a mental map as he studied the wary old herder. The roads had looped around the base of the huge mountain, but there would have been tracks leading directly over the ridges that would have been much shorter. Trinle had been in a hurry even before the truck had stopped. They had been racing toward this very place, but not because they knew Nyima had been attacked. Shan nodded toward the patch of ground the Tibetans were staring at. "What have you found?"

Trinle did not want to answer. He glanced uneasily at his wife Lhamo, who stood with the ring of Tibetans, then stared at a black crack in the ground.

"It has found us!" cried out a middle-aged man Shan recognized as a farmer who lived near the town. "A ghost has summoned us to its entrance! A *bayal!*" he exclaimed, referring to one of the mythical paradises that were said to be hidden underground, revealed only to those of great virtue. "Nyima heard it call out from the ground yesterday, then again this morning. *Hal lei lu jah*," the man said and touched the *gau*, the prayer amulet, that hung around his neck. Knotted into the cord of his *gau*—knotted or stuffed into every *gau* visible to Shan—was a twisted piece of green paper.

"I don't understand," Shan said.

"It is for the pure of heart," the woman beside the farmer replied, as if to explain Shan's ignorance.

"*Hal lei lu jah*," the farmer repeated. "It must be what the ghosts say, to summon us. Yesterday, and again today, the same time each day. We have all come to hear it, so we can learn their secrets at last!" The old man pointed to the narrow opening in the earth. "At last it is time for us to cross into it!" He turned to the woman beside him. "Should we prepare a bag of food for the journey?" he asked her.

Shan paced along the little crevasse, which revealed nothing but deep shadow below, then surveyed the plateau. "What is this place?" he asked. The Tibetans near him looked away uneasily.

"The Plain of Ghosts, of course," Lhamo said. "No one would ever come here. It's taboo. Except now we are called, after all these years."

Shan dropped to his knees, exploring the grass-lined edge of the opening, then pulled up a tuft of grass to reveal the straight edge of a carefully chiseled stone. The tuft had not been rooted there; it had only recently been pushed into the loose soil covering the stone as if to conceal it.

"Blessed Buddha! It's a door!" the farmer exclaimed and dropped to his knees, pulling more tufts. His wife knelt beside him to help scoop away the soil, then a third man bent to help. Soon they had revealed a carefully cut stone slab, eight feet long and nearly six wide.

"*Terme!*" one of the women said, meaning Buddhist relics and teachings that had been buried or hidden in Tibet during earlier centuries, waiting to be found by the devout of the future.

"A *bayal*," the farmer insisted. "The paradise we have waited for."

As Shan walked around the slab a great foreboding seized him.

Rikyu, the young nun, had run to Nyima to report the discovery and was now sprinting back, her robe streaming behind her. "Don't!" she gasped as she reached Shan. "You can't!" She grabbed his arm. "Make them stop!"

"Who attacked her?" Shan pressed. "Why assault an old nun?"

Rikyu's anxious gaze turned to the circle of Tibetans. The farmer was arranging men at either end of the slab. "No! You don't understand!" the nun shouted. "You must stop!" From beyond them came a frantic cry, then weeping. Nyima was trying to crawl toward them but had collapsed in pain. "Stop!" she shrieked from the ground. "You'll bring the long night back!"

"Stop!" Jengtse took up the cry, with surprising vehemence. He grabbed the arm of one of the men, who resentfully shook him off.

No one seemed to hear. The farmer grabbed a shepherd's staff, inserted it into the crack, and began prying up one edge of the stone.

"Please don't!" Rikyu pleaded. "I beg you! He is a saint!"

The farmer with the staff gestured for the other men to grab the slab as it rose on his lever. "Not even a saint could get out of that hole by himself," he muttered.

Suddenly Shan saw Lieutenant Jinhua standing a few feet away, staring with a predatory expression at the stone slab. "Wait!" Shan called out, and pushed through the Tibetans to intercept the knob officer.

But it was too late. The lever had raised the stone high enough for the excited Tibetans to grip it, and they were lifting the slab. They groaned, staggering under the weight, then lowered it onto the grass beside the hole.

One of the women screamed and staggered backward. Several of the Tibetans began running away. Others grabbed their prayer amulets or rosaries and began urgent prayers. Trinle collapsed onto his knees, staring wide-eyed.

The lama lay in a wide tomb carefully lined with more stone slabs, his hands folded over his belly, the lids of his closed eyes painted vermilion, his mummified face, like all his exposed skin, covered with gold gilt. It was a burial of the distant past, probably hundreds of years old, the kind indeed reserved for the most saintly of teachers. The mantras changed and grew louder. The remaining Tibetans weren't making the traditional request for compassion now, they were asking for forgiveness.

Only Lieutenant Jinhua moved, shoving past the stunned Tibetans. He knelt at the edge of the tomb, then lowered himself onto his belly to study the mummy. "He was calling out," the knob observed.

"There was a sound from the grave, that's all," Shan said. "An animal fell inside, perhaps."

"No," the knob insisted. "I mean he was calling out."

Shan followed Jinhua's gaze to the folded hands. He stopped breathing for a moment, then, as the lieutenant twisted and lowered his legs over the edge of the tomb, Shan roughly grabbed his collar. He pulled Jinhua back, then quickly dropped into the tomb himself. He pulled out his own prayer amulet, as if to show it to the long-dead lama, then, pushing down some of the tattered ornate rug that covered much of the body, so large it was bunched against the sides of the tomb, he stepped closer and reached out. Clenching his jaw, he pried up the topmost hand. The long-dead lama was holding a cell phone.

Shan retrieved the device and, ignoring Jinhua's outstretched hand, pressed the large green button. As the screen sprang to life, he stared at it, disbelieving. All the words were in English. He pushed the button for the ringtone. "Hallelujah," sang a chorus.

He looked up into a circle of confused faces.

The young nun was the first to find her voice. "Cover him! He is a saint, not a spectacle!"

Shan let Jinhua reach down and grab the phone out of his hand, then lifted the old carpet in each hand to fling it forward, and froze.

The Tibetans, including the nun, backed away, gasping, some now clutching their bellies. Jengtse cursed and lifted the staff as if for protection. Shan, dropping the carpet, found himself flattened against the end of the tomb, his heart thundering.

"Like you said," Jinhua observed in a tight voice, "just one miracle after another."

The hideous, desiccated body Shan had exposed to the left of the lama was that of a Chinese soldier, dead not for centuries but probably for decades. The one on the right was of a Western man, dead for only hours.

CHAPTER TWO

The procession down from the Plain of Ghosts was not so much mournful as angry. Rikyu, upset that the grave of so obviously a holy man had been opened, was even more furious that it had been desecrated with other bodies. The remaining Tibetans, except the ever-steady Trinle, were most unhappy over being drafted by Shan to help carry the two bodies, now wrapped in blankets, down the path.

"Where is the ice cave?" Shan asked Rikyu as they reached the bottom. The nun answered only with a silent glare.

"Just a hundred paces down the ledge," Trinle offered, nodding toward the north.

Shan glanced uneasily at Lieutenant Jinhua, who had lingered, studying the little plateau, before trotting down the embankment to reach Shan's side. "To the cave," he told the Tibetans, then turned back to the young nun. "Get help to carry Nyima down and make her comfortable in the back of my truck. I will take her to town."

Jinhua gazed uncertainly at the bodies as they were carried toward a deep shadow in the face of the embankment. "There is no morgue in Yangkar," Shan explained, then gestured toward the flat where their vehicles were parked. "And lots of room here for Public Security vehicles, even a helicopter or two."

The officer seemed surprised. "Helicopters?"

"The word that Yangkar has discovered a dead Westerner will

echo all the way to Beijing. It is going to be quite a circus. Dozens of Public Security officers combing the crime scene. Bureau of Religious Affairs demanding to control the tomb. Ministry of Foreign Affairs insisting on dealing with the body. And of course there will be an investigative team from his home country once we determine that."

Shan hesitated, studying the young lieutenant, who sometimes seemed so arrogant, at other times just puzzled. He had been around enough murders, and enough knobs, to know that Jinhua should be excited, ecstatic even, over such a sensational find. It could easily earn him a promotion, and certainly reassignment to one of the glamorous eastern cities. But instead Jinhua seemed troubled by Shan's words. He watched the Tibetans carrying the bodies along the grassy ledge.

"Westerners sometimes fall off Tibetan mountains and die, do they not?" Jinhua asked after a moment. "He had on climbing boots."

"They don't fall into ancient graves and cover themselves with granite slabs," Shan pointed out.

"And that soldier died long ago. The liberation of Tibet was not bloodless."

"Dangerous words for an ambitious officer, lieutenant. Our history books say the Tibetans draped Chinese soldiers with flowers to celebrate the end of their servitude."

Jinhua ignored him. "He was no doubt reported dead decades ago. It seems impossible his body was even preserved like that."

"The Tibetans would say it was the influence of the saint beside him. Like an attendant lying in the holy man's aura." Shan weighed his own words. The two dead men had indeed been laid out like attendants. Why would anyone go to the trouble of disposing of dead men in such a fashion? Why would it have been done twice, so many years apart?

"More like the cold and the dryness," Jinhua observed. "Desiccation without decay. It happens in high altitudes. So we turned up an old soldier's grave, the way a bulldozer turns up old bones when making a new apartment building. You drop the bones into a new hole and move on."

"If you choose not to file a report, lieutenant, I will be forced to," Shan pointed out. "If you prefer, just move on with your prisoners and forget about this."

"Of course I will file a report, comrade," the knob officer shot back. "And I forbid you from doing so before me. Just as soon as we know what to say. Or should we just compose it now? Some herders found some buried antiquities, which of course belong to the state. The bodies are already removed. No real evidence of crime other than mishandling of a corpse, and no doubt the Tibetans would want to avoid all that official fuss. Let Religious Affairs take jurisdiction."

Jinhua saw the doubt on Shan's countenance. "Fine," the lieutenant offered, "tell the army a careless soldier fell into a hole decades ago. Tell the Foreign Ministry the foreigner was looting a grave and had an accident, then some of those hill people replaced the slab hoping to avoid government inquiries." He frowned as he noticed Shan's impassive expression. "You have a better theory, comrade?"

"They call it the Plain of Ghosts. Maybe we just say the same ghost killed all three, in different centuries."

His words seemed to strangely disturb Jinhua, who turned away and stared down at his car.

"This will be taken out of my hands," Shan explained. "I'd rather that happen sooner than later. I need to call Lhadrung. The governor's office."

"Somehow I didn't peg you as the sniveling bureaucrat," Jinhua challenged. An unexpected resentment had entered his voice. The lieutenant paused and studied Shan. "Look at you. A worn-out public servant wearing what looks like someone else's uniform. You fell hard, didn't you? You're being punished. And from here there's nowhere else for you to go except into your own hole in the ground."

"Something like that," Shan agreed.

"I will be glad to dig it for you if you are going to behave in such a spineless manner. The motherland needs us to show fortitude in times of crisis."

"I'm confused, lieutenant," Shan declared. "Is it a crisis, or is it a nonevent? You're just a bystander. It was just coincidence you were here at all."

Jinhua seemed oddly deflated. "I am Public Security," he asserted in a voice that had lost its confidence.

Shan pushed past the knob. The herders carrying the bodies had disappeared into a crack in the side of the hill. The tall, jagged opening was barely three feet across, but it quickly widened into a broad passageway that led into a cavern. The temperature plunged as they stepped into the chamber. His hand lantern illuminated a glassy section in the center of the far wall. It was what the Tibetans called an ice root, an underground spring that had been frozen. Shan tried to recall the map on his office wall. There was a glacier nearby, perhaps a mile to the north, and this must be one of its underground tentacles.

In the center of the chamber several rock formations had been leveled off years earlier to create flat, table-like surfaces. The Tibetans laid the long bundles on the two largest, then hurriedly retreated out the passageway, leaving only Trinle and Lhamo. A flame flickered behind Shan. Jinhua had followed Jengtse inside and was lighting a cigarette.

Trinle whispered to his wife, who set off down the passage. "Lhamo will bring butter lamps and a brazier from Nyima's cave." Shan hesitated, then realized he should not be surprised that the two old Tibetans, who spent much of their lives hiding in the mountains, knew the hermit nun. "I can stay for a few hours," he said in a pointed tone. Even for strangers the death rites should be spoken. The old herder stepped into the shadows and returned with a small tripod stool, shaking the dust off it, then, cocking his head, studied the walls of the cavern with new interest.

"Hold it still, damn you!" the lieutenant snapped to Jengtse, who was nervously holding a flashlight over the hideous remains of the soldier. Jinhua had opened the blanket, covered the face with a handkerchief, and was examining the uniform. He paused over a tarnished pin on the soldier's pocket, a yellow enameled star inside a red wheel.

"A sergeant," Shan said, pointing to the red rectangle with three stars sewn onto the soldier's collar. He pulled at a corner of dusty paper that extended from the dead soldier's pocket. It was a much-folded letter, the paper brittle and crumbling, the writing so faded it was almost invisible. Jinhua grabbed it out of Shan's hand and stuffed it into his own pocket.

Trinle settled onto the stool between the two bodies and took up what sounded like a slow, cadenced prayer. "I think these two are long past saving," Jinhua observed.

"He's reciting the Bardo," Shan explained. "The rites of passage for the release of souls. Those who suffer sudden deaths have difficulty finding their way to the next plane of existence. Their spirits could linger, confused, for years."

Jinhua drew deeply on his cigarette and exhaled the smoke over the dead soldier's head. "I don't think there's much left of this one in this world or the next. Past helping."

"Then why study his uniform? Why take his letter?"

"Three men in a grave. He was the only Chinese," he said, as if it were an answer. There was challenge in his voice. He inhaled again and blew his smoke at Shan. His confidence had a tide, rising and falling from minute to minute. Shan had the sense Jinhua was performing, though he had no idea what his script might be.

"We have to take the old nun to a doctor. You're welcome to stay."

"Stay alone with two dead men and a senile Tibetan?"

"And the others."

"Others?" Jinhua finally noticed that Trinle was staring intently toward the entry wall as he recited the ritual words. He followed his gaze, then grabbed Jengtse's light and held it high, aimed at the wall over the entry, below the soot-stained ceiling. "*Ta ma de!* Damn!" Jinhua cursed and stepped closer to Shan.

The four images over the entry were very old, the plaster on which they had been painted chipped and cracked, but the fading colors only gave the monsters a more ghostlike appearance. They were what the Tibetans called wrathful deities, protectors of the faithful, and they explained why the rock formations in the cave had been chiseled into level surfaces. The stone tables were altars. The dead men had been brought into a *gonkang*, a secret shrine where senior nuns and lamas once kept spirit demons in check by paying homage through prayer and ritual.

"We should go," the knob whispered uneasily, his eyes fixed on the demons. He held his cigarette behind him as if to hide it from them. "The old nun needs help, you said."

"We are not stopping you," Shan replied, still studying the protector demons. Even through the grime of centuries the images retained an unsettling power. Below them, on either side of the entry, smaller creatures were painted with the heads of monkeys and snakes, their attendants.

"I don't know if I can find the way back to town," Jinhua confessed. "I have to follow you."

"Wait for me at your car," Shan said and motioned for Jengtse to escort the knob. When the two men had disappeared down the passageway, Shan stepped to Trinle's side. "I worry about leaving you and Lhamo alone. I can't explain these deaths, and we don't know who attacked Nyima."

Trinle nodded toward the images on the wall. "We have an understanding with them. They are watching too now," the herder said with a confidence that sent an unexpected chill down Shan's back. The old man clearly had not been in the cave for many years, but he just as clearly knew of the demons. "We have been waiting all these years. Now the dead awaken them."

Every mile he drove back toward Yangkar with Nyima brought Shan closer to the end of his short career as a constable. A small army of knobs would soon arrive, trucks and sedans filled with crime investigators and political officers who would filter all reports. Furious army officers would come soon thereafter. The Bureau of Religious Affairs would be summoned to haul off the gilded saint, and though they would promise to take it away for study, it was likely the body would be taken to a crematorium where the mummy would be reduced to ashes while the officials waited for the golden puddle on the furnace tray.

But all that agony paled by comparison to how Colonel Tan, the tyrannical governor of Lhadrung County and Shan's reluctant patron, would react. Tan had elevated Shan as constable in the farthest point of his county to keep a tighter rein on Shan, who had too often dragged Tan and the county into scandal. Tan wouldn't punish Shan, he would punish Shan's son Ko, an inmate in the hard-labor prison where Shan had formerly been incarcerated. The only concession Shan had won in accepting the blue tunic was that for the first time in years his son would be allowed brief home paroles, five days in the custody of the Yangkar constable every three months. The thought of at last seeing Ko outside of his gulag prison had preoccupied Shan from the moment he had entered the dusty, worn-out constable's station. Now Tan would cancel the parole.

"Can't you hear her?" Jengtse asked, shaking Shan's arm. "She's been pounding on the window for half a mile!"

Shan shook away his gloom and saw Rikyu waving from the back, yelling for him to stop. He pulled over and watched in confusion as the young nun helped Nyima out. They were nearly a mile from town, and the only structure Shan could see in the fading light was a run-down farmhouse a quarter mile off the macadam, at the top of a grassy ridge that ran parallel to the road. Jinhua pulled his car in behind them and impatiently blinked his lights as Shan climbed out.

"There's a nurse in town," Shan said to the Tibetans. The farmhouse looked abandoned.

"Here is the healing she needs," Rikyu replied stiffly, then she stretched the old nun's arm over her shoulder and began walking with her up the path to the farmhouse. Shan watched for a moment, tempted to join them.

Jinhua began blowing his horn.

. . .

In the station the prisoners were lying on cots and pallets in their cells, some asleep, others quietly whispering their beads. Empty noodle bowls were stacked on a tray left on a chair by the door.

Mr. Wu, sitting vigilantly at the table in the cell room, saluted Shan and asked in a hopeful tone if the committee should order badges for its members to cover such occasions. Shan hesitated, reminding himself that the committee was the closest thing to an arm of the Communist Party that existed in the township. "There were some old army caps in the used clothing stall at the market," he replied. "Less expensive. The chairman has called for austerity in public spending," he reminded the town clerk, a plump, balding man who never spoke more than a few words about anything that did not relate to the township account books.

"For the motherland!" Wu affirmed with an enthusiastic nod and left the office with new vigor in his step. Like most other officials in Tibet, Wu had served in one of the vast bureaucracies of an eastern city and had been enticed to Tibet by hardship pay and the prospect of being a senior official in a small town.

"Get the lieutenant settled in the guest house," Shan told Jengtse, then pulled a cellophane bag out of his desk. "Tell him I must have that phone from the grave. Put it in this evidence bag. Bring it to me and go home for some rest. I'll take the first shift. Be back in six hours."

Jengtse gazed at the bag uncertainly. "That was the bag you carried your lunch in yesterday."

Shan took a marker from the desk and wrote EVIDENCE in big characters across the bag and handed it back to Jengtse. "Don't come back without that phone."

His deputy was back in five minutes, looking relieved. "He was asleep, passed out on the sofa. But fortunately he had taken off his tunic. It was in the pocket, with this," Jengtse added in a grim tone, and laid a business card on the desk beside the phone before backing away. "Six hours," he confirmed, and slipped out into the night.

Shan stared at the card. LIEUTENANT JINHUA GUO XI, it said, over the logo for the Public Security Bureau. The words at the bottom struck a chill in his heart. *Office of Special Investigations, Central Branch*, Beijing.

Most of the prisoners were asleep when he checked again. The woman with the green eyes lay curled up, her heavy felt dress draped around her like a blanket. But her hand was tightly clutching Nyima's bloody rosary. On her dress was pinned her only identification, the number 12, meaning she had been the last prisoner taken. He had seen her plainly for only an instant when she had grabbed the *mala*, but her expression had not been the same as those of her cell mates. The eyes in her strongly featured face, the strangely green eyes, had been more watchful than fearful.

Shan turned out the lights in the cell room and closed the door, leaving it ajar for light to filter inside, then locked the station door and stared toward the cells. He had become one of those he had loathed for so many years, a jailer of Tibetans. After several painful moments he stepped back to the cell room door and stood there. The man he had become in Tibet, nurtured and taught by so many lamas and gentle men like his old friend Lokesh, wanted to go inside and speak with the prisoners, to comfort them, recite prayers with them, perhaps even help them escape. But there were soldiers and a knob officer just outside the back door. One phone call from Jinhua or the sergeant would end any chance of his son being released on parole, could even put Ko back in solitary confinement. He looked down at his hand, which had begun to tremble, then squeezed it with the other to stop the tremors, and went back to his desk. From a bottom drawer he extracted a stick of incense, dumped out the tin can he used to hold paper clips, lit the incense, and set it in the can. He stepped into the cell block just far enough to set the burning incense on the table. The fragrant smoke meant the spirits would be watching over the Tibetans.

He lifted the phone taken from the grave. It could have belonged to the dead Westerner, or to his killer. Setting the volume to the lowest setting, he played the ringtone again. *Hallelujah*, sung by a chorus.

He knew it from his childhood, when his father had still been permitted to own Western books and recordings, from the Sunday afternoons when his uncle would visit just to listen to their phonograph. It was from Handel's *Messiah*.

There was no cell phone service in Yangkar, and surely none in the remote mountains above the nun's cave, yet somehow the phone had been activated in the tomb. The gilded lama had been a miracle of the sixteenth or seventeenth century. The sound of a Western prayer had been a twenty-first-century miracle, summoning Tibetans to the deaths. They had somehow been waiting for word from the Plain of Ghosts, and the word had been from a long-dead German composer.

Although the colonel had sometimes insisted Shan carry a borrowed phone, he had never owned one of his own. They had come into use during his long years of imprisonment, and even today Tibet only had narrow pockets of reception around population centers and along its few major highway corridors. Most older Tibetans distrusted them, convinced that the Chinese government heard every word spoken over them, which, Shan knew from experience, was not too far from the truth.

Although the phone's applications had been set to English, it was a domestic brand, purchased in China or Hong Kong. He experimented with the keys. There were a few games, simple games of the kind people played to while away time. There was a program that converted traditional English measurements into metric units. He pressed an unfamiliar icon of little stars and discovered an application that reported the location of stars, planets, and satellites. The list of recent calls numbered only a dozen and went back less than a month. Most were to one of two numbers, with exchanges for Lhasa and Hong Kong. He dialed the Lhasa number on the phone on his desk. "Palace Hotel" came the answer, first in Chinese, then in crisp English. He hung up. He stared at the phone for a long time, then, feeling fatigued, stepped out into the cool air. Night had overtaken Yangkar. Half the streetlights around the square were burnt out, giving the center of town a lonely, abandoned feeling. A scrawny dog ran from one shadow to the next. A broken gorse bush tumbled down the street in the rising wind. The lonely call of a nightjar echoed from the old stone tower by the entrance to the square. He sat on the steps of the station, his back against the door, and shut his eyes.

The future is what happens when you wake up from your dreams. The words had been spoken by an old man at the brutal reeducation camp where Shan and his parents had been sent when he was a young boy. His mother had been furious at the man, a professor whose university had been burnt down by Mao's teenage mercenaries, the Red Guards, and chided him for trying to steal away Shan's hope. For years now Shan had been unable to visualize the man, but he recalled perfectly the raspy voice that spoke the words now echoing in his mind. In his early years he had dreamed of so many futures, of a contented home with his parents, then of a happy life with his bride and son, then of success in his career as a Beijing inspector. But his parents had been branded intellectuals, enemies of the people, and he had lost them; then his wife had become a strident, ambitious Party member and left him; and he had finally investigated the wrong politicians and been condemned to the gulag.

He clung to much smaller dreams now, of a reverent, remote life with Lokesh. They would read old books and cut barley in a golden field. Most of all he dreamed of Ko being freed as Colonel Tan had promised, five days every three months. For weeks Shan had lain in the dark before sleeping, constructing those days, thinking of what they would do, and say, and eat. But Shan had awakened again. Ko would not come now. The town would be flooded with bullying knobs, who would, as always, be tempted to arrest more Tibetans. And everyone, from his son to Tan to every Tibetan in town, all would blame Shan.

Something nudged his knee. He opened his eyes to see a grinning Tibetan boy of perhaps ten years sitting at one side on the steps, a shaggy brown and black mastiff at the other. They were both staring at Shan.

"Raj pulled me away when those soldiers came," the boy announced.

Shan reached out and stroked the dog's massive head. "Raj is wise in the ways of the world, Lodi. Best do what he says."

Lodi extended a small brown paper bag to Shan. "I told Uncle Marpa that you were working late."

"Have you done your reading?" Shan asked before accepting the bag. He and the boy's uncle had been teaching Lodi to read Tibetan script, which was banned in his school.

The boy beamed. "Twenty pages, like you said."

Shan took the bag and opened it, revealing half a dozen large *momos*, meat dumplings. Lodi's Uncle Marpa, who ran the noodle shop, had raised the boy since he was a toddler, after his parents had been arrested on suspicion of supporting the exile government. Shan carefully laid two of the *momos* on the boy's knee, two on his own, and two in front of the dog. Raj was a cheerful, inquisitive creature, who for some reason always brought a smile to Shan's face. The mastiff looked up to the sky. It never ate before doing so, as if offering a prayer. Shan suspected the boy had taught the dog to do so, but Lodi insisted it was the act of the reincarnate spirit who inhabited Raj. The people of Yangkar were deeply set in the old traditions of Tibet, and more than once Shan had noticed the unusual connections between humans and animals in the town.

"Full house tonight," Shan said after taking a bite. The boy and his dog often slept in the guesthouse when there were no visitors.

"No problem. We'll go to the stable up above the carpet factory. Sometimes Trinle's old bull wanders down and lies with the other yaks. He lets me curl up against him. We call him the lama yak, since his gaze seems so wise."

Raj's head shot up, and the three of them watched a solitary sheep trot across the square. From an apartment window down the street came the sound of a Chinese rock-and-roll singer. A motorcycle sped along the far side of the square, its headlight illuminating for an instant a young couple on a bench.

"The moonrider!" Lodi exclaimed.

"Moonrider?" Shan absently asked. His gaze was fixed on the pay phone box in the shadows beyond the couple.

"He only rides at night. I bet it's the best motorcycle in town. Probably doesn't have a permit, so he rides in the shadows," the boy added with an awkward glance at Shan.

"Lodi," Shan asked, "did you see the man in the gray car?"

"You mean the knob?"

"The officer of the Public Security Bureau," Shan corrected. He reached into his pocket and handed the boy a few coins. "If you are sleeping in the stable you'll be up at dawn. Come back to the square and watch the phone."

The boy's eyes lit with excitement. "You mean another job, like Mrs. Weng's onions?" The month before, Shan had asked Lodi to watch the garden of Mrs. Weng, who had loudly complained of a Tibetan thief raiding her garden. After a few hours Lodi had discovered the culprit, a rock squirrel that was building its winter larder on the slope above town. They had patched the hole in the fence and saved her garden.

"Right, without the vegetables and rodents. I want you to tell me if that officer makes a call on it." Jinhua would be leaving with the prisoners in the morning, so he would not have much time to report to his superiors. He could not use his cell, and if he used the station phone Shan would know, and know what he said. That left the pay phone.

He sent the boy and his dog on to the stable and stayed on the steps, studying the night sky. The lights of Yangkar were so dim he could clearly see the spectacle of the sky even from the center of town. The stars seen from Tibet were like nowhere else in the world, the thin, high-altitude atmosphere making them so bright and so crisply defined Shan sometimes thought he could reach out and touch them. From the window of his barracks behind the razor wire of the 404th People's Construction Brigade, nearly a hundred miles to the south, he knew Ko often tried to look up at the sky before sleeping. From his remote hidden sanctuary where he served the exiled government, Lokesh would often do the same. Every devout, loyal Tibetan had his or her own secrets, little personal rituals that defined their world, Lokesh had once told him, and this was one of Shan's. He imagined that they were looking up at the same stars. Shan would sometimes catch himself pointing at a meteor as if one of them were beside him.

When Jengtse finally returned for his shift, Shan drove up to the old farmhouse above town that he now called home, one of the many abandoned structures that dotted the Tibetan landscape. Although he was entitled to quarters in the government house, he preferred the quiet of the orphaned farm, and he knew neither Ko nor Lokesh would be comfortable visiting him by the jail. In his spare time he had patched the stucco, painted the outside walls the traditional maroon, and was coaxing the shriveled garden back to life. He made tea on his brazier, then tried to read one of his books, Sung dynasty poetry, but his gaze kept drifting toward his constable's tunic hanging on a peg by the door. He had been so worried about telling Lokesh of his new job when the old Tibetan had first visited that he had worn civilian clothes to meet him. Only after a long meal, filled with exuberant descriptions of Lokesh's work at his secret monastery deep in the mountains, and an hour of stargazing, had Shan explained the bargain Colonel Tan had forced him into.

"A father needs to see his son," was all his old friend had said, and had spoken no more of it that night. But Shan had awakened in the small hours of the morning and discovered Lokesh at the peg, forlornly fingering the brass buttons of the tunic. Each was embossed with Beijing's seal. The same buttons had adorned the uniforms of the guards who had made life so miserable for them and the other inmates of their hard-labor prison. The disappointment on his friend's face had been like a blade in Shan's heart. He had crept back to bed before Lokesh noticed him.

Twice since Lokesh's visit Shan had thrown the tunic on the table and cut off every button. Twice, in the light of the next day, he had sewn them back on. Now he rose, threw the tunic into the shadows, and dragged his pallet out to gaze at the stars.

When Shan arrived at the station at dawn, Jengtse had already made barley gruel on the jail's hot plate for the prisoners' breakfast and was serving it to them. Shan whispered to his deputy, who rolled his eyes and then went into the outer office to keep watch as Shan spoke to the Tibetans about what to expect when they reached their internment camp. They would be kept together as families for two or three weeks of political indoctrination, he explained, and he begged them to submit to the lectures without resistance, or risk being sent to a real prison. The three children in the group were clutched by their parents as he explained that the children would then be sent to boarding schools, and no amount of protest would prevent it. But he told the children to be brave and to find ways to secretly speak Tibetan to their friends, to keep their language alive. He did not have the heart to explain that the children would receive new Chinese names and many would have difficulty speaking Tibetan with their parents when they were reunited years later. He did warn that the schools would not allow prayer amulets, but in a whisper, holding the shoulders of the youngest child, he suggested they could hide prayers inside candy wrappers or pieces of foil and keep them inside their shirts like secret *gaus*.

He explained that the factory complexes in Lhasa and Shigatse were expanding, and if the adults proved submissive there was a chance they would be assigned there instead of some distant Chinese city. Finally, Shan passed out cards with his address. The last day together, when internees were sent to their new assignments, was often confusing, and they might not learn where other family members were sent. If that happened, he told them, they could send word to him and he would coordinate as best he could. One of the women immediately opened her *gau* and stuffed his card inside.

As he finished, Jengtse rapped on the door and Shan opened it just as Jinhua and the sergeant entered the station. The army truck was parked at the front entrance, the soldiers waiting to load their prisoners. The frightened Tibetans filed out, several of the older ones offering worried nods as they passed Shan, the mothers fiercely gripping their children. One of the soldiers called out their assigned numbers as they climbed into the truck, and the sergeant kept tally on a clipboard. When the sergeant confirmed all twelve were loaded, he gave a sharp command and the guards jumped into the back. Moments later the truck pulled away in a cloud of exhaust smoke, Jinhua closely following in his gray sedan.

As they left the square Shan darted back into the cells, saw they were empty, and returned to watch the little convoy disappear down the road. Twelve prisoners had boarded the truck, but the woman with green eyes had not been one of them.

CHAPTER THREE

Two small horses, tattered saddles on the ground beside them, grazed on the thin grass outside the ice cave beside a dozen sheep. Shan did not recognize the shepherd boy who watched them until Ati, Trinle's great-grandson, sprang up and ran to help Shan with his armful of equipment. Jengtse had energetically helped Shan locate kerosene lanterns, blankets, and a basket of food, never looking Shan in the eye. Shan's deputy had no explanation for how the green-eyed woman had escaped, and no suggestion of who would have been so brave, or so foolish, as to replace the woman among the prisoners.

Trinle still sat chanting between the bodies, or sat again between them, for Shan could see a pile of quilts that had been used in the night. His wife Lhamo was coaxing embers to life in a small brazier, blowing on them as she added chips of dried dung. Shan stacked his supplies on another of the flattened rocks and lit the lanterns, whose bright light brought the features of the dead men out in macabre detail.

The faces of both dead men had been cleaned. Small columns of pink salt, as long as Shan's thumb, sat beside the head of each man. It was a traditional offering in the region. As Trinle paused to take the bottle of water Shan offered, Shan put a hand on his shoulder. "Take Lhamo outside, my friend. Both of you need a rest. If you see Public Security coming you need to leave, up into the mountains." He felt guilty over allowing the feral family to stay when he knew other authorities might arrive at any minute.

The old herder nodded and rose, but hesitated before following his wife down the passage. He bowed his head to the savage gods above him, then turned back to Shan. "The golden saint needed this to happen, Shan," he said. "I'm sorry. He's been waiting with Acala for too long." Acala was known as the wrathful king among the old deities, a fierce gatekeeper invoked in images at temples and monasteries. "They wanted us to stay away all these years. But now they want something different," Trinle said, with a bow of his head to the dead men. It was almost as though he were thanking them. "*Lha gyal lo,*" the old Tibetan added. *Victory to the gods.* Then he backed down the passage.

Shan pulled away the blanket covering the dead Westerner, releasing a faint scent of decay. The ice cave was slackening his decomposition but not stopping it. He clenched his jaw and gripped the man's arm. The chill of the grave, then of the cave, had slowed the release of rigor mortis so that there was still a degree of stiffness in the limbs. The phone had been first heard two days earlier, and certainly could not have kept its charge for much longer. The Westerner had probably been killed not much before then. He paced around the body. The man's light brown hair, long enough to cover his ears, showed hints of gray. Shan guessed he was well into his forties, though with his slim muscular build he could have passed for someone ten years younger. He wore heavy olive-colored trousers and a dark green flannel shirt, which seemed light for the cool air of the high mountains. His boots, with the heavily cleated soles favored by foreign hikers and climbers, had been stripped of their laces.

Shan dropped onto his knees and brought a lantern closer as he studied the man's head. There were two dark bruises on his temple, others along his jaw. He pulled up the man's sleeves, exposing bruises on his forearms and rings of abrasions around his wrists. Their discoloration was diffuse, meaning the tight bruising of his hands had likely happened hours before his death. He had been beaten. He had raised his arms to defend himself. Shan paused as he reached the man's hands, an icy knot forming in his gut. The hands had been mutilated, each palm pierced with something sharp. The dead man had resisted too much, and his assailants—surely there had been more than one to subdue him—had immobilized his hands by driving nails into them.

Shan gazed into the dead's man face, knowing now with certainty that his death had not been accidental. He felt somehow he should apologize to the man. Foreigners always came to Tibet with wildly unrealistic expectations, whether it be a paradise of wise men, an exotic distraction, or a landscape of peaks that when climbed would bring glory and self-discovery. This one had come from the other side of the world to this impossibly remote, almost unknown place only to be tortured and killed.

He had still not found the deathblow. He suppressed a shudder as he realized he would have to strip the man's clothes. As he began unbuttoning the man's shirt Trinle stumbled into the cavern, his hands raised at his side, his eyes wide with fear.

"Keep moving, you old fool," Lieutenant Jinhua ordered in Mandarin as he pushed the shepherd forward, then pointed with his pistol to the sheet of ice at the back of the chamber. "Over there, where I can keep an eye on you."

"His Chinese doesn't go much beyond hello and good-bye," Shan observed.

"More the fool for not understanding what century he lives in," Jinhua snapped. He frowned at the bodies. "I thought you would have seen the sense of putting them back in the ground by now," the knob growled.

"You aren't with the prisoners going to Lhasa," Shan stated to the young lieutenant. "But then you never were with the prisoners, were you?" He stepped between Trinle and Jinhua, then motioned the old Tibetan back outside. "Put your gun down, lieutenant."

Jinhua looked at his pistol, then shrugged and returned it to its holster. "That army truck and I traveled the same unfamiliar roads. Safer to travel in numbers. Like the old caravans."

"Or concealment in numbers," Shan replied. He was having a hard time controlling his anger. "You were with them for cover. What are you doing in my township?" he pressed. "You didn't come here expecting to find these bodies. But something about them caught your interest."

Jinhua stiffened. "Surely even some mud-encrusted slug of a constable understands not to meddle in the secrets of the motherland! Public Security shares its secrets with ministers of state, not with the likes of you."

Shan stared at the knob for several silent breaths. His bravado seemed forced. There was an uncertainty in his eyes that he was trying to hide from Shan. "This is a chapel. A holy place," Shan said. "Do not raise your gun again in front of them," he stated, and gestured toward the demons above the entry.

Jinhua had no reply. He just stared in confusion at the old gods.

Shan turned back to the dead foreigner, probing the dead man's pockets, which yielded a few Chinese coins, a waterproof container with matches in it, and a small black box, an electronic device smaller than a cell phone.

"GPS," Jinhua said over his shoulder. "Expensive. American. Probably illegal in China."

American. It was the truth Shan had been trying to ignore. Dead Americans inevitably brought reporters, nosy diplomats, and, worse, furious officials from Beijing, who tended to read intrigue and subversion into the presence of every American in Tibet.

"Why wouldn't the killer take it?" Jinhua wondered, gesturing toward the device.

"Because it would stand out, it would be too noticeable. No one in this township can afford such an instrument."

"Meaning he was killed by someone local," Jinhua asserted.

Shan frowned but had no reply. He did not want to believe that anyone in his peaceful township could engage in such savagery. He finished unbuttoning the man's shirt, pulling it down over his shoulders. There was a tattoo on each shoulder, one of an anchor, the other of a crescent moon cradling a small sun, a Tibetan good-luck sign.

"We need to roll him over," Shan said. "There's still no evidence of a deathblow."

"Call it a heart attack. Altitude sickness." Jinhua bent over the bruises on the man's arms as he spoke. "It struck with a sudden paralyzing spike of pain in the head. Then he fell on a mountain trail at the edge of a cliff or steep slope, flailing out with his arms, hitting them on rocks on the way down."

Why, Shan wondered, was the young officer so eager to find a label other than murder for the crime? Lodi had reported that Jinhua had appeared in the square but had only studied the solitary stone tower at the entrance to the square and not used the phone. It was as if he wanted to keep the crime to himself. "Altitude sickness usually results in edema," Shan declared, "swelling in the extremities then swelling of the brain. The optic nerve expands. Capillaries burst in the eyes. He shows none of those signs. And it doesn't explain his hands."

Jinhua lifted a lifeless hand and murmured a curse as he saw the piercing.

Shan stripped away the shirt, pausing to examine the label. It was from a store in Pittsburgh, Pennsylvania. He tossed the shirt to Jinhua, then rolled the body over and brought a lantern closer.

"Not altitude sickness," he announced. The cut in the flesh appeared to be a thin slice at first but as Shan stretched and probed it he saw the grisly truth. A heavy knife had been thrust downward into the spinal column and twisted.

"He was immobilized by having his hands nailed to something," Shan explained, a new hoarseness in his throat. "A table. A bench, maybe a long plank. This was an execution." He found himself looking up at the wrathful gods on the wall above the passage. The one over the passage seemed to be smiling at him. Its mouth was curled up in the same hideous smile as that of the mummified soldier.

Jinhua pushed past Shan and picked up the shoulder of the dead Chinese sergeant. The rotting fabric of the tunic fell away. He pushed at the leathery neck then gasped and stared. He seemed to have stopped breathing.

Shan stepped to his side and followed his gaze. The desiccated flesh was still intact enough to clearly show the deep stab wound at the base of the skull. The two men, dead fifty years apart, had been executed in exactly the same way.

After spending another half hour studying the bodies, Shan found Jinhua by the saint's grave, pacing along the little plateau the Tibetans called the Plain of Ghosts, using his Japanese camera to take photographs of the grassy flat, the mountains above, even the track leading toward the distant highway. The lieutenant had been struck dumb by their discovery in the cave, backing away from the dead soldier before fleeing down the passage, the revulsion on his face replaced by something like fear. Shan had assumed the knob officer had driven away and had not bothered to check for Jinhua's sedan before climbing up to the grave. Now he fervently wished the knob had fled.

Three old women in fleece *chuba* coats kept vigil at the tomb, one working her rosary, one tying *khatas*—prayer scarfs—to the surrounding bushes, and the third whirling an old hand-held prayer wheel. The stone slab had been pushed halfway across the tomb to give the saint shelter. It was as if the gilded lama had died again and needed solace. When Jinhua began taking photos of the tomb, one of the women hurled a stone that squarely hit his camera, cracking the lens.

"*Ta ma de!*" Jinhua cursed. "Damn! She could have hit my head! Look at this! One wild throw and she takes out my camera!"

Shan put a hand on his arm, pulling him back. "Those women use stones to hunt game for their stew pots. I think she hit exactly what she was aiming at. You are on sacred ground, no place for photographs."

"Sacred ground? You just proved in that cave that we are on a killing ground, a crime scene." Jinhua stared at the half-open tomb. "If there is indeed a man inside that suit of gold we should determine how he died."

"No. We should not," Shan replied. "In the world he lived in no one would even dream of murder." He stepped between the officer and the women at the grave, who had settled back into their praying. The devout in Tibet had learned to ignore all distractions, whether wind, hail, or uniformed Chinese. In the strands that held their *gaus*, twisted pieces of green paper had been knotted.

Jinhua sneered. "How nostalgic. Revisionist even. The has-been constable protecting has-been indigenous louts and their grotesque idol." He inched around Shan. "With the bodies removed I can call Religious Affairs to clean up the site. They have special disposal teams. It's what they are trained to do. You know, pick up a box of Buddhist rubbish here, a bag of Buddhist bones there."

Shan would not be goaded. "We have enough for a good investigator to work with, lieutenant. A heavy knife, double-edged. Near the hilt it was an inch and half wide. Not a household knife. A fighting knife. A camper's utility knife. Perhaps a mountain climber's knife."

"What do you suggest, comrade?" Jinhua shot back. "A metal detector?" He made a sweeping gesture toward the ranges that swept to the horizon. "I'll do the first ten miles, you do the next?"

"Travel records," Shan continued. "A clever foreigner might slip unnoticed into this wilderness, but he wasn't invisible when he arrived in Lhasa. Take photos of his face with your phone. Go to Lhasa, work the airport, canvas the travel service offices, the train station."

Jinhua narrowed his eyes at Shan. "This from a man who spends his time pulling yaks from the mud? Who the hell are you, Shan?"

"The constable of Yangkar Township. The face of the government that every Tibetan loathes."

"You've got it all wrong. You are the king of Yangkar Township, with hundreds of subjects at your mercy."

Shan turned and looked out over the mountains, reminding himself that Jinhua was from the Office of Special Investigations in Beijing, which dealt with dangerous secrets and inflicted secret punishments. On a distant peak an ancient *chorten*, freshly whitewashed, glowed in a little pool of sunlight. Soon a flood of men like Jinhua would arrive.

He wanted so badly to rip off his tunic and flee. But if he did it could be years before he saw his son again. "There's at least one murderer in my township. He needs to be stopped."

"A murderer who strikes every fifty years? Perfect. Write out a warning and we'll put it in a time capsule. Your golden saint can hold it."

Shan motioned him toward the path. "Tell me, lieutenant, why does this crime seem to frighten—"

Suddenly thunder rumbled in the east. Jinhua turned and stiffened. It wasn't thunder. Several dark specks below the clouds were becoming bigger, and louder. Shan counted four small attack helicopters, used by the mountain commandos, escorting a larger transport helicopter. The Tibetan women bolted, running for the safety of the outcroppings on the upper slope. "The army does training up here," Shan explained over his shoulder. But there was no one to listen. Jinhua was gone.

After a moment the helicopters slowed, then hovered, half a mile away. He descended the hill and warily confirmed that the nervous knob officer had driven away, then waved to Ati, now petting a solitary horse, and approached the plank door, adorned with images of auspicious signs, that led into Nyima's home. He extracted his flashlight and lifted the worn iron latch. The shallow cavern was surprisingly comfortable inside, with a tattered but still colorful carpet covering the floor, and a low sleeping platform on which blankets were neatly folded. He lit two candles on a shelf above a small altar of burnished wood, elegant in its simplicity, which held a bronze image of the goddess Tara, mother protector of Tibet, flanked by two more of the little columns of pink salt. Everything was in its place. Someone had tidied the chamber.

A horse was gone, he realized. There had been two. Trinle and Lhamo had spent the night in the cave and Ati had arrived that morning. The boy would not have come alone. His mother Yara had been there, and probably had hidden here when Shan arrived.

A *peche*, a book of Tibetan scripture, lay open on a low wooden table, the wooden case for its loose leaves of text on the floor beside it. As in many Tibetan houses, the old carpet told the tale of domestic habits. The carpet was worn threadbare in front of the altar and in front of the little reading table. Although he had never encountered the old nun until the day before, Shan felt a connection to her. In his mind's eye he saw Nyima sitting there, reading, praying, working her *mala* and prayer wheel for hours at a time, year after year, ignoring the distractions and fears of the world below.

Why here? he wondered. Why did she choose this lonely wind-swept slope that was miles from any other habitation? The ice cave and its wrathful protectors were nearby, the dead saint above. The Plain of Ghosts was haunted, a place taboo to the local people. Tibetans stayed away from it, all except Nyima the hermit, and now a few with green papers in their *gaus*. He recalled her desperate protests when the grave slab was being pried open. She had known about the golden saint. Was that what had kept Nyima here for so many years? Why had the hermit been attacked now, a day or more after the American had been killed? If it had been the killer, why had she been left alive? Had Yara or her grandmother cleaned the chamber out of respect for the nun or to conceal evidence?

He studied the chamber with an investigator's eye, then carefully moved the low table and rolled back the carpet. In a rectangular indentation chiseled into the stone floor was a folded piece of black felt. Inside was a large key, resting on a worn red silk wallet fastened with a button. The key was stamped with the words PALACE HOTEL in English and Mandarin and the number 619 across the top. The dead man had called the Palace Hotel repeatedly. If the key was his, why leave it here? Why call his own empty room? He opened the wallet and extracted a black-and-white photograph, several old Tibetan coins, and a thin silver ring, set with coral and turquoise. The ring was delicate and small, probably for a woman's finger. The photo was of a smiling Tibetan woman standing at the corner of a stone building cradling an infant in one arm while a boy of perhaps two sat in the other, an arm hooked around the woman's neck.

He stuffed the key and photo into his pocket before returning the coins and ring to the wallet and setting it back in its hiding place. Retrieving his binoculars from his truck, he climbed up to the plateau once more to scan the landscape for signs of the helicopters. He found them on a wide flat over a mile away, or at least the transport helicopter and three of its escorts. Tiny figures were sitting at a table, as if the army had simply gone on a picnic excursion.

Pausing at the head of the trail, he studied the rocks where Nyima had been beaten. The attack on the nun was a piece of the puzzle that would not fit with the others. Why the delay between the killing and the beating? Why had she not been killed? He considered the position of the rocks where she had been found relative to the tomb of the golden saint. She had been backed into the rocks from the direction of the tomb. Her assailant had used a club. Shan bent to retrieve a small white object. It was a chip of bone, old and dried bone. He leaned closer into the little niche where the nun had been found and picked up a small, broken column of pink salt and a rounded brown object that reminded him of a double bead. At first he thought it may have come from Nyima's prayer beads, but as he held it close his gut tightened. It was a phalanx, a finger bone. She had fought with her assailant, but the skeleton demon had beaten her down with his bone club.

Shan drove slowly back toward Yangkar, having confirmed on his map that the nearest military reserve, of which there were so many in Tibet, was twenty miles to the northeast, just above the county line. It was the kind of remote base where special, clandestine projects were conducted, and secret weapons tested.

He was watching a small herd of antelope on a grassy slope as he drove when suddenly they started, dashing for the cover of a thicket. As he slowed, a distant whine rapidly became a rumble, then a deafening thunder directly over his head. He slammed on the brakes and a small black helicopter roared over his truck, only feet above him. It veered about as it rose, then hovered for a moment, so close Shan could plainly see the two men in the small cockpit. The pilot of the attack helicopter was laughing as he aimed his finger repeatedly at Shan, as if firing a gun. The officer beside him, a silver-haired man wearing aviator sunglasses who looked too old for active duty, did not share his amusement. He stared impassively at Shan until the helicopter pulled away.

Half an hour later he parked the truck on the side of the road and started up the track toward the run-down farmhouse where Rikyu had taken Nyima. Its barley fields had gone to weeds. The stone walls of its half-dozen livestock enclosures had collapsed in several places. Only the one closest to the house had been kept in repair, where a *dre*, a milk yak, and a few goats grazed.

Shan was a hundred feet from the house when a furious barking erupted. He froze as four large mastiffs charged him. A single guard dog could mangle an appendage in seconds. It was not unheard of in Tibet for packs of mastiffs to tear intruders apart. He tucked his hands under his shoulders and waited. They circled him with low, threatening growls, pausing to make false lunges with bared teeth.

He slowly withdrew his hand and touched the *gau* that hung from his neck, then began reciting the *mani* mantra to the animals. First the one who appeared to be the oldest quieted, then another, until they all sat, cocking their heads uncertainly at him. "I am going to the house now," he explained, then, taking up the mantra again, took a tentative step forward. He aimed for the front door, which was slightly ajar.

"If you drugged my dogs, damn you, I'll complain to the county authorities!" growled a stocky man who appeared from around a corner of the house. He was a middle-aged Tibetan but spoke in perfect Mandarin.

"I doubt there's enough drugs in all the township to slow them down," Shan replied, forcing a smile. As his fear faded he saw that the dogs were magnificent creatures, whose thick hair and broad shoulders gave them what looked like lion manes. "I came to see Rikyu and Nyima."

The man glared at Shan, clenching his jaw so tightly that the deep scar along his left cheek whitened. "Rikyu left for town before sunrise." His vest swung open as he stepped to block the door, revealing a long knife in his belt.

"I could bring medicines for Nyima," Shan offered.

The stranger, who had an air of self-confidence that was unusual for Tibetans of his age, gave a snort of amusement. "Chinese medicines for Chinese wounds."

"I couldn't tell how severe her injuries were," Shan tried.

"Severe enough," came a voice from the shadows inside. The door swung open, revealing an elderly Tibetan with a wispy beard of gray hair. "She was fortunate to have you transport her," the man said. "A trip on her donkey could have pushed one of the broken ribs into her lungs."

The surly man blocking Shan's path sagged and stepped aside.

"Put on some tea, Dingri," the old man at the door suggested. "For all of us." The man named Dingri winced and slipped around the side of the house.

"You are an officer of the People's Republic," the stranger with the beard observed. His voice was slow and melodious, like those of lamas Shan had known.

"I was asked to put on the tunic of the man who used to be constable. I haven't decided if it fits me." Shan unbuttoned his tunic and dropped it on the bench outside the door.

The old man offered an appreciative nod and gestured Shan inside. The building seemed much the same as nearly every farmhouse Shan had ever visited in Tibet, a compact two-story structure built for accommodation of livestock on the ground floor, with a stair leading up to the living quarters. But his host opened what Shan took to be a small closet door to reveal a narrow stair ladder descending to a level that was built into the back of the hillside, making it invisible from the road.

Shan followed him down into a chamber that was much larger than the floor above. It was brightly lit by a row of mismatched windows overlooking a well-tended herb garden, with four cots below the windows, on one of which Nyima slept. The walls were covered with shelves holding dozens of wooden cases, the long ones used for storing Tibetan manuscripts but also many smaller ones with hand-written labels. Between the shelves were *thangkas*, painted hangings bearing complex images and symbols. Shan recognized the Tree of Treatment on one, depicting the interconnected branches of medical cures, and the Tree of Diagnosis on another, flanking an intricate *thangka* depicting the Palace of the Medicine Buddha.

"I am called Dorchen," the old man said and gestured to Shan to sit at a low table. "You must be Constable Shan."

"Amchi," Shan said with a respectful nod, using the Tibetan word for doctor.

"A pale shadow of a true *amchi*, I fear," Dorchen replied. "In the land I grew up in no one took that title without graduating from one of the great medical colleges." The old Tibetan shrugged. "But my education was curtailed when the schools were destroyed. Tibet has become a land of partial people, because complete education has been prohibited. Incomplete teachers, incomplete artists, incomplete monks. I am an incomplete doctor."

"Chokpori?" Shan asked, referring to the most famed of the Tibetan medical schools, located on a mountain overlooking the Potala in Lhasa. It had been leveled by the Chinese army more than fifty years earlier.

Dorchen smiled and turned toward Nyima. "Two fractured ribs, a bruised kidney, two broken fingers. Apparently she would not release her beads until someone stomped on her hand." He paused, as if considering his own words. "It's an old thing, thinking a Tibetan is stronger when holding a *mala*."

Shan fixed the old doctor with a questioning stare. "The grave of the gilded saint was hidden to the world but she knew it was there. I think that's why she has lived in the cave near it all these years. The place is said to be haunted, taboo even, but she chose to live there. Why?"

Dorchen gazed at his sleeping patient as he replied, "It would be a violation of the state's rules to not report the discovery of religious antiquities."

Shan began pointing to three elegant figurines that lined one of the shelves. "Like a silver Buddha Shakyamuni, a bronze Tara, and a jeweled *dakini*. If you visited my own house I could show you a dozen more such violations. My friend Lokesh and I restore such finds and get them to safekeeping with the devout. When I was younger I used to keep a copy of the Chinese constitution, because it gave me such hope. It says religions are guaranteed protection by the state. So, long ago I decided that the laws that take away the instruments of religion must be unconstitutional."

Dorchen impassively returned Shan's gaze, then looked down at the *gau* that had slipped out of Shan's shirt. "Have you considered that you may be in the wrong line of work, constable?"

"All the signs seem to indicate so, doctor. At best, I am an incomplete policeman."

A grin slowly grew on Dorchen's countenance, then he glanced over Shan's shoulder. "Ah—the tea!" His unhappy assistant entered from a door at the end of the long room, carrying a wooden tray bearing three steaming mugs and a bowl of dried apricots. "You haven't been formally introduced to my assistant Dingri." He turned to Dingri. "Constable Shan is concerned about our patient."

Dingri twisted his mouth as if he had bit something sour. Outside, one of the dogs barked.

"Just Shan. I was wondering what you can piece together about the attack on her."

"Her fingers were crushed under a boot," Dorchen said. "Heavy tread marks were still in the flesh. Her ribs were broken with the swing of a club or pole. The bruise left on her rib cage suggests it was something that ended with a ball or knot of wood. She regained consciousness for a moment, and I asked who had done this. She said the demon misunderstood when it used the thigh bone club." He shrugged. "A hermit often dreams of demons. Once a lama told me that's what hermits do in Tibet, camp on the fringes of the world to struggle with the demons who would otherwise overrun us."

The tea was a delicate green, smelling of jasmine. Dingri glared at Shan as he drank. Dorchen pushed the bowl of fruit toward Shan. "Your home is very cleverly designed," Shan observed as he studied the outer wall. The windows did not match and the wall beams were of salvaged lumber.

Dorchen smiled again. "When I arrived for a visit a few years ago, the townspeople said they needed a doctor. I said I came to the mountains for solitude. I was up in a cave when they came to get me. They had built this for me, using wood from abandoned houses."

"First they had Nyima bless each piece to exorcise the demons," Dingri inserted in a needling voice. "There's a reason so many houses are abandoned in the mountains."

"The reason no one goes up there," Shan suggested. "Too many demons?"

Dingri seemed to welcome Shan's question. "Exactly. Those mountains have been haunted since before memory. Something in the earth there doesn't like us."

Shan hesitated over the words, but resisted the temptation to press the doctor's assistant. He turned to Dorchen. "Can you keep her here for a few days?"

"She certainly needs to rest, for a week or more. But she is a creature of the wild mountains. She talks with deities in the night. I am not sure I could restrain her if they call her away."

"A man was killed on the mountain above her cave. A Westerner."

"I have heard. Not the business of Yangkar. And surely not Nyima's business."

"Who beat her if not the killer? She lived up there for how many years? And she is only attacked at the same time an American is killed?"

"You said a Westerner at first. Now it's an American. Why would an American trouble himself over Yangkar when the rest of the world forgets it?"

Shan had no answer. "She is in danger, I fear. I need her safe, for her sake, and for the information she can give me. Her attack had something to do with that old tomb."

"There are looters everywhere in Tibet."

"The attacker left behind gold along with the dead American."

"We live with danger every day of our lives. We must embrace our impermanence."

"She shouted something when I approached the tomb. 'You'll bring the long night back.' What did she mean?"

Dorchen did not answer for several breaths. He looked back at the nun. "Just her way of saying we must embrace our impermanence."

"You would have her embrace a knife driven down into her spine? That's how the American died."

Dorchen visibly shuddered. He exchanged a long glance with Dingri before turning to Shan. "There are infusions I could give her to keep her subdued while the bones knit."

"What do you know about the cave where she lives?" Shan asked. "The old tomb above her was not constructed there at random. I think there must have been a shrine over it, perhaps one of those little temples that used to be built by farmers."

Dorchen drained his cup before answering. "The Plain of Ghosts. It's a cold, windy place, I hear."

"Why would she live there," Shan asked, "when it is taboo for other Tibetans?"

The doctor shrugged. "She is a hermit. Choosing inhospitable places is what hermits do. It's all about sacrifice and conquering the burdens of mundane existence, is it not? Once, monks would lock themselves up with demons to test their inner strength."

Shan rose and stepped to the back wall as the *amchi* examined his patient, checking the pulse in Nyima's ankle. On the long shelf below the paintings lay a line of curious metal objects, one looking like a sharpened spoon, and several small silver spatulas ending in leaf-shaped blades beside upended glass cups with rounded bottoms. He paused at a small, aged painting on silk, depicting a turtle whose shell had been divided into little rectangles, each with a Tibetan inscription inside it. Tibetan doctors were renowned even centuries earlier for their skill in diagnosing through external examination. He had seen such a painting before. It was a chart used in evaluating urine. He took another step and paused by a tray of long needles, each ending in a small corkscrew shape. They were what Tibetans called golden needles. Fragrant leaves or scented wool were fastened into the corkscrew and burned while the needle was inserted into the crown of the skull. Lokesh had sworn it was the best treatment for relieving the pressure of bad spirits in the brain. Shan was tempted to jam one of the needles into his own head.

He heard a clink of metal and found Dingri standing an arm's length away, an icy grin on his scarred face. In his hand the Tibetan held one of the sharpened spoons. "Know what this is for, constable?" he asked with a predator's gleam. "Tibetan surgery." Dingri made a dipping motion with the spoon. "A good *amchi* could scoop out your heart while you are still breathing."

Shan found his deputy asleep again in one of the cells. "He's a former soldier, I'm sure of it," Shan said to Jengtse after explaining his visit to the doctor. "His name is Dingri. He carries a big knife."

Jengtse rubbed his eyes. "That angry bastard who runs errands for the *amchi*?"

Shan nodded. "He would have preferred to feed me to his dogs rather than let me see the doctor."

"I've seen him around. Keeps to himself."

"Two former soldiers in the People's Liberation Army living in Yangkar and you don't know more about him? Old soldiers have a bond."

Jengtse stood and stretched with careful disinterest. He disliked being reminded of his army service. "He's a son of a bitch. A one leg butcher, though they say he gives all the meat to his mastiffs." So many

Buddhists preferred not to take part in killing animals that in many towns the butchers were Muslims. Otherwise older men, often unmarried, played the role, taking one leg of the animal as payment.

"I need to find Rikyu. She knows something. And that woman with the green eyes you let escape."

Jengtse frowned. "Twelve prisoners got out of that truck. Twelve prisoners went back into it the next morning."

"That woman who took her place is now in the internment camp, about to become slave labor at some factory. Surely she didn't understand the price she was paying."

Shan's words sparked an unexpected defiance in his deputy's eyes. "What part would she misunderstand?" Jengtse asked as he pulled on his tunic. "The submachine guns aimed at her? The jail bars? It was a weight she chose to carry. Maybe she knew she could take it better." Jengtse lifted his mug, a souvenir from Chengdu bearing the image of a dancing panda wearing a soldier's cap, and drained it.

"Mrs. Weng stopped by," he reported to Shan. "She wanted to remind you that the Committee of Leading Citizens requires monthly reports on activities of this office. They recorded in their minutes that you still haven't responded."

Shan suppressed a groan. "So do a report."

"I wish I could, just to shut the bitch up. But she anticipated that, said it must be from the constable himself." Jengtse glanced out to the street, where the truck was parked. "There was a report of a yak pushing down highway signs again," the deputy said. "Can I take the truck?"

Shan threw him the keys.

Jengtse paused as he put his hand on the door to the street. "He was always splitting the seams," he said. "You can see the threads where he repaired them."

"I'm sorry?"

"The tunic, left by old Constable Bao before your predecessor came. Too big for you, too small for Constable Fen. But the station only gets new uniforms every four or five years. Unless you want the dress one out in the guesthouse closet. Fen only wore it on May Day and the Chairman's Birthday." Jengtse cocked his head at Shan. "Didn't they tell you anything about Fen?"

"My predecessor died in an accident. Driving at night in one of those sudden ice storms. The roads are treacherous, even in the best weather."

"A herder came and took me to the body. It was a mile from the nearest road. Legs and arms broken, skull crushed open. His eyes had been scooped out."

Something icy gripped Shan's spine. "Surely you're mistaken."

"No doubt. The Public Security report concluded it was a tragic accident caused by his own negligence. He shouldn't have been driving in such conditions. They decided that his body had been dragged away by wolves and vultures took his eyes. Off to the crematory to spare his family in Hunan the agony of his disfigurement." For a moment Jengtse's eyes seemed filled with warning. He shrugged and broke away from Shan's gaze. "No one wanted to go up with me to get the body. Taboo, they said. The gods hate any human who dares to go beyond the first ridge. Funny thing. The wolves dragged him a long way before feasting, and up a steep path to a haunted place called the Demon's Den. Clever wolves. Just made people all the more scared when they heard that. There's been demons in the hills since time began. Not our concern. Settling disputes between yaks and highway signs or chasing goats from the town square, that's what proper constables do." Jengtse opened the door and took a step across the threshold.

"I once made a promise to an old lama before he died," Shan said to his back. "I vowed I wouldn't waste my life."

The deputy turned once more. "I hear you have a son, constable," Jengtse said, in a tone of uncharacteristic sympathy. "And you have that old man who visited, your Tibetan uncle, people call him. Those two may want you to stay alive. Aim for goats, not demons," he said and pulled the door shut behind him.

CHAPTER fOUR

An hour later Shan stood in the evening shadows at the side of a long, low building that was composed of several old stables in a row that had been joined with cement block walls. The air around the carpet factory was filled with the pungent, vinegary scent of freshly dyed wool hanging on lines behind the compound. Brightly colored carpets hung on poles to dry after their final washing.

He leaned against the wall, listening to the town retiring for the night. A *dre* brayed from a stable, asking to be milked. A dog barked on the slope above town, stirring finches from their roost in the gorse thickets. From somewhere in the darkness came the creak of one of the old barrel-shaped prayer wheels being turned. Closer by, Shan heard a splash, followed by two more in quick succession. He followed the sound to the end of the structure and discovered Ati and Lodi tossing pebbles into a barrel under the gutter that slanted down from the roof. When he tossed a pebble himself, Raj bounded out of the shadows, tail wagging, and the boys turned, smiling as they recognized Shan. He pulled a small sack of candy from his pocket and handed it to the boys before removing his tunic and balancing a flat rock on the lip of the rain barrel. He gathered a handful of pebbles and wondered aloud which of the boys could knock the rock into the water from ten paces away.

Delighted with the new game, the boys threw the pebbles in turn as Shan, kneeling, stroked the back of the big dog. In his prison, de-spairing monks and lamas had sometimes killed themselves despite the certainty that they would be reincarnated as a four-legged crea-ture. Whenever they encountered a mastiff with a deep, penetrating stare, many of the prisoners were convinced they were seeing a monk who had, in the parlance of prison culture, taken four.

The owner of the little carpet factory favored the off-paper Tibet-ans who worked for the lowest wages—usually those who just lacked proper domicile papers for the town but sometimes, on the night shift, ferals with no registration at all. Shan heard soft voices singing at the far end of the complex where wool was being carded under freshly lit lanterns. He sat and watched the boys until the workers took a break.

Lhamo, the younger boy's great-grandmother, appeared and lit a hand-wrapped roll of tobacco. The coarse tobacco from India was a favorite of some of the older Tibetans, who had few vices other than their cigars.

Yara appeared and went to the barrel, washing wool fibers from her arms and then sluicing water over her head. Her grandmother energetically worked her tobacco, exhaling great clouds of smoke. She had exhaled a perfect ring and turned to show her great-grandson when she saw Shan in the shadows. The old woman whistled, and Yara grabbed her son's arm, as if she were going to flee from the uni-form, then she recognized Shan and the fear left her eyes. Yara whis-pered to her son, sending him to Lhamo, then approached, shaking the water out of her long black hair as she walked.

"Soldiers and knobs will be coming," Shan announced. "Don't be in town when they arrive. And don't go back to Nyima's cave."

The young woman's eyes flickered with surprise, then she slowly nodded and looked back at her grandmother and son. Yara might be willing to take risks on her own, but she worried about her family.

"Nyima will recover," Shan said. "But she is staying with the old *amchi*. She's not going back to her cave, not this week."

"We're not frightened of the ghosts. We have lived with them for years."

Shan hesitated, not certain of her meaning. "I'm sure you've nothing to fear from ghosts," he replied. "Where is the woman with the green eyes? I need to speak with her."

Yara looked away. "I just mind my family."

"You came to the jail with Nyima's bloody *mala* and fled when you saw the soldiers. But you were there for the woman with the green eyes. Is she part of your family? Was she captured near the Plain of Ghosts? If you came to the jail to warn her, tell me why. Tell me where I can find her. She needs help. If she fled back up into the mountains she needs to know a murderer is loose."

Yara watched her son as she replied. "I found some bloody beads. I came to the constable's office with them as was my duty."

"No. I left you on the slope south of town, climbing toward the mountain. But that messenger on the horse changed that. You galloped to town instead. You never came to my station before. Why would a feral Tibetan risk such a thing? If someone had questioned you, you would have been thrown into a cell yourself."

"So now I understand," Yara declared in a defiant voice. "I will never go to your office again."

The words brought an unexpected pain. At another time, in another age, Yara and her family could have become his close friends. But the tunic he was forced to wear would never permit it. "Please. Think of your son and your grandparents. The longer the knobs are here the greater the danger to you. An American was murdered. The violence isn't over. Help me stop it. Who found Nyima's beads? That rider must have come down from the Plain of Ghosts with them. Why did the woman with the green eyes have to see them so urgently?"

She looked up as the moon emerged from behind a cloud. Her uplifted face glowed in the soft light and for a moment she looked more like one of the beautiful *dakini* goddesses depicted in Tibetan paintings than any woman he had ever met. But through her physical beauty, through her defiant strength, there was something else that he had seen too often, the flaw in her beauty. Her strength was hollow, because there was no hope behind it.

"Leave it alone, constable. It was just something that happened in the hills. Happened again. Storms blow hard, then they pass."

"Happened again? What do you mean?"

A sad smile crossed Yara's face. She ran a finger along one of the washed carpets. "My mother's sister was famed in all the herding camps as a healer of sick animals. The abbess of a great convent heard and asked if she could come visit us, to give a blessing to the herds and drape a holy scarf around my aunt's shoulders. It was a great honor, and the camp prepared for it as if for a festival. We saw the abbess coming way down the valley, riding on her donkey, and my aunt trotted out on her own donkey to meet her.

"I was very young, but I will never forget. A terrible black cloud slid out of the mountains. It began dropping hail the size of your fist. My aunt's daughter and I watched from under the rock ledge where we camped. There was nothing we could do. They tried to gallop away, but their donkeys were struck and killed in seconds. They then ran themselves and were hit but got back up on their knees and crawled. They had no chance. They died in front of us. Ten minutes later the sun was shining."

"I fight back in hail storms," Shan stated after several silent heartbeats.

"Then you're a fool. Only an unbalanced soul resists the gods' wishes."

"I don't fight gods, I fight men who steal justice."

"An even greater fool then, in this land."

"The dead American was looking for something. Someone didn't want him to find it. Was it the tomb itself he sought?" Yara looked away as he spoke. He leaned closer to her ear. "A blade was stabbed down into his spine, the way they kill laboratory animals."

Yara visibly shuddered. "In the old days there were summer pastures in the mountains. For a hundred miles nothing but summer pastures, just rich meadows of sweetgrass and wildflowers. Herds of wild yaks and antelope. There used to be a way station for the herders in the center of it, a beautiful high valley along the northern pilgrim's

trail where the herding clans would meet, not far above what's now
the county line. But you can't go there anymore. It's where the new
demons live."

"The new demons?"

"One of those secret bases was built there. They have helicopters.
They test the equipment used to detect people who try to cross over
the Himalayas to freedom. You know. Automatic machine guns. Laser
beams. Trip wires that activate gas bombs. The People's Liberation
Army, they call themselves. Beijing has quite a sense of humor."

The words twisted Shan's gut. Someone whistled from the wool
shed. Lhamo carefully crushed out the embers of her cigar, preserving
it for the next break.

"Just above the house where I live," he said to Yara's back as she
stepped away. She hesitated. "There's an old stable by a stream, shel-
tered by high outcroppings. If you sense trouble, take your family
there. You'll be safe there. In the garden you'll find onions and cab-
bages."

She did not reply. As she disappeared into the shed, Raj stepped in
front of Shan as if to block him from following.

Back at his house, Shan picked at his dinner and then gave up and
dumped the plate on a flat stone, knowing the rock mice would have
more interest in the meal. For perhaps the hundredth time, he reviewed
and refined the list of activities for his son's visit, then wrote up the
report for Mrs. Weng. Finished, he again dragged his pallet outside to
find comfort in the heavens.

He slept fitfully, waking before dawn, his heart hammering, out of
a nightmare in which Lokesh was being marched in front of a firing
squad. Knowing he would find no more rest that night, he pulled out
his bike and set off down a moonlit trail. Half an hour later, with a
hint of gray in the eastern sky, he reached the old salt caravan trail

and stopped by a row of figures carved from salt mined from the deposits in the surrounding hills.

Shan was not certain why he found the eroded, almost shapeless sculptures of the salt shrine so calming. It must be because they were so old, yet seemed to live again, he had suggested to Lokesh when they had walked along the four-foot-high figures.

His old friend, who made a point of whispering into the ear of each eroded saint—or at least into the middle of each amorphous head—had laughed. "Not live again, Shan," the aged Tibetan had corrected. "It is because they have lived all these years. These were placed before the Buddhist came. They are Bon," he explained, referring to the animist religion that had preceded, then blended with, Buddhism in the land. "From when all gods were gods of nature and all creatures rejoiced that they were instruments of the gods." He affectionately stroked a rounded, pinkish head. "They may be asleep but they have not abandoned us, despite our lack of respect."

The old man with the bright eyes had stroked his wispy white beard, then gestured Shan to bend before one of the weather-beaten figures. "Listen!" he had instructed. "It speaks to you."

Shan had earnestly tried to hear something as he lowered his ear to where he supposed the mouth should be. "I guess I don't speak the language," he had conceded at last. "What does it tell me?"

"Be!" Lokesh had declared with a hearty laugh. "Just be! Exercise the gift of life granted to you! Be joyful, be honest, be true! Be the god that lives within you!"

Shan now stood before the same salt figure and bent, trying in vain to hear its wisdom. "I'm sorry," he murmured. He had been losing his connection to the god inside ever since he'd been pushed into the constable's job. He was being forced to be someone he didn't want to be, forced to be an arm of the government he loathed, forced to be the voice of authority when he had spent years defying authority.

Lokesh had seen the struggle in his eyes. His friend had paced along the line of salt figures and then finally rested his hand on top of one whose only identifiable features were the indentations of his eyes. "Here he is," Lokesh had announced. "The constable saint."

Shan had grinned at his friend's gesture. "Surely there was no constable saint."

"Surely," Lokesh replied, "in all the ages, for all the souls, there has had to be. The truth seeker. Your patron. Your protector. Creator of justice where no justice ever existed." The old Tibetan, himself now one of the ever-threatened ferals, had extended a piece of incense, laid it on a rock before the lumpish column of salt, and lit it with one of the stick matches he always carried for the purpose.

Now Shan walked along the row in the rising light and found the constable saint, marked by the ashes of Lokesh's incense. He lit one of the small incense cones he often carried in his pocket and sat before his patron. He did not remember when he had felt so inadequate, so adrift. Not only was justice impossible for the crimes he had discovered, the victims themselves were impossible.

"Striving too much is as destructive as not striving at all," his old friend had often reminded him during their years together. He had spoken the words again there at that very spot. Shan was too logical, too methodical, too committed to solving problems and inequities that were best left to the gods. It was the closest Lokesh would come to suggesting that his new responsibility would become a terrible burden, a shadow across his eternal spirit.

"It's the only way I can see my son," Shan had protested.

Lokesh had shrugged. "The gods will have you listen," he had said, and pointed to the eroded salt face. "Learn to give your problem to the gods, Shan." Then he had taken Shan's bicycle and launched himself down the steep trail, coasting at breakneck speed. Shan ran desperately after him, convinced he would crash at the sharp cliff-top curve, but finally halted, out of breath, and just listened as the Tibetan, more than eighty years old, howled with laughter all the way to the bottom of the ridge.

Shan smiled at the memory, then began to softly chant a mantra to the constable god, losing himself in the rhythmic chant, listening to the song the wind made in the rippling grass. When he closed his eyes he kept seeing the golden saint. *The gods will have you listen.*

The sun was just venturing over the horizon, casting its early rays on the treetops, as Shan entered the kitchen door of the noodle shop. The little café would not open for another hour, but Ati's uncle, Marpa, was always happy to make him a bowl of porridge. Big pots of water already boiled on the stove. Marpa, whose deep black eyes were usually lit with a smile, paused in his task of measuring out spices to pour a cup of tea for Shan, then gestured him into the empty dining room.

On his one visit to Yangkar, Lokesh had insisted on joining Shan at the window table every morning at dawn. Shan's former prison mate enjoyed speaking with Marpa, but most of all he was enchanted by the view of the snow-covered peaks to the north, framed perfectly by the buildings at the end of the square. When the sun first hit them, the summits would glow like diamonds hovering in the sky, then the mountains would gradually emerge out of the grayness.

"It must be the way the world was formed," Lokesh had exclaimed the first time he witnessed such a sunrise. He had seen the confusion on Shan's face.

"But Lokesh, that would be upside down," Shan pointed out.

"Not at all!" Lokesh patiently explained. "Because the gods would start with the pieces closest to heaven!"

Marpa brought Shan's porridge on a tray with some pickled vegetables, then sat with his own cup of tea.

"You've been in Yangkar all your life?" he asked the cook.

"Except for the empty years."

"I'm sorry?"

"When they dragged people off to one of those big collective farms near Lhasa." Marpa grinned. "I was just a boy, but they insisted we all work the fields. Some fools in Beijing decided we had to grow cotton and maize. We told them it was too dry and the growing season wasn't long enough, but that didn't matter because the Chairman had willed it. Every plant shriveled up and died. At the end of the first year when officials came for inspection, the Chinese in charge brought in a truck-load of cotton and ears of maize from Szechuan and put them in our storehouse. Then the inspectors awarded us a medal for best produc-tivity in the county, though they made sure to distribute a truckload of beer first so we would be too drunk to protest." The men ex-changed a long glance. Marpa made it sound like some sort of theater of the absurd, but they both knew that life on the early collectives had been a living hell. The Tibetan tipped his cup to Shan and drank.

"Was there much fighting here when the army arrived?"

Marpa took so long to answer Shan thought he had not heard. "First the Red Guard, the teenagers with guns," he finally replied in a near whisper. "A few months later the Red Army. If a Tibetan could find a weapon there was fighting."

"I mean here, in the mountains around Yangkar."

Marpa pointed toward the range framed by the square. "I heard Mrs. Weng explain to a tourist who asked about the name of the Ghost Mountains. She said they were called that because they look like ghosts in the twilight."

"But that's not the reason."

The Tibetan sipped at his tea. "It was a long time ago, Shan. No concern of yours."

"The ghosts aren't a trick of the light," Shan pressed.

Marpa gazed back out the window. "They called it a clearance, like they're doing now with the herders from the high plains. Guard posts were set up, maps were handed out. No one allowed within a zone in the mountains to the north, about twenty-five square miles. They trucked a few out, old ones and children mostly. They nailed notices to the buildings here, nailed one to the main gates, nailed an-other to the knee of the huge carved Buddha that sat where the square is now. Funny thing was that the notices were only in Chinese and not a soul in town could read them. We didn't understand until the next day when a herding family began taking a flock of sheep into the pastures up there. An army sniper stood on top of the old tower and killed them one by one. I don't think they understood why their loved ones were suddenly dropping. They had never seen that kind of rifle, only old muskets that shot a hundred yards at most. They just stopped, looking back toward town in confusion as the bullets ripped into them. Wouldn't even let us go collect the bodies, wouldn't let us even go into the temple here to pray for them."

"Temple?" Shan asked. There was no temple in Yangkar.

"Like I said, that was before. Not long after that they hauled us away."

It was Shan's turn to stare into his cup. "But it's not army territory today. When did the restrictions get lifted?"

Marpa shrugged. "People are still scared to go up there. At first, when people were allowed back, a few went up. They found old camps with skeletons. Of dogs, of yaks, of people, just their bones circled around campfires. Killed where they lay in sleep, I guess. No one would go up after that. It was a black place, a soulless place. Then the demons came. Not often, usually on nights of a full moon. But herders still say they see demons dancing on the ridge. Demons of bones, demons with bull and horse heads, shaking bone clubs and rattles. No one dares go up anymore. A black place. A death zone. Might as well be the army's. This is Lhadrung County," he added with another shrug.

"What do you mean?"

"How many counties still have a military governor? How many have so many prisons run by the army? That bastard Colonel Tan runs this county like his personal fiefdom. If he wants something the army takes it."

Shan looked back out toward the snow-covered mountains. The bodies of the murdered men were out there, in a cave below a gilded saint. Once that saint had lived there. It had not been a soulless place then. "Tan is getting old," he ventured. "He's been sick." Shan saw that Marpa was confused by his words, and he flushed at the thought that they may have been taken as an apology for the despised colonel. He lifted his spoon and focused on his porridge.

Marpa rose, then hesitated. "Is it true?" he asked. "That there has been more killing up there?"

"No Tibetans," was all Shan said.

Marpa gave a satisfied grunt and retreated. He was halfway across the room when he halted, muttering, then hurried back into the kitchen only to reemerge with a small paper sack that he dropped on Shan's table. "Almost forgot. Baked porridge with raisins," he explained. "Shiva sent word," he declared. "Can't let the furry lama go hungry."

The door at the end of the narrow cobbled alley was flanked by painted images of a hare and a moon, a peacock, and half a dozen other astrological signs. As Shan lifted the iron latch of the door the strong scent of incense wafted outside. Shiva, a diminutive Tibetan woman of seventy years, was sought out for her skills of prediction, and when she wasn't working on a specific commission she made sample horoscopes and *sipaho*, protective charms hung on doors to fend off demons. Inside the door was painted a tortoise with twelve animals on its shell, the foundation diagram used for Tibetan horoscopes.

The old woman sat cross-legged on a small carpet, working at a low easel with delicate brushes, jars of pigment scattered around her. Her face, wrinkled like a worn leather sack, lit with a smile as Shan appeared and extended the bag. She rose, tossing a cloth over her work, then motioned him toward a glass box, an old aquarium much patched with tape and wooden slats, that sat in the sunlight before the room's only window.

"My uncle was very hungry last week," she said and drew up the remnant of carpet that covered the open top of the cage. A small, long-legged, brown rodent squirmed out of the deep layer of sand and looked up with huge, moist eyes. Shiva was convinced that her great-uncle, once a lama, had been reincarnated in the gerbil. She had carefully explained to Shan in one of his first days in the office that in

Yangkar there had been a long tradition of having all food for animals blessed by the local abbot in a weekly ceremony. Yangkar had apparently always had a special relationship with its four-legged residents, and there seemed to be quite a few who were identified as reincarnations of holy men and women.

Shan emptied the bag from Marpa onto one palm and placed the other palm over it. *"Om mani padme hum,"* he murmured self-consciously. There were no more abbots in the township, and Shiva had decided a constable who wore a Buddhist prayer amulet around his neck was the best substitute.

Shiva pressed her hands together in gratitude, then took the baked porridge, broke off a small piece, and dropped it in front of the gerbil. Instead of eating it, the animal stared at Shan with its large nocturnal eyes. He seemed to be accusing Shan of being a fraud. Shan backed away from the intense gaze.

"Birth or death?" he asked, nodding at the easel. Most of the astrologer's charms were for the families of the newly born or newly dead, either of whom needed special protection as they embarked on new spiritual journeys.

"You forget I also do protective banners," the woman replied. She hurried to the doorway. "Did you see I painted a peacock? They say it is a favorite of the Green Tara." Shan considered her nervous gesture toward the new image, then made a quick step to her easel and, ignoring a gasp of protest from Shiva, pulled away the cloth.

It was a death chart, composed with extraordinary skill. He knelt and studied it, confused by the imagery. Such charts reflected the life of the deceased and were meant to set forth the propitious days for disposal of the body and mourning rites. Shiva had provided for a dozen small rectangular panels on the chart, half of which already contained intricate images or elegantly scripted prayers.

Shiva's red apron touched his shoulder. She had retrieved the cover and meant to return it to the painting. "I get letters sometimes from far away, with money tucked inside and a request for a chart. There's not many of us left, you know."

Shan scanned the traditional prayers on the chart, then pointed to a panel containing a bird. "What is this?"

"It's common enough to put vultures on a chart, indicating the sky burial to follow. Or *garudas*," she added, speaking of the sacred bird that protected Tibetans against serpents.

"This is no *garuda*, Shiva. And vultures don't have white heads. And what is this?" he asked, pointing to what looked like a semicircular fortress with high poles extending above it.

The astrologer turned away from him. He read the other words on the half-finished death chart. The burial was to be the following week, and the words for comforting disturbed souls were to be spoken for forty-nine days. When he straightened she was standing at the glass cage by the window. Her eyes were filled with moisture.

"I never asked you your uncle's name," he observed.

"Kapo. Uncle Kapo."

Without really knowing why, Shan reached down into the cage. The gerbil jumped onto his palm, and he readily let Shan stroke the back of his head.

Shan lifted Kapo up and held him close to his chest. "How can you trust me to protect your Uncle Kapo's immortal spirit, Shiva, and not trust me with a few simple explanations?"

As the old woman saw how Shan and Kapo both patiently stared at her, she smiled through her tears. "I'm scared, constable, scared for all of us."

"Shan. Just Shan."

"He came from far away. A nice boy. But nothing good ever happens when people from far away arrive in Yangkar."

"American. It's why you painted that white-headed eagle."

Her nod was slow and melancholy.

"What is the fortress?" Shan asked as he lowered Kapo back into his cage.

Shiva stepped to a clay pot and extracted a postcard. *Pittsburgh, City of Steel*, said the caption across the top of the glossy photograph. It showed a cluster of skyscrapers above a point of land where two great rivers met. On the river bank opposite the towers was a large semicircular stadium that vaguely resembled the image on the chart. "His greatest joys were ships and going to that sports arena. It was like his temple. Now I have to draw a ship. But I've never seen a ship. I've never even seen the ocean. A world of nothing but water, they say."

"Ships sail the ocean the way clouds sail the sky," Shan offered.

The astrologer replied with a solemn shake of her head. "I can't settle my mind around that. Everyone knows water never stays in one place. Where does it all go?"

"You met the American?" Shan asked after a moment.

"Not for long. There was going to be a feast later, next week, they said, for all of us in . . . for all of us. He promised he would have much more time to spend with me when we met again. He was in a hurry."

Shan had no stomach for interrogating the woman. "But someone else came later. Who asked for the chart?"

"Her news made me weep. He was so young. A new kind of Tibetan, the kind we need now . . ." Her voice drifted away, then she looked up at Shan. "This is not for you, Shan. The gods will deal with it."

"You wouldn't write a chart without a name. I would say a prayer if I knew his name."

"Jag . . . Jagob." She struggled with the syllables, then pulled a slip a paper from her apron and handed it to Shan. "I can't read English, but I said I would make those letter shapes."

Jacob Taklha, he read in neat Western letters. He stared at the name in confusion. Taklha was Tibetan. "That can't be," Shan said. "He was American."

Shiva kept her eyes on the gerbil. "Just a name for the death chart. Sometimes people use a nickname, even a code name."

"What did you mean, a new kind of Tibetan?" he pressed.

Shiva was not comfortable lying. She returned to the window and silently stroked her Uncle Kapo's back.

"When?" Shan asked. "When were you asked to do the death chart?"

Shiva hesitated. "Three days ago."

Shan's mind raced. They had opened the tomb of the golden saint two days before. Someone had known the day before, which was likely the very day the American had died. Someone had seen the body before it had gone into the tomb.

"What was your payment?" Shan tried.

The astrologer reached into the jar again and produced a simple gold band, a small elegant ring. "I protested that it was far too much. She said keep it, she didn't need it anymore. Buy incense, she said. Ransom a goat in his name, build a *chorten*, she told me."

Ransoming an animal to save it from slaughter was something Tibetans did to gain spiritual merit. It was not something foreigners would know about. "Where did she come from?" Shan asked. The ring had the look of a wedding band.

"I went out to eat lunch in the stables. The animals keep me calm. When I came back they were here, waiting in the alley, watching the street. She was wiping away tears. I gave her the hem of my apron and said dry them, dear girl, because I wanted to see those beautiful green eyes."

CHAPTER FIVE

As Shan reached the uneven pavement of the town square, a walnut landed by his foot. He looked up to see Lodi waving to him from high in a walnut tree and absently waved back. Then, seeing that Jinhua's car was still parked by the station, he walked a slow circuit of the square. The little *chorten* at the far end remained only half painted. Neither Rikyu nor any of the townspeople who helped her had been there since the day the prisoners arrived. The young nun had escorted Nyima into the doctor's house but had hurried away once the doctor had confirmed the old woman would survive. Shan realized he had no idea where Rikyu lived and would have to wait to ask her more about the attack on Nyima.

He slowed as he completed the circuit. Raj the big mastiff sat at the base of the walnut tree, looking up at Lodi with a distinctly worried expression. The boy did not respond when Shan called up to him, just kept looking toward the eastern sky, and Shan realized he had not thrown the walnut in play but to summon Shan. He mounted one of the concrete gaming tables and followed the boy's gaze. Seeing nothing at first, he cupped his hand above his eyes. He thought the black dot must be a vulture but then he realized it was not moving. It was a helicopter. The army was watching Yangkar.

Shan lowered himself to sit cross-legged on the little table, built in the Chinese style for chess and mahjong players. His hands seemed to

move on their own, clasping together, his index fingers forming a steeple. It was a *mudra*, one of the hand gestures used in Buddhist meditation. This one was called Diamond of the Mind, meant for focusing
the mind. He stared into it, trying to strip the facts to the bone. He
could not understand any of the events of the past few days. Something terrible was unfolding in Yangkar and he was helpless to stop it.

A walnut hit his arm, another his knee. He looked up to see Lodi
standing a few feet away now. "You look like some old statue up there
on your pedestal," the boy said. "Raj has challenged you to see who
can hold stiller."

The big dog sat beside the boy, staring at Shan. It spoke, with a
long rattling sound that had the tone of a question.

"Sorry," Shan said to the dog, "I don't speak your—" He stopped,
then jumped down from the table. "You win," he said as he patted the
dog's head, then motioned the boy closer and whispered.

When he returned to the station he instructed Jengtse to take the
truck out to the little crossroads inn a dozen miles to the south to
make sure the inspection certificate at the fuel station was current.

"Now? I'll miss lunch," his deputy groused. "I could just call."

Shan extracted a crumpled currency note from his pocket. "The
innkeeper runs a kitchen for the truckers. Buy yourself some soup and
dumplings."

Jengtse sighed and took the keys off the desk. As he drove away
Shan raced to the top of the stone tower at the edge of the square. He
watched as the truck sped down the switchbacks that led to the highway. The helicopter broke from its hover and followed the truck of
the Yangkar constable.

Lodi was waiting at the town's garage when Shan arrived, wearing an
uncertain grin. "What do you mean you need a car?" snapped the
young mechanic. "You think you can just send a boy with instructions
and I'll kowtow? I don't care if you wear a badge!"

"I only want to borrow it for the day," Shan answered evenly. "Is your father here?"

"I don't need my father to—" The youth's reply was cut off as the door from the inner office opened and a middle-aged Tibetan in oil-stained coveralls emerged. He swatted the young mechanic with a rag.

"Constable," the mechanic greeted Shan in a cheerful tone.

"Tserung," Shan acknowledged with a nod. "I have a favor to ask."

The younger man muttered under his breath, and Tserung cuffed him on the shoulder.

"This is Constable Shan, boy. He's the one who located your brother. After all these years, we found him," the man said with a smile aimed at Shan. "How rough are the roads you will travel? How long?"

"All paved. Back in the evening sometime."

Tserung's older son had been arrested years earlier, but no one in the government had ever responded to the family's requests about the location of his prison. Shan had spent a morning on the computer and located the son's name on a list of inmates at a prison in Gansu Province. With Shan's help in affixing the proper address in Chinese, Tserung had been able to open a correspondence with his son, who had been told his family had all died.

The Tibetan garage owner pointed to an old Red Flag sedan, a mainstay on Beijing roads decades earlier. "I'll put a can of water in the trunk. She tends to overheat, but she's still a steady workhorse. And an extra can of gas." He took a step toward a shelf of gas cans and paused to turn to his son. "Gyatso, make sure there's no sheep droppings in the backseat," he whispered, with an embarrassed glance at Shan.

Shan had just turned onto the connecting road to the north-south highway, fifteen miles above Yangkar, when he slammed on the brakes and pulled onto the shoulder. In a narrow turnout several portable trestle road barricades were stacked, each bearing a faded sign reading NO PASSAGE BY ORDER OF THE PEOPLE'S LIBERATION ARMY. They were used to seal roads for the passage of military convoys or, just as often, the long convoys transporting Tibetans between prisons and internment camps. He knelt with the sun behind him and studied the soil around the barricades, then the tire marks leading up to them. A heavy truck had turned around recently, rolling over the narrower, lighter tire marks left by a sedan.

He paced along the edge of the turnout. The tracks had been made since the last rainfall five days earlier. The detainees had been diverted to Yangkar because the road to the highway had been closed. Before he returned to the driver's seat he took off his tunic, placing it in the trunk—chicken feathers blew out as he opened it—and pulled on a sweater.

It was early afternoon when Shan finally reached Lhasa. He parked the car on a side street and looked for tour buses, mingling with the tourists. From a street vendor he bought a cheap plastic camera bag with an image of the Potala on its side and a visored cap imprinted with a cartoonish panda riding a yak. He found the Palace Hotel a few blocks away, but instead of entering immediately, he sat with a pot of tea in a café across from it, studying the building, the cars parked around it, and the cameras on the utility poles aimed at its doors. There was always surveillance on hotels that accommodated foreigners, but when there was no special cause for concern Public Security would likely just rely on the cameras, and then only monitor them from time to time. He waited until a bus arrived, disgorging Chinese tourists into the hotel, then pulled his cap low, crossed the street, and pushed into the throng of noisy tourists as they entered the lobby. He entered the elevator with a half a dozen of them, riding up to the sixth floor. Room 619 was at the end of the hall, with a DO NOT DISTURB sign on it. He waited until the last of those in the hall entered their rooms, then inserted the key.

The chamber was comfortable, though far from luxurious. Its thin beige carpet was in need of replacement, the heavy drapes over the window in need of washing. The Palace was a mid-tier hotel that catered to affluent domestic travelers and low-end Western tour groups, with many Tibetans on its staff, the kind of place where foreigners and locals could meet inconspicuously. Two black nylon duffel bags were under the bed. A garment bag hung in the small closet. Half a dozen books were stacked beside the small television. There was no dirty laundry, no cigarette butts in the ashtray, no crumpled linens or any other sign that the room had recently been used.

He examined the books, all with Chinese covers. A history of the Eighth Route Army, as told from the perspective of liberated peasants. A report on the successes of collectivism in agriculture, and one of the lesser biographies of the Great Helmsman. But the books inside the covers were not as advertised. None were in Chinese. *Sky Burial*, a tale of the death of Tibet, read the first title page. *In the Service of My Country* read the second, then *In Exile from the Land of the Snows*. They were books about the suffering of Tibetans at the hands of the Chinese, books that were banned by Beijing. They had been glued inside the covers of Chinese propaganda volumes. The remaining books were a Tibetan-English dictionary, a book on mountain climbing, and a dog-eared book on Tibetan Buddhism published by an American university. Beside them on the table was a sheet of paper on which had been written *Potala 12523, 1.3.*

He searched the duffel bags, stacking their contents on the bed. Clothes of a size that would fit the big American. Two dress shirts, bearing the same Pittsburgh label as that of the shirt the man called Jacob Taklha had been wearing when he died. At the bottom of the first duffel was a cardboard carton, a cube eight inches to a side. Inside were pieces of bubble wrap and several rubber bands. Whatever had been in the box had been valuable or fragile, or both, and the American had taken it north with him.

The second bag was nearly empty except for a sweatshirt labeled Steel City Rowers and two heavy plastic bags. One contained a pair of needle-nosed pliers, a set of small screwdrivers, and a roll of black electrician's tape. The second contained what had been a small, cheap Chinese radio receiver. It was not a complete receiver, he saw as he turned it over and peeled away the black tape that held it together, but rather the case for a receiver. The American had used it to conceal something inside.

He lifted the garment bag and searched its pockets, then the tweed sports coat and trousers inside it, finding only chewing gum, matches, and receipts for taxis in Hong Kong from two weeks earlier. He ran his hand along the high shelf at the top of the closet beside a stack of folded towels and pulled away a flat cloth pouch embroidered with Buddhist signs. Inside were two plastic sheets and a notebook. The sheets each held pockets for half a dozen photographs, two of which remained. The first was a black-and-white image of a stone house with a large stone barn behind it, with a big American sedan from the 1960s parked under a spreading tree to the left of the barn. A young man wearing wire-rimmed spectacles and a graceful woman, both with dark hair, stood before the house with a dog sitting between them. The couple was too far away for him to make out details of their faces, but the woman looked Asian. Only the dog was clearly recognizable. It was a Tibetan mastiff.

He pulled out the photo he had taken from Nyima's hiding place, in which a woman with two children stood in front of a stone wall. Stone walls were like fingerprints, no two were alike. It was the same woman, a few years older, and they stood before the same stone house in the United States.

The second photo was more recent and in color, of a smiling family group by the same barn, of five adults and three children. In the center was the same bespectacled man, his hair graying, beside a man of about thirty years with his arm around a red-haired woman, standing behind three blond and red-haired children, none older than nine or ten. At one end stood a tall man of about forty wearing a military uniform, and at the opposite end an athletic-looking woman, a few years younger, with brunette hair and wearing what appeared to be a dark blue uniform. Along the white border at the top of the photograph, names had been penciled in over the heads. The row of adults was listed as Jake, Dad, Ben, Susan, and Jig, then for the children, Samuel, Madison, and Caleb. Shan held the photo closer to the light to study the man in the uniform, recalling the anchor tattooed on his shoulder. The jacket was double breasted and had two narrow gold stripes at the base of each sleeve. Shiva had said one of the American's passions had been ships. Jake was Jacob. The dead man had been in the American navy.

His gaze shifted to the black-and-white image, considering the paths that might have taken a young Tibetan woman to America so many decades earlier. The man and wife stood proudly in front of their stone home. Shan tried to recall the American history his father had secretly taught him decades earlier. Pennsylvania was one of the original colonies, where the founders of the United States had met. It would have old houses made of stone. The second image had to be of children and grandchildren, but the mother was missing. She was likely the one behind the camera.

The spiral notebook had pages torn out at the back, and the rest of the pages were filled with drawings, numbers, and efforts at writing Tibetan script. The Tibetan writing at the front was rough and clumsy, sometimes illegible, but toward the back the strokes became more fluid and the words perfectly clear. He gazed at it in surprise.

Jade green pool, spring water clear, it said. The writing exercise was repeated again and again. It was in Tibetan, but the text was from the eighth-century Chinese poet Han Shan.

Some of the drawings were of buildings, groups of *chortens* and clusters of structures that called to mind *gompas*, the traditional monasteries of Tibet. Others appeared to be hand-drawn maps, some of them of broad regions with mountain ranges marked, others close-in depictions of building compounds. One had four *chortens* on four separate peaks surrounding what he guessed to be a *gompa* on the side of a mountain. The *chortens* would be dedicated to demons who protected the residents of the monastery. Another showed a ring of twenty *chortens*, inside of which was a cluster of elegant buildings, framed by several high peaks in the background. He leafed back and forth, gradually recognizing that the drawings were in two different hands. Some had a bold, measured style, made with a thick pencil lead, like the work of an engineer, while the others, on paper slightly yellowed from age, were softer, crafted with a firmer hand, and included shadows adeptly shaded in with the side of the pencil lead.

The numbers in the notebook seemed to be variations of the same sets, pairings of six and six, with differences only in the last two or three digits, followed by question marks. He considered them for several minutes, trying to imagine them as phone numbers, then alphabet codes, before realizing they were latitudes and longitudes, done by someone who was speculating, who was not certain of the exact location of what he sought, though knowing it was in the vicinity of Yangkar. He looked back at the drawings. With a good map the American could have lined up known geologic features, like the peaks in the first sketch of the *chortens*, to ascertain an exact location, but good maps were not available in China except to the military. The government's public maps distorted features and provided only rough approximations of entire regions. If he had descriptions, even sketches of several peaks as seen from a given location, the American could have constructed a map by pinpointing such landmarks. Shan looked back at the sketch of the *gompa*. Jacob had died with a GPS device in his pocket. It seemed a laborious, unlikely way to locate a set of buildings. Suddenly Shan understood. The buildings no longer existed. The American had been trying to find the site of buildings that had been destroyed by the Chinese.

On the last page was a different map of sorts, of a road or perhaps river intersected by a perpendicular line drawn with a straight edge. At the point where the line cut across the road was a sketch of what looked like a tall tree, with an arrow pointing to the top beside the single English word "Red." Along the bottom were numbers: 700, 1300, 1900.

Shan closed the notebook in frustration. It did not seem possible that the dead man could be so anonymous. He picked up the duffels, searching the straps now, at last finding a small tag integrated into the strap itself. JACOB T. BARTRAM, it stated in block letters, US NAVY

RETIRED, then UNIVERSITY OF PITTSBURGH. Shan stared at the name. Jacob Taklha was the name Shiva had been given for her death chart. The dead man was Jacob Taklha Bartram.

He sat on the bed, pulled the phone directory from the nightstand, and a moment later lifted the phone. "China Travel Service, Lhasa office" came the brisk female voice at the other end. He identified himself as a police officer from Shigatse, since it was one of the few towns where foreigners were permitted. As provider and coordinator of tourist visas, CTS was charged with knowing the whereabouts of all foreigners in China. After a hold of less than a minute the woman confirmed that Jacob Bartram of the United States had arrived in China on a tourist visa over two weeks earlier. He had spent four days in Hong Kong, where he had booked the agency's seven-day Wonders of Tibet tour, then joined at the Beijing airport for the flight to Lhasa. The clerk was interrupted by someone at her end, then quickly amended her report to explain that on arrival Mr. Bartram had canceled his tour, citing altitude sickness, even though he had been warned his prepaid fee was not refundable. If Mr. Bartram was now in Shigatse, he should be reminded that private unescorted travel was not permitted outside the approved localities. Shan thanked her and hung up.

Shan paced in silence, studying the room, then launched a new search, checking the window drapes, inside the pillow cases, under the mattress and seat cushions, finally lifting the towels off the closet shelf one at a time. Inside the folds of the bottom towel he found a small packet of letters tied up with green silk ribbon, like a gift. He untied the ribbon and counted out a dozen letters, arranging them on the little desk by date of postmark. All were in the same hand, not Bartram's, all with the same return address in Pennsylvania, and all were addressed to simply *Taklha* in Yangkar, Tibet, in English and Tibetan. The early letters were dated a year apart, starting in 1969. Then they became more sporadic, the last ending in 2010. The envelopes of the first six, all on the onion skin paper once favored for international air mail, bore multiple legends affixed with official rubber stamps.

DELIVERY DENIED, read the largest, in Mandarin and English, then COUNTRY DESTINATION INVALID. The addresses all defiantly read "Tibet" with no reference to the People's Republic of China. The last six bore no official rejections, because they had never been mailed. Not one of the letters had ever been opened. Inside would be the answers to at least some of his questions about the dead American.

He lifted the first, feeling a stab of guilt for even thinking of breaching their confidences, then glanced at his watch. It was late and the drive up over the mountains during the last leg of his trip would be treacherous in the dark. He straightened the room to leave no sign of his presence, stuffed the letters into his tourist bag, and left. It took him nearly an hour to escape the Lhasa traffic. He was held up not by the emaciated Tibetan man who was progressing along the pilgrim path to the Jokhang Temple in slow prostrations, lying on the ground before each step, but by the crowds of laughing Chinese tourists who were snapping photographs of the solitary, determined pilgrim.

By the time Shan cleared the pass that led down into Yangkar Township, a large gibbous moon had risen. The rugged landscape was washed in pale silvery light, the summer snow on the peaks glowing against the night sky. On his visit to Yangkar, Lokesh had spent much of his time locating old pilgrim trails that led to forgotten shrines in the mountains. Pick up the thread in the passes, Lokesh always explained, and indeed they had found the traces of a trail along a high ledge only a hundred yards from this very road. He parked the car on the shoulder and by the light of the moon climbed to the cairn they had built at one of the small flats where pilgrims would have once stopped to pray.

He began gathering some dried heather and brush for a small fire, then abruptly stopped. Facing west, framed by the pass, he could see a blinking red light. The north-south line on the crude map on the last page of Bartram's notebook had been the Lhasa highway, and it had not been a tree beside the perpendicular line, it had been a tower capped by a red light. He turned and studied the shadowed landscape. The line had been drawn to the east and the marks on it had been the high points on certain ridges of the Ghost Mountains. The numbers had been times, expressed in military format. 700, 1300, and 1900. Six-hour intervals, like a military check-in. 7 A.M., 1 P.M., and 7 P.M. Back in his office he would draw the line on his own map, but he already guessed it would intersect the tomb of the gilded saint. The crude map marked a line of sight from the cell tower. Yangkar had no cell service, but Bartram had discovered that a cell signal could be found along that line. The Tibetans had heard the Hallelujah prayer slightly after midday. Someone had been following his instructions and calling the dead man's phone.

Shan lit the fire and sat, cross-legged, beside it, then scooped soil into a mound. He extracted a small cone of incense from a pocket, lit it in the flames, and set it reverently on the mound. As the fragrant smoke rose toward the moon, he raised a hand to the north, for Lokesh, and then to the south, for Ko, and took out the letters.

"Forgive me, Jacob Bartram," he said in the direction of the ice cave, then opened the first letter. September 1969. The message had been sealed away for decades, crossing the Pacific unopened three times. It was all in Tibetan, and loving hands had turned it into a work of art. Little images were skillfully drawn along the edges, in the fashion of illuminated prayer books. Some were auspicious signs like a lotus and conch shell, but there were also songbirds, a deer, an acorn, and a pumpkin with a carved face. *Cherished family*, it began,

I have taken up my pen many times these past years to write you but it always felt as though I could speak of only an incomplete journey, of a story without a real ending or at least a meaningful stopping place. But I have at last found my place, in a beautiful and fertile land called Pennsylvania, in America. I have a husband who is a professor at a great university and a home with enough room for you and all our cousins if the troubles find their way to Yangkar.

The letter went on for five pages. He flipped to the back and read the closing: *May Mother Tara watch over you.* It was signed *Pema Taklha Bartram.*

He turned back to the front pages and leaned over the candle, reading the rest, piecing together the tale of a woman who had escaped across the Himalayas with five friends to obtain a blessing from the Dalai Lama for their struggling families. Three of the party had died on the journey, but Pema and one other had survived, only to be rounded up with other Tibetans and sent to one refugee camp after another, first in Nepal, then in India. After several months she had made it to Dharamsala, home of the exiled Tibetan government, where she had at last received the blessing of the Dalai Lama but was then asked by him to take on a job teaching in a school for Tibetan children. She had worked alongside an American volunteer, a young professor named Daniel Bartram, and there, in the shadows of the Himalayas, they had fallen in love. She had grown despondent over his inevitable departure, knowing how difficult it would be to visit him in America, but then he had explained that the answer was for them to marry. They had done so before an old lama, then, after they had arrived in America, a second ceremony had been performed in the church of Daniel's parents. After a year in a city apartment they had moved to an old stone farmhouse on the side of a mountain.

The last page comprised a list of questions. How many calves had Pema's favorite old *dre* birthed since she left? Has the abbot finally had his cataracts remedied? Has Father finally repainted the old stable? Has brother Kolsang received his yak hair whisk? Did Dolma finish her rainbow carpet? If the Chinese ever found Yangkar, she advised, tell my brother to be respectful and patient. She was sure they would not stay for long.

Shan returned the letter to its envelope and stared at the dying fire, then gazed out over the vast shadowed landscape. He hated himself for playing the voyeur to the family's secrets. He hated the killers for forcing him to do so. He wanted to shout out across the ocean, across the years, to beg this gentle, loving woman to hide her eyes, to stop looking toward Tibet so she might think of it only as she remembered. Most of all he wanted her never to know the son she had sent to Tibet had been murdered.

He slept fitfully that night, awaking to a nightmare vision of the gilded saint chasing him with a ritual dagger, then gave up sleep and spent the early morning hours cleaning his house for Ko's visit, only three days away now.

The breaking of the day was sometimes quite literal in Tibet. He had dozed off, leaning against the plastered wall of his house as he watched the stars. A terrible cracking sound abruptly woke him. The air seemed to be splitting over his head. As he shook off the fog of sleep he realized that a small, intense storm was passing over the mountain, pressing down patches of the long grass in its passage as if with giant footsteps. It grabbed the land with claws of lightning as it traveled down the valley. As was often the case in the high, dry air, there was more thunder and lightning than rain, although for a few seconds the ground around his house was pelted with half-inch stones of hail. In less than five minutes the sky overhead was clear and the sun was edging over the horizon in a blaze of gold and purple. To the southwest he could still see the pocket of black cloud, touching the earth with its fire. He lifted the hail stone and rolled it in his fingers, looking up at the violent sky. It was no wonder so many Tibetans still believed in the earth deities.

He filled a bucket from the hand pump outside his door, washed, then made a mug of tea and opened the second letter from America. Pema had again illuminated the margins, this time with more images of her new home, including a small rendering of the stone house he had seen in the photographs, a tractor, a dove, and a cat. Every day she said prayers for each of the family in Yangkar, Pema reported. She wondered if she sent American money whether Dolma could use it to get a new loom. Were Mother and Father's old coats, she asked, still warm enough for the winter?

Her husband was very successful at his university post teaching eastern religions and Asian literature, she reported, beloved by his classes, and they often entertained his students on weekends. A German woman down the road was teaching her knitting, and she was making them all scarves. She told them the American post office used special codes and suggested that their letters must not be getting through because no one in Tibet would know such codes. She wrote the five numbers out and underlined them to be sure they would know for their next letters. She had started a garden, and they would be amazed at the unusual vegetables that could be grown in Pennsylvania. She would try to send some melon seeds. She was making *Aunt Nyima* a new felt hat embroidered with one of the protector dragons.

Nyima and the dead American were of the same family. The news haunted Shan as he drove into town. Pema had sent her son, the sturdy former military man, to reconnect with their family, to find his lost relatives, but, he suspected that, except for the old nun, they were alive now only in her heart. With the frailest of hope, he went to the office of the town clerk at the end of the square. Mr. Wu enthusiastically pulled out ledgers of registrations and tax rolls. He handed one of the heavy books to Shan and then opened one himself. "Annual lists," Wu explained, "back for twenty-five years." The clerk hesitated, then darted to his desk. "This came for you, Comrade Constable, in a package from Lhasa." He handed Shan an envelope marked MINISTRY OF THE INTERIOR. Shan quickly pushed it into his pocket and opened the ledger.

He started with the oldest entries, and the two men bent over the books in intense examination for a quarter hour. "Nothing, Comrade Constable," Wu finally said. "No mention of a family named Taklha.

But then I guess we wouldn't find it, would we? Anyone who agreed to move back to the restored town was assigned a Chinese name. And there are those damned ferals. They wouldn't be anywhere on the books, unless for arrest warrants."

Shan considered the clerk's words and realized the horrible truth. Pema, who had bravely left her beloved home to bring her family a blessing from the Dalai Lama, had been writing for decades to dead people.

Over a late breakfast he asked Marpa about a young woman named Pema who had left to meet the Dalai Lama many years earlier, but his friend only shrugged. "It was one of those dreams that gave people hope in the dark years. A blessing would come back from the Dalai Lama and our lives would change. But no one ever came back."

Shan asked about the family name. "Taklha?" Marpa repeated the name and stroked his bristly chin, then stepped back into the kitchen to confer with the old Tibetan who washed dishes. The old man dried his hands and bent to write something. "One of those families who were landowners here above town," Marpa reported. "One of the big farms that kept the monks fed. But . . . you know how it was. . . . It didn't go well for landowners when the Red Guard came through."

"Where did they live?" Shan pressed.

Marpa brought out the dishwasher, whose nervous smile revealed several missing teeth. When Shan repeated the question the old man grunted and pointed toward the hills above town, then flattened his hand and made a sharp cutting gesture.

"I don't understand," Shan said.

"I thought you knew," Marpa explained. "He's mute, but makes himself understood well enough. I think he means the places are gone." The old man pointed to Shan, then put his hands together and rested his head on them.

"My house?" Shan asked.

The old man nodded, then held up two more fingers and pointed once to the east and once to the west.

Shan drew a rough map on a napkin, showing the town and the

ridges above it, then handed the old man his pencil. "Show me the others." The aged Tibetan chewed on the pencil a moment, then quickly made two X marks and pushed the napkin back to Shan.

"One branch of the family had the little burnt-out house in the valley," Marpa said, pointing to the first mark. "And the bigger one, the manor house as it were," he began, shaking his head as he examined the map. "No good."

"No good?" Shan asked.

The old man took the napkin back and used the pencil again, then returned the map with an apologetic expression. He had drawn two tiny skeletons on the ridge above the larger house.

"The ghosts," Marpa explained in a tight voice. "The demons. That's where they live. They're real, Shan. I've seen them myself."

"Surely you haven't seen demons walking the hills, Marpa."

"On my sacred soul, yes!" his friend insisted. "In the light of the full moon the skeletons dance, shaking old rattles and waving human bones. The old ones say it's always been like that. Just stay away and no one gets hurt."

Shan studied the Tibetan. Marpa was a steadfast man, not particularly superstitious, and not prone to flights of fancy. "You never told me."

"Last time was long before you came. I told Constable Fen. He wrote it all up, like a crime report, as if he were determined to catch the demons and put them in jail."

"How close did you get?"

"Fifty paces. Close enough. I got away fast. Stay away, Shan. It's the gate to the Plain of Ghosts, people say. You need to understand, Shan. It is forbidden by the demons to go past that old farm. Fen went up, and Fen died."

Shan stared at the map as Marpa cleared the table. He didn't realize the old mute was still there until the man thrust another napkin in front of Shan. The scorpion he had drawn was surprisingly detailed. It had eyes on each of its extended claws and its tail. Flames rose out of its mouth. It was a very old thing, a scorpion charm, a protection against demons. When he looked up, the old man gestured to Shan's *gau*, which was visible under his shirt. Shan opened the *gau* and placed the charm inside.

Shiva was asleep when he returned to her house, with her gerbil curled up on her belly. The death chart was nearly complete, with a rendering of a ship surrounded by clouds. He looked through her box of paints and brushes and found a small notepad of green paper tucked into one side.

"I drew the ship for him," came the astrologer's dry, sleepy voice. "I could only visualize the ocean as a sky," she added as if in apology.

"It's perfect," Shan assured her. "The sky is where he sails now." He lifted the pad. "You must have been busy that day, making so many protective charms."

Shiva turned her eyes away and began stroking her uncle's head.

"I saw the people riding hard up over that ridge. They were coming from the direction of town, but most of them lived elsewhere. It's because they had to go into the forbidden land. They had to get a special charm first, to protect them. Was it Nyima who first heard the sound from the tomb? No one else was up there."

"Some shepherds tried to use the pastures there a few years ago but their sheep always got sick," Shiva said in a distant voice, then shrugged. "She rode her donkey to the nearest farm with the news and said she would tell others when she came to the market."

"She didn't make it to the market," Shan finished. "But she had already told the green-eyed woman that the American was dead and they came for the death chart." He hesitated, seeing in his mind's eye Nyima's cavern home. The American had been there. She was his great aunt. She had known he had died, because she had asked for his death chart, yet she had not known he had been placed in the tomb near her home, meaning she had not been on the Plain of Ghosts the day the killers had hidden the body. Where had she been? What had she seen? "She didn't make it to the market but she had already been to town," Shan suggested to the astrologer. "She was the one who came with the green-eyed woman. Nuns don't have a family name. Just Nyima, or Ani Nyima, or Sister Nyima. But she was of the Taklha clan. Aunt Nyima."

Shiva said nothing.

"They came down for the chart and went back up into the mountains. The next day Nyima was attacked and the green-eyed woman was snared by the army."

"I was going to ask Nyima at the market," Shiva murmured, her voice brittle with pain. "If the gods are speaking out at last, does that mean the curse is finally lifted? Otherwise I will need a lot more paper."

He drove up an unfamiliar, overgrown track until he reached a washout that had left a deep rut across the road, then he leapt across the gap and followed the track on foot. In a few minutes he crested a low rise and discovered the ruins of the house. The Taklha clan had lived in a surprisingly large structure, or rather, he saw as he approached, two houses that had been joined as one by construction of walls between them, framing a large barnyard. The family had expanded, and prospered, through the years.

The compound had been ruined by fire, and explosives. In half a dozen places the walls had been shattered, stones ripped apart, and in front of the entry there was a small crater. Decades earlier the house had been shelled by a mortar or small howitzer. Most of the beams and posts, except those of the main doorway, had been salvaged for reuse elsewhere. Those few that remained had been propped in a corner to form a small lean-to shed. He knelt at the circle of stones beside the shed, running his fingers through the ashes in the ring. The ring showed signs of long use, but the ashes on top were not compacted by rain, meaning the fire had been made recently.

Shan ducked his head and entered the lean-to, which made a surprisingly effective shelter against the wind. Snagged in the wall were
clumps of wool, and along one side dried grass had been piled and
slept on. In one corner was a stack of dried dung for fuel. The lean-to
had been used not just by sheep but by humans as well, despite the
taboo.

Back in the old farmyard, he sat on a squared stone, a mounting
block, imagining the life of the extended family that had once lived
here. *Had Father repainted the stable?* Pema had asked. He looked at
the remains of a building across from the bigger house. It had once
held stalls, and scorched, shattered planks on the ground before it
bore faded paint. *Was Mother's coat still warm enough?*

Thinking he should light some incense in memory of the inhabitants, he found only an envelope in his pocket. His drifting mind
abruptly returned to the present and he eagerly opened the envelope
from the Ministry of the Interior. With a flash of excitement he spilled
the contents onto his open hand.

He had stayed awake many nights fretting over the safety of Lokesh.
The old Tibetan had destroyed his identity card and dedicated himself to secretly working for the exiled Tibetan government. If arrested
for not having a card, he had told Shan, he would declare himself
subject only to the authority of the true government in Dharamsala,
which would guarantee that he would spend the rest of his life in
prison, or worse. Shan smiled at the new laminated card in his hand.
The only chance Lokesh would have would be if Shan could intercede,
showing this new identity card as evidence of Lokesh's loyal citizenship and apologizing for any misunderstanding caused by his aged
friend's mental infirmities.

With a satisfied nod Shan returned the card to his pocket and
surveyed the compound again. He was not sure what he hoped to find.
Land records, like Buddhist church records, had been destroyed wher-
ever the early occupation government found them, insisting on a clean
break with the past. There would be no family photos here, no sign
saying TAKLHA HOMESTEAD. But then he turned and found one.

Leaning on a tiny ledge made by an oversized wall stone was a small drawing. It showed the structure before the destruction, a lovingly drawn rendering in pencil of the double house, with yaks grazing on the rising slope behind it. It was torn from the notebook he had seen in Jacob Bartram's hotel room, in the hand that he now knew as Pema's.

He paced along the crumbling walls. In the shadows of another corner he found a flagstone leaning against the wall. Behind it was a sleeping bag in a blue nylon bag and a nylon stuff bag holding a dozen energy bars with labels in English.

Bartram had been here, and slept here, then gone into the mountains expecting to return here, to the home of his ancestors. He had been found only in a thin shirt. A veteran of the American military would not have gone up to the higher elevations without more equipment, more clothing. Where had he been? Where had his killers found him? What was his solitary mission in the high country? What secret had caused him to become another ghost of the haunted mountains?

Shan felt the need to go back to the American's body, to explain to Bartram why he had to open the old letters. He was lost in thought as he drove, recalling the notebook drawings Pema had made of the old shrines, when suddenly an army truck pulled out from behind an outcropping to block his passage. Two soldiers darted from the shadows, waving him out with their submachine guns. When he hesitated, the nearest soldier emphasized the request by leveling his gun at Shan.

A loud whine filled the air as Shan followed them around the rocks, into a sudden cyclone that churned up a blinding cloud of dust. One of the soldiers shoved him forward, pushing his head down, and a helicopter appeared in the cloud. The soldier helped him into the machine, buckled his seat belt, slammed the door shut, and tapped on the cockpit glass. With an abrupt lurch the helicopter rose.

They had flown toward the east for perhaps ten miles when a second, waiting helicopter appeared, which led them southward. Shan struggled with his fear. He was given no headset, so he had no way of speaking with his captors. The army hated people like him, Chinese who had become too Tibetan. The resistance groups told stories of people who proved too great a nuisance sometimes being taken up into the sky and simply thrown out. Old soldiers mockingly referred to it as sky burial. There were also special, invisible prisons on military bases from which no one ever emerged.

Shan attempted in vain to see who might be in the lead helicopter. They went fast, as if charging into battle, and as they progressed into the central region of the county he began to recognize the landscape. A complex of buildings enclosed with high fences appeared below them, then another, and another. Some counties in the People's Republic boasted of bumper rice crops or famous peaches. Lhadrung's leading crop was prisoners. In another five minutes he saw the familiar rows of run-down barracks and sheds that was the 404th People's Construction Brigade, where he had spent five years of his life. So far his son Ko, drug dealer and leader of what Beijing called a hooligan gang, had spent nearly four.

On the northern edge of the town of Lhadrung, new buildings were being constructed and bulldozers were scraping out a long runway. The county seat was becoming a major depot for the prisons and army bases. An asphalt apron by three new hangars was already completed. They landed by the hangar closest to the road, where several utility vehicles were parked.

Shan sat motionless as he watched a man in a stylish black flight suit climb out of the first helicopter. The dark lenses of his aviator glasses and black-visored cap set off his silvery hair. Shan had seen him before, staring at Shan after his attack helicopter had nearly taken the roof off Shan's truck.

But it wasn't the man in the flight suit who caused Shan to shrink back in his seat, it was the tall, gaunt man standing at the front of the hangar. Officially Colonel Tan was the governor of the county, but Shan had come to think of him more as the last of the fierce warlords who had controlled vast regions of China a century earlier. Lhadrung County was Tan's kingdom, and he was given all the latitude he needed to run it because he kept his prisons secure and well hidden. Lhadrung had become a model county as far as Beijing was concerned, because Tan stomped down every problem before it spilled over Lhadrung's borders. He controlled over three thousand prisoners, and although fatalities were common among them, especially at the hard-labor camps like the 404th, there were never escapes, never a scream heard outside the county. Tan may have taken Shan out of his prison years earlier, but Shan still considered himself Tan's prisoner.

The colonel raised his head toward Shan. Shan obediently unbuckled his safety belt and climbed out.

"Not even three months yet!" Tan spat as Shan approached. He didn't finish the sentence before turning to shake hands with the silver-haired visitor. *Barely three months and you've already put a stick up my ass,* he meant. Shan hesitated. Surely Tan could not yet know about the bodies hidden in the mountains.

"General Lau Lujou of the 34th Mountain Division," he heard Tan say, and Shan realized he was being introduced. "Constable Shan is responsible for police administration in Buzhou Township. An old soldier in the motherland's battle for justice."

Lau took off his glasses and grabbed Shan's hand with an approving nod. "I never trust a soldier without scars," he observed in a smooth, refined voice. His accent was that of Shanghai. "Your watcher in the mountains," he said to Tan, his eyes fixed on Shan in a cool, assessing gaze. "It takes a hero to serve in such a forbidding landscape. Like the men I used to leave in Himalayan bunkers for weeks at a time."

"I've grown fond of the mountains," Shan replied impassively. "Highest land in Lhadrung County. Closest to the gods, the Tibetans say."

Lau gestured toward the sky. "There are no more gods up there," he declared with a gloating grin. "I shot them all down." He put a hand on Shan's arm and steered him into the hangar. Once out of the bright sunlight Shan saw that the building contained no aircraft, only a table in the center, laid with linen and set for four. One orderly was arranging covered dishes on the table, another opening a bottle of wine. Lau pulled out a chair for Shan.

"Like the American Wild West up in those ranges," the general observed as the food was served. "You must have your hands full."

Shan shrugged and put his hand over his glass as the orderly tried to pour wine. "A missing yak, a stolen road sign. The Wild West was tamed before I arrived," he said pointedly.

Lau's face lit with amusement. "I like him, Tan!" he exclaimed to the colonel. "A good soldier never commits until he knows the landscape." He dipped his glass at Shan before draining it. "Or is it just until he knows the mind of his master?" he asked Tan, his very white, very straight teeth shining through his smile. He lifted his chopsticks and studied Shan again. "The colonel and I go way back, comrade. War games. His mechanized infantry against my commandos, my Snow Tigers. Sometimes he won, sometimes I won. I know his moves. He would insist on deploying a wily old tiger to guard his northern border."

Shan glanced at Tan, not certain how to take the colonel's silence. "I feel old," he admitted.

Lau laughed. As he raised his glass to be filled again, his black jacket folded back, exposing a pistol on his belt. A Russian Makarov. It had been a favorite of army officers two generations earlier, although the general's had been retrofitted with pearl handles.

"Ah, Captain Yintai," Lau announced as a sinewy man in combat fatigues appeared out of the shadows. "My aide de camp," he said in introduction. Yintai turned his shallow eyes to Shan and nodded. His neck was ravaged by a thick, jagged scar that ran down into his shirt. As he sat, a thin grin grew on his face, as if Shan reminded him of a private joke. There had been two men in the helicopter that had buzzed his truck. One of them had pretended to shoot Shan.

They ate to a guarded banter about the weather, always too cold and too dry, and the progress of Tan's new military depot, as impressive as anything Lau had seen in Tibet. In his new, slower life in Hong Kong, Lau had taken up golf and suggested Tan should add a golf course for officers. The colonel replied that he would enjoy shooting the balls with his pistol. Lau's laughs were as short and well-manicured as his fingernails.

Tan very deliberately avoided Shan's gaze, staying focused on Lau as they exchanged tales of military life on the frontier. Shan began to see subtle lines around Lau's eyes and the slight puffiness around his lips. He was older than Tan and had taken up semiretirement in Hong Kong, where golf courses and plastic surgeons were abundant. Shan realized he had seen his face before, in Beijing newspapers. Think about a move, Lau urged Tan. "An old horse should not die in harness, but prancing about sweet pastures. I could make you a director of one of my companies, even give you a small apartment building to boost your pension."

Tan gestured toward the airfield construction. "I have responsibilities to the army."

"And the motherland kneels before you," Lau declared in an imperial tone.

Finished with his meal, the general lit a cigarette, an American Marlboro, and tossed the pack to Tan. Without hesitation the colonel lit a cigarette, exhaling the smoke toward Shan as if to cut off any reminder that he had lost a lung to cancer the year before. Lau's pilot, who had been pacing along the front of the hangar as they ate, caught Lau's attention and motioned toward clouds building in the west. Yintai rose and jogged toward the helicopters.

The general snuffed his cigarette out on his plate and rose, gesturing Shan and Tan in the direction of a side door. He led them into a squat, heavily guarded building behind the hangar, around the corner of which Shan saw the heavy transport helicopter he had seen in the mountains above the gilded saint's grave. Had the general brought cargo to Lhadrung?

The building was an arsenal. Lau paused at one of the weapon racks that lined the walls and lifted out a semiautomatic rifle. He worked the mechanism with a satisfied smile, then looked up at Shan and abruptly tossed the weapon to him. Shan awkwardly caught it by the barrel, pushing down his loathing of the cold, deadly metal. He had never carried a weapon as an inspector in Beijing and kept those in the constable's office under lock and key.

Tan stepped closer as Shan gripped the stock and leveled the gun, as if he worried about Shan's reaction.

"Do you have any idea what a good AK-47 costs?" Lau asked Shan. "More than a damned Tibetan makes in a year. Then there are the machine guns, grenades, artillery, battle tanks, troop carriers, barracks, aircraft, and airfields, not to mention the costs of transportation and maintenance. Tibet is the most expensive operating theater in the country." He relieved Shan of the gun and mocked a series of aiming motions, toward the door, toward a poster depicting a charging soldier, then, for an instant, at Shan. He laughed and returned the rifle to the rack, then led them toward a rear corner of the chamber, where a temporary partition of hinged panels blocked the view from the entrance.

"But you know the most expensive thing of all?" the general asked, not waiting for an answer. "Our glorious soldiers. The motherland makes an investment of years in every man, worth hundreds of thousands." He pushed the partition aside. "I despise wasting resources."

The two metal tables in the corner each contained the body of a soldier. Tan clamped a warning hand around Shan's arm and stepped past him. "This is my county, Lau!" he growled. "I should have been told!"

Lau shrugged. "Not your men."

"Nor yours!" Tan shot back.

"From a signal company attached to my Snow Tigers. One of our patrols found them, stretched out on a trail as if waiting to be found. I devoted thirty years to the Snow Tiger brigade," Lau declared. "Once a Tiger, always a Tiger." When he turned to Shan his expression was icy cold.

"Where exactly was that trail?" Shan asked. "My township has no military reservation."

"You tell me, constable. All of Tibet is a military reservation."

"When?" Shan asked.

"You tell me."

Shan ignored Tan's furious gaze. Puddles were forming under each table. The bodies had been frozen and were thawing out. They both wore black-and-gray camouflage uniforms, the kind used in the mountains above the tree line. "Dead three or four days, though if you kept them in a refrigerator the timeline may be longer. Each has cuts and blows on their heads that never bled. Meaning they occurred after these men died."

The general stepped aside, as if to invite Shan to continue.

Shan did not move. "I have no authority to act in military matters." He was certain he was being led into a trap. But was he the bait or the prey? Tan paced around the tables, his countenance as inscrutable as stone.

"Of course you don't," Lau agreed. "I confess that we do lose men in training exercises. Real soldiers need real adversity to keep the edge on their skills. Maybe one or two a year in all of Tibet. But two together? In your township," Lau reminded Shan.

"On a military assignment," Shan ventured.

Lau shrugged. "The nature and location of training missions is classified."

"I think you have me confused with Public Security or the army investigation office. I'm in charge of broken fences and traffic accidents."

"Colonel Tan says you are a man who can pierce through impossibilities. I don't want Public Security or military inspectors. They will want to tell Beijing it was an act of the Tibetan resistance, and Yangkar Township will become home again to a brigade of troops. No. I want a man who is not afraid of impossibilities."

Shan hesitated. The general had said Yangkar, not Buzhou, as if he had been familiar with the township in the past. "As in it is impossible that a conscientious general would record two deaths as accidents," he asked, "when he privately believes otherwise?" Why, Shan asked himself, would Lau care whether a brigade of troops camped in Yangkar?

"We are taught to adapt, are we not, Comrade Constable? We are taught to learn the truth in the way it best serves the people. The truth is that soldiers are not murdered in Tibet. Impossible."

Shan weighed his words. "Meaning you suspect murder but don't want the murders solved in the real world, only in your world."

Lau gave an exaggerated smile. "Ah!" he exclaimed. "Someone who understands the opera of modern China!" He rolled his hand toward Shan, encouraging him to continue.

The older victim had a tangle of blood-matted hair on his crown, angled toward the back. A loose bandage, brown with dried blood, hung over a wound, inflicted not long before his death, on his shoulder. The second man's right hand had been frozen in an unnatural position, folded back against the arm. His wrist was broken. His still-open eyes were red from burst capillaries. Shan probed his skull, then his neck, with his fingers. "The first suffered a concussion, struck from behind with force enough to leave him unconscious, perhaps enough to kill him, though I doubt it. Not a fall, or he would have had broken limbs and scrapes." He pointed to the younger soldier. "This one suffered from asphyxia."

"Suffocated?" Lau asked. "There's no marks on his neck."

"Something soft, like a rolled-up cloth. The thyroid cartilage is fractured. If he had fallen onto rocks hard enough to do that his neck would have been broken as well." He looked up. "These were not climbing accidents." Shan realized he had had a similar conversation with Jinhua in the ice cave. "The injuries to the front of their skulls might have killed them. Except they were already dead." He leaned over one of the soldiers and with the tip of a pencil pried out a squarish shard of glass from his forehead. "Shatterproof glass from a windscreen," he announced. He turned to General Lau. "Someone staged them in a vehicle accident." He paused, considering the gleam in Lau's eyes. "But you already knew that. And you knew any forensic examiner would say the same thing." Lau wasn't looking for forensic advice; he was looking for Chinese opera.

Shan folded the dead men's hands over their bellies. "You said they were on exercises, general. You mean like war games?"

Lau glanced at Tan. "Theoretically."

"That must be the answer," Shan declared. "Theoretical murders by a theoretical enemy. Write it up like something from a training manual."

Lau silently stared at Shan before speaking. Shan was well aware that the general had not really explained why Shan had been summoned. "I'm not sure I follow, Comrade Constable."

"Seize the initiative, don't give anyone a chance to challenge your report. Surely you can find an army doctor to say they were indeed climbing accidents, brought on by altitude sickness. Look at their features. They were from the lowlands of southern China, Fujian or Guangzhou perhaps. Their bodies would not adapt well to the altitudes. No need to be bound by what we actually know, not if they are cremated soon. Like you said, general, the truth should be what the people need.

"Make them a statistic," Shan continued as he paced around the bodies. "Beijing has made an art of depersonalizing murder." Shan felt Tan's hot glare but did not look at the colonel. "No one worries about justice for a statistic. They were the stars of a war game, well aware of the risks of playing their parts too aggressively, but knowing that was how younger troops learned. They died for the sake of their beloved army, the latest martyrs for the motherland. Send medals back to their families." Shan fixed Lau with a level gaze. Surely the general did not need help in disguising inconvenient deaths.

As Lau returned the stare, a smile grew again on his refined features. He turned to the colonel. "Only a constable, Tan? This one should be running your entire police force."

As he realized Tan was actually contemplating an answer, Shan interrupted by pointing to the pilot, who was trying to get the general's attention. The whirl of helicopter rotors could be heard. "If we

don't lift off in two minutes we'll be spending the night here," the pilot shouted over the rising noise.

Lau threw a casual salute toward Tan and trotted toward the runway, leaving the colonel staring after him. Shan quickly lifted each
corpse and examined the back of their necks, then saw his own pilot
urgently waving and darted toward their helicopter.

As they rose into the air, Shan saw Colonel Tan standing at the
hangar entrance, staring at Lau's departing helicopter. He too would
have thought of the other impossibility Shan had not mentioned. It
was impossible that a retired general would leave his life of luxury in
Hong Kong to trifle with two deaths in forgotten Yangkar.

CHAPTER SIX

Shan sat in the town square gazing at his station and the Public Security sedan parked in front of it, trying to make sense of his visit to Lhadrung. He could not fathom why Tan had been so subdued. The colonel should have been furious over a retired general encroaching on his authority, and the Tan Shan knew would have raged at Shan for causing the embarrassment.

He became aware that a sturdy woman in a worn felt dress was standing before him, patiently awaiting acknowledgment. When Shan forced a smile, she pulled a young girl from behind her. The girl's shy smile revealed dimples on her rosy cheeks as she extended a lamb toward Shan.

"For her naming day my granddaughter asked to ransom their newborn lamb," the Tibetan woman nervously explained and extended a length of red yarn to Shan.

With a lurch of his heart Shan understood what was being asked. Ransoming an animal was a great spiritual gift. Tying the red yarn on it meant it would be forever immune from slaughter. "You have me confused," he said, "I am no monk. This is a task for someone wearing a robe."

"There is no monk or nun in Yangkar anymore. They have abandoned us," the woman explained, her face tight with emotion. She was scared of Shan, but her love for her granddaughter had brought her to the square. The girl, still smiling, pushed the lamb closer to Shan. The animal bleated, then cocked its head toward Shan.

For a moment he was gripped by an overwhelming sadness, then weakly returned the girl's smile and gestured her to a patch of grass. He pulled out his *gau*, knelt on the grass, and put one hand on the lamb's head and one on the prayer amulet, then had her place her own hands over his. He recited the *mani* mantra ten times before solemnly tying the yarn around the lamb's neck, then cradled the animal's chin in his hand a moment and told it that its duty was to lead a long and virtuous life and provide thick wool to warm those who provided for it. When the girl realized he was done, she gave a squeal of joy and hugged the lamb to her chest. *"Lha gyal lo,"* the pleased grandmother whispered, then quickly pulled the girl away, leaving on the grass a plastic bag stuffed with nuggets of dried cheese, her payment.

Shan watched them until they disappeared around a building, then steeled himself and headed for his office.

"Buddha's breath!" Jengtse exclaimed. "They said the army took you away into the sky. I didn't know if we would ever see—"

Shan cut him off. "Where's the lieutenant?"

His deputy pointed to the back room. Jinhua was sitting at the table by the cells reviewing a stack of files. Surprise flickered on his face as he saw Shan, then he gestured to the files. "Did you know Buzhou used to be an important seat of government, the most important town for scores of miles? Now it's nothing. A remote place of yak dung and barley fields. Why is that?"

Ignoring him, Shan stepped into the cell nearest the door. "Something happened in here that night you arrived," he declared as he pulled up the pallet on one of the cots. "Hidden messages may have been passed." He bent over the frame of the cot as if intensely searching for something.

Jinhua was instantly at his side. "Check the other bed," Shan told him. As Jinhua leaned over the second cot, Shan backed out of the cell and closed the door.

Jinhua's surprised grin faded as Shan locked the cell.

"Officer Jengtse," Shan announced to his deputy. "This man is under arrest. His possessions are confiscated."

Jinhua darted to the cell door, shaking it, as if not believing it was locked. "You can't do this!"

Jengtse stood in the doorway, his confusion turning to amusement as Jinhua pounded the bars. He no doubt thought he was witnessing Shan's self-destruction. "What charge?"

Shan returned Jinhua's disbelieving gaze as he replied. "Impersonating a Public Security officer."

Jengtse, clearly relishing the scene, shrugged. "I'm not sure we can just—"

"Do it, deputy!" Shan snapped. He lifted the phone from the table and set it on a stool by the cell. "Get the arrest form. If he's engaged in official business he can clear this all up and settle the score with me, by making one phone call." Shan extracted Jinhua's card from his pocket. "Or maybe he would prefer that I call. I have the number. Office of Special Investigations, Central Branch."

Jinhua's legs seemed to grow unsteady. He lowered himself onto a cot.

"You rolled into Yangkar with the army," Shan recounted, "making everyone quake with fear. But I think you lied to the army. I think you blocked the road yourself and told them the road was closed, so you could arrive in Yangkar with an escort of armed soldiers at your disposal. You discover the murder of a foreigner, the kind of case investigators dream of, the kind that means promotion and celebrity, but you don't report it. You're the one who should be going away in a helicopter."

Jinhua dropped his head into his hands.

Jengtse reappeared, extending a form to Shan. "Not this one!" Shan barked. "The one with that special address in Beijing. For enemies of the state."

Jengtse's face twisted in confusion. Shan waved him back into the office, then sat at the table and withdrew a blank sheet of paper from the drawer. He slowly recited the full name on the card as he pretended to write. "Jinhua Guo Xi. Address?" he asked. Jinhua seemed not to hear him. "Let's say Township Jail, Yangkar. Work assignment? Have to leave that one blank for the inquisitors to work with. Class background? Let me guess. Defiant offspring of ambitious Party members. An unrepentant hooligan in sheep's clothing. Your parents will be thrown out of the Party, of course. But that's just the beginning."

Shan rose and paced along the cell as he spoke. "What a field day Beijing will have. What exquisite choices you will present them. I can hear the conversation in the minister's office. Do we just lock the fool up for pretending to be an officer?, Public Security asks. No, that would never be enough, the minister scolds. There's that dead American to deal with. So let's charge him with the murder. All we need is a motive. Black market feud perhaps? Two smugglers fought over what they thought was a golden statue, not knowing it was just a bag of bones, as you described it. But then we are admitting we have foreign smugglers operating in the motherland. I have it! Jinhua and Bartram were both spies for America. Our heroic forces were hot on their trail. The American was killed by our gallant soldiers. Perfect! That way there's no danger of Jinhua causing future embarrassment. Just put him up against a wall. One nine millimeter round in his cerebrum and order returns to our world. You'll just become another morality tale for the propaganda artists. The chairman is so fond of blaming everything on the Americans."

"I *am* a Public Security officer!" Jinhua protested.

Shan pointed to the phone. "Then call. Right now. If you are what you say, they will put me in jail. Surely that must be reason enough to call."

Jinhua took a step toward the phone, then sagged and retreated to the cot.

Shan returned the phone to the table, tucked the files under his arm, and closed the door as he stepped back into the office. He stared at the door for a long time, then moved to the map of the township on the wall by his desk. With a pencil he sketched the old paths he had discovered with Lokesh, then the straight line from the cell tower the dead American had drawn. They were all converging on the ridge that held the tomb of the gilded saint, on the Plain of Ghosts. Yangkar held secrets from the past, and he was convinced that the key to the murders lay in that past. He turned to Jinhua's files, now on his desk, and sat before them.

The files were so encrusted with dust that Shan could plainly see the recent marks left by Jinhua's fingers. He leafed through them, confused as to their content and even more confused as to how Jinhua might have found them. The top third of the stack of paper was in Mandarin, everything else in Tibetan script. Those in Mandarin were letters and reports, all marked at the top DIRECTOR YIN FU, BUREAU OF RELIGIOUS AFFAIRS, YANGKAR BRANCH, with an asterisk after the name, which was explained at the bottom as BY APPOINTMENT UNDER EMERGENCY ORDER. All the documents were dated in 1966 and 1967. A shiver ran down Shan's spine. Most Tibetans wouldn't even speak directly of those years, referring to them with special coded terms, the most descriptive of which was the *Years of Chinese Terror* or simply the *Black Days*. More chilling were the words used by some of the old lamas in Shan's prison barracks: *The Ending Times*.

Jinhua would have been reading only the documents in Chinese, all of which appeared to be inventories and dispositions of what were characterized as "cult material" or "feudal artifacts." The government had its own special language for dealing with Tibetan culture. The Chinese lists reflected what must have been a very large *gompa*, a monastery that would have been a center of life for the region. There were inventory entries for "books" numbering in the thousands. There had been stored grain, farming implements, horses, sheep, yaks, thousands of tubs of butter, thousands of incense bundles, metalworking tools, religious statues, carpets, looms, and bolts of cloth. The dispositions had begun in the second half of 1966. Most of the foodstuffs had been shipped east, where famine was beginning to spread. The animals had gone for slaughter to the military and to camps of the Red Guard, Mao's surrogate army of fanatical teenagers who committed massacre and mayhem in his name. The books had gone to the same barracks and camps, as well as housing compounds being set up for Chinese officials in Lhasa. Toilet paper had been in scarce supply.

The Tibetan documents, none of which seemed to have been touched by Jinhua, were all from the early 1960s, routine administrative records reflecting life in a busy monastic community. Prepared by the monastery's clerk, they were accounts of purchases and contributions for the many supplies needed to sustain a sizable population. Five hundred bushels of barley in one week's accounts, two hundred the next, hundreds of blocks of black tea, and always butter, butter for buttered tea, butter for lamps, and butter for the *torma*, the small ritual figures sculpted of butter that were used, and often burned, on special festival days.

He looked up to see Jengtse inching toward the outside door. "You just gave these to him." Shan rose and blocked the door. "Without consulting me."

"He demanded old records. The clerk's office has nothing. He said that wasn't good enough. He's Public Security. I mean . . . isn't he?"

"I don't know what he is. He's acting more like a fugitive. Where did these come from? How can such old records magically appear?"

"You know," Jengtse said and gave one of his characteristic shrugs. "It's an old country."

"One more time, deputy. I have two cells. Where did they come from?"

"Tserung's garage was built on an old foundation. Out in his junkyard there is a stairway. Down the stair are some old things. Forgotten papers. Nobody's papers. The sooner the lieutenant gets what he wants the sooner he leaves, that's what I figured."

"Who else knows about the papers?"

"Nobody," Jengtse replied, then broke away from Shan's intense stare. "Tserung and his son Gyatso. Gyatso and I go down there sometimes to play cards since his father forbids him from gambling. Maybe a few of the old ones. But they weren't here, so probably not."

"Weren't here when?"

"When the town was reshaped." He rolled his eyes at Shan's confusion.

"Are you blind? Why do you think the town is laid out in nice blocks like one of the new Chinese towns? Every man, woman, and child was taken away, for years. When they returned, the old *gompa* had been destroyed and the new town constructed. The army told everyone there had been a terrible fire and as a gift the motherland had built a beautiful new settlement for them. The square outside was the courtyard of the old *gompa*. The main gate framed the mountains, like the buildings off the square do now."

Marpa had spoken of the empty years when the townspeople had been hauled away to a collective. He had not said it was virtually every inhabitant. "The guesthouse out back is old," Shan pointed out.

"It was just a stable. No one cared about it. They kept that old stone tower too, which had been part of the gate."

Shan considered his deputy's words. "You mean it wasn't a fire. The army and Religious Affairs destroyed buildings they wanted forgotten." He went to the window and stared at the square and its surrounding buildings. Structures aged fast in the gripping cold and pounding winds of Tibet, and patchwork repairs of cinder blocks and galvanized sheets rendered many buildings difficult to age, but he realized for the first time that other than the solitary tower at its entrance, which would have made a convenient watch tower for the army, not a building on the square was likely more than fifty years old. Lodi had reported that Jinhua had taken special interest in the tower on his first morning in Yangkar. Shan had indeed been blind.

When he turned Jengtse was staring at him. "Go to the garage," he ordered his deputy. "Block that stair so no one else gets in. Now!"

Shan waited until his deputy had crossed the square, then stepped outside and circled around to the guesthouse. Jinhua's only luggage consisted of a nylon overnight bag packed with two changes of clothing, toiletries, and a tourist's guidebook to Tibet. In a zipped pocket inside the lining, he found an envelope with four sheets of paper inside. The first page held a series of dates, beginning in 1963 and ending in 2005. Each date had a location beside it. 1960 was Harbin, the industrial town in Manchuria. Then 1962 said Aksai Chin, the site of the short, intense war with India over the Himalayan border. 1964, 1965, and 1966 simply stated "Tibet," then 1968 Hanoi, 1972 Kunming, 1975 Hainan, followed by years marked as London, Washington, and finally Beijing. The next was simply a list of banks in Hong Kong. The third was the address of a cemetery in the Beijing suburbs, and clipped to that page was one of the usual burial contracts, signed by Jinhua, agreeing that the body of Bin Shi would be exhumed and cremated after five years. The dead were only given short-term quarters in the capital. The last page held a series of questions, some illegible. Shan made out *Reaction timing of lime on flesh? Flight manifests on indirect flights to Hong Kong?* and *Taxi drivers at airport?* Clipped to this page was a forensic lab receipt for what was termed "biological evidence from cement plant," on the back of which was a series of phone numbers with Beijing exchanges.

Back in his office Shan tried the first number. "Inspector Shan calling for Lieutenant Jinhua," he tried when a professional-sounding woman answered.

"We have nothing more for the lieutenant," came her impatient reply. "I told him again and again that DNA is only useful when we have something to match against."

"I was hoping to find him there."

"Haven't seen him for three weeks," the woman snapped. "Try his office at Central. Tell him we had to dispose of his evidence. There's rules about lab sanitation. And tell him to stop wasting our time."

Shan tried the other numbers. One was for an office at the Military Archives, one for the Bureau of Religious Affairs, Office of Buddhist Relations, one a private number that rang with no answer, the last a fax machine. He went on his computer and found a general number for the Ministry of Public Security in Beijing. He dialed it and nervously asked for Central Investigations. Central was the office that handled politically sensitive investigations, the office that had taken over Shan's own former office of Internal Investigations after the scandal that had led to his own imprisonment. Lieutenant Jinhua, he was politely informed after being transferred four times, was on extended family leave to care for his ailing mother. Shan stared at the receiver for a long time before returning to the cell block.

His prisoner was lying on the cot, one arm over his eyes. Shan pulled the little table under the light bulb in the center of the room and arranged a chair on either side. When he opened the cell door Jinhua sat up.

"Okay. You win, Shan," he said. "I'll leave. I'll just get my—" His words died away as Shan shoved the remaining chair under the knob on the door to the office to keep anyone from entering. Shan gestured him to the table, then sat down. The color left Jinhua's face as Shan opened the drawer and extracted a hammer and pair of pliers.

"You wouldn't dare!" Jinhua gasped.

Shan wrapped his fingers around the hammer. Jengtse had left the tools in the drawer after trying unsuccessfully to hang curtains in the cells the month before. "Sorry to hear about your mother," he began. "How does she fare?"

Jinhua stared at the table as he spoke. "My mother died two years ago. Tuberculosis. The fools shipped her to a clinic in Inner Mongolia. A land famous for its dust storms. She just coughed until she died."

"At last something with a ring of truth," Shan observed. "Does anyone in Beijing even know you are here?"

Jinhua shrugged. "Yangkar was one of the places listed on a report I filed. My boss called me into his office so I could witness him burn it in his wastebasket."

"A concerned mentor."

"Right. He taught me I had given the report to the wrong person."

It was Shan's turn to look down at the table. He had once given a report to three of the ministers of state for whom his tiny, very private office had worked. The first had laughed at him and thrown it back in his face. The second had shredded the report and ordered him never to speak of such things again. After he gave it to the third, he had been terminated, prosecuted in a secret trial, and left to die in the Tibetan gulag.

"There were two more murders committed up in the mountains," he said when he finally looked up. "Both victims were soldiers."

Jinhua seemed to brighten. "Snow Tigers? From the 34th Mountain Commando brigade?"

Shan ignored the question. "If you are waging war with the army, I want the battlefield moved out of Yangkar."

"I didn't bring it here."

"What does General Lau have to do with it?"

"Everything. Anything that touches Lau becomes all about Lau. Glory and corruption. Glory and wealth. Glory and murder. It's his mantra." Jinhua saw the impatience on Shan's face and took a deep breath before beginning his story.

"Lau was a major in the war against India, in Aksai Chin. His unit rolled over the Indians and advanced fifty miles in one day, taking hundreds of prisoners. He was made a colonel for that. He was sent into Vietnam to be a shadow commander of the antiaircraft batteries around Hanoi that began shooting down American planes. They made him a general for that. Ran the war college. Ran secret missions with the North Koreans. Military attaché in London. Still has an apartment in London. Owns buildings in Hong Kong and a military supply company that sells to the army. Came from a peasant farmer family but left the army as its richest pensioner ever. Not shy about spreading his wealth. They don't call him a retiree, they call him general emeritus. Still enjoys all the privileges of rank."

"Like taking command of active duty troops if he chooses," Shan inserted.

"Of course, for short periods. Unscheduled exercises, he calls them. He always had the best-trained troops, so the army considers it important to showcase his talents. He was awarded the Order of the Heroic Exemplar by the Chairman himself. Ten years ago the Order of the Republic. A dozen years before that the Order of the Red Star. An official Hero of the Motherland. A living saint as far as Beijing is concerned. There was an article about him last year in the *Beijing Daily*. It called him one of China's living treasures. Last month he was brought in to christen a new destroyer in Fujian."

"And today he christened me by taking me to Lhadrung to show me two dead soldiers. I still don't know if I should feel honored or terrified."

"Terrified," Jinhua rejoined in a hollow voice. "Always terrified."

"Why Yangkar?"

"After the war with India, Lau arrived in Tibet a colonel struggling to support a young family in Shanghai. A year later he had bought his wife and children a villa on the coast. After two years in Tibet he had opened a huge bank account in Hong Kong. Soon he had a mistress and his own apartment building there."

"And Captain Yintai?"

"His aide de camp, since the Indian campaign. A weapons instructor who excelled at hand-to-hand combat. Past retirement age but Lau pulled strings to keep him in, though he never seems to have official assignments anymore. Still acts like Lau's deputy and bodyguard."

"Why Yangkar?" Shan repeated.

Jinhua reached inside his shirt and extended a small, worn notebook, opened it to the first page and pushed it toward Shan. Inside the front cover someone had sketched a *gompa*, an elegant monastery drawn with a view through its tall front gate, showing a large *chorten* in front of a series of temples. On the opposite side were two maps, the first showing what appeared to be the same *gompa*, then a smaller site with a building complex inside a circle of *chortens*.

"The large shrine in the center," Jinhua said, pointing to the *chorten* in the first sketch, "was said to be covered in gold."

"It could be anywhere. Surely Yangkar never had such wealth."

"I have a list of possible sites, all at intersections of the routes of the two groups that liberated resources in this region. I checked three already. None of them fit the description as well as Buzhou—as Yangkar," he added, as if finally conceding the Tibetan name to Shan. "Look at this—" He folded the drawing of the *gompa* along an existing crease, covering the gate opening, then placed a hand down to cover the *gompa* wall. "It's the tower," he explained. "They took it all down but the one tower."

"You said two groups?"

"A Red Guard unit that called itself the Hammer of Freedom. And the commando brigade that later became known as the Snow Tigers."

Shan felt something icy growing in the pit of his stomach. "The Party signed off on the official history of Tibet long ago, lieutenant. You aren't going to change it. The communists liberated the long-suffering Tibetans from the slavery of the Buddhist cult."

When Jinhua closed his notebook and looked up, there was a bitter smile on his face. "I had a partner. Bin Shi. I hated him at first. A moody guy who would brood for an hour over his failed career, then burst into some rock-and-roll song. But he was smart, tenacious as a fox once he got the scent of a crime. He became my best friend. We were assigned to the Chairman's campaign to root out corruption in the central government. Operation White Jade, they called it. We weren't senior enough to get anything too sensitive, just corruption at the law enforcement level. We caught the director of a statistics office who paid a bribe to get a drug case against his daughter dropped, then found a customs inspector who had been taking bribes for years from officials who imported German cars without paying duties. Twenty-five convictions in that case alone. We were stars. My captain gave us commendations and told us to dig deeper. He gave us new authority to secretly review the banking records of high-level police and correlate any unusual payments with dismissal of sensitive cases. One of those we found was a hundred thousand paid from a Hong Kong account to a detective lieutenant.

"Two days after the payment he dropped a case involving the assault and rape of a young secretary in the Ming Garden Hotel. Bin and I went to talk with the lieutenant. He said the charges had been brought against some visiting businessmen from Hong Kong, who fully cooperated. It had just been a misunderstanding, everyone said. There had been a party in their suite. When they discovered she had taken drugs, they took her down to the lobby and told the manager to let her sleep it off somewhere else. It was their cover-up. They had abused her, then pumped her full of drugs. When we asked the lieutenant for her name, he couldn't remember. When we asked for the file, he said closed cases were sent to the archives, out in a big warehouse in the suburbs. He gave us a case number, but when we went to check there was no such file. A few days later the lieutenant we spoke with had died of a massive heart attack. We asked for an autopsy, but the body had already been cremated. We went to the hotel to interview the staff, one of whom remembered the woman's name. Bin tracked her down, set up an appointment for us to meet her. She rode a bicycle to work. On the way home that day a dump truck hit her, ran right over her body with its wheels, like it was aiming for her, a witness said. Crushed into the pavement. She was dead before the ambulance arrived.

"I was scared. I said maybe this was a case we just had to drop. But Bin was furious. He went back to the hotel and demanded to see the records of the guest registered in the suite. It was Captain Yintai, but there had been an older gentleman with silver hair staying in the second bedroom in the suite. The desk clerk had recognized him, because he was a celebrity. The famous General Lau Lujou. The next day Bin spent hours on the phone with Hong Kong. He got very excited, booked a flight to Hong Kong for the next day. He said this was the case that would make our careers, that the Chairman himself would soon hear of us.

"I never saw him again. Bin never got on that plane. I searched for two weeks, retracing all his steps. I found a body at a morgue that I thought could be his, but it had been recovered at a cement factory in a mound of lime. No fingerprints left. No face left, almost no skin anywhere left. I ordered DNA testing." Jinhua's voice became hoarse. "I paid one of the doctors to stay after hours for a more detailed, unofficial exam. She found a cause of death. A stab wound at the base of the neck."

Shan left him staring at his notebook, went into the office, and switched on the electric kettle. "You were right," he said when he returned with two cups of tea. "A case that must be forgotten. You should leave. Go back to your mother's home to put some flesh on your alibi, then wander back to Beijing looking duly bereaved. Forget it all, if you ever want to have a career in Beijing."

Jinhua cocked his head at Shan. "By the gods!" he gasped. "Now I understand you. You once had a career in Beijing."

Shan ignored him. "Drop the case. It never happened. For the sake of your career, for the sake of your life, drop it."

Jinhua sipped at his tea before speaking. "I could never do anything with the rape charges. So I made the general my personal project. I didn't dare try a frontal assault, so I began piecing together his story. From public records, the few military files made available to corruption investigators, bank accounts. Company records in Hong Kong." He set his cup down and looked up at Shan. "He was worth forty million Hong Kong by the time he left Tibet."

"A tale of war booty taken decades ago won't get any traction in Beijing."

"You don't understand. I found a survivor of that Red Guard unit, the Hammer of Freedom. It was a youth brigade from Tianjin. It had been like a rolling party at first, he said, cruising through the Tibetan countryside, taking whatever they wanted in the name of the revolution, demolishing shrines and schools, staging trials for landlords then executing them. But after the first year or so, they grew weary. He went back to Tianjin, on leave, because his father was dying. Three months later he returned to Tibet, tried to reconnect with his friends. But they were gone. The Hammer of Freedom had disappeared without a trace. Forty-five Red Guard cadres, gone without a word. His last contact had been a letter from his girlfriend, who had sent him that sketch of a huge *gompa* they had discovered high in the mountains and spoke of tales of phantom treasure in the hills above it, protected only by a circle of the idolaters' shrines. He said others in the unit had called him a slave to reactionary values for going back to his family, but he knew that if he had not gone he would have disappeared too.

"He said he wandered around, trying to re-create the path of the Hammer of Freedom, showing people this sketch. No one would talk with him. Tibetans would run away. Chinese officials would laugh and say there were always casualties of war, and the Red Guard was so disorganized no one could keep track of the units anyway. By then the Guard was no longer in favor in Beijing, and he could find no one in authority who would help. Some said there had been Tibetan guerrillas in the hills who had been savagely resisting. In a few more months nearly all the Red Guard units had gone home, replaced by regular army units. But none of his friends ever returned to Tianjin. It haunted him all these years."

Jinhua reached into his pocket. "His girlfriend had sent this as a memento with her last message. She said everyone had taken one, as a souvenir of their greatest conquest. He was going to melt it down but never did, said he began to feel it was cursed so didn't dare." He tossed an inch-high Buddha on the table. Shan lifted it. It was solid gold.

"The famed General Lau never took heavy casualties. Not in India, not in Vietnam, not anywhere else in Tibet. But a company of his men went missing, never accounted for. Twenty-four men. I found the list of their names in a military archive and thought at last I might find some witnesses. But then I discovered that Lau had reported that while pursuing guerrillas up in Kham Province, scores of miles to the north, an avalanche had swept their convoy into a deep crevasse. No survivors, and it was too dangerous to recover the bodies.

"Everywhere I looked I hit a wall. It had all begun to seem like some terrible nightmare, part of an investigator's psychosis. There was no hard evidence anywhere, except that tower in your square. Then we found that crumbling letter from the dead sergeant's pocket. I cleaned it up, studied it with a lens, and finally made out the addressee. Sergeant Ma Chu. One of the twenty-four soldiers who went missing fifty years ago lies in that ice cave with the dead American. Dead from the same wound that killed my partner four months ago."

CHAPTER SEVEN

They left before dawn so they could not be tracked from the air, Shan and Jinhua in the front of the truck, Jengtse stretched out among the tools in the back. The sun was edging over the eastern peaks as they reached the empty plain where the golden saint slept. The tomb was now surrounded by *khatas*, white prayer scarves fixed to the low bushes and heather in homage to the saint. The gap where the stone slab had been slid open was covered by a heavy felt blanket. On the crest of the next ridge above them a solitary man on horseback watched them. Jinhua and Shan exchanged a reluctant glance.

"Give me your flashlight," Jinhua said. "I'll go in."

"No," Shan replied, looking at the sentinel on the ridge. "I have to do it. Stay close," he added, then stepped to the end of the tomb.

Jengtse pulled away enough of the blanket to allow Shan to lower himself against the rear wall. To his relief the face of the gilded saint had been covered by a *khata*. He straightened the thin carpet over the saint's shrouded feet, then touched his *gau* and whispered a prayer before beginning his inspection.

Along the right side, where the American's body had been laid, he found a few clay offering pots, their contents long ago turned to dust. Near the stone wall was an American quarter, dropped from Bartram's pocket. Shan held it in his palm a moment, then leaned it upright on the wall so that George Washington stared at the dead saint.

He inched his way around the tomb, his back to the wall, to reach the other side, where Sergeant Ma had lain for fifty years. There were more clay pots, all smashed. The soldier had been dumped into the grave, whereas the American's body had been carefully laid out. Whoever had done it had pushed Bartram's cell phone into the saint's desiccated hands. Had that simply been an act of glibness by a callous murderer, or had there been a message in that placement? Surely the killers had never expected that the tomb would be reopened. It was, he had come to realize, the perfect hiding place for a body, since only Tibetans knew about it. The devout Tibetans of Yangkar would never open the sacred tomb, and certainly would never tell Shan or any other Chinese about it. At the head of the tomb Shan spied a lump of dirty canvas he had not seen before. He knelt by the shoulders of the saint and reached for it. The rotting fabric began to disintegrate at his touch, though he was able to pull away a large piece. It held the stenciled initials PLA. *People's Liberation Army.* It was a small backpack, and its meager contents lay in a dusty pile on the stone floor of the tomb now. He made out a small tin bowl with a pair of bamboo chopsticks that must have constituted the sergeant's mess kit and, leaning against the bowl, a compact wire-bound notebook. Flakes of rust fell away from the wire binding as he opened it. Inside the thin cardboard cover was written SERGEANT MA CHU, TUNXI, ANHUI PROVINCE.

The first several pages had congealed into a single mass, but the rest were readable enough for Shan to realize it was a running letter to Ma's family back home in Anhui. He glanced up, hearing Jengtse and Jinhua speaking at a distance, then propped his light between his arm and body and turned the pages. The sergeant missed his parents terribly and hoped to see them in a year or two. He prayed they had been able to make their long-delayed pilgrimage to the famed sacred peaks of the province, and he looked forward to making offerings of gratitude on one of the summits when he returned. Tibet, Ma observed, was a difficult land, and its people much more resentful of the Chinese than he had been told to expect.

Shan skipped to the last few pages. Ma complained of how his commander had asked him to do the impossible, to build a twenty-mile-long road at over ten thousand feet along a long ridge in less than two weeks, which was when the Bureau of Religious Affairs was to arrive to take over administration of Yangkar, then use his bulldozer for a special project at the terminus of the road. Later, *the ridge was flat, the progress from the northern base faster than expected, except we lost a tread and had to stop for repairs.* There was a gap of ten days before the final entry. *I want to come home,* Ma wrote. *I am sorry for the wise ravens. I wish they could have just taken wing. Tomorrow we will be gone from this accursed place, not a day too soon. I cannot live with the ghosts.*

When Shan pulled himself up from the tomb, Jinhua was fastening crime scene tape to metal pins that Jengtse was driving into the soil around the slab. On the ridge above, the sentinel had been joined by another figure on horseback, and three women in the black felt dresses favored by the herding women.

"No!" Shan stated.

"This is an official crime scene," Jengtse protested. "They should stay away. No contamination of the evidence. I will put up signs on the slope above."

"No," Shan repeated and lifted a pin out of the ground. "We will satisfy our curiosity and leave." He nodded toward the Tibetan watchers. "This is more their place than ours."

As Jinhua pulled the blanket back over the tomb Shan collected the pins and tape, then motioned Jengtse toward an outcropping by the brush near the western edge of the plain. "Watch from up there," he instructed his deputy, then tossed one of the pins to Jinhua and lifted another for himself. With his back to the tomb he began walking in an arc, stopping to tap the ground with the pin every five paces. Jinhua took up a parallel path a few feet away.

After a dozen steps Jinhua paused to consult the map sketched in his notebook. "No way of knowing the scale," he pointed out. "Even if there is a ring of buried structures, we don't know its dimensions."

Shan jumped onto the tall rocks where Jengtse kept watch and studied the wide shelf before him. He had watched for traces of paths from the helicopter before they landed back in Yangkar and now had his own map, in his mind, of the pilgrim paths that climbed up from the valleys below. He had passed an hour in his office the night before, studying the lines he had already sketched on his big wall map, then adding those he had seen from above and transposing all the lines onto the military map he had furtively taken from the helicopter. Only the military maps had reliable topography marks. Paths never ran straight in the mountains, they followed the land. When one of the paths ran into a compressed set of lines that meant a cliff face, he had extended it along the base, then more tentatively up the most gradual slope toward the ridgeline. But the wise men who had laid out such paths centuries earlier would also have taken pilgrims past spiritual places of power, often where springs emerged within pockets of trees, which were not marked on such maps. He longed for Lokesh as he worked, for the old Tibetan always had an instinct for how pilgrims moved through the Tibetan landscape.

One of his lines descended from the high ice passes to the north, leading from the rugged lands of the old Kham Province in the north to loop the peaks above, along a long, flat ridge that would have been the likely route of Sergeant Ma's road. The other paths came from east, west, and south, from every direction. He was convinced this was their convergence, the destination of ancient pilgrims. Pilgrims had been coming here for centuries. It had not always been the Plain of Ghosts.

The northern edge of the little plain, half a mile long, ended with a sheer drop into a chasm that extended hundreds of feet before disappearing into black shadow. When he climbed down from the rocks, he led Jinhua across the grassy plain to the chasm. The lieutenant took one look into the abyss below and backed away. "It's the kind of meditation site many monks would prefer, sitting by a shrine at the edge of emptiness," Shan explained. He counted five steps from the cliff face and tapped the ground again with his pin. After two more steps he halted and repeated the motion, raising a hollow echoing sound from below.

He knelt, scratching with the metal rod enough to expose a stone slab, then loosened soil along its side to reveal its chiseled edge. The slab of granite seemed identical to that which had entombed the gilded saint, and all but confirmed that they had found the mysterious site of circled *chortens* that had been drawn by a Red Guard cadre decades before and the building complex they had enclosed. The *chortens* had been built over tombs. If this was the boundary on the north and that of the saint on the west, then the ring of shrines was much bigger than he or Jinhua had expected.

Jengtse whistled to Shan and pointed toward the slope. The Tibetans were approaching the plain. He could not hear what they were shouting, but their anger was unmistakable.

Pushing the soil back into place, he erected a small cairn of stones to mark the slab, then continued his probing, walking an imagined arc that connected the two known tombs. Jinhua soon joined him, tapping the ground on a parallel path. Within a quarter hour they had discovered two more slabs, marking each with small cairns. Shan could see that the tombs were arranged in an oval that extended at least six or seven hundred paces at its longest axis.

He watched Jinhua continue, feeling a sudden emptiness. He desperately wished that Lokesh were with him. The old Tibetan had warned him again and again not to be deceived by appearances. This was not just some barren, empty cemetery lost in the vastness of the mountains. There was an essence here that Shan could only glimpse, a power that he could not name, and that the old Tibetans watching him would never share with him. He felt inadequate to the homage he sensed the site deserved. More than anything he wished he could sit with Lokesh at his side and meditate, perhaps recite mantras, and touch the ancient spirits of the place. But all he had was a resentful deputy and a nervous Public Security officer.

After Jinhua had located two more slabs, Shan called him back, concerned about giving too much away and even more about the onlooking Tibetans. He was not certain Jinhua had even recognized their resentment. Certainly he had not noticed the stones landing twenty feet away, thrown by an angry old woman.

He dropped Jinhua and Jengtse at the station, then, saying he had forgotten that he promised Mrs. Weng to patrol the southern roads, sped back out of town. He headed north, stopping at the base of the first high ridge that defined the forbidden zone. Demons were striding those hills, the Tibetans believed. The American had drawn a map that, without his knowledge, led directly into the heart of their lair.

Shan sat in his truck, studying the yellowed finger bone he had found where Nyima had been attacked. It seemed so genuine that he had first taken it to be an actual bone but later, under a lens in his office, he had seen that it was an intricately carved wooden replica of a bone. He had seen such fingers, such hands, even entire wooden skeletons before, usually sewn onto backing of black fabric. They had been designed for the elaborate demon dancers that had once featured prominently in Buddhist festivals.

Beside the wooden bone in the rocks where Nyima had been attacked had been a broken column of pink salt, like the one he had seen left as an offering with the dead men in the cave and on Nyima's altar. He knew of only one place locally where pink salt was found. He stepped out of the truck and began climbing. At the top he took out his compass and the map he had found in the dead American's room, the line-of-sight map for the cell tower. Shan penciled in the two sites he already knew, the mountain pass and the Plain of Ghosts, then surveyed the landscape and set out toward the northwest, to intersect the line.

After half an hour he reached an old trail and, minutes later, rounded an outcropping and froze in alarm. The construction before him was built like an archway between two of the highest rock formations, made from thin limbs bound with leather straps. From it hung a human skull, several human arm and leg bones, and over a dozen pieces of cloth. He grabbed one of the windblown cloths. It was a crudely drawn image of an angry leopard god, a curse. All of the tattered pieces of cloth held similar curses. He was standing at the entry to the forbidden land, on the most likely trail from Yangkar.

The taboo wasn't a mere legend or rumor. The bones and curses made it real, or at least made it clear the taboo was being enforced by flesh-and-blood humans. To either side of the arch were more charms, inscribed in paint on the flat faces of rocks. He bent over each, trying to understand. The charms on the stones were different. They were demon destroyers. Someone was actively opposing the demons. He hesitated over the last of the countercharms, positioned so it would only be seen by someone who had walked through the gate. The silk prayer scarf on which the charm was written was tied through the eye sockets of a sheep skull, which was nodding in the wind, balanced on a Chinese bayonet.

Minutes later he found what he had been looking for, a recently made cairn that lined up with other marks on his map. Under the flat rock at the top of the cairn was a paper torn from a notebook with three numbers: 700, 1300, and 1900. Jacob Bartram had left a reminder at the cairn. Along the bottom of the paper was a short note. *See you soon, Jig girl.* Underneath, in a different hand, was a penciled note. *OK*, it said. *700.*

Jacob Bartram had waited there, and while waiting had cleared a small circle around the cairn, even dragged a flat rock to the edge as a seat. Shan sat on it, studying the circle, then investigated a glint under a small heather bush. A pack of chewing gum with an English label had fallen underneath. A foot away he found an elongated wooden bulb. It was another carved finger bone, a bigger one than that he had found where Nyima had been attacked, as if from further down the same finger. Did the demon even know one of its fingers was separating? Once the tip of a finger on one of the old suits was removed, the others, held on by knotted threads, would be easily loosened.

On the opposite side of the circle he found several clumps of broken heather. Underneath one he discovered three unused cigarettes, of cheap, acrid tobacco.

He paced the circle and let the pieces fall into place. The *Jig girl* Jacob had expected had arrived and had written a confirmation for a call the next morning. But then she had been attacked. Had she successfully defended herself? The demon had lost a finger bone and three Chinese cigarettes.

On the cairn he discovered a pinkish smudge. He wet a finger and tasted it. Salt. Once salt in Tibet had been the most valuable commodity in trade, the reason for months-long caravans, a source of wealth and a source of offerings. Now, somehow, it had become a link between murders and demons.

He reached the salt shrines after another steady climb and looked down on the curving cliff-side trail he used to reach it on his bicycle. He walked along the line of eroded salt saints, pausing to give a mantra to the one Lokesh had dubbed the constable saint, then followed the line formed by the row of saints, for the first time exploring the terrain above the shrine. He quickly discovered a fallen statue, which had been lying on the ground so long its salt was leaching into the soil, killing the plants around it. He searched for similar circles of dead plants and found three more. When standing, the figures would have defined a slow arc pointing toward a cliff face with a dark shadow in the center of its base, a cavern.

The entrance in the cliff was flanked by two more of the salt sculptures, eroded so severely he could only discern the vague suggestion of heads and arms. Inside the entry chamber were dozens of the small salt offerings and the wooden molds used to make the cylinders. To his surprise two butter lamps burned inside, making the pink walls glow with warm, soft light. He lifted one and ran a finger along a wall. It was salt.

Extending the lamp, Shan followed a passage, its air growing strangely warmer as he walked, then emerged into a huge cavern. *Thangkas* hung from the wall, old paintings of the Tara goddess in

her many forms, their edges encrusted with salt. More lamps illuminated the center of the chamber, and to his great surprise he saw a
large pool from which wisps of steam rose. Oddly, he smelled tobacco.

"I don't think a Chinese has ever been in here," a woman said.

The words echoed off the walls, and it took a moment for Shan to
realize they had come from the pool. Only Lhamo's head was visible
above the surface of the thermal water.

"It's the ancient healing spring," she explained with a grin, "used
by the caravans."

"I have read," came another voice from the shadows at the end of
the pool, "that they brought sick sheep in too, the sheep that carried
their bags of salt. The warm mineral water is a restorative." The voice
grew louder, and Trinle appeared, his head gliding above the shimmer-
ing surface.

"We are in the forbidden zone," Shan observed.

"We've been coming here since long before that taboo," Trinle replied with a grin that showed his missing teeth. "We have an understanding with these gods."

Shan walked along the edge of the pool. "You are the ones who
put the countercharms at that gate," he suggested. The two old Tibetans offered silent, serene smiles. "The skull of a sheep on a Chinese
bayonet. I am not sure what demon you meant that for."

Trinle began rubbing a block of pink salt on his wife's shoulder.

"If you think it is mere mortals scaring people, why don't you tell
the town? Why keep the fear alive?" Trinle grinned again and Shan
answered his own question. "Because you are ferals. You oppose the
men who pretend to be gods but you don't fight the taboo."

"A forbidden land is a sanctuary to us," Lhamo confirmed.

Shan turned back to the wall and paced along the old *thangkas*.
"A forbidden land is also a sanctuary for old secrets," he suggested. He
paused at a hanging that presented a depiction of the local geography,
centered around the cavern and salt shrine. He could clearly see the
line of salt saints, painted oversized to emphasize their importance.

They all actually had faces. To the southeast he saw something that seemed to be a fortress that must have been the *gompa* at Yangkar, to the northwest a small flat plateau. He pointed to it. "The Plain of Ghosts?" he asked.

"No, no," came Lhamo's voice. He heard the water dripping, and the aged woman was beside him, pointing to another plateau, slightly more distant, with a solitary temple painted blue. "When this was done it was only the Temple of the Pure Water, where a different type of healing was being done. Later it became the famed college."

Shan heard a wheezing laugh from Trinle. He turned and recoiled, backing away from Lhamo as she faced him. "Did you see where I put my cigar, constable?" she asked. The old woman was naked.

When he arrived back at the town square, the aged Red Flag sedan was in front of the clerk's office, the motor running. Inside the office he found the mechanic's son, Gyatso, with a piece of thin paper over the framed map of central Tibet, tracing a route from Yangkar.

Wu, the town clerk, nervously looked up from his desk. "Gyatso says he has to visit a sick aunt near Lhasa."

The young Tibetan spun about and stuffed the paper in his pocket. "Good maps are hard to find," the youth said in an uneasy voice. He seemed to always wear a guilty expression in Shan's presence.

"Have you been here the entire time?" Shan asked Wu.

"Yes, yes," Wu said, then hesitated. "Except when he asked for a tax form from the back office." The clerk saw Shan's frown. "His family does own a business, constable," Wu reminded Shan.

Shan just turned and left the building, quickening his pace as he heard the mechanic's son hurrying behind him. He reached the car just in time to pull a piece of paper from the dashboard. It was a hand-drawn map of back roads just north of Lhasa, leading to a cluster of barracks-like buildings enclosed in a large square. Shan looked up in surprise at Tserung's son, who carefully avoided eye contact, then stepped aside to pace around the car. He opened the rear door.

"I have heard of old monks and nuns with charms that could make them invisible," Shan said to the figure trying to crouch low on the floor, "but I'm afraid you haven't mastered the art, Shiva."

"She didn't understand," the astrologer blurted out as Shan helped her from the car.

Shan waved the paper at her. "This is the big internment camp by the Kyichu River. I've been there. It's crawling with Public Security and Religious Affairs officers. If they catch you trying to interfere with a detainee they'll grab you. They can put you behind wire for a year without even asking a magistrate."

Shiva stared at Shan's prayer amulet as she replied. "I did a chart. There are bad times coming to that camp. We can't let a young nun just throw herself away. . . ." Shan followed her eyes as they shifted toward the pile of blankets on the backseat. He pulled away the top blanket to reveal Nyima curled up on the seat. Her bandages were soaked with blood and her gaze was clouded with pain. She had escaped her doctor's care.

Shan approached Tserung's son, backing him against the sedan, and extracted a piece of carefully folded paper that extended from his pocket. It was a blank piece of official stationary from the clerk's office.

"What were you going to write?" Shan demanded.

"Not me," Gyatso mumbled, not looking at Shan. "Shiva. She knows Chinese."

Shan turned to the astrologer. "Nyima said she was going to ride her donkey to Lhasa," Shiva explained. "It would have killed her. She said she didn't care, that there always had to be a young robe to take over for the old robe or all is lost."

Shan stared at the astrologer as realization struck. Someone had been substituted for the green-eyed woman in the detainee truck. Rikyu had been missing since that day. He waved the empty sheet in front of Shiva.

"Mr. Wu does tax records," she explained. "Just a note to say tax records have been located for prisoner twelve. If she paid taxes she can't be unregistered, right?"

It was, Shan had to admit, an imaginative ploy. He stuffed the letterhead into his pocket. "The first thing they would do is call Mr. Wu for confirmation. It wouldn't just mean a year's administrative detention for you, it would be forgery of state records. Five years hard labor at least. And you," he stated to Nyima, "an unregistered nun committing conspiracy against the government. You would never survive the sentence they gave you."

He gazed at the frightened Tibetan women, so wise in the ways of the spirit and so innocent in the ways of the world, but always so relentless in their hope. "Gyatso," he said without looking at the young Tibetan, "you will drive Nyima back to the *amchi*'s house. Nowhere else." He turned to Jengtse, who was watching with amusement from the steps. "Did you say my predecessor had a dress uniform?" he asked his deputy.

"Constable Fen? Sure, he kept it in the back closet in the guesthouse."

"Brush it off. I'm going to Lhasa in the morning."

He waited until two hours after nightfall before knocking on the back door of the garage. Jinhua waited outside as Shan spoke with Tserung, listening as the mechanic argued, then silently followed as the Tibetan, muttering his disapproval of a knob entering his vault and cursing his stone-brained son for ever letting Jengtse know about its secrets, led them through his junkyard. The compound, surrounded by high stucco walls, extended farther than Shan expected, and as they reached the back the junk changed. Old car parts and rusty truck bodies gave way to appendages. Shan stepped over a graceful six-foot-long bronze leg, passed a heavily dented statue of a seated Buddha, then found Tserung waiting at the rear wall beside a pair of bronzed hands pressed together. The hands were nearly three feet long, meaning the statue of the deity they had belonged to must have been massive. Tserung disappeared into the shadow behind the hands and Shan followed, discovering a narrow set of stairs that led to a crude, rough-hewn door set in a narrow, irregular opening that seemed to have been chiseled through a stone wall. Inside the door he found himself on a landing at the top of a second flight of stone stairs, cupped from centuries of use, that to the left led back under the junkyard. To the right stones and earth had collapsed into a passage, cutting off what must have been a connection with the old *gompa*.

He recognized the smell of long-neglected chapels, the dust and musty air mixed with faint scents of the jasmine, aloe, and cardamom used in incense, cut by the slightly acrid smell of butter lamps. Tserung pulled the door shut behind their small party and joined Shan at the bottom of the stairs. Jinhua turned up the flame in the lantern he carried, revealing a long corridor whose walls and vaulted ceiling had once been adorned with colorful images. Although faded and cracked, with several sections of plaster fallen to the floor, there were enough claws, talons, fierce eyes, and flaming bodies to tell them they were passing along ranks of protector demons. The underground complex had not always been an archive. It had been a labyrinth of *gonkangs*, small chapels where the most savage of the demon deities were worshiped, where, the devout had believed, the fierce deities actually resided. In the old *gompas* novices were never allowed near such *gonkangs*, for they were not trained sufficiently to deal with the terror. In many, graduation to the higher orders required spending a night alone in such a chapel.

Tserung guided them to the end of the hundred-foot corridor, which ended not in more sacred images but a wall of debris. Shan turned. They had passed six separate chapels, three on each side, and a quick glance inside each had shown them to be lined with makeshift shelves, each jammed with records. The chapels had been urgently turned into a secret archive, which had then been sealed by the collapse of its passages into the *gompa*. At the entry to each chapel the stubs of unlit candles sat jammed into heavy iron lug nuts.

"The only records in Mandarin are in the first chapel, nearest the stairs," the Tibetan explained. "Everything else is older, in Tibetan."

Shan looked at the oil-stained mechanic in surprise. He spoke like a curator. "How are they organized?" Shan asked.

In answer Tserung led him into the nearest of the chapels. The shelves, constructed in front of elaborately painted walls, held scores of *peche*, Tibetan loose-leaf books, each in a long wooden box or wrapped in its own silken cover.

"The ones in blue and red cloth, or in boxes, are the usual scriptures or teachings of the lamas," the Tibetan said. "But the ones in brown wrappers seem to be administrative records. Anything that's been read has gone right back where it was found on the shelves."

"You've studied them then?"

Tserung seemed embarrassed. "I was the firstborn son. For as far back as memory goes my family always sent the firstborn to be a monk." He shrugged. "I come down sometimes with a thermos of tea and some candles when the wind howls at night. It's quiet here. I read what I can. My mother would like that," he added self-consciously. He put a hand on one of the covers, raising a cloud of dust. "Time for them to go, I guess."

"Go?" Shan asked.

"Religious Affairs will come for them now, with one of their cleanup crews. I don't blame you, constable, I understand. It's your job. It was only a matter of time."

Shan hesitated, hurt by Tserung's conclusion. "Religious Affairs will only come if someone reports these," Shan observed, and turned to Jinhua, who had followed them. "Are you going to report this discovery, lieutenant?"

Jinhua stared hard at Shan, then shrugged. "Report what? A bunch of scrap paper buried under a yard full of scrap? What's the point? They are already in a junkyard."

Surprised delight rose on the mechanic's face.

"When we leave tonight," Shan said, "pile more debris over the stairwell." Tserung's grin blossomed into a wide smile. "Meanwhile,"

Shan said, "let's see if the books can make the past live for us." He pulled a small flashlight from his pocket as Jinhua began lighting candles. "Room by room. Jinhua in the first, with the Chinese records. I'll go to the last. Take an hour, and we'll meet by the stairs."

"What are we looking for?" Tserung asked.

Shan and Jinhua exchanged a glance. "Records of particularly valuable artifacts," Shan ventured. "Inventories of the *gompa*'s property. Evidence of what the *gompa* was like in, say, 1960. And evidence of who was here in 1966."

As Shan probed the manuscripts, he felt Lokesh at his shoulder, urging Shan to slow down, to study the elegant little birds painted in one margin, the gold-leafed lotus blossoms worked into the title page of another. The old Tibetan would spend weeks in such a place, studying this archive of the spirit, as he called collections of old *peche*. He found himself whispering an apology as he quickly scanned another book, whether to the old scribes who had labored over it or to Lokesh he was not sure. After opening several aged sutras he tested Tserung's theory, confirming that the brown shrouds covered records related to the business of the *gompa*. He studied the stacks and lifted out the book on the bottom shelf, from the farthest corner.

He stared at the date recorded at the bottom of the parchment page. 1959. It seemed much older. Suddenly he realized it would have been stated in the Buddhist calendar. He did a quick calculation and with a thrill realized the book had been written six hundred years earlier. He lowered himself onto a three-legged stool, the only furniture in the chamber, and eagerly began to read. The writer interspersed Buddhist poems and proverbs between reports on construction of buildings. A train of four hundred mules laden with squared building stones and timbers had departed for the Pure Water monks, he read, then an account of payments, usually made in measures of barley. The passage was followed by verses from Milarepa, the poet saint, then an account of artists arriving from Lhasa who were waiting for the blessing of the abbot before proceeding up the trail. A list of villages that had sent laborers came next, and a description of the huge camp set up to accommodate them. There were calculations in the margin, then the text continued with a description of how thirty strong men were assigned to each of the huge beams that had arrived from the forests of Kham. It was, he gradually realized, a report by one of the engineer monks who had been responsible for construction of the thousands of shrines, temples, and *gompas* that had once dotted the Tibetan landscape.

He rewrapped the journal in its cover and lifted another volume wrapped in dirty silk. It was dated sixty years earlier than the prior volume. The construction of the main *gompa*, described as one of the most beautiful in Tibet, was still under way. A sculptor from India had arrived in Yangkar and was carving stone *dakinis* that would grace the corners of the main sanctuary, teaching Tibetan apprentices as he did so. Shan lingered over a sketch of a *chorten* surrounded by seated monks with a lama laying a hand on the rounded dome, as if blessing it.

Three more manuscripts related to the early years of the great *gompa* of Yangkar and the construction of structures in the mountains called the Temple of Abundant Life, the Healing Shrine, and later the Pure Water Sanctuary.

By the time he joined the others, Shan had reviewed another dozen volumes, all of which were similar construction chronicles spanning three hundred years. Jinhua had found reports from the eighteenth century about great caravans of the sick arriving in Yangkar, several bringing scores of the sick and one bringing the Dalai Lama with his ailing dog. Yangkar, and the Pure Water complex in the mountains, had become a center for healing all creatures.

Jinhua had made some sense of the most recent records. "All Religious Affairs and the army," he reported, pointing to notebooks inscribed in Mandarin. He had made two stacks, one of the Chinese records, one of what Tserung had told him were the most recent Tibetan records. Shan pointed in query to the solitary *peche* between the two stacks. "That's exactly how it was in the stacks, between the Tibetan and Chinese," the lieutenant explained.

Shan opened the brown cover. "From more than a hundred years ago," he said, then made another silent calculation of the exact date. 1897. "Why would that be here?" He paused, looking at the Chinese notebooks. "And who brought the Chinese records into this vault?"

Tserung spoke from the doorway. "I did. Years ago, when the town clerk had thrown them in the trash." The mechanic motioned them into the corridor, where he had brought two wooden chests, each twice as long as the usual *peche* container. From the first he produced a manuscript cover carved with intricate images of gods and goddesses. From the second the mechanic pulled a large square of silk over six feet on each side. In its center dragons had been embroidered, surrounding two crossed *dorje*, the thunderbolt symbol used in Tibetan ritual, done in golden thread.

"A throne cover," Shan declared in an awed tone. "Very old. It could have been used when the Dalai Lama was—" His words died away as a piece of plaster fell out of the ceiling. With a terrible ripping sound three long cracks suddenly appeared in the walls. Tserung tossed the cloth to Shan and bolted up the stairway. Shan dropped the cloth into the chest and quickly followed the mechanic up into the cool night air, spying Tserung as he ran toward the street. The rumbling of heavy engines and metallic screeching filled the night. From somewhere a woman screamed. Shan abruptly halted, his chest tightening as he saw Tserung freeze at the head of the alley, then collapse onto his knees. An army tank rolled past his garage.

Shan walked the streets in the cold gray dawn. The army was gone, leaving cracked roads and quaking Tibetans in its wake. In the night one of the nameless couriers who carried letters to Lokesh's secret home had stopped at his house. With a stab of pain, Shan had handed him a message telling his friend to forget about coming during his son's visit and to stay away until he wrote again.

He kicked a piece of loose asphalt to the side of the street and turned toward the sound of weeping. In an alleyway a man was trying to console an old woman, who was sobbing into his shoulder. The tank had run the length of the main street, to the far end of town, turned, and rumbled back again, leading a parade of two turreted assault vehicles and two troop carriers. Yintai, General Lau's brutish aide, had stood in a smaller open vehicle, surveying the town with a sneer on his face, holding the roll bar in one hand and a pistol in the other, raising it against his forehead in salute as he spied Shan watching. The Tibetans of Yangkar still showed panic on their faces. Shan had tried in vain to convince a family there was no need to flee, then watched forlornly as they finished tying their possessions onto a donkey and hurried toward the mountains.

Mrs. Weng was sweeping debris away from the front of her shop. She looked up with a furious expression as he approached. "You did this! I told the Tibetans to stop building that shrine on the square!" she declared in a simmering voice. "It was too reactionary, I told them. And you did nothing! How can we have a proper town when you let people behave the way they do? We need seminars, constable, we need some of those firm teachers from Religious Affairs who can explain the new world. The Committee of Leading Citizens is writing to Lhasa today! We shall offer the town's formal apology and petition for the instructors!"

Shan saw that the big plate glass window of her shop was broken, and bricks had fallen from the top of the front wall. She leaned on her broom and sighed, her anger burned away. "Sometimes I think I should just go live with my sister in Nanjing. But they make you pay back the pioneer bounty if you leave early. And I spent all that on my shop."

Down the street Tibetans were futilely trying to fit pieces of macadam back into the holes chewed up by heavy treads. A tree listed precariously over a building, one of its roots snapped by the tank. Another tree in the square had fallen, crushing one of the gaming tables.

Shan avoided the station, going straight to the guesthouse where, feeling strangely numb, he put on the dress uniform. He felt a melancholy detachment, as if preparing for a funeral. He had survived by living on the fringe, out of the jaws of the machine that chewed up the souls of China. But now that machine was here, in Yangkar, and it was impossible for him to flee.

He paused outside the building. The vibration of the equipment had shaken loose some of the stucco on the converted stable. Underneath, some of the original paintwork from the days of the old monastery could be seen. A large, solitary eye stared at him, the watchful eye of Buddha that had once adorned many Tibetan buildings. His hand trembled as he touched the ancient image with a finger. He *would* flee, he *had* to flee to save his soul. He would go into hiding with Lokesh, become another feral Tibetan. He began unbuttoning his tunic.

"They should have called," came a frightened voice over his shoulder. Jengtse was standing in the back door of the station. "He's never done this before. The tank was just to soften us for his teeth. He's going to chew us up and swallow us bit by bit."

Shan pushed past his alarmed deputy, straight through the station. As he stepped out the front door, two big blocky sedans pulled up to the curb. An aide rushed to open the rear door of the first and a thin, almost gaunt figure emerged. He paced angrily along the street, studying the ruin in the square before turning toward Shan.

"Your town is a disgrace, constable," Colonel Tan observed in a brittle voice.

Shan found himself refastening the buttons of his tunic. An older Chinese woman climbed out of the second car. It was Amah Jiejie, Tan's steadfast assistant and closest confidant.

"The army came," Shan replied as Amah Jiejie, leaning into the car, coaxed someone to join her. A lean, nervous figure climbed out. "A battle tank sent by . . ." Shan's words choked away. Standing there in ill-fitting civilian clothes, without manacles, was his son Ko.

CHAPTER EIGHT

"This is my county!" Tan roared. "I sent no tank, no soldiers at all!" He spoke to Shan's back as his constable looked out the window of his office. Tan, stating he had business with Shan, had asked Amah Jiejie to escort Ko to the noodle shop.

"He wasn't due until tomorrow," Shan said, his voice strangely hoarse. "I thought I would have to go get him."

"I was coming up," Tan shot back impatiently. "It seemed more efficient. It was her idea. Then she asked to come, said I wouldn't know how to speak with the boy."

Shan fought down a wave of emotion and turned to face the colonel. He struggled with his words. "I didn't know if you were still going to let him—"

"Where did the soldiers come from?" Tan interrupted. "What unit?"

"The general's aide, Yintai, was in charge. They must have come from the commando training base north of the county. Lau probably just called it night maneuvers. The Tibetans were terrified. Everyone was terrified."

"Why?" Tan demanded. "This town is nothing to him. You are nothing to him. Why bother with Yangkar?"

Shan had been asking himself the same question ever since the army paraded out of the town. He had no reply, just returned Tan's intense gaze.

A sound like an angry growl rolled out of the colonel's throat. "In the hangar just before you left, you lifted up the heads of those dead soldiers."

The colonel had just answered his own question. "Who else saw?" Shan asked Tan.

"The pilot from that transport helicopter was on a cot in the far corner, in the shadows. I thought he was asleep, but as soon as you left he sprang up and followed you outside. What was it you found so interesting?"

Shan lowered himself into his chair. His heart seemed to shrivel. The fear and chaos of the night before, the terror that had driven Tibetans into the hills, had all been caused by him. "It's all about what is not there," he said in an absent tone. "What's useful about a window is what is not there. The hole. There's a chapter of the *Tao Te Ching* about the importance of holes."

"I'm not so clear on the Tao philosophers," Tan declared in a simmering tone. "Humor me."

"Lau doesn't care about two dead soldiers, even if they were murdered. What concerns him is the little hole at the base of each neck."

"Meaning?"

Shan found himself looking back out the window, toward the noodle shop. "My son looked like he was in shock. He could barely speak." Shan's son had mumbled a greeting to his father but kept his eyes on the colonel. Amah Jiejie had patted Ko's shoulder and led him away with a motherly air.

"The fools at the prison had forgotten to tell him," Tan explained. "Amah Jiejie said he probably thought he was being dragged out for another trial."

Shan turned toward the colonel. "By you? More likely he thought he was going to be shot."

"We gave him civilian clothes," Tan said, as if that should explain everything. He shrugged. "She insisted on the second car so she could ride with him, steady him. She checked his record. He hasn't been outside a prison in years." Tan seemed to check himself. Expressions of sympathy were a foreign tongue to him. He clenched his jaw. "If he's not back on the fifth day, Shan, he will be considered an escapee."

Shan nodded. It was Tan's way of saying their bargain still held.

"We were talking about holes in soldiers," Tan pressed.

"Knife wounds. A single expert thrust, directed down the spine at the base of the neck."

Tan lit a cigarette and took several long draws before speaking. "Like you told Lau, it's a military matter."

Shan emptied the little stone bowl he used for paper clips and pushed it across the desk for Tan to dump his ashes in. "Except I have two more bodies, killed exactly the same way. A helicopter has been watching the place where they were found, which I suspect is close to where Lau's dead soldiers were found. The only reason Lau would be concerned is because he knows something about those bodies. A connection with his own bodies."

A rumbling sound rose from Tan's throat. "You were at Lhadrung and said nothing! When you were going to tell me?"

"You would have had me tell you in front of Lau? He didn't exactly give us time alone."

His response took the fire out of Tan's eyes.

"And Public Security was here," Shan pointed out. "Surely it should have been for them to make any official report."

"The knobs? They've said nothing. No report has been filed."

The skin over Tan's already thin face drew so tight he looked almost skeletal. He hated Public Security almost as much as Shan did. The colonel inhaled a last time on his cigarette and crushed it in the bowl. "I have to come all the way up here for the pleasure of hearing that my county is being fucked in the ass by Public Security?" he hissed.

"You had already decided to come to Yangkar," Shan reminded him. "And not to bring my son," he suggested as he studied the colonel's rigid countenance. "You came to find a way to get a Hero of the Motherland out of your county."

Tan lit another cigarette and exhaled twin plumes from his nostrils. "You were always quick to grasp the subtleties. Maybe that's why I put up with you. Everything is a game for Lau. He's been a pampered pet of the Politburo for decades. If he sees a new gun he has to fire it. Put him by a new helicopter and he jumps in the cockpit like a teenage boy with a motorcycle. Leaves wrecks in his wake. Sports cars. A state minister's young wife. He filled a fountain at a casino in Macau with whiskey and lit it on fire. Used to be a squad of old sergeants who would follow him around just to clean up his messes."

"He offered you a fat retirement," Shan recalled.

Tan hesitated, then nodded. "Now I understand why. A bribe on account."

"Meaning he anticipated a mess the governor of Lhadrung County might have to clean up."

Tan's eyes narrowed. "What bodies?"

"A man like Lau will never be defeated in a frontal assault," Shan said in a wary tone.

"Defeat? Who said anything about defeating him? He is a general, an exalted hero. I am a lowly colonel."

"My mistake. More like teaching one wolf to respect another wolf's territory."

Tan did not argue. He rose and paced along the wall, silently studying the large map pinned there. The old campaigner quickly focused on the pencil lines Shan had drawn, converging toward the Plain of Ghosts. "What bodies?" he asked again, still facing the map.

"Two men dead in the mountains. One was an American. Both left in the same Tibetan tomb."

Tan did not turn. Shan saw the veins bulging on the side of his neck. The colonel's hand reached down blindly to the little table by the wall and closed around Jengtse's prized panda mug. With a quick violent motion he slammed it against the far wall. It shattered into a dozen pieces, leaving a blot of tea that dripped toward the floor.

"You!" Tan whispered. "It's always you."

This was a new Tan. His fury, which could burn like a bonfire for

hours, had flashed white hot and was gone. The colonel sat back in
the chair in front of Shan's desk. "What's that word the Buddhists
use? Karma. Is that what this is, Shan? The disgraced investigator only
gets the investigations that ensure more disgrace. Allowing criminal
elements to run wild in your mountains and commit four murders,
including a foreigner? How can you not be blamed? I gave you the
quietest post in my county, so remote no one would ever hear your
howls of desperation."

They stared at each other, two old fighters tired of the world.

"Karma," Shan said at last. "It's like divine justice. That's the only
kind that will ever reach General Lau."

Tan cocked his head. "Surely Lau is not implicated. Don't even
bother to suggest it. Lau would never kill soldiers. He just sees some
kind of opportunity in this. He's bored in retirement. He found a di-
version."

Shan looked longingly out the window toward the café where his
son sat. He wanted so to be there eating with him, to take him home,
to walk with him on a quiet mountain path, to rejoice with him in his
temporary freedom and begin the list of activities he had planned for
his visit. He glanced at his watch. "Give me a couple hours of your
time," he said instead.

Tan, who had followed Shan's truck to the little flat below the ice
cave, left his driver with his car and walked in silence up the path. As
they reached the ledge with the caves, the colonel turned to look back
down at the car. "Lau's man Yintai bribed the sergeant who drives me.
The sergeant told me immediately, saying he wanted to throw the
money in Yintai's face, but he couldn't offend the famous general. I
told him to keep the money and to demand more next time because
he was going to earn it." Tan replied to the question in Shan's eyes.
"He won't say a word to Lau's men except those he and I agree on.

Lau will not be denied his spies. Better to know who they are than not."

"Then you were never here," Shan said.

"Persuade me," Tan shot back.

Shan first took him up to the Plain of Ghosts and showed him the tomb where the bodies had been found. The tomb had been sealed again, the slab not only pushed back in place but also covered with little cairns and *khatas* anchored with stones. Tan paced about it once, surveyed the plain with the eye of a battlefield commander, and turned expectantly to Shan. "The bodies?"

Shan did not have to warn away the shepherd who now guarded the ice cave, for the instant the young Tibetan saw Tan's uniform he bolted up the slope. Tan pretended not to see him and said nothing as they passed the cave with the crude door where Nyima lived.

Shan picked up one of the lanterns by the entrance to the cave, lit it, and led the colonel inside.

"Like the breath of some cold hell," Tan muttered as the frigid breeze hit them in the tunnel. Shan looked up in surprise. Did he sense a contemplative tone in the words? Although the colonel would never admit it, his long years in Tibet were changing him.

Half a dozen flickering butter lamps lit the chamber with the bodies, which were still covered with blankets. Someone had laid flowers beside Bartram's head. It was not a Tibetan custom. Shan pulled the cover from the American. "His name is Jacob Bartram. He had Tibetan relatives. I think he came to look for them."

Tan put an inquisitive hand on the ice of the far wall, then turned and pointed to Bartram's feet. "Climbing boots. Another foray up a forbidden mountain." They both knew that when Westerners were found in remote, prohibited parts of Tibet, it was usually because they had been trying to furtively climb a mountain to add to their lists of conquests. "They never learn. Shortness of breath, dizziness, then they black out. Down they go." He was already postulating the logical cover-up.

Shan lifted the man's head and held his lantern close. "The blade was wide and razor sharp. One slice downward, precisely positioned." The colonel leaned toward the wound, froze, then slowly straightened. The impatience in his eyes faded.

"If it were one body I'd say maybe just a lucky stab in a fight. But with so many . . ."

"But what?"

Shan shrugged. "It's professional. A precise kill by a professional who is proud of his work."

Tan walked around the dead man. When he halted he was staring at the images that flanked the entry. "Who did those?"

"Tibetans, a very long time ago."

"Monsters?"

"Minor deities. Deputies to the monsters," Shan replied, then aimed his lantern toward the top row of images. "Those are the monsters."

Tan made a sound like a snort. He studied each of the savage heads with great interest. "What are they called?"

"Protector demons. Savage deities. They defend the Buddhist faithful. Some of the old Tibetans say they sometimes sleep for centuries, but when they wake up the unpure will tremble."

"What's that he's holding in his other hand?" Tan asked, pointing to a fanged, black-faced figure with a raised sword in one hand.

"A skull filled with blood. He is one of the gods called blood drinkers."

Tan's mouth curled up in a lightless grin. "Demon gods," he said in an approving tone. "Looks like he's proposing a toast." He turned to the second body. "One was American, you said. The other?"

"Not American. Not Tibetan," Shan confirmed. He pulled away the blanket.

Never in all the years Shan had known him had he ever seen Tan exhibit surprise, until now. He was many things, but above all he was an old soldier now, looking at the remains of a fallen comrade.

"He's been dead fifty years as far as I can tell," Shan explained. "Sergeant Ma Chu, from Anhui Province."

Tan stared, transfixed, into the desiccated face with the sunken eyes and twisted grin, as hideous as those of the demons. "Not a police matter," he said at last. "He's a damned archaeological project."

Shan pointed to the pocket of the dead soldier's uniform. "His unit badge was a star inside a wheel."

"An engineer," Tan observed.

"But assigned to a mountain commando unit, Lau's I think, although no emblem of the Snow Tigers."

"That came later," Tan said in a near whisper. "First time I saw one of those Snow Tiger badges was in a funeral procession for Chairman Mao. 1976." He reached out and touched the dried, dead hand, as if to reassure Sergeant Ma, then bent over and gazed into the hideous face for several long breaths. "Sergeant Ma," he repeated, then saluted the dead man before turning back to Shan.

"The men in the monasteries usually surrendered peacefully," the colonel observed. "But there were others, Tibetans in the hills, who fought like crazed warriors. Of course there were casualties. Who but Tibetans would put him in a Tibetan grave?"

When Shan lifted the shoulders of the corpse he heard a brittle bone snap. "Hold the lantern," he instructed Tan and pulled back the collar at the nape of the neck.

A slow hiss escaped Tan's throat as he saw the stab wound at the base of the sergeant's neck. "Impossible!" He retreated, nearly to the wall of ice at the rear of the chamber. "You!" he uttered for the second time that morning. It had the tone of an accusation.

Shan silently covered the dead with the blankets. He lit one of the sticks of incense left by the Tibetans and jammed it into the little cairn of pebbles that held several burned-out sticks before facing Tan.

"Take them, colonel. Put them in your trunk and dispose of the bodies on the way back to Lhadrung. You and I can only lose."

"Me?"

"Mention this dead soldier and you embarrass the army, and worse, you embarrass General Lau. No one likes those who open old wounds. If word leaks outside the army you will be accused of disloyalty, even of encouraging the resistance. You know better than any that Tibet is a powder keg. The fuse is long and slow-burning, but it is still a powder keg, ready for the final spark. That might be the death of the Dalai Lama. Or perhaps just a new spotlight on the atrocities committed in the 1960s."

Tan extracted a cigarette but then looked up at the savage demons and put it back in his pocket. "Why do you have them here, together?"

"They were together in death, in that old tomb. That slab was laid down hundreds of years ago but lifted fifty years ago to bury Sergeant Ma, then again a few days ago."

"Meaning what?"

"Meaning the killers knew about the tomb. They went out of their way to put the American there, then they covered it up with dirt and weeds. Killers, because one man could never move that slab."

"You mean the ones who killed the American knew about Sergeant Ma."

Shan nodded. "There is a connection I am trying to understand."

Tan gazed at the mummified soldier. "The sergeant should have an honorable burial," he declared.

"There are twenty-three more."

"More?"

"A company of Lau's men went missing. Twenty-four men. Lost in an avalanche in Kham, Lau reported. One of those missing was Sergeant Ma."

"So it was a massacre by Tibetan guerrillas in these hills," Tan said and cocked his head. "That's why Lau's so upset. The only smear on his perfect record. Now one of those guerrillas has surfaced, and he threatens to expose Lau's lie."

"Maybe. That doesn't explain the dead soldiers in the hangar."

Tan grimaced. "Then what?"

"Lau came into Tibet a poor soldier and left a wealthy man."

Tan shrugged. "Officers took things, sure. Times were different. A gold figurine, a few jewels pried off an altar. It was just going to be recycled by Religious Affairs, so why not let those who did the real work get the benefit."

"Lau had forty million in a Hong Kong account by the time he was reassigned."

"You can't possibly know that."

Shan gazed up at the deities as if for help. He would never have shared what he had learned from Jinhua with the Tan he had met years earlier. Could he take the risk? he silently asked them. He looked back at Tan, seeing again the intense way he stared at the protector gods, and began to explain. Tan was not frightened of the demons. He had recognized some of his own kind.

Shan drove toward Lhasa in something of a daze, reliving his brief moments with Ko and thinking again of how they would spend the few days they had together. They would take a lunch up to the waterfall on the slope above Shan's house. They would have long, slow meals, just the two of them, and Shan would tell Ko about the wonderful grandparents, uncles, and aunts his son had never known, as they used ink and new brushes Shan had bought to write out ancient poems the way his own father had taught Shan. He would have Ko write a long letter to Lokesh, the closest thing to a grandfather Ko would ever know. Shan would translate into Tibetan and send both versions to his old friend. Each time the anticipation put a smile on his face, a shadow quickly crossed it, a blurred image of a killer with a heavy knife. He had brought his son home as a murderer was roaming the hills.

He switched on his radio, listening to a Chinese opera and then a local newscast. A hailstorm had wiped out barley crops south of Shigatse. Two German climbers had died on Mount Everest. The famous General Lau, Hero of the Motherland and personal friend of the

Chairman, had graciously led the opening ceremony for a new school in Lhasa.

CAMP NEW AWAKENING, announced the brightly colored sign at the gate of the huge internment facility. On the high walls that lined the road to the compound offices were painted murals of smiling steelworkers, soldiers waving rifles, parading schoolchildren, even beaming parents holding babies aloft toward Chinese spaceships. Along the front of the headquarters building hung a banner that declared WITH ARMS UPRAISED WE CONQUER THE WORLD.

Inside the headquarters office the fashionably dressed Chinese receptionist acknowledged Shan with the same smile he had seen on the propaganda wall outside. She directed him to an empty conference room in the rear of the building, left him a thermos of tea, and closed the door behind her. He stood at the window, staring out at the compound, so huge that its razor-wire fence, enclosing over fifty barracks-like buildings, disappeared over a hill in the distance. Trucks and buses disgorged Tibetans in tattered clothing along one side road lined with armed guards, and more waited at a gate on the other side to receive reclothed, renamed graduates for the long relocation ride into the bowels of China. The steel mills of Manchuria awaited, and the endless miles of chemical and textile factories in Guangzhou. The farther the relocation, recited Party planners, the more Chinese the subjects would become. Nomadic shepherds by the thousands were being dragged from their centuries-old way of life on the wildly free plains of Tibet to work in huge, suffocating factories where orders would be shouted to them in a language they couldn't speak. Once, Africans had been bound with chains and dragged into forced labor far from the land they loved. At least that had been honest. Those slave drivers never pretended to have the interests of their slaves in mind. Tibetans too were dragged away and forced into labor, but they were told it was because the motherland loved them.

He had expected a long wait, even hours of tedious argument with camp administrators, but after only half an hour the door opened to admit a well-fed matron holding a clipboard and leading the young nun, Rikyu, clad in what looked like brown pajamas. She seemed a pale shadow of herself. Her eyes, always so full of defiant energy, were sunken and filled only with fear. Her uniform was stained and had the unmistakable stench of prison, a smell that still shadowed Shan in nightmares of his own confinement.

The gasp that escaped her when she recognized Shan seemed to confirm to the matron that she had brought her charge to the right man. The woman nodded with a cool grin, had Shan sign a form on her clipboard, and quickly departed.

"We need to go," Shan told the nun. "No questions for now."

Rikyu kept her eyes fixed on the floor.

"Shiva and Nyima were going to come, but I told them I had a better chance," Shan tried.

She did not reply.

"Please," he said and pulled a set of manacles from his pocket.

She looked up, a dim spark now in her eyes. "I am already in prison."

He poured her a cup of tea. "You are not under arrest, we just have to make it seem so. I told them you were a suspect in a criminal case." She seemed not to listen. "And this place is a resort compared to a real Chinese prison," he declared. "You are going back to Yang-kar. Nyima needs you."

The nun grabbed the cup and drained it.

"The little *chorten* on the square needs to be finished," Shan added. "And Lodi looks for you every day in the alleys."

"The Chairman is not my god," she declared. "And my name is Rikyu." She was frail, but her defiance was returning.

Shan paused, confused, then glanced outside and understood. He took a pad of paper and a pen from the sideboard and set them before her. "Write it down. Write the Chinese name they gave you here. Don't speak it."

She hesitated, not understanding, but followed his instructions. He pushed an ashtray toward her and extracted a box of matches from his pocket. "Burn it," he instructed. "Burn it and it will be dead. The woman going back to Yangkar is Rikyu the nun. Ani Rikyu."

She solemnly obeyed. They watched the paper shrivel to ash, then she let him fasten the manacles on her wrists and escort her out of the building.

Five minutes after they left the gate of the internment camp he pulled over at a crossroads. "We are going to Yangkar," he promised, "but not with you like this. The smell of your clothes brings overpowering memories, hard for me to bear."

"Memories?" the nun asked.

"Never mind. You don't want to go back to Yangkar like this. I know a place," he added before she could react, and turned toward Lhasa. He had intended to somehow get her to the hotel, to discover her reaction to the photographs, but his words were no subterfuge. The fetor of the internment camp was on her, and it was opening long-shut doors in his mind, resurrecting painful images of lamas dying of slow starvation and monks being beaten for praying.

As the city streets came into view she grew more nervous. "In the glove box," he said, "I brought them for you. Just plastic, but it's the full one hundred eight, not the pretend ones they sell to tourists."

Rikyu opened the box and pulled out a strand of prayer beads, which she instantly pressed to her heart. "*Tuchachay,*" she whispered in a voice tight with emotion, then began to urgently recite a mantra.

He parked a block away from the hotel and at a tourist kiosk bought two cheap windbreakers and a cap for Rikyu, then a skewer of roasted crab apples, which the nun ravenously consumed. She saw the wink the doorman cast at Shan when they entered the hotel, then boldly put her arm through his and walked across the lobby.

The American's room was darkened when Shan opened the door. Rikyu pushed past him as he hesitated, trying to remember if the drapes had been closed on his first visit, then groped for the light switch. He sensed a sudden motion from behind the door, then a shadow swung through the air and slammed into his skull. He dropped to the floor.

When he came to, the drapes had been opened a few inches, casting a dim light over the room. The shower was running in the bathroom. He was bound to the chair with the bungee straps that had been in Bartram's duffel bag, one tightly fastened around his chest and arms, another pinning his legs to the frame of the chair.

"I saw you before," came a voice speaking in English from the shadows beside him. "You're the policeman who put me in that damned jail." He twisted to see a woman sitting on the bed, her back against the headboard. She was swinging a sock that appeared to be half filled with sand. She turned on the bedside lamp to study Shan. He looked up into her green eyes.

A dull pain throbbed in Shan's temple. "I guess I should be glad you didn't fill that with stones," he observed. She seemed surprised, as if not expecting him to understand English. "Improvised weapons are the best when you travel. Airport security is so damned inconvenient, even when you have the correct paperwork."

It wasn't her anger that surprised Shan, it was her air of confidence. "You attacked a Chinese law enforcement officer."

"Who had concealed his uniform and forced his way into the room of an innocent American tourist. What do you expect a girl to do?"

Shan tried to shake away the pain in his head, then studied the woman. He had not connected the young woman in Bartram's photographs to the frightened countenance he had briefly seen in his cell, but now, in better light, he saw the strong jaw and bright, intelligent eyes of the woman at the end of the row of adults in the group shot. She even wore her hair in the same braid over one shoulder.

"Jig," he said. "What kind of name is that?" he asked in English.

The woman frowned, then lowered the sock. "Jacqueline. When I was born my brother couldn't pronounce it, always just said Jig. It stuck."

"Brother," Shan repeated. "I thought maybe husband. You left a wedding band with Shiva."

The American woman grimaced. "Just an experiment that failed. I should have taken it off a long time ago."

"You wore a uniform once yourself. Your brother was in the navy. Yours looked more like a policeman's."

The American sighed. "That photo was more than ten years ago. Now I carry a federal badge. U.S. Marshal. I go after fugitives. People who don't want to be found." She swung her legs onto the floor and leaned toward him. In the photograph the younger woman had been pretty and had somehow seemed joyful. The face before him was older—she was in her late thirties, he guessed, stronger and more sober. The joy had been replaced with a grim determination. "I want my brother's body," Jig Bartram declared.

"I want his killers."

She fixed him with a lightless smile. "No. You're the uncertain new constable that nobody trusts. You don't have a chance. The killers are mine."

"And you'll catch them by hiding in a comfortable hotel room three hours away?"

"I came down on a bus, hoping to blend in and find a way to rescue Rikyu." She hesitated, glancing toward the bathroom. "I should thank you for that at least. Now I can get back to battle."

Shan weighed her words. "You sound like the killers are waiting for you."

"I hope so. I gave them my calling card. And discouraged one up on the mountain."

"Calling card?"

"They know I moved those dead soldiers so they would be found. You wouldn't have had the balls to do that."

The words silenced Shan. It had been part of the test Lau had put him to in Lhadrung. When were they found? Shan had asked. *You tell me,* Lau had replied. Where had they been found? *You tell me.*

"You have no authority," he pointed out.

"You have no power," the American shot back.

Suddenly Rikyu was beside him, rolling up his sleeve. She turned his arm into the light to read the serial number tattooed there, then stepped back in surprise. "It's true," she whispered. "A former prisoner."

After a moment Shan felt the cord around his chest loosen. "I guess that makes you two perfect partners," the nun observed as she stepped around the chair. She was wearing a new shirt and denim jeans, no doubt borrowed from the American woman. Her hair was still dripping from the shower. "When do we leave for Yangkar?" she asked, holding up the bungee cord.

The city had disappeared behind them before Shan pressed the American woman, who sat beside him as Rikyu slept in the backseat. "Your mother Pema is from Yangkar," he ventured. "You and your brother were trying to connect with your relatives there and deliver some letters she's been writing. Pema," he repeated when she did not reply, "who lives in a stone house in Pennsylvania."

The American looked out the window. "It was her blessing for us, she said, to experience Tibet for ourselves. Ever since we were young, she always wanted us to visit Tibet, said it couldn't be as bad here as people said. She hadn't heard from her relatives for decades, but she fervently believed they weren't dead, just silenced. Jake had been in the navy and I was with the federal police. If anyone could find them, she insisted, it would be us."

"Why didn't she come herself?" Shan asked.

Jig Bartram grew silent. "You misunderstand everything," she said at last. "My mother died. Last year, of cancer. We came to bring her ashes home."

Shan felt a flush of shame. The kind, passionate Tibetan woman whom he had grown to admire through her letters was dead. He stared straight down the highway and asked no more questions.

It was half an hour before the American spoke again. "My mother would tell us bedtime stories about Yangkar and the mountains she grew up in. It seemed a magical place. The beautiful monastery where wise old men debated the mysteries of the human spirit and artisans brought the amazing Tibetan gods to life. The home of the great doctors in the sanctuary in the hills. There were archery contests at the summer festival and for years my grandmother always won. Great caravans of sheep and yaks carrying packs of salt would pass through, and little statues of the gods were carved in salt blocks at a shrine where they prayed for safe passage. Her aunt was one of the nuns who helped at the medical college. They were our heroes when we were growing up. Her great uncle often corresponded with the Dalai Lama, who had promised to visit on his eighteenth birthday. My mother's older brother Kolsang was the pride of the family, famed for his knowledge of scriptures and ability to communicate with animals. He loved mules, and as a boy put on shows at festivals with them. He was going to be the abbot of Pure Water College when the old one died."

Has brother Kolsang received his yak tail whisk yet? Pema had asked in a letter. A whisk was a sign of office for an abbot.

"Jake and I were going to travel together to bring her ashes home but I had a delay. So Jake went ahead, two weeks earlier than me. He called me before I left the U.S. He said I shouldn't come, that everything was different than mother described. Nothing fit her descriptions, it was like the earth had shifted, he said. No one had even heard of a medical college. He said he would just spread the ashes in the mountains. He said he had brought a Chinese cell phone, and he would call when he was free of Tibet. That's what he said, like Tibet scared him somehow."

Shan remembered the small square box in the hotel room, just the size for a container of human ashes. "But you came anyway."

"Of course I did. He knew I wasn't going to stay away. I called him from Hong Kong. He had left a key for me at this hotel and told me to buy a signal booster for my cell before leaving for Lhasa, that there would be a map in the room showing where I might be able to use my phone to reach him, and when to call."

"7 A.M., 1 P.M., and 7 P.M.," Shan said and saw her nod. "On a line from the highway cell tower."

"He was more excited that last time we spoke. He said he made some amazing discoveries, that we still had family in Yangkar after all. There were things I needed to know, things he didn't dare talk about on the phone. I got to the first point on his map as fast as I could and called. He never answered. Not then, not six hours later, not the next day."

Hallelujah. It had been a call from the murdered American's sister that had excited the old Tibetans, not a summon from the gods.

"But how could you have been on that truck that came to the jail?"

"I was sloppy. I knew foreigners were prohibited in Lhadrung so I traded clothes with a woman in the first town I came to outside of Lhasa. That old dress and a beat-up old wool cap. But I had no papers. After having no luck reaching him the first day I went back up to that mountain pass, closer to the tower, and tried again. I was sitting on a rock, studying that map Jake left me to see if I had done anything wrong when that damned lieutenant came up behind me. I can't speak Mandarin, only Tibetan and English, so I couldn't answer his questions. I didn't dare speak English to him. He gestured to my pockets and when I could produce no papers he pulled out his gun and took me to a wide place in the road where he made me help him put barriers up. Then that truck came up full of Tibetans guarded by soldiers and they shoved me inside. He must have passed them earlier, because he was expecting it."

Shan had already discovered that Jinhua had used subterfuge to arrive at Yangkar with an escort of soldiers, but he had not fully understood the scale of the lieutenant's subterfuge. Jinhua had seized a

Tibetan, or a woman he had thought to be Tibetan, as part of his cover. Shan chewed on her words. "But you had already come to Yangkar. You didn't find those dead soldiers by accident. You were trying to find your brother." Someone else had discovered the dead soldiers, Shan suspected, someone in her family.

"You and I may be the only people interested in finding the truth," he said when she did not reply. "I know things you do not. You know things I do not. But if you lie to me I can just take you back to my cell."

The American turned her head back toward the side window as if to avoid answering.

"I could always just call Public Security," he stated. "An American law enforcement agent in disguise in Tibet. They will have a field day."

She looked out the window a long time, then back at the sleeping nun. "I told you," she said. "My mother's sister was a nun. I never cry. But I was weeping like a little girl when she spread her arms out to embrace me, before I had a chance to introduce myself. She said she would recognize my mother's eyes anywhere."

"Nyima," Shan said. Jig Bartram glanced at him in surprise, then nodded. "She became a solitary nun after . . . after everything. But she was not exactly a hermit, for she was the spiritual shepherd to all the farmers and shepherds who lived in the mountains, especially the ones without registrations, the ferals. We stayed awake all night in her cavern home, with her telling tales of her youth with my mother. They were only ten years apart in age, and the two of them had been best friends when young. She had tales of the two of them frolicking with lambs, the two of them stealing butter to make a lamp so they could explore the caves, the two of them carrying incense at my Uncle Kolsang's side when he first joined the monks. She said one of my mother's favorite things was going to his classes when he became a teacher and turning the *peche* leaves for him as he read scripture to the novices and questioned them on its meaning. Later he would take her out to the mules to speak with them. Every mule had a name and would come when he called."

"Your brother was there that night?"

"No. He had met Nyima a few days before but had gone out to explore the mountains, said there was something he had to understand. I think he was still trying to find the location of the old medical college. My mother wanted her ashes spread in the herb garden of the medical school. All her life she never asked us for anything. Just the one thing. Bury my ashes at Pure Water College, in the Medicine Mountains, she said, and the most amazing people mother had ever known were the lamas and nuns who worked there, healing the sick. 'Plant me with the medicine herbs my brother Kolsang uses to heal people,' she told us. But no one, not even Nyima, will talk about it, not even acknowledge the existence of Pure Water College. And they say there is no such thing as the Medicine Mountains. Something's wrong in Yangkar, something disjointed, dark secrets that haunt everyone. They are deeply scared of something, and think speaking of it will bring it back. I think there was something terrible about the destruction of the medical college, something more than the routine destruction of other temples."

Jig looked out the window for several breaths before speaking again. "Nyima said Jake must have gone too far, and decided to sleep in a cave for the night. The next morning she showed me where to hide my car, in a grove of trees off the road, then I climbed up to a cairn he had built, a cairn Nyima told me about, to reach the cell phone signal, to make the call at 1300."

"Where a skeleton stalked you." She did not respond. She did not trust him enough, he realized. "He didn't answer," Shan tried.

"No. Never again."

They found her car still in the grove of trees, behind a thicket of juniper. "Your brother's body is not being kept for me," he said as she extracted the keys from a hollow in a tree. "It is for him, for the Buddhist rites to be spoken."

The American woman studied Shan a moment and then looked away. "Bardo," Jig whispered.

"Yes. The rites for passage to the next life. Those who are murdered often have trouble finding the path."

"Shiva says it has to be done in the next six days."

Shan realized they were not talking about the rites now. "The Taklha clan would have used the services of the *ragyapa*, the traditional way."

The American wiped a tear away. "The flesh cutters, yes. That's what the clan wants. Feed my brother to the vultures."

"It should be your decision, Jig. Taking an American body out of the country or even cremating here would prove—" Shan searched for words. "—problematic."

"They break him into pieces like butchers with a cow." She scrubbed at an eye.

"They reverently give what he left behind back to the circle of life. I once heard a Tibetan say the vultures are reincarnated monks."

She offered a small, bitter smile.

"You should follow me to town. We can leave your car at the garage and cover it. A late model rental is too conspicuous."

She started the engine, opened the window, and handed Shan a long object wrapped in cloth. "Are you scared of demons, Constable Shan?" the American asked, then sped away. He flipped open the top fold of the cloth and almost dropped it in his shock. It was the hand of a skeleton. The American had given him the hand of a skeleton god, missing two finger bones.

Numbed with fatigue, Shan opened the door of the station and collapsed into his chair. He was painfully aware that he had been absent for most of his son's first day of parole. If Marpa was still in his café he would gather some food, he decided, and was about to wearily rise when he heard the metallic click of the door lock.

Mr. Hui, the dentist, stood silently at the entry, looking at Shan with an earnest, almost apologetic expression. He pointed to the cell chamber. Shan considered ignoring the usually taciturn Chinese dentist, but instead followed him into the inner chamber. Hui closed the door behind him.

Five chairs had been arranged in a circle between the empty cells. Mrs. Weng, Mr. Wu the town clerk, and the town's Chinese barber sat beside her, joined a moment later by Hui. Shan was looking at the Committee of Leading Citizens.

"I didn't realize we had an appointment," Shan stated, glancing at his watch.

Mrs. Weng took a deep breath. "Affairs of state do not wait on the calendar." She gestured Shan toward the remaining chair.

"We have affairs of state in Yangkar?" Shan asked and motioned toward the phone. "I should call Beijing."

"Affairs of Yangkar Township," the town clerk inserted and rose to pull the empty chair out for Shan.

"The army invades our town and you disappear," Mrs. Weng impatiently declared. "The town totters on disaster and its constable disappears."

"I have been conducting an investigation in the field with Colonel Tan. Perhaps you want to speak with him?" Shan suggested.

"The colonel left before noon."

"Investigation in the field," Shan said again.

"A lie. You brought back that nun and set her free."

Shan choked down his reply. He had let Rikyu out by the tower on the square. The committee had been watching him.

"The constable was specifically appointed by Colonel Tan, Comrade Chairman," Mr. Hui reminded Mrs. Weng.

She seemed not to hear him. "A score of Tibetans left today, fleeing to the hills. A score of customers for my store. A score of patients for Dr. Hui."

"Is that what this is about?" Shan asked. "Selling socks and tooth fillings?"

"If the army comes again, it could be fifty, even a hundred. A third of the town even. Our economy would collapse."

"The army is entitled to conduct maneuvers where it sees fit. Our citizens understand that. If you are truly concerned, I can find a form for complaints."

"Investigations involving violent felonies are to be led by Public Security."

"Public Security is here," Shan observed.

Mrs. Weng made a dismissive wave of her hand. "That young pup? He acts more like a frightened tourist."

"You've never heard of undercover work?" Shan shot back. "The whole point is to appear to be someone you're not."

Weng seemed to stumble on her words. "Undercover?" she whispered, as if to herself.

Hui leaned forward. "Comrade Constable, do you actually know the army was on maneuvers?"

"Unequivocally. Perhaps the committee can prepare a handbill to explain that. Claims for damages can be submitted to my office."

Hui seemed relieved. He smacked his knee. "Exactly the thing!" He looked at his fellow committee members. "We can all sign it, offer to help the Tibetans fill out the proper papers."

Weng, a new determination on her face, was unimpressed. "We have the right to know what you are doing."

"No, you don't," Shan insisted. "Pending investigations are strictly confidential."

"We are the Committee of Leading Citizens," Weng countered.

The committee of pompous busybodies, Shan almost said. "When the results are about to be released I would be happy to brief you before the story is published."

Weng was not satisfied. "You don't fit with this town, Shan."

"If you have a complaint, write to Colonel Tan," he replied in a level voice.

"I am not convinced you embrace the ways of democratic socialism," Weng declared.

Shan hesitated. She was pushing him onto treacherous ground. "I am ever a humble servant of the law," Shan said. "I strive eternally to become more skilled in the political dialectic, Madame Chairman."

"They say people died up in those mountains," she observed.

"They were called the Ghost Mountains long before I arrived."

Weng sneered. "Next you'll say you're scared of all that taboo mumbo jumbo."

"There are things in Yangkar that frighten me," Shan admitted.

"You fool! I don't know what Tan sees in you. He only hires puppets and bullies," she added, as if to answer her own question. "And you don't have the balls to be a bully."

"Just a simple servant of the motherland."

Weng shook her head. "We're going to need to take an elevated role in this town," she announced to her colleagues.

Wu looked uneasy. "The constable had a constructive suggestion about a handbill. It shows proper respect for the collective consciousness, as the chairman in Beijing encourages. I can make up a form for damage claims."

Weng winced and threw up her hands. "Public order disintegrates and you talk of handbills. A town of sheep without any shepherds."

Shan drove carefully up the hill to his house, wary of spilling the contents of the containers with the supper he had brought to share with Ko. He could not understand the strange anxiety he felt as he approached the house. It wasn't happiness or gratitude or paternal love he felt, it was fear. Never in their troubled lives had Shan and Ko been together like this, just the two of them, away from razor wire and guards with guns at the ready, alone with time to openly talk. How much did he really know of his son? When Tan had first brought Ko to Lhadrung from a prison outside Tibet, his son had been a sullen, insolent young hooligan who mocked his father and the Tibetans. Had he really changed that much? How could two people ever get to know each other in the short, worried conversations on prison visitation days? Ko had been kept in solitary confinement for weeks at a time, sometimes just to punish Shan. No prisoner came out of solitary unaffected by it. Shan had seen men shrivel up inside after frequent visits to the harsh cells used for solitary.

The images of his son that often came to him at night flooded his mind's eye. Ko the foul-mouthed gang leader who had been dragged into the 404th Construction Brigade compound. The angry, desperate Ko who had tried to escape more than once, and been beaten until bones had been broken for the attempts. The mute Ko with drug-glazed eyes whom Shan had rescued from a hospital for the criminally insane, hours before a lobotomy was to have been performed. More recently there was the Ko Shan sometimes watched from outside the wire, unknown by his son, supporting an old lama on his shoulder as they stumbled together toward a meal.

He called his son's name as he entered the little farmhouse, then, thinking him asleep, set down their dinner on the small rough-hewn table and pushed aside the curtain that led into the sleeping quarters. The two pallets inside were empty. The little brazier he used in his kitchen was cold. Replacing his tunic with an old tattered coat that hung on the peg at the back of the door, he stepped outside, fighting an unnatural fear. Ko was not in the woodshed, not at the little shrine Lokesh had built of flat rocks by the stream.

Shan's heart wrenched as he heard a scream from the outcroppings on the slope above. He ran. The sound came again, a high-pitched shriek from behind high rock formations along the stream. He slowed to grab a piece of wood to use as a weapon and circled the last of the big boulders, club raised, his heart pounding.

He made out Ko in the shadow of an old juniper, moving at an odd hopping gait. The cry came again, and Shan stared in confusion as he saw now that there was a boy on his son's back. He lowered the club, not understanding. It had not been a scream, but peals of laughter he had heard. The smell of cigar smoke wafted toward him, and he turned to see old Lhamo sitting on a ledge, watching Ati as Yara laid out laundry on the stone fence of the old stable. Shan had forgotten that he had invited the family of feral Tibetans to use the building.

"He's a good yak, your son," the old woman explained with a grin as Shan approached. "If he keeps it up I may ask him for a ride," she chuckled. Shan declined the cigar as she offered him a puff.

The old images of Ko fell away. Here was a new Ko, an impossible Ko, a happy Ko. As his son spotted him he straightened. The Tibetan boy slid off his back and ran to his mother.

"I brought dinner but I couldn't find you," Shan began, and self-consciously dropped the club. The embarrassment in his son's eyes somehow hurt him, and he looked away. "You've met," he said, with a gesture to Yara and her son.

"They told me how you helped them when their yak got stuck in the mud," Ko explained in an awkward tone.

"It wasn't the mud I was worried about," Yara put in, "it was the soldiers and the knob who arrived. Your father kept us out of their grip." She hesitated and looked at Shan with a question in her eyes. "But there were more soldiers in town last night. We ran up here from the carpet factory."

"You're safe enough here," Shan assured her. He saw that Ati was wearing the new T-shirt he had left in the house for Ko.

"You said something about dinner?" Ko asked. There was a tentative, almost adolescent quality to his voice. Everything, from the ability to walk about without guards, to the laughter of the boy, and the notion of eating when he wanted, was new to him.

Shan smiled. "We'll have to stretch it. Soup and *momos* from Marpa. I have some rice we can add."

The Tibetans heartily agreed to join the meal, though only if the grandparents took turns watching the road. It was the way they lived, he realized, always watchful, always ready to run.

As Yara and Ko lit the brazier, Shan went into his sleeping quarters and came out with a wooden box that he set down on the bench outside beside Trinle. The old man was watching Shan more than the road, with his gaze sometimes drifting toward the truck with the constable's insignia on it.

From the box Shan extracted four small sculptures, the first a small Buddha carved of jade with a silver-inlaid necklace, then a four-armed *dakini* encrusted with dirt, and two corroded demons cast in bronze. "My friend Lokesh and I find these, or I take them from the storerooms of Religious Affairs when I can." The old man's confused gaze shifted from the figurines to Shan. "We clean them, restore them the best we can. Then we get them to Tibetans who know safe places, hidden shrines. Do you understand what I am saying?"

"I understand it is against the law."

"And you could turn me in."

The old man scratched his head. His tongue worked against his dry lips and twice he seemed about to speak but didn't. Slowly, like the sputtering of a stubborn wick, his leathery face lit and the shadow of worry fell away. He lifted one of the corroded demons. "Best thing for this," he suggested in an earnest voice, "is to soak it overnight in a bucket of yak urine."

"I haven't tried that," Shan confessed.

"I'll bring our big yak for you, the lama yak we call him," Trinle said, staring without expression at Shan. "I saw him drink for near ten minutes straight, not two hours ago."

Shan returned the stare for a moment, then quite unexpectedly burst into laughter.

The old man grinned, exposing his missing teeth, and pounded Shan on the back.

As the tension broke, Trinle enthusiastically lifted each of the figurines, studying them with great interest. When he was done Shan extracted the little gold Buddha Jinhua had given him and placed it on the bench. Trinle did not touch it, only stared at it with a distant, forlorn look. "That one," he said, "cannot be restored," and he gestured for Shan to take it away.

It was not the meal Shan had hoped for, but perhaps it was the one he and his son needed. The old woman took over the cramped corner that served as a kitchen, ordering Shan to retrieve a bucket of water and the old man to bring onions from Shan's meager garden, while Ko and Yara prepared the table with Shan's mismatched utensils and bowls. Shan was too exhausted and Ko still too stunned by his abrupt freedom to join in much of the dinner conversation, and they were halfway through when Shan realized his son must not be able to follow the Tibetans' discussion. When Yara warily asked about Ko's life in prison, Shan was about to translate when to his surprise his son replied in Tibetan. "I break rocks and I haul rocks from when the sun is low in the east until it is low in the west." His pronunciation was rough but quite understandable. He had been learning from the old monks. "They put me right at the back of the truck where the road dust always coats me, thinking it is punishment, but they don't know I like it. The morning ride is the best part of my day. I can watch the birds. There are always birds. If it has rained they show us where the worms are."

"You catch worms?" Ati asked. "Why?"

Ko glanced at his father. "You know, so we can say a little prayer, help them on their spiritual journey." Two years before, Ko had lost a tooth to malnutrition. Shan had himself often seen prisoners fight over worms, a favorite source of protein.

"The farmer on the next hill has horses," Yara said, sensing the need to shift the conversation. "Do you ride horses?" she asked Ko.

Ko smiled. "I think these days are about trying things I have never tried before."

"I found a special *mani* stone," Ati interjected. "Very heavy. Grandfather says it may be sky metal—you know, a meteorite. It sings when you hit it just right." He stepped to the pouch his mother had left by the door and heaved the heavy stone onto the table. It was a flat block almost a foot long, with sharply defined, squared edges, with one side notched at the corners, the opposite side having two pieces that extended from each corner. It was covered with lichen, into which someone had scratched the *mani* mantra. Shan lifted it. It had the heft of iron. He balanced it in his hand a moment, then congratulated the boy on his discovery. "Where did you find such a treasure?"

Ati extended an arm toward the back window. "Along the trail from the north, two ridges above here, along a long row of junipers," the boy explained. "There's more. We could show you."

"I would like that," Shan said.

Yara's countenance stiffened. "I'm sure you have more important things to do, constable." She was a feral, Shan reminded himself, and instinctively not inclined to spend time with officials, however minor.

Shan smiled at the boy and tossed him an apricot. "Like Ko says, these days are about trying things we've never done. I've never seen a shrine of singing *mani* stones."

Ati clapped his hands in excitement. His mother told him to help with the clean-up, and soon the family slipped away into the shadows, back to the old stable.

Shan and his son sat in the dark, on the bench outside his front door. "I haven't seen the whole sky at night for years," Ko observed. "Just patches of it, out the window, sometimes through a hole in the roof."

"When I was in the 404th," Shan explained, "an old lama had loosened a section of the metal roof and would slide it off at night to speak with the stars. But after a few weeks the guards found out and nailed it shut, saying it could be a means of escape. The old lama laughed and said that the guards didn't understand, that we had already done that, that we escaped every night into the stars."

"I was trying to get Lokesh to come," Shan said after a few more minutes of silence. "But I had to send a message not to come now, because of the problems here."

"You said he tore up his registration card. So he's feral like Yara and her family."

"It was his choice to make."

"I couldn't bear his being arrested on my account," Ko stated. "If he were sent back to prison he would never get out again. I will write him a letter. I have been practicing my Tibetan script."

"It would be a wonderful surprise, for him to get a letter from you in Tibetan."

"I will tell him you have found new ways to help Tibetans."

"Just let him know you are well, and getting a taste of normal life."

Ko made a sound that may have been a laugh, and looked back up at the stars. "My life is all guards and prisoners. Before today I can't even remember the last time I spoke with a woman other than Amah Jiejie. When Yara started talking to me I just stared like some fool. I came here with Colonel Tan. I spent the day with a family of ferals. I have no idea what normal life is. Can you tell me what normal is?"

Shan had no reply.

"My mother left you by getting the marriage annulled on the grounds it was never consummated. Technically I don't exist. By definition I can't be normal."

The knowledge of Ko's wretched childhood with his unloving, Party-zealot mother was a scar on Shan's heart. The greatest happiness, Lokesh had taught him, was unconscious, spontaneous happiness, the kind most humans experienced only in childhood. Ko had never been given a chance for such happiness. "Ko, never think—"

His son held up a hand. "I understand. It's just that they make us take courses on Sundays about life after release. The classroom walls are covered with those banners and posters. The teacher made me stand and she pointed to a steelworker—you know, with a red helmet and a raised hammer. She said that could be me. I wanted to say if that was me then take off the helmet and hammer my brains in."

"Does she still make that clucking noise when she paces around the room?" Shan asked. "We called her the old hen."

"Cluck, cluck, cluck," Ko imitated, with a laugh. "The motherland is our happy nest."

Shan joined in the laughter. "I don't know what normal is, Ko," he said, "but you and I were never destined to join it."

"*Lha gyal lo,*" was his son's reply.

. . .

They made a strange procession the next morning, Yara and Ati leading them up a steep track above his house that Shan had never used
before. Lhamo and Trinle lingered behind, as if reluctant to join them.
They were moving into the mountains along the edge of the zone the
Tibetans feared.

After nearly an hour they reached a high ridge that ran east and
west, connecting the Ghost Mountains with the peaks to the northeast. They passed an outcropping and suddenly were on a path that
was defined by more of the oblong lichen-covered stones, identical to
the one Ati had shown Shan. Shan turned to the east and studied the
landscape. The shadows cast by the low sun outlined a path that might
have been otherwise invisible, a track much wider than the typical
pilgrim's path. It had not seen heavy use for many years, but its packed
earth inhibited the growth enough for him to make out its course
toward the eastern horizon. He bent to examine a drying stem, broken several days earlier, then saw another, and another, all apparently
broken along a line at the same time. He moved back and forth until,
finally, in the slanting morning light he could make out two parallel
trails of broken stems extending along the top of the ridge. The old
road may not have seen heavy use for decades, but a light vehicle had
driven down it recently. He paused, studying the stems again. They
were all broken in the same direction. He saw no evidence that the
vehicle had returned.

Yara saw the intense way he studied the landscape. "I don't understand," she said. "Are you here as a pilgrim or a constable?"

Shan bent and lifted one of the oblong *mani* rocks, identical to
thirty or forty more he could see along the track. "I would prefer as a
pilgrim," he replied, "but this is not a pilgrim's path." He tossed the
block against another. Their thin coating of lichen only slightly muffled the ringing sound. "It's an invasion path."

As Ko bent to lift the block, Shan opened his pocketknife and extended it to him. Ko shrank back and Shan quickly knelt, clumsily

pretending that he had meant to use the blade himself. Prisoners were forbidden anything that could be used as a weapon.

He scraped at the block with the flat of the blade, peeling away the encrusted lichen to expose a steel surface, with squares cut away at the top corners and square extensions at each of the bottom corners. When he saw the confusion that remained on his companions' faces, he cleaned off another block and fit them together, the notches on the bottom block fitting neatly into the extensions of the top. *The ridge was flat,* Sergeant Ma had written in his notebook, *the progress from the northern base faster than expected, except we lost a tread and had to stop for repairs.* "A tank tread!" Ko exclaimed.

"Pieces of a tread. Not a tank, I think. A bulldozer. This terrain was tough even on the heaviest vehicles. A tread was lost near here, its pieces scattered."

"But there's nothing here," Ko observed.

"Nothing here," Shan agreed, then pointed ahead and began walking up the track.

In another mile they reached a sharp rise where the ledge rock had been blasted to create a more gradual gradient for heavy vehicles to climb. A cluster of crumbling buildings sat where the sharp rise began. For the first time in Tibet the ruins Shan was looking at were Chinese.

Ko suddenly pulled at his arm. A solitary figure had appeared on the opposite ridge, above the old structures. Shan pulled out his binoculars and watched as Jig Bartram descended toward the buildings.

As Ko took a step toward the ruins Lhamo grabbed his arm. "We don't go there. Not ever," the old woman said. "The worst of demons, insatiable blood eaters, live there." She held her hand out to warn young Ati away.

Shan studied the buildings, then pointed to a sturdy stone structure set away from the others, higher up the slope. "That does not belong with them."

"A pilgrim shed. When I was a girl my mother would bring me there to pray sometimes, by its beautiful juniper trees. There was a grove of rhododendron beside it, a meadow of poppies beyond," she said, pointing to where a bulldozer had sliced into the earth. "It was once a place full of birdsong and butterflies in the summer. But after those children came, the flowers never grew again."

Ko seemed very interested in the old woman's words. "Children?" he asked.

"That's all they were," Lhamo replied. "Chinese children playing with guns. Playing with lives. They needed a good thrashing, but if you even looked at them funny they shot you. They lined people up in the town and made them repeat Chinese slogans. Of course none of us understood a word."

"You mean this was their base," Shan suggested and studied the windswept, barren landscape. "Why here?"

"The main military road from the north was only twenty miles to the east, with no ravines or chasms blocking the way. No one had ever driven vehicles into Yangkar before then. This was the best way into Yangkar. Otherwise you had to take the old salt caravan routes over the high passes. None of those new macadam roads existed. They held their meetings here, with the communist bosses, out of sight of the town. They were here only three or four months, then the army took over." As Lhamo spoke Jig Bartram reached the buildings and began climbing up to join them.

Shan studied the ruins, where rusted corrugated roofs lay in pieces over poorly constructed timber buildings. Other ruins would have been stripped of usable materials, but these had not been touched for all the long decades. "Where did they go?"

"Everyone in town was rounded up by then. The rest of us fled deep into the mountains. Didn't come back for five winters. When we did come back it was a new land. Everything had changed. People said the land demons had been released when so many temples in Tibet were destroyed." She pointed to the road that had been sliced into the ridge. "They severed the land. They took away the buildings in the town. The *gompa*, the old storehouses. Our famous Buddha Shakyamuni statute, the giant in the courtyard who blessed all the people of the mountains. The grove of apple trees where we sang to call in the butterflies."

The American reached them and, to Shan's surprise, embraced the two old Tibetans. She gestured toward the ugly slice up the ridge. "The road continues to the Plain of Ghosts. Why would the Chinese army have built a road to the gilded saint?"

Lhamo grimaced but did not answer. "Don't go," she warned, nodding toward the camp. "They can snatch a word right out of the air and jam it back down your throat so hard you can no longer breathe."

Jig gazed in mute alarm at the old Tibetan.

"There is evil in this world, girl. There is evil so great you may not speak of it. People die for speaking of it. It's done. It's gone. That was another world."

"But my aunt," Jig said. "Nyima lives at the tombs. She lives in that world."

Lhamo shrugged. "Some demons embraced her. Some demons hated her." The herder woman cast a melancholy glance at the ruined camp. "Don't go in, I beg you. Come with us to the pilgrim's hut. Your mother and I used to go there and make little cairns. Come with me and we can make cairns together."

"We have to go, grandmother," Shan said. "We have to know the truth of those who lived there."

"Then may mother Tara protect you," the old woman said. "We will go around," she added after a moment, making a circular motion that indicated she would take her family to the hut near the top.

Most of the buildings had no roofs left, and the elements had ravaged them, leaving only a few rusty metal cots, corroded pails, and irregular piles covered with lichen that proved to be rotting blankets. Only two buildings had their roofs intact, though they were riddled with holes. Jig, Shan, and Ko walked into the nearest, which, judging by its benches and tables, had apparently been a hall used for meals and assemblies. Several of the tables and benches were upturned, old and covered with the same layers of dust, as if there had been a fight in the chamber long ago. Bowls and tin mugs sat on several tables, and a long platform along the wall held several large pots beside a rusting brazier.

"They left in a hurry," Ko said as he examined one of the pots. He held it up. "This crust on the bottom was once porridge, enough to feed twenty or thirty. They left their breakfast uneaten, but they packed up their personal equipment? There's no sign anywhere of personal possessions."

Half a dozen bowls on the tables still held traces of food, some with spoons cemented into the hardened contents. Jig paced slowly along the walls, uncovering nothing but more pots and dishes. She paused at a dust-caked photo on the wall and blew on it, revealing a group picture of Chinese teenagers clad in green uniforms, some with fists raised high, several clutching hammers. Those in front held a banner that read HAMMER OF FREEDOM.

Shan found Ko outside, behind the building, where the flat face of a ledge still showed the scorch marks of a bonfire. His son dragged his heel in the earth, exposing a layer of burnt soil and a half-burnt shoe, then he knelt and with a flat rock began scraping away more dirt. The ground quickly yielded the charred remnant of a belt, a moldy green cap, and the burnt remains of Mao's Little Red Book.

"I don't understand," Jig said, then knelt with another scraping rock and exposed two half-melted, dirt-encrusted toothbrushes.

"They ran away from their breakfast and their personal possessions," Shan said. "But later someone burnt those possessions."

"The way a fugitive burns everything so he can't be traced," the American marshal suggested.

"What fugitive leaves his toothbrush?" Shan asked. Jig had no answer. He kicked up a melted pair of eyeglasses. "Or his spectacles?"

The American silently followed him to the most intact of the buildings as Ko continued to search the patch of burnt soil. With shelves on the walls and a long table bearing dusty file folders, it had the air of an office. A door to what appeared to be a closet was closed, its knob broken off, the door stuck in the jamb. Around the table were several chairs and upended crates. At one end stood a high stool.

The folders were all empty, although several bore neat, handwritten labels. *Yangkar Landowners* said one, *Yangkar Peasant Farmers* said another, *Dispositions* a third. The shelves held a few volumes, mostly compilations of Mao's speeches but also, oddly, a book on world geography and another on algebra. Not all the students who formed the Hammer of Freedom brigade had abandoned their studies.

On the wall was a large piece of sheeting on which, written in thick brush strokes that mimicked the Esteemed Chairman's famed hand, was a list that read like a manifesto:

— Revolutionaries embrace Mao Tse-tung's invincible thought for the purpose of turning the old world upside-down

— Mao Tse-tung thought is a demon-exposing spotlight

— To rebel is always justified

— We will make China and Tibet red from the inside out

— Our Revolutionary State shall last 10,000 generations

Along the ceiling over the shelves hung a faded banner that declared OUR HEARTS ARE RED LIKE FIRE. A lump of ice rose in Shan's heart. He reached to the back of one of the shelves and pulled out a lump of cloth, then snapped it against the edge of the shelf to break its crust of dust. It was an armband with *Zaofan!* printed on it. *Rebellion!* He paced along the wall, then lifted another encrusted object from the floor. With a lurch of his heart he recognized it as a tall conical cap.

He did not know how long he stared at the cap, his hand shaking, but finally Ko touched his arm and stirred him from his trance. His son pointed to Jig Bartram. She was on her knees under the table, staring at a length of brown cord joined by knots.

"He was here," the American woman said. "His bootlaces were tied around his wrists." She pushed the frayed ends together. "You saw his body. It matches the marks on his wrists," she said as she slowly sank into a chair.

"Perhaps," Shan said as he saw now how the dust at the end of the table had been recently disturbed. "We can't be certain."

"It's certain," Jig declared in an anguished voice and pointed to two marks on the rough table, then placed an outstretched palm beside each.

Confused, Shan bent over her hands. A chill ran down his spine. Two freshly made nail holes were framed by the thumb and index finger of each hand.

"There had to have been more than one of them." Moisture filled her eyes. "Jake broke away, but they overpowered him. Then they nailed his hands to the table. It would have taken a gun to his head to make him sit for it. Who has guns in Tibet?"

"Soldiers. It could have just been a knife to his throat."

"No. He won awards in personal combat training. He would not have stopped for a knife unless it was cutting into his throat. There were no marks on his throat. And those two soldiers died. Jake wouldn't kill soldiers." As she stared at the table a tear spilled down her cheek. "Why? Why here?" she asked.

"Maybe it's the same question," Shan said. "This place is a mystery in itself, tied to the mystery of the tomb and the Plain of Ghosts. For all these years someone had made sure it was taboo for Tibetans to come here. I think your brother discovered answers from fifty years ago, the reason this land has been forbidden all these years."

"My mother's favor to us, she said," Jig whispered, her voice cracking.

A groan of wood scraping wood broke the silence, and Shan turned to see Ko standing in what appeared to be a storage room on the other side of the jammed door, which he had pried open.

Shan did not understand the stricken expression on Ko's face until he reached his son's side and followed his gaze toward the wall. In the light cast by a hole in the roof he could see dozens of nails that had been driven into the rough wood of the wall. From each hung two or three *gaus*. Every prayer amulet was different, every one worn from years of devout use. Some hung on the braids of yak hair used by shepherds, others on straps braided of leather or red thread, greased string, and even silver chains. The Hammer of Freedom had a trophy room.

"The *gaus* would have had prayers and relics inside," Jig said over his shoulder, as if she needed to explain to Shan.

"Probably still do," Shan whispered. The owners of the *gaus* would have clung to them with their last breaths.

The American reached out and with a tentative stroke of her finger brushed away the dust on a *gau*, exposing an ornate cross-hatching of silver and copper. "You can't tell," she said.

"The Party zealots scream about the poison of religion," Shan explained, "and they are eager to confiscate *gaus* and prayer wheels. But I have never known one to actually open them because of all the tales of the deities that protect such things. They are a superstitious lot. Always hedging their bets."

Jig shook the *gau*. Something rattled inside. She stared at it in surprise, then a look of reverence rose on her face. "We should do something with them. For them. Maybe some of the owners are in the town."

Shan had no heart to correct the American. The *gaus* were souvenirs of the Red Guard's savage, short-lived war. There would have been mock trials of landlords, merchants, officials, well-off farmers, and senior nuns and lamas, all charged with the crime of supporting the notorious Four Olds—old habits, old customs, old ideas, old culture—making them reviled reactionaries. In Tibet the punishment had almost always been a bullet, and often a child of the accused had been forced to pull the trigger as their baptism into the new order. "We should do something," Shan agreed.

Jig took out her cell phone and photographed the wall.

"Why would they leave them if these were trophies?" Ko asked, then lifted a piece of canvas that been nailed to a beam and gasped. The canvas had served as a cover to a cache of more trophies. On a narrow makeshift shelf behind the canvas sat over a dozen little golden Buddhas, identical to the one Jinhua had been given by the despairing survivor of the Hammer of Freedom.

Shan lifted one, took the American's hand, and set it in her palm, then closed her fingers around it. "They were given to the monks and nuns who successfully completed their studies. Like your Uncle Kolsang. They would have been handed down to their families."

Jig stared at the little figure, then solemnly nodded as she extracted a wool cap from a pocket and scooped the remaining Buddhas into it. As she did so a new sound arose, a low, hurried chant from the outside door. Lhamo was standing there, her face pale, taking mincing steps forward as she clutched her *gau*. After all these decades the old Tibetan was braving the place of demons.

Lhamo visibly shuddered as she saw the banners on the wall, then with clenched jaw marched to the cloth painted with the manifesto, ripped it off the wall, and stomped on it. When she reached Shan's side and saw the wall of *gaus* she froze, then raised a trembling hand and began pointing to individual amulets. "Nagri Tawun, Dolma Puntsok, Rabten Denpa," she intoned, grief thick in her voice. "Tsewang Rigzah, fat Tarpa, Kola the runner." She pointed to a *gau* with a tuft of wool woven into its cord. "Gyatso Lomo, the herder who refused to let them take his goats." Tears streamed down her face.

Lhamo was paralyzed with grief. Shan and Jig each took an arm and led the old Tibetan out of the building. Ko had already reached the rest of her family, fifty paces up the slope, and was sharing out some of the food they had packed that morning. Clear of the compound, Shan released Lhamo's arm to return his son's wave, then heard Ko shout something that was lost in the wind. As Yara ran down the track toward them, Ko shouted more loudly. Lhamo halted and turned back toward the compound.

"The abbot!" the old woman cried and broke into a run toward the building they had just left.

"No!" Yara screamed. "PLA!"

Shan stared at the frantic young woman, then followed her pointing arm back toward the east and froze. Jig Bartram, several steps above Shan, broke into a desperate run to intercept Lhamo. As the American passed Shan, he grabbed her arm and threw her down, protesting, behind a boulder.

The two helicopters of the People's Liberation Army flew low and incredibly fast. Shan was prepared for the soldiers to buzz them, to frighten them away as they laughed in their cockpit seats, but not for the blaze that erupted from each. The ruined buildings began to explode as the rockets found them. Lhamo seemed unaware of the explosions or the debris that rained down around her as she reentered the long building. The helicopters veered away and then turned and hovered, aiming and firing their weapons more precisely. The rock face above the patch of scorched soil erupted into flame, then the site of the old bonfire itself exploded.

"*Nooooo!*" Yara shrieked as she ran to save her grandmother. Shan leapt up but Ko was faster, and in a long flying tackle brought the young Tibetan woman to the ground.

They watched in horror as the far end of the headquarters building exploded and machine guns began to rip the ground beside it. Incredibly, Lhamo dashed out of the door, seemingly unscathed, clutching something to her breast. She was thirty feet away when a final rocket penetrated the open doorway and exploded. The old woman's body jerked as shrapnel struck her. She was thrown through the air like a limp rag doll.

CHAPTER NINE

It was nearly two hours before they reached the *amchi*'s house, and Lhamo remained unconscious for the entire journey. More than once as he probed for a pulse Shan thought the worst, but as he and Ko laid her on the doctor's table, she emitted a long moan and her hand rose to the bloody gash along her temple. Dorchen pushed her hand away, and Yara pulled back her grandmother's hair so the doctor could wash the wound.

"A bad concussion, a broken arm, cracked ribs on the right, torn cartilage, and a ragged flesh wound on the left, but praise Lord Buddha, the shrapnel didn't penetrate the rib cage," the *amchi* explained as he completed his exam. He paused to look up. "Mother Tara give me strength!" he exclaimed in chagrin. Shan followed his gaze out the window and saw Nyima, leaning on Dingri's arm as she played with his dogs. "He helps her too much," Dorchen groused. "He may act the surly bully with most he meets, but he has been doting on that woman like she was his long-lost mother." With a frustrated sigh, the doctor tapped on the window and gestured them inside, then pulled off Lhamo's shoes to check her lower pulses.

Nyima was entering the room, one hand on Dingri's shoulder, when Dingri stopped her. He glared at Shan, then stepped away from the nun as if embarrassed to be seen helping her. Nyima pressed a hand to her side and limped a few more steps, then froze as she saw the woman on the table. "Lhamo!" she cried and rushed to the co-matose woman.

"There was"—Shan looked toward Jig Bartram as he struggled for an explanation—"an explosion at the old Red Guard camp." He could offer no other words. He had no idea why Lhamo had darted back into the building as it was being attacked.

"But she would never go there, she knows better than . . ." Nyima's words choked away as her gaze fell on the prayer amulet still clutched in the old woman's hand. With some effort she pried the *gau* from Lhamo's fingers, then rushed to the window and held it up to the sunlight. With a deep groan she sank onto the nearest bed, still staring at the worn copper and silver box, and began weeping.

Shan warily approached her and was about to comfort her when he saw the smile on the old nun's face and realized he was seeing tears of joy.

"It is his!" Nyima declared. "It still lives!"

"I don't understand," Shan confessed.

"This *gau*, it is his! It was hidden away by the curse, don't you see? That was the key, the secret we didn't know. But the curse doesn't bind foreigners! It is his!" she repeated.

"Who?"

"The abbot of Pure Water College! The *gau* is from the founding of the great medical college! It was given to the first abbot by the Great Fifth Dalai Lama, who blessed it and named it the seed of the sacred teachings. Inside is a relic of an ancient saint given at the con-secration of the college. It's a sign! So long as it exists, the college can be born again!" She held up the *gau* with the cross-hatched silver and copper pattern for Shan to see. "I told them. They didn't believe, but I told them!"

"Told whom?" Shan asked.

Nyima held the *gau* against her forehead a moment, then glanced up. "The old constables. Constable Fen and Constable Bao before him."

. . .

Shan left Ko with Lodi, asking the Tibetan boy to take him to Marpa's café for some lunch, then stepped inside the station to make a call to Tan's office. Jig lingered long enough for Shan to explain his intentions.

Five minutes later, he found his son at the café door. "Jig says we are going to Lhasa," Ko observed.

The door opened and the American woman appeared holding bags of food.

"No," Shan declared. "It is too dangerous. Not us. Me."

"I promise not to knock you unconscious this time," Jig said with a grin.

"I need you to protect my son."

"I will. In Lhasa."

"I thought you were searching for your brother's trail, what he was investigating."

"Aunt Nyima says one of the most joyful events in my mother's life was a visit to the great temple in Lhasa. I want to see it, I want to experience it as my mother did. This is probably my only chance."

"No." Shan spoke more firmly now. "He is not allowed to leave the county."

"You're the constable."

"I could tell everyone in the barracks about the temples," Ko suggested. "It would keep the old ones entranced for a month."

"No!" Shan insisted.

"I will be there to watch him as well," a voice said over his shoulder. Shan turned to see Jinhua standing there. "Just give me a moment to get my own bag of dumplings."

Half an hour later they were on the highway in Tserung's big old sedan, with Jig and the lieutenant both asleep in the back seat.

"In that building today," Ko suddenly said, "you held that piece of cloth like it had paralyzed you. I didn't understand. For a moment I thought something had bit you."

Shan offered a sad smile and turned back toward the road. "Your grandfather was a learned man," he began after a minute, "a professor of Western history and literature at one of the big universities in

Shanghai. His students adored him. His classrooms were always crowded, often with people standing in the aisles who were not even registered for the course. But when the Red Guard started targeting intellectuals, they first went after anyone with Western connections. He maintained correspondence with professors in America and Germany. That meant his name was one of the first on the lists of enemies. They put him on trial, though in the early days they just called them dialogues about proper Mao Tse-tung thought. He wasn't worried; he had a kind, gentle heart that always gave everyone the benefit of any doubt. He even invited my mother and me to the session. I think he really thought it was going to be just a robust philosophical debate, which he always relished.

"The Red Guard had taken over the university by then, painting slogans on every wall. Making bonfires for the old paintings, school records, everything that could be stripped out of the classrooms. They put him on a stool in his classroom and demanded whether he knew the university had been started by Western missionaries in the prior century. He said, of course, it was a well-known fact, that there was a plaque on the old administration building that declared to the world as much. They demanded that he confirm that half the books in his school office were in English. He said of course, since many important Western books had not yet been translated. They declared him a puppet of the running dogs of the West and then put a dunce cap on him. That was what I found today. Once of those dunce caps the Red Guard put on those they persecuted. He said that if more of them had done their homework they would recognize that there were great truths in many books, both Chinese and Western, and reminded them that he was also a scholar of Confucius.

"My father didn't know that Confucius had also been declared an enemy of the motherland. By then they had unearthed the grave of his direct descendant, the great Duke Yanghang, and hanged his corpse. When they reported that to him, he said that they were being very foolish and disrespectful and it was time to return to their studies.

"'We are mightier than the Shang, the Han, the Tang, and the

Chin!' the student in charge shouted to my father. 'Shame on you,' my father replied, 'mixing up the dynasties like that.' That's when they started beating him. They had a basket of willow switches, which they passed out, insisting my mother and I each take one.

"They had a ritual. They would ask a question and then everyone had to hit him once with a switch. By the end of the first round they had knocked off his spectacles and crushed them underfoot. When it came to mother's turn she refused, so they brought another stool with another dunce's cap and they hit her too. She scolded me when I refused and insisted I hit them both with the switch. She nodded her approval even as the tears streamed down her face.

"After the first round my father just stared at the wall and repeated the same thing, in English. 'She Shamefully Chose Chinese Hand Jingles and Sinfully Sweet Tango Songs, You and Me, Chickadee.'"

"I don't understand," Ko said.

"It was a memory aid, a mnemonic device he taught in his English language courses to help foreign students learn the dynasties in order. Xia, Shang, Chou, Chin, Han, Jin, and so on." The scene was seared into Shan's memory so deeply he could still smell the choking mixture of chalk dust, blood, the smoke of the endless Red Guard cigarettes, and the stolen beer that fueled many of the interrogators. His words tore at the scab over the old wound.

He did not know how long he had lapsed into silence. "We got sent away," he said at last. "We were part of the Stinking Ninth—that's what Mao called the intellectuals—and all the Ninth that weren't killed outright were sent away for reeducation." He looked over at his son, who was staring at him. "I'm sorry. It was a long time ago."

"In that building with all those *gaus*," Ko answered. "It was just yesterday."

Shan walked past the little shop in Lhasa twice before stepping inside. GENUINE TIBETAN MEMORIES, said the sign over the door, in

English, Chinese, German, French, and, in much smaller letters, Tibetan. In the window were plastic nesting dolls garishly painted like a laughing Buddha, framed photos of the Potala, a painting of a giant yak standing beside Mount Everest, and, incongruously, a series of deities painstakingly carved out of walnut shells. He glanced uneasily in the direction of the Jokhang Temple. Jig Bartram had assured him she would not let Ko leave her sight, and Jinhua had vowed to watch over both. "Let the boy be a tourist for a while," the American had cajoled and assured Shan that his son was safer there than in Yangkar as she led him toward the temple complex. Shan pulled his windbreaker tighter over his tunic and stepped inside the shop.

He feigned interest in a rack of postcards as a cheerful, elderly man waited on a Western tourist. The proprietor seemed a weary but patient man, whose balding head held patches of gray hair along the temples. Shan had been surprised that the address given to him over the phone by Amah Jiejie had been in the commercial district, but then he had realized that the meager pension of a constable would never by itself support living in the city.

When the tourist left, Shan chose four postcards of Lhasa's shrines and stepped to the counter. He exchanged small talk with the owner about the weather—the sun was welcome, but the wind was, as ever, too strong. As Shan extended a handful of coins, the shopkeeper hesitated a moment, then quickly glanced outside as if expecting Shan to have a companion.

"Have you come far, then?" the man asked in a level voice.

"From the north," Shan ventured. "The land of buried treasures."

The owner moved around the counter and paced along the front window, studying the street before turning to Shan. "Are you here to arrest me or just interrogate me?" he asked. "If it's arrest then I would like to feed my cat first."

Shan cocked his head, and the shopkeeper pointed to his wrist, where his windbreaker had slipped up his arm, revealing his tunic. "I'm the one who sewed up that tear on the sleeve. I seem to recall it was made by one of those overzealous hounds of the *amchi*." The old man stared at him expectantly.

"I'm sorry," Shan said. "My name is Shan and you must be Constable Bao. I just have a few questions on a matter of mutual interest."

"Not an official visit, then?" the retired constable asked.

"You were the constable of Yangkar for two decades until you retired four years ago. I became constable less than four months ago. The last constable should have lasted much longer."

Sadness grew in the old man's eyes. Bao studied him in silence, then stepped to the door, inserted a CLOSED sign into a slot by the handle, and gestured Shan toward the curtain behind the counter. "Business is, as ever, slow. I can't afford a place on the busy shopping streets. Most of my customers are tourists who have lost their way. Let's have tea."

Shan followed Bao into a sparsely furnished chamber that was a combined sitting room and kitchen. Through a gap in a narrow curtained doorway, he glimpsed a bed with a large cat sleeping on it. He sat at the small table and answered Bao's questions about mutual acquaintances in Yangkar as his host prepared tea. Was Mr. Hui still trying to grow poppies in his garden, was the carpet factory still spinning its own wool, and did the Mao statue in the square still anonymously acquire a blindfold of prayer scarves every few weeks?

Bao had an easygoing, unguarded nature, and Shan liked him at once. They laughed over the clumsy efforts of the Committee of Leading Citizens to assert authority and the way Chinese language signs often went missing along the roads. As he poured a second cup of tea, Bao saw the way Shan gazed at a little Buddhist altar near the bedroom entry.

"My parents' marriage was arranged by the government," Bao volunteered. "My father was a soldier from Manchuria who signed on to the pioneer program to get land in Tibet if he agreed to settle here. When he went to sign the papers, there was a line of former soldiers and a line of Tibetan women. As each man signed, he got the next woman in line." Bao shrugged. "They learned to love each other, in their own way. When I was ten, my father dismantled the altar my mother always kept in the kitchen, saying it was a bad influence on me. My mother said the gods would punish him, and he said the Tibetan gods had been defeated by the motherland's army. She said he obviously didn't understand the way of the gods in our house, and she went to sleep with the sheep in the stable. Every night for a month she slept with the sheep, then that altar magically reappeared. She came back to his bed, and there was never a word spoken about it. Later on she began taking me to shrines every few months." He tipped his cup to Shan. *"Lha gyal lo."*

"Lha gyal lo," Shan echoed with a grin.

Bao put his cup down, crossed his hands, and waited.

"Constable Fen had been your deputy," Shan began.

"For a dozen years, yes. Colonel Tan wasn't sure about my recommendation that he succeed me, said he was too Tibetan. But I assured Tan that Fen was loyal enough to get the job done." Bao paused and fixed Shan with a meaningful gaze. "It wasn't in his nature to work hard, but he was always an honest policeman. The people felt comfortable with him."

"Tan criticizes me as well. He loathes what he calls my overactive imagination."

"Which you came here to demonstrate."

Shan sipped at his tea. "What if we imagined Constable Fen didn't die in a road accident?"

Bao's face remained impassive. "What if we imagined that a miserable hard-labor prisoner could be redeemed and established as a constable, if only in forgotten Yangkar?"

Shan had been a fool to think Bao would no longer have friends in Lhadrung. "Colonel Tan never stops finding new ways to punish me."

"So you are here to pay him back." A grin slowly formed on Bao's face. "A noble cause!" He rose and retrieved two small glasses and a bottle of cheap *bai jin* whiskey from a cabinet. He did not speak until he had served out the liquor and downed a swallow. "But because I like you, Comrade Shan, I tell you that matter is closed. Public Security investigated and recorded it as a traffic accident. Public Security's word is final. That is our truth, as they would say whenever I tried to argue with them."

"It is not officially possible to murder a constable," Shan agreed.

Bao looked into his glass. "I had a debate once with Marpa at the noodle shop," the shopkeeper declared. "He said he was struggling to understand this strange Chinese notion of murder. He said when someone was destined by the gods to die, they died, that one cause of death is much the same as another."

"Maybe it depends on which gods."

"Sorry?"

"Did Constable Fen die because he offended the gods of Tibet? Or was it the gods of Beijing?"

Bao slowly shook his head and sighed. "You must have balls the size of Everest."

"Do you know Nyima?"

"The hermit nun who lives up in the Ghost Mountains?"

"She was beaten nearly to death. Nearby we found a murdered American hidden in a tomb with a Chinese soldier who died fifty years ago."

Bao's breath caught. He lowered his glass. "That's quite a mouthful, comrade. You do have an impressive imagination."

"I think they died because of the same secret that killed Constable Fen."

Bao stared into his glass for several breaths before looking up. "Drop this, Shan, I beg you. There is no possible good that can come to you or to Yangkar."

Shan returned his level gaze. "But you wouldn't have dropped it."

Bao sighed. He lifted the bottle as if to fill his glass again, then reconsidered and screwed the cap back on before rising to lock the back door. "Talk to me."

Half an hour later Shan had finished his story and Bao was making a fresh pot of tea. He filled Shan's cup, but before sitting he retrieved an envelope from his bedroom. "Fen came to me a week before he died," Bao began. His voice was a near whisper. "He was always excitable, but I never saw him so worked up. He had grown very fond of the people of Yangkar, would talk about what they called the empty years, even drew sketches of how he imagined the old *gompa* to look, though the townspeople and I discouraged it. No one in Yangkar talks about the old times, the old places. People sealed their memories up in a vault in their minds and threw away the key, just as Chinese refuse to remember the years of famine caused by Mao. It was like Fen wanted to rip open old scars.

"But he wouldn't stop. An aged Tibetan came to him one night, a stranger who had signs of hard travel and was anxious to move on. He just said he had made a promise to a friend and handed these papers to Fen, then walked back into the night." Bao wrapped his hand around the neck of the *bai jin* bottle, looking at it longingly, then rose and returned it to the cabinet.

"Fen said what he had would change everything. He said he couldn't stay, but wanted me to have a copy of the papers. He turned to go and said the spirits of the Ghost Mountains had been asleep too long. I was alarmed. I asked him to stay the night. He wouldn't hear of it. 'It's a miracle,' he said, over and over. 'It's a miracle, it's a miracle.' Just as he opened the door to leave he stopped, then ran back and traded, gave me the originals and took the copies. 'It's a miracle,' he whispered one last time, and I detected fear in his voice. I never saw him again."

Shan opened the envelope and withdrew five sheets of paper, arranging them side by side starting with the topmost on the left. The papers seemed heavily used, even worn thin in places, but the penciled drawings were neat and clear. The first was of a large complex of elegant buildings, surrounded by an oval of *chortens*, each on a large slab of squared stone. The largest structure was not in the center but at the northern side of the compound, and although it reminded him of a traditional temple, its windows and balconies indicated it was more likely a building of classrooms or sleeping quarters. It stood at the head of a courtyard with walkways around carefully tended plantings, in the center of which was a row of large prayer wheels on a

wooden frame. All the other buildings were smaller, traditional structures with inwardly slanted walls and hash marks sketched on the
roofs that seemed to indicate tiles.

The artist had drawn tiny images on the walls, apparently repre-
senting the traditional symbols often painted on the walls of treasured
buildings. Shan made out an eye, a half moon, and what may have
been a lotus. There were smudged words along the bottom of each
page, and smudged images along the sides. He made out clouds and
birds and what may have been a turtle with a snake in its mouth. Over
the largest building a rectangle had been drawn with a tree inside it.
It reminded Shan of the trees of medicine used by medical instructors.

His heart raced with realization. He was looking at the phantom
medical school, Pure Water College.

The next sheet showed the large building missing, as well as the
six northernmost *chortens*. In the lower left corner was inscribed the
Arabic numbers *239*. The remaining structures had been sketched in,
though without the fastidious detail of the first drawing. The third
page showed half the remaining buildings and *chortens* gone, with the
number *249* in the corner. The fourth, with the number *259*, showed
only one building left, a squat structure near the southern end of the
compound, and only empty slabs where the *chortens* had stood. Over
it was an unfamiliar symbol that looked like two crossed feathers. The
last drawing was markedly different and seemed to have no connection to the others. It simply showed three rows of dancing figures,
depicted top to bottom, the first of humans wearing robes with arms
outstretched, the second of horses with their legs extended, the third
of what looked like crows. Shan stared at the drawings a long time.
The crows weren't dancing, he decided, but struggling to fly. "Do you
know exactly when the Red Guard and army were in the Ghost
Mountains? It would have been sometime in 1966."

Bao gestured to the papers. "I think I know when they left. Late
September. Say after the twenty-fifth."

Shan looked back at the sets of three digits. *259* could indeed be
the twenty-fifth day of the ninth month.

"And these?" Shan asked, pointing to very small pairs of numbers he discovered at the bottom right corner of each page. *29* on the first, *45* on the second, then *37, 78, 94.*

"No idea. It looks like they were added later, as an afterthought, perhaps by the messenger." Bao reached across the table and gathered up the papers. "Leave it, Shan," the old man said as he returned the sheets to the envelope. "The Tibetans believe the Plain of Ghosts is a powerful spiritual place. Some spirit places reach out to humans with signs. There is a place in the north that is said to speak to humans with rainbows of different colors and sizes. There is one to the west that expresses itself with sounds, moans from the center of the earth, though I suspect it's just a trick of the winds. The Plain of Ghosts expresses itself in death, that's how it sends its messages."

"But that leaves the essential question," Shan said.

"What question?"

"Are the messages for the dead or the living?"

"Meaning what exactly?"

"Do we just accept the deaths and ignore their message? Surely the mountain doesn't simply want to teach us how to mourn."

"Over a million have died in Tibet of unnatural causes these past decades, Comrade Shan. Tell me why any of them died."

"I am not talking about statistics. I am talking about one man. Fen was a friend of yours. And you know why he died. He discovered that a witness to the atrocities at the Plain of Ghosts was still alive."

To Shan's great relief he found Jig Bartram and Ko drinking tea with Jinhua in the Barkhor Square café they had selected as their rendezvous. The smile on his son's face burned away the foreboding that had gripped Shan since visiting Bao, and he gladly accepted their offer for him to join them for another pot before the long drive back to Yangkar. Ko spoke enthusiastically of playing the tourist with the American in the Jokhang Temple complex, and Shan nodded gratefully to Jig for allowing his son a couple hours of normalcy. Perhaps, he considered, the American too needed the escape, for he knew she was still deeply shaken by her brother's death.

As Jinhua turned to signal for the check, he froze, then grabbed Shan's arm. "He's from Yintai's squad!"

Shan's heart sank as he followed Jinhua's gaze toward a table at the far side of the café, where one of the men he had seen in the general's escort sat. His gaze was not on their table, but on the street from which Shan had just entered the square.

"Bao!" Shan gasped. He pulled the envelope Bao had given him from his tunic, pushed it against Jinhua's chest then tossed him the car keys. "Get to the car! Keep this safe. If I am not there in half an hour leave without me!" he ordered, then slipped around the end of the café.

He ran hard, loathing himself for the danger he had thrust onto Bao. As he rounded a corner and the shop came into view, he halted, his chest heaving. The street seemed as quiet as before. Down the block, tourists were taking photographs of a building painted with traditional symbols. Three boys rode by on bicycles. He slipped into the shadows along the side of a construction site and reached the alley that ran behind the shop. The back door was open. He could hear the sound of breaking glassware inside. Inching up the steps he saw a man in a dark sweatshirt violently searching the chamber where he and Bao had sat thirty minutes earlier, scattering dishes off the shelves, slamming framed photos against the wall above Bao, who sat on the floor, looking dazed, blood streaming from his nose.

Shan slipped off his windbreaker and stepped into the chamber.

Yintai stopped and eyed Shan with amusement. "Perfect. All of our questions can now be answered."

Shan darted to Bao's side. The old man gave a weak grin then coughed and winced, holding his side.

"Your turn, constable," Yintai said to Shan. The large kitchen knife in his hand cut a circle in the air.

"You're good with knives, I see," Shan observed. The scar on Yintai's neck seemed to be turning darker. "Did you pick that skill up before or after someone slashed your throat?"

"He died. I didn't."

"Do you know there are more police per capita in Lhasa than any other Chinese city?" Shan asked as he maneuvered in front of Bao. "The government is constantly on alert for protests. I called them before I came inside."

Yintai frowned. "Pathetic. You don't even have a phone, comrade." He took a step closer, still carving the air with the knife. "Did he give them to you? Please tell me you ate them so I can gut you to confirm." Yintai thrust the knife forward but hesitated at the sound of porcelain breaking underfoot. He spun about in time to glimpse the piece of lumber that Ko slammed into his head.

Shan had destroyed his son's life. It was all he could think about on the endless drive north. The envelope from Bao was safe, and Bao himself, shaken but steadfast, had agreed to go visit a brother in Gansu for a few weeks to be out of the reach of Lau's henchmen. But Ko, now silently staring out a rear window, had committed a crime to protect his father. Shan had not only permitted him to break his parole, meaning it would be years before he was trusted out of prison again, but he could be charged with an assault that could add another fifteen years to his sentence. Shan's plans, the hopes that allowed him to persevere through each day were like the shards that had covered Bao's floor. Ko was the gravity that had kept Shan's feet on the earth for years. Without him, Shan was not sure he could hold on.

Jig and Jinhua had arrived moments after Ko and carried the unconscious Yintai as close to the construction site as they dared before dumping him in the shadows. Jinhua had run to buy a bottle of cheap sorghum whiskey, then poured half the contents over the man's clothes and put the bottle in his hand. Jig had even rubbed some of the blood from the man's temple onto a brick by his head. They had quickly cleaned Bao's home as he packed, stacked crates to block the back door, and driven the constable and his cat to the Norbulingka bus station before heading north. Shan feared for Bao, but the sturdy old man, more angry than frightened, insisted he would be safe and would call Shan's office in three weeks for an indication of whether he could return to his shop.

It was late evening by the time Shan had dropped Jinhua behind the station and returned Ko to his house, where Yara and Jig began making dinner. He reminded them that he had to return the car to the garage and told them not to wait for him. Now, an hour later, he eased his truck onto the shoulder of the road outside town and extinguished its lights, then climbed into the cargo bay where Lodi and his dog Raj sat on a blanket. Shan settled beside the Tibetan boy and the mastiff squeezed in beside them, resting his head on the boy's leg and a paw on Shan's. Shan pointed out a fast-moving satellite and Lodi listened attentively to his explanation of how it orbited the planet.

"It's good that you have strong beliefs from the world you come from," the boy said in an earnest voice when Shan finished.

"Beliefs?" Shan asked.

"In the world I live in, when something is thrown up into the sky it always comes down. Moving stars can't just fall forever. Nothing falls forever," the adolescent said, suddenly sounding like a lama. It was the way of many orphans in Tibet, Shan had learned, for they had to grow up too quickly. "There is always a reckoning with the earth."

Before Shan could find an answer, the boy pointed toward a solitary headlight that suddenly appeared in the darkened fields. "There . . . It was easy after Gyatso told me he repairs a Japanese motorcycle sometimes at the garage. It's painted orange, because it is quick as flame."

"When you saw it that night on the square you called him the moonrider."

"He rides when the moonlight is good. Mostly stays off the roads, and can't see the trails without moonlight."

"But he has a headlight," Shan pointed out.

"Not usually. Watch."

Moments later the headlight was extinguished. The sound of the engine trailed off to the south.

"He keeps it in an old shed below the ridge, not far from the *amchi*'s house. He can go down into the dry river bed and ride for miles. I bet he has a girlfriend, a secret he keeps from the *amchi*."

"You're sure it is Dingri?"

"Only two people live there, and the *amchi* would never leave when he has patients."

Shan gazed for several breaths in the direction the motorcycle had disappeared. There wasn't much to the south except a few farms, the inn ten miles away, and the road to Lhadrung. He stood and climbed out of the truck, then helped Lodi down. "I trust you," he reminded the boy.

"You don't have to trust me, just trust Raj. Don't you know? He's the lord of all the four-leggeds in Yangkar."

They were only thirty or forty steps from the house when the bushes along the path came alive with angry, growling animals. Shan could make out at least four of the big guard dogs and was considering whether the door would open in time if he tried to run through them when Lodi spoke out. "Walu, Gosi, Wosar, Duba! You're being silly. It's just us." Raj pushed close to Shan's leg, and at his bark the growls instantly turned into lower rumbles. The mastiffs approached, sniffing the boy, wagging their tails, then pressed tentative noses toward Shan and let him pass.

To his surprise it wasn't Dorchen who answered his knock. Rikyu cracked the door, then bowed her head to him and gestured Shan inside. Lodi faded into the darkness, off to watch the motorcycle shed.

Downstairs, Nyima was at Lhamo's bedside, feeding the old woman spoonfuls of porridge. Dorchen was sitting on another bed, his head against the wall with a book on his lap, asleep. He jerked up at

Rikyu's touch, then greeted Shan with an amiable nod before stretching and rubbing his eyes.

As they made tea, the *amchi* confirmed that although Lhamo seemed to be responding to his treatment, she slept very restlessly, talking in her sleep to long-dead family members and waking long before dawn in screeching nightmares that kept her sleepless the rest of the night.

"Is there a place we can talk?" Shan asked as Dorchen poured his tea. The *amchi* led him through a door at the end of the ward into a dim chamber. As Dorchen began lighting candles, Shan saw that two walls were lined with more old medical *thangkas* and the other two with shelves of books, equally divided between long, loose-leaf Tibetan *peche* and Western-style bound books. The old Tibetan motioned Shan to a table in the center and began clearing the books that covered it, the topmost of which was a well-used volume with color plates titled *Botanical Medicines of the World*. Dorchen, to Shan's surprise, read English.

"Speaking with dead people, you said. How do you know they're dead?" Shan asked.

"There was her mother, who died in a lightning strike when Lhamo was a teenager. The abbot of the medical college and his deputy Kolsang, who was her cousin."

Shan hesitated. "Lhamo is of the Taklha clan?"

Dorchen nodded. "They haven't used the family name for years. The Red Guard didn't just execute the older members fifty years ago, they outlawed the name as well. Lhamo's family used to manage the herds that fed the *gompa*, just as Pema's branch of the family managed the grain supply. She and Pema were close friends and often did chores for the monks, sometimes with Nyima," Dorchen continued. "On festival days they always helped with the ceremonies. I remember young Pema holding a parasol for the abbot as he read scripture to the monks gathered in the courtyard." Dorchen looked expectantly at the envelope now in Shan's hand. Shan silently laid out the drawings on the table, lining them up in front of the doctor just as Bao had presented them to Shan.

The *amchi* stopped breathing. He was so still, for so long, that Shan was about to reach out to touch him when he finally spoke.

"I was a young boy of six years when I first went up the mountain to the Pure Water school. We traveled for five days, with my sick mother bent over in the saddle. She couldn't even stand up because of the agony in her belly, but my father insisted that the legendary doctors on the mountain would cure her. We stopped at every pilgrim's station to pray, always climbing higher. The last day we were in thick fog for hours, then suddenly we found ourselves in a patch of brilliant sunlight with the buildings and *chortens* before us, glowing like they had halos, a serene island in the sea of fog. I truly thought we had reached some way station to the heavens."

Dorchen wiped at an eye. "The Hall of Abundant Life, that was the main building. They called it a temple but it was really a big hospital. The old lamas who were the senior doctors seemed so wise, so compassionate, that I was convinced they were all *tulkus*, the perfected souls who chose to stay on earth to help mere mortals. It was only much later that I learned that many *tulkus* had indeed taught there over the centuries and were buried under the *chortens*." The old man looked up at a *thangka* on the wall, on which a god rode a white yak.

"To express his gratitude for their healing my mother—they never demanded payment—my father offered to leave me with them, to act as a servant. But they always treated me as a student, from the very first day. As I grew older and realized they were just highly educated humans, all I ever aspired to be was one of them, a Pure Water doctor, serving in the Hall of Abundant Life." For a few moments, Shan saw a distant contentment in the old man's eyes. "I always thought that was the perfect name, as if handed down by the gods. The college was all about life, even the lowest forms. They were famed not just as healers of humans but of animals as well." He sighed and pointed to the words written along the bottom of the fourth drawing, as if to demonstrate his point.

"The writing is so small and smudged along the edges I cannot make much out," Shan said.

Dorchen ran a finger along the writing. "'Faithful hooves, faithful hearts,'" he read. "Legends say the college started centuries ago as a rest stop for the caravans. There were healing mineral springs down at the salt shrine, but there were special springs said to be the gift of the mountain god above them, on the plain that became Pure Water. The plain became a long-term encampment for convalescence where sick herders and sick animals stayed to recover. Some of the songs sung in college assemblies were just old caravan songs. This was one of those songs, in praise of the mules who made all things possible in construction of the college by bringing heavy loads up the mountain, year after year. *Beam by beam, stone by stone. The most steadfast of all our monks have four legs,* that was the first verse. The refrain was *Faithful hooves, faithful hearts.*"

Dorchen sipped at his tea. "You had to succeed as a novice at the *gompa* in Yangkar before the final years of training as a doctor, and after two years they sent me down the mountain to the *gompa*. It was the happiest day of my life years later when I made that long walk back up with the sack of my meager worldly belongings and entered the gates as a medical student. Did you know that they had a tame snow leopard that freely walked the grounds? He was like a guardian spirit. When it purred the sound echoed through the courtyard. The old ones said it was a heart sound that came from the earth god, using the leopard as its messenger." The sad smile faded. "That was the first thing the Chinese did when they arrived. They shot the leopard."

Dorchen gathered up the drawings and handed them to Shan. Shan returned the second, third, and fourth to the table in front of the *amchi*. Dorchen would not look at them.

"Whether or not you believe in the tale that demons curse even memories of the old college, Shan," the *amchi* stated, "surely you can understand the agony and hate such memories stir. We are taught that the pure of heart can forgive anything. But there are none so pure in Yangkar."

"People are still dying because of what happened there," Shan replied. "Help me stop it." The doctor still did not look at the drawings, but he returned Shan's gaze. "How did you survive?" Shan asked.

"Survive? I would hardly call it that. Survival implies healing, and moving on. The best parts of me died up on that plain. For fifty years it has been a raw wound in my soul. It will never heal."

"But it's the only soul you have."

Dorchen's eyes flared for a moment, then he sank his face in his hands. "What do you want from me?"

"I want you to look at the drawings. Really look at them."

The *amchi* grimaced but complied. "Fine. Someone drew a memorial of the lost medical college. It could have been anyone. Hundreds went in and out of Pure Water every year. Probably someone who lost a loved one there drew something in honor of the dead. Shove it in the pages of some history book for posterity."

"Where were you, doctor?" Shan pressed. "How did you survive?" he repeated.

"I was still two years away from completing my studies. I needed more work on diagnosis. I could read the first six pulses quite well but not the others. I had been sent to study with a specialist at Chokpori," the old man explained, referring to the famed medical college in Lhasa, which eventually had also been reduced to rubble.

"And if you were to draw a memorial what would it be? Why draw it like this, in three phases?"

"Maybe it's a drawing of the sequence in which it was built. It seems quite likely that the first building would have been a stable. The numbers that look like dates could just be the dates they were drawn."

"That's the solitary building, a stable?" Shan hesitated, looking at the drawing with the single building. "But the buildings were constructed centuries ago," he added. "No one alive would have known the sequence of construction."

"Who could know what this person intended? No one thinks clearly about the old place anymore."

"I think someone does. Someone who has the original perspective."

Dorchen slowly raised his head to meet Shan's gaze. "I don't follow."

"This isn't a memorial. This is a chronicle of what happened. From an eyewitness. It is not some fanciful drawing about construction, it is about destruction."

Dorchen straightened, then finally looked down at the drawings again. "Impossible. The army scoured those mountains. Not a soul was left alive, on two legs or four."

"Constable Fen had copies of these and was taking them to someone in the mountains the night he died." Shan pointed to the images penciled along the left margin of the first page. "I can make out an alms bowl, a lotus, a fish, and other sacred symbols. But there are more." He pointed to the center of the column. "That reminds me of a pistol, though surely that can't be. And the next seems like a pick ax. Then what looks like three inverted skulls."

Dorchen pushed the drawing closer to the light. "Skulls, yes. The drinking skulls used by wrathful protector gods, followed by some tiny images of what we used to call the sleeping gods." He looked up. "The artist had some experience with illuminated manuscripts."

"I don't think any image on these pages is meant to be decorative," Shan said.

Dorchen rummaged around the books at the side of the table and found a magnifying glass, then bent over the row of little symbols on the right margin of the first drawing. Slowly the skepticism in his eyes was replaced with an expression of intense curiosity. His brow wrinkled and he leaned still closer, the lens close to his eye.

"This isn't just anyone . . ." he began, then faltered, his eyes widening. He abruptly shot up and hurried out the door.

Moments later he returned with Nyima, directing her to the chair he had been sitting in. He spoke to the old nun in excited whispers, too low for Shan to make out.

The two old Tibetans huddled over the table for several minutes, exchanging urgent comments. "I know of only two people alive who know these symbols," Dorchen finally explained. He gestured to the old nun. "Nyima had begun training as a nurse and had gone up to attend to some sick herders when the trouble started. She never went back."

"Two people know these, you said," Shan observed. "The two of you."

Nyima nodded as Dorchen explained. "I have heard that in the West doctors once communicated between themselves in Latin, their own secret language in a way. These signs were similar, used by advanced students and their teachers at Pure Water to focus for diagnosis of a specific ailment. These symbols are a diagnosis for a heart troubled with grief and confusion. Heartwind, they used to call it."

"They were included to authenticate the one who drew," Shan suggested. "You thought there were only two alive who knew how to read them. Now we know there are three. Someone else survived."

Before he parked his truck on the empty square, Shan dropped off Lodi, who had not seen the orange motorcycle return, at the stable on the edge of town. The light was on in his office. He found Jengtse sitting at the little desk opposite Shan's staring at a blank sheet of paper. He tossed down his pen as he saw Shan.

"I'm sorry," Shan's deputy said. "At least you're here. I didn't know how to write the message."

"Who called?"

"It was a bad idea, constable, to take him out of Lhadrung County."

"Who called?" Shan demanded.

"Captain Yintai, General Lau's aide. He says your son attacked him, that he had to seek treatment in a hospital. He mentioned something about a phosphorus prison, whatever that is. He says they are coming at noon tomorrow to take custody of your son."

CHAPTER TEN

Shan watched from the open top of the old gate tower as the two black helicopters landed on a field outside of town. He felt utterly drained. His life had been built around his son, at first aimed at just keeping Ko alive in China's cruelest prisons, later at creating the barest spark of light at the end of the miserable tunnel that was his imprisonment. But he had failed his son. He had extinguished that light and thrown his son into the jaws of Lau's vengeful machine. Military prisons in China forced inmates into a merciless, medieval servitude. A man like Lau would think nothing of creating a file that labeled Ko a soldier, a deserter perhaps, branded as a violent, unpatriotic repeat offender. If the general took him, Shan would lose all touch with Ko, would have no way of learning where he was, no way of knowing if he lived or died.

"It is a chess game," said Jinhua, standing at his side. The two men had stood in silence, waiting, for so long that Shan had forgotten he was there. "Lau and Yintai play chess games. Not every trap results in checkmate." The young lieutenant, at first so bold, then so fearful, now had a somber determination in his eyes. Shan had repeatedly tried to convince him to leave, but Jinhua insisted that his duty to his dead partner would not let him flee. He would stay as long as Lau stayed.

Shan knew the Public Security officer was trying to calm him, but

Shan was beyond being calmed. "A chess game where the captured pieces die," Shan rejoined. He turned back toward the square, where a beat-up old cargo truck was parked, and signaled to the figures gathered there. When they had faded into the alleys, he gazed back toward the field where the helicopters had landed. Lau had dispatched a utility vehicle to meet his aircraft, and Shan watched as four figures climbed into the distant car before descending the worn stone stairs. For centuries the tower's gate had welcomed the Dalai Lamas with entourages of holy men, who healed the sick. Now it was for demons in dark fatigues who sapped the souls of men.

Shan forced the emotion from his face and greeted Captain Yintai with an impassive nod as he climbed out in front of the station. Yintai made a show of pointing to a bandage on his head. Lau emerged with his security detail, lit a cigarette, and made an impatient gesture toward his aide. Yintai and Shan stared at each other. The only movement was by Lodi, who was inching forward from the alley, showing a boyish curiosity over the soldiers and their weapons. Yintai glanced irritably at the boy, then reached into a pocket for a pack of cigarettes. As he pulled it out, a small disc fell out of his pocket and rolled toward Lodi, who scooped it up and darted to Shan's side.

Yintai extended his hand to the boy. "Give it back," he growled.

Lodi did not comply but instead lifted his hand to his mouth and murmured into it. Yintai angrily grabbed his wrist. "This is Yangkar, not Buzhou," the boy stated. Shan placed a hand on the boy's shoulder, frightened now of the strange game the boy was playing.

Yintai pried the hand open then spat a curse and stepped back. There was no disc in the boy's hand, but rather a large black beetle. "Yangkar, not Buzhou," the boy repeated defiantly, then raised his palm as if offering the beetle to Yintai. For a moment the cruel arrogance that seemed permanently etched on Yintai's face was replaced with an uneasy confusion, then he raised a hand to strike the boy.

"Enough!" Lau snapped. Lodi broke away and ran toward one of his climbing trees in the square. Yintai stepped to Lau's side, a lightless grin back on his face.

"The general is prepared to be generous," the captain declared in an oily voice. "You can stay in office. If there's no more trouble we will return your son to Tan's prison in two years."

"You were ravaging the home of a respected citizen in Lhasa, a former law enforcement officer. There are judges who would throw out a case against someone who inflicts injury in stopping a crime."

Yintai seemed to relish Shan's resistance. "A prisoner convicted of violent crimes on brief parole from a hard-labor camp, traveling without authority outside his county, was caught looting a home. I could have shot him and no one would have complained. One less worthless hooligan to deal with."

"You mean no one would have lived to complain. Like that woman in Beijing? She was only twenty-three. When she got on her bike that morning, she never expected to end her day as a smear on the pavement."

Yintai hesitated, glancing at Lau, then cocked his head, staring at Shan with a new, intense interest.

"The constable is distraught, captain," the general observed in an airy voice. "Unhinged even. We should finish our business and let him nurse his bitterness in private."

"You didn't come to Lhadrung County because you heard about two dead soldiers," Shan said. "Their bodies weren't even discovered until the day you arrived. You came because a foreigner was reported in the Ghost Mountains. I keep wondering, how could you have known? It's like one of those old riddles that keep you awake at night. Then you discover the answer, and it seems so unlikely it keeps you up another night. How could you have known? How could you have come so quickly? It's because you communicate with ghosts. Most people would lie awake because they fear ghosts. But you, you own your own ghosts, who conduct your unfinished business here."

A thin smile creased Lau's face but he said nothing.

"The army has hard-labor prisons that are chemical factories," Yintai put in. "A phosphorus plant, that's my personal favorite. Little dollops of phosphorus solution splash from the machines. When they dry out they burst into white flame. You can't extinguish it, just have to let it burn out. Every inmate has scars over scars. Most have their hair burnt away in the first few weeks. Once when I visited, there was a prisoner who had some splash into his ear. It started a fire inside his skull. My god, I've never heard such screams. Took him an hour to die."

"I was in prison when an official sentenced for corruption arrived," Shan replied. "He had been living in a penthouse in Macau, paid for by bribes. He mocked the other prisoners for eating insects and worms, even told the guards to stop the filthy practice. But three months later he was on his hands and knees, fighting over grubs with the others."

Lau gave a soft laugh. "What an amazing creature you are, Shan. So fearless. So perverse. You could have been my strong right arm," Lau suggested. He shrugged. "But you made other choices." He glanced at his watch. "You've said your good-byes? We'll take him now."

Shan glanced at the window of the station, where Jinhua now nervously watched. The plan had been his suggestion. "Your man awaits you in the truck," Shan stated, pointing to the cargo bay.

Yintai gestured to one of the guards, who leapt up onto the bumper and pulled back the canvas that covered it. The man glanced inside, then glared at Shan, who gestured for him to look more closely. He stepped inside and pulled back the blanket that lay on the floor, then instantly recoiled, stumbling against the bench that lined the bay and collapsing onto it.

"If he's unconscious, drag him out," Yintai snarled. The soldier stared at the floor, seeming not to hear. Yintai muttered an expletive and leapt inside. He too froze, then backed away from what was under the blanket. Lau spat a curse then climbed in himself. The cigarette dropped from his fingers as he saw the mummified remains.

"His name is Sergeant Ma Chu," Shan declared. Lau seemed not to hear. "As near as I can tell he died in 1966. I would guess September."

Lau's face was still pale but his voice was full of fire when he finally turned to Shan. "You insolent fool! I will crush you! I don't need your son, I will take you! To hell with your colonel! I will put you in such a—"

"1966," inserted a new voice, thin but firm. "You must remember it, general," Colonel Tan stated as he stepped out of the alley to Shan's side. "September was when the Snow Tigers suffered their biggest combat loss ever. In Kham, two hundred miles north of here. You reported Sergeant Ma among the dead in that incident. Imagine our surprise when we found him here in the Ghost Mountains. Buried with a saint."

Lau leapt out of the truck and advanced, his hand on his pearl-handled pistol. Bystanders were gathering, watching from across the street.

Shan returned his stare without expression. "Never leave a man behind," he stated. "Part of the Snow Tiger creed."

Yintai and his companions appeared at Lau's side, their fists clenched, waiting for the word from Lau. "General," Yintai murmured, as if to encourage Lau.

Tan shrugged. "1966," he repeated. "A chaotic year. Who could expect accurate records to have been kept? The recovery of an old hero is cause for solemn celebration. If you like, I can take him back to Lhadrung myself for the ceremony. Full military honors. An article in the Lhasa paper. An honor guard for the funeral, after the forensic exam is done."

Lau stiffened. "Like the constable said. We leave no man behind."

"General!" Yintai urged.

"Stand down, captain. We will take the noble sergeant with us."

Tan murmured a command and one of his own aides appeared, dangling a set of keys before tossing them to Yintai. A minute later Sergeant Ma was being driven away, rejoined after five decades with his comrades-in-arms.

Tan stared silently until the truck and Lau's car disappeared, then stepped across the street and lowered himself onto a park bench.

Shan followed and sat beside him. "He deserves better," Shan said. He glanced toward the ridge that rose behind the town, in the direction of his house. He had insisted that Ko stay there, far from Lau's grasp.

"He?" Tan asked.

"Sergeant Ma. They'll probably discard him in some ravine."

"Your sense of justice is truly pathological, Shan," Tan said as he lit another cigarette. "Lau will stay away now. We're not worth the trouble. That's all I want. He can go commit his perversions elsewhere. Just not in Lhadrung."

"There's probably records somewhere, of Ma's family."

"By god, Shan, it's over. Let him go." Tan nursed his cigarette a moment. "You said part of the mummy fell off when you carried him to the truck."

"One of his feet must have dropped off in the cave. We didn't realize it until we reached town."

"So bury his foot. Make a monument. Tomb of the orphaned foot. Grave of the hero appendage." Tan stared at his cigarette, then flicked it onto the street. "I'm hungry," he declared.

Shan looked again up at the hills where he had left Ko. He had longed to pass his parole in long quiet discussions. He gestured toward Marpa's café. "Noodles or dumplings?" he asked.

"Three of us. I want that knob you mentioned to join us."

Jinhua reluctantly accepted the invitation, relying on Shan's less than confident assurances that Tan only wanted to hear his evidence, and the three of them soon sat in the front room of the café, alone, at the window table. Marpa had offered to clear out the room but had not needed to, for with one glance at Tan, every other customer had disappeared.

"You're not convinced Lau's gone for good," the colonel declared to Shan as Marpa set a tray of food on the table.

"We simply raised the stakes this morning," Shan replied. "I don't think Lau has ever surrendered in his life."

"Meaning he has unfinished business here."

"The business he began in 1966," Shan said and gestured to Jinhua.

The young Public Security officer, once he overcame the intimidation of sitting with the notorious bulldog of Lhadrung, spoke in hushed tones of what he had found out about Lau and his men, from the connections between his tour in central Tibet and sudden wealth in Hong Kong to the deaths of the young secretary and his own partner in Beijing, including the bribes that covered up Lau's crimes.

"You call them bribes," Tan said as he helped himself to another dumpling. "Lau would call them mere expediting payments, for the more efficient administration of justice. He would never be convicted. Why waste all that time on investigations and court proceedings?"

"He killed people," Jinhua asserted.

"People who touched his sphere of influence died. Not the same thing. Lau is royalty. The imperial court always had deaths in the shadows that surrounded it."

"And now those shadows fall on Lhadrung," Shan observed.

"I'd say you cast a pretty harsh spotlight into those shadows this morning." Tan suspended his dumpling in his chopsticks. "I like these. Do I detect a hint of curry?"

"What if he killed twenty-four of his own soldiers in your county?"

"Ridiculous. He's a greedy son of a bitch, but no traitor. He is as devoted to the army as I am." Tan turned to Jinhua. "Lieutenant, I consider your business here complete."

Jinhua glanced uneasily at Shan before replying. "But I've accomplished nothing."

"Nonsense. You helped frighten Lau. You convinced Constable Shan of your earnestness, no small accomplishment in itself. You've even managed to stay alive."

"So Lau's payment for all the murders is a momentary fright," Jinhua shot back.

Shan's gut tightened. Jinhua had never experienced one of Tan's eruptions.

"This is Tibet, comrade," Tan said in a chill voice that set Shan's nerves on end. "Tibetans believe that eventually all sins are paid for. Lau is old. He will die soon enough and come back as a cockroach. You can stomp on him then."

"It wasn't Lau who killed two soldiers last month," Shan said.

"Like you said, Shan, a military matter."

"I'm pleased you acknowledge it. So someone with access to military channels should have no trouble with the obvious tasks."

Tan frowned. He folded his chopsticks over his plate and drained his tea. "Good-bye, lieutenant. Enjoy the scenery on your long drive home."

Jinhua stood, then hesitated, as if wondering whether to offer a hand. He brushed a finger along his temple in what might have been a feeble salute, then left.

Tan waited until he saw Jinhua on the street before speaking. "Tasks?" he asked Shan.

"What was the mission of those two soldiers? They weren't in the Ghost Mountains by coincidence."

"And?"

"An assignment for someone who knows the old record systems. Bosses come and go, but bureaucrats live forever. I once saw records for construction of the storm water system for Kaifeng in the Sung Dynasty." Shan poured Tan more tea. He might dismiss outsiders and profess interest only in keeping trouble away from Lhadrung, but in his heart the colonel was a warrior, and he had not had a good fight for years.

"But you're concerned with the Mao Dynasty," Tan suggested.

Shan nodded. "Also the service record of Sergeant Ma. Whether Lau requisitioned heavy trucks when he was operating here, and where did they go. Whether his unit actually did move north into Kham in fall of 1966."

Tan stared out into the square. The remains of the tree that had fallen had been cut and piled, awaiting a bonfire. "You don't think Lau is giving up. What could possibly interest him about this place?"

"He suspects there is more treasure still hidden in these hills."

"What's more treasure mean to him? He's as rich as an emperor."

"He is a man who must have more. There's always one more thing to buy. A bigger yacht. An island. A city. A country. But what really festers isn't so much the missing treasure, it's that Tibetans successfully concealed it, cheated him. His business here was never finished. It's why he left agents here."

"For fifty years?"

"There was an army outpost here in Yangkar until ten years ago. Only since then. One of them killed my predecessor."

Tan frowned. "That was a road accident."

"When a law enforcement official dies in Tibet, Public Security has two sets of forms. Death by heart attack or death by road accident. Pick an option and complete the name."

Tan watched a tumbleweed blow across the ragged square. An old woman led a donkey past them, baskets of dried dung on its back. He shook his head. "It's like the land itself resists," he said. "Stomp them all down and they just grow back again like some stubby weed. You begin to wonder who is stomping whom."

Shan gazed at the old officer. It was somehow disturbing to hear Tan equivocate about anything.

"When I was assigned to Lhadrung," the colonel continued, "it was supposed to be just for a few years. My destiny was as a battle leader, in a war with India or Taiwan. That's how I viewed myself, a battle commander in a temporary assignment. Thirty years on temporary assignment," the colonel added with a hoarse laugh.

Shan studied Tan. He seemed to have aged since Lau appeared in his county.

"Orders came from Beijing," Tan continued. "We are to assign troops to community rehabilitation. Show the friendly face of the Chinese soldier. This place is a disgrace. How many should I send for cleanup? The projects can be assigned by the local civil authority."

Shan returned his pointed stare. He was offering to post his men at Shan's disposal. Shan shook his head. "The local authority has to conduct this particular cleanup."

He stayed at the table as Tan's weathered limousine appeared from an alley and the colonel climbed inside. "Day after tomorrow," Tan reminded Shan in parting. "I'll tell them your son is expected at sunset tomorrow instead of noon. A few more hours. Try to keep him from assaulting anyone else."

Marpa, a towel in his hand, appeared at Shan's side and watched as the Red Flag drove out of the square. As he turned, Shan saw movement in the pocket of his apron.

"Just our friend," Marpa explained. He inserted his hand and briefly lifted a brown furry mass in his cupped hand. "Shiva's in the mountains and asked me to watch him."

Shan reached out and stroked the gerbil's head. "I'd like to take a meal home tonight," he said. "For half a dozen. Something special."

Marpa nodded as he set the gerbil back in his pocket. "I found a book on the great Tibetan poets. Maybe you want to show your son. A good boy." The townspeople had been unusually friendly to Ko, except for the members of the Committee of Leading Citizens, who cast suspicious glances at his son. Shan had seen Mrs. Weng watching from a doorway, her face pinched in a frown as she wrote in a notebook.

Marpa brought the volume of poetry from the kitchen, then hesitated. He glanced nervously at Shan and looked away. "I didn't want to say anything," the café owner began, "but Lodi's my nephew. Neither of us have anyone else."

"Lodi? What's wrong?" Shan was still troubled by the boy's strange actions with Yintai.

"Nothing wrong. It's just that he spends so much time in that tower these days."

"The tower?"

"Sometimes hours every day. It's better not to fill his head with wild ideas."

Now Shan was worried about Marpa himself. "Marpa, I have no notion of what you speak about."

"He's been keeping a vigil, as it were. He's watching for his parents, Shan."

"I never told him—"

Marpa raised a hand. "He tells me most every day recently. Constable Shan can bring people back. Constable Shan brought Tserung's dead son back to life."

"I swear, Marpa, I never—"

"I can't bring myself to tell the boy. They're never coming back. He hadn't mentioned them for years. But then that Gyatso in the garage started talking about his lost brother being found, and he began spending hours up on that tower, watching for them. Childhood is short enough in Tibet. He should be living it, not groping among the ruins of our past. That fool Gyatso told him he had to do something to be noticed by the gods, something bold and defiant, to make it clear to them the boy was still a good Tibetan."

Shan shut his eyes a moment. *Yangkar, not Buzhou,* Lodi had shouted at Yantai. "That stunt on the street. He's lucky he wasn't pistol-whipped by the captain."

"I should have kept him in his room."

"I'm sorry," Shan said to his friend. He could find no other words. "I'm sorry," he repeated, then gestured to Marpa's apron pocket. "I've been meaning to ask why Shiva thinks her uncle would be reincarnated here, in Yangkar."

Marpa, half listening, was stacking dishes on a tray. "Here?"

"She only came here a few years ago, she said. I mean why not in the town she came from, her family's town?"

"But he was from here. Her Uncle Kapo ran the forge for the old *gompa*, I hear."

"But she was not from—"

Marpa put down his tray. "She'd be scared to tell a policeman the truth. She was one of the few who dared to return. No one speaks about them."

"Them?"

"Buddha's breath, Shan. The original ones. Haven't you ever wondered about why there are so few old ones here? Only four over sixty-five in the entire town. They told us it was because it was to be a new pioneer town back in 1973. No one over twenty allowed back. Meaning no one who had been more than fifteen before we were sent away. Only a handful of the older ones dared to come back. The astrologer, Trinle and his wife, and Nyima."

"The Americans' mother was Nyima's niece. And Lhamo is a cousin."

A surprisingly loud chattering noise rose from Marpa's pocket. "He's hungry," Marpa announced. "Shiva even gave me a little horoscope, a chart, to show how her uncle's diet should change on certain days. I taped it inside one of my cabinet doors."

"I want to see it."

Shan followed Marpa into the kitchen, where he opened several doors before finding the chart. "Okay, a little bit of apricot on the third day, some fresh barley on the fourth." Marpa turned to Shan. "What did you want to see?"

"His name. I think she would have used his full reincarnate name."

Marpa ran a finger down the chart and stopped near the bottom. "Taklha," he announced, cocking his head a moment in confusion before looking at Shan. "Kapo Taklha."

All the old ones who had returned were from the Taklha clan. Were they there as the keepers of the faith in Yangkar? Shan wondered. Or had they returned to exact secret revenge?

CHAPTER ELEVEN

Shan arrived at his house an hour before sunset so he could have hot embers on the brazier to warm the feast Marpa had sent. He put the book of poetry on the windowsill and was lighting incense on the little altar when he heard a yelp of joy.

He found Ati sitting on a boulder, bouncing with excitement as he watched two figures on horseback racing along the trail that ran to the next farm, a mile away. "Go! Go! Go!" the boy shouted as the rear rider whooped and began passing the first.

Shan gazed in mute amazement. His son was the second rider, and he was passing Yara. They were mounted on two sturdy mountain ponies, galloping at breakneck speed across the rocky terrain. "They went for butter," Ati explained. "The farmer is an old friend. My mother must have asked for the loan of the horses."

Ko didn't know how to ride. Ko was going to fall and crack his skull. A dozen fears shot through Shan's mind, but then he saw the joy on his son's face and he forget all else. His son was due back in prison soon enough, and he was cramming every hour with experiences. Shan was painfully aware of what Ko would return to. These were the memories that would sustain him, memories that would strengthen him more than meat and noodles. He would lie awake at night and forget his empty belly and the bruises of the guards' batons by dissecting each of these minutes and living them again.

"A tie!" Ati shouted as the horses wheeled up in a cloud of dust. Ko was off his horse in an instant and at Yara's side, helping her dismount. The Tibetan woman tossed her son a sack that had been tied to her saddle, then showed Ko how to fasten the reins over the saddles. She whispered into the ear of each horse, turned their heads, and playfully slapped them on their haunches. The horses shot off at a trot, back to their stable.

"There's a pilgrim trail Yara showed me," Ko reported, "with a prayer station by a waterfall. If you drop a white pebble in the pool you get a wish."

"I was going to take you," Shan said, his voice strangely tight.

Ati squealed with laughter as Ko swung him onto his back. "What's that?" his son asked Shan.

"Never mind. I have food. If we can just find your grandparents," Shan said to Yara.

"Not here." She didn't look Shan in the eyes. "Up with the herds." In the mountains, Yara meant. Shiva too was in the mountains, and he expected Nyima had joined them. The Taklha clan was secretly meeting as their tormentors from 1966 roamed the same mountains. Ko was already in the house. "There's chicken!" he called out. "Real chicken!" He was already eating out of a container as Shan stepped inside. Yara seemed to recognize the disappointment on Shan's face and playfully chastised Ko, telling him to set the table.

"It's a feast! We need a bigger table!" his son laughed.

"I wanted you to eat well on your . . . vacation," Shan clumsily offered.

"Parole." Ko gestured to Yara and Ati. "They know. Vacation from the 404th People's Construction Brigade, where I am the meanest rock smasher in the camp."

Ati laughed. Ko threw a noodle at him.

They passed their dinner with lighthearted talk of horses and the old festivals where horse races could last for hours. Ati fell asleep at the table, and Ko carried him to his own pallet in the adjoining room. As Shan cleaned up, the boy cried out and Yara sat at his side, stroking his head as she sang an old Tibetan lullaby. When he finished with the dishes, Shan turned to see Ko sitting against the frame of the door to the bedroom, where he had been watching the boy and his mother, who now lay beside her son. All three were asleep.

Shan opened the book of poetry and read by candlelight, but his heart wasn't in it. He set the book by the pens and paper they had also not used. At the table he sat so he could see the sleeping figures. He doubted Ko knew there were bounty hunters who looked for ferals like Yara and Ati. He had warned them to stay hidden. Had he been a fool also not to tell his son that Lau had been bent on destroying him? After what Shan had done that morning to protect his son, the general was likely now to try to crush Shan as well. The calm of their little remote house was a delusion. None of them were safe. They had no happy future. They might have no future at all.

It was the most Tibetan of scenes. They had to live in the contentment of the moment, wearing this hour's peace of mind like a cloak, for the world could erupt in new pain and disorder at any moment.

He rose and took a long walk in the cool night air, then, still restless, settled back at the table with one of the bronze *dakinis*, coaxing away its dirt with a small brush. He found himself whispering to the little goddess as he worked, a habit he had picked up from Lokesh. He was liberating the deity within the crust of dirt, Lokesh would insist, and soon it would be gleefully dancing in the air around him.

Do I just make it worse by releasing you? he wondered to the goddess, looking into her lapis eyes. *Or would it have been more merciful to keep you in the cave where we had found you, blind and half buried, so you might wait to be released into a better world?*

Suddenly he saw his son was sitting at the table, studying him with a quizzical expression. Shan realized he had spoken the questions aloud.

Ko picked up a second, smaller figurine on the table and began working on it with a little wooden pick from Shan's tool kit.

"They will want to know everything about my days here," his son said after several minutes.

Shan hesitated. Was his son worried about interrogation by his prison guards?

"Every little thing. What people are eating, whether they seem healthy, whether people still have altars inside their houses. Some haven't been outside for thirty years or more. And no one has been released for only a few days, not from the 404th, which everyone knows is the dumping ground for all the hopeless cases. They asked me about television and most can't understand how it is possible. Some think I am touched in the head when I speak of things like television and cell phones. I wish I could take them one of these deities back for the secret altar in our barracks. But it would just be confiscated."

"Then you will have to give it to them in words," Shan suggested. "The first years I was there, a couple times a week after lights out someone would ask me to describe some aspect of life in Beijing. I remember one night talking about fast food. One of the monks was confused. Was it called that because you had to travel fast to get to the restaurant, or because it consisted of animals that had been fast on their feet, he asked."

A melancholy grin rose on his son's face. Shan motioned to the figurine in Ko's hand. "That one is Kalika, one of the sixteen elders, the first disciples who went out into the world to teach the word of Buddha. They are venerated even in China, where they are called *arhats*. You can still see them in temples in the east."

"Kalika," his son repeated. "Proof that not all Chinese run prisons."

Shan nodded. "I'm sorry, Ko," he said after they had silently worked on their gods for several more minutes. "I had intended to spend more time with you. I got you home at last and then I just leave you here."

"People need your help. I wouldn't want to interfere with that. It is what you do. They still talk about you in the 404th. The Chinese Rock, they call you, because Public Security and the guards kept inflicting pain on you and you just let it bounce off. There's a place where you had a top bunk, where you whittled *Lha gyal lo* in the ceiling a dozen times. The oldest of the lamas covered it with a piece of canvas, as if to stop a leak, and takes it off on holy days. *Lha gyal lo, Xiao Shan,* he recites, all twelve times."

Shan felt his throat tightening. Xiao was the old form of address for the younger generation, as an uncle might call a favored nephew.

"One of the old monks began calling me the Chinese Pebble last year when I was released from solitary. It was weeks before I realized it was a term of honor."

Shan felt his eyes fill with moisture. He felt somehow shamed. He was free, wearing the uniform of the government the prisoners loathed, while most of the wise, gentle Tibetans in the 404th would never be out in the world again.

Not knowing why, he set his *dakini* down and extracted the drawings they had brought from Lhasa, then explained to his son everything he knew about the murders and the old medical college. "There is something important here," he said, "something my predecessor died for."

Ko pointed to the solitary building on the last drawing of the complex. "Why that one, why is that left standing?"

"I don't know. I think it was a stable."

Ko pointed to the blurred image above the building. "What is the symbol above it? Looks like feathers."

"I don't know."

"And the words below it?" Ko asked. "I can't make them out."

"It's a song, a kind of blessing for mules. An old thing, from the days of the trade caravans."

"Stables were used as storehouses for caravan goods. One of the old lamas talks about going on caravans as a boy."

Caravans. Shan saw the excited way Ko studied the drawings. "You can't sleep?" he asked.

"There will be time enough for sleep when I am back inside."

"Then put on your shoes. I will give you a story our friends in the 404th will treasure."

. . .

Tserung had hidden the entrance to the underground archives behind a new labyrinth of broken statuary, tires, and vehicle bodies, and Shan was obliged to use his hand lantern to find the way. They found Jinhua in the first chamber of the sublevel, studying the most recent of the records. Ledgers and *peche* were strewn about the table where he worked under the light of half a dozen candles.

Shan gestured to the ledgers with a look of inquiry.

"Very disorganized in the early months of the Chinese arrival," Jinhua explained. "But then the bureaucrats arrived. Director Yen Fu of Religious Affairs was fastidious. I can tell you how many sacks of rice were ordered for the Bureau of Religious Affairs officials here, and the size of the temporary dormitory built for truck drivers and demolition crews here. They left the one gate tower up as an observation post. Not a word about the medical college. Then in late 1966 Director Yen disappears. All references to him stop. Except a month later there is a note that someone should write to the family of Yen Fu, as if he had died."

Shan realized Ko was not listening. He was pacing along the racks of *peche*, wide-eyed. "Forgive me," he said to his son. "Let me give you a proper introduction to the centuries."

They left Jinhua working at his table and ventured into the other chambers, sampling manuscripts in each. Ko grinned with pleasure as Shan uncovered a two-hundred-year-old *peche* and read of the summer horse festival, where horses raced around obstacle courses or over the mountains on courses that sometimes took hours to complete, and archery contests were held every day, some reserved for lamas over seventy years of age and some for adolescent girls or novice nuns, who were awarded prayer beads blessed by the Dalai Lama. When Shan finished, Ko found a volume containing nothing but prayers for injured animals and a three-hundred-year-old treatise on the shapes of clouds, written by a monk who insisted clouds never changed or faded away, that all clouds that ever lived still floated, just in different parts of the sky.

By the time they returned, Jinhua had organized his findings. He had three books in front of him. He put a hand on the first, a Tibetan *peche*. "Tserung says no entries after April 1966." He touched the last of the books, a ledger all in Chinese. "Last entry December 1967." He indicated a pile of paper bound with a length of twisted wire that pierced the top left corner of each page. Shan sat and leafed through the mismatched pages. Half the makeshift book seemed to consist of pages torn from Chinese ledgers, half were *peche* leaves that had been torn in half or in some cases folded.

"I discovered it hidden on the top shelf, out of sight," Jinhua reported. "Someone has been doing the same thing we are, though with a lot less respect for the records. Someone who reads both Chinese and Tibetan." He saw the uncertainty on Shan's face. "Looking for evidence of shipments, inventories of anything that might be called treasure. They seemed convinced something was hidden. Some of these report how a special team of Lau's soldiers tore out walls in chapels. And there's this one," Jinhua said, resting a hand on the brown-wrapped older book that had been in the middle of the 1966 records. "The mysterious out-of-place 1897 volume. I asked Tserung to look it over. It's mostly about the huge earthquake that happened that year. There's a page annotated." Jinhua rummaged through his notes, then lifted a slip of paper on which he had recorded the passage in Chinese and recited, "The earth deities woke briefly last week. We lost a temple wall, three *chorten* steeples, and the well. We bid good slumber to the beloved gods."

The words faintly resonated in Shan's mind, and then he remembered that Dorchen had revealed that several of the images on the margin of one of the drawings had been of sleeping gods.

Jinhua motioned to one of the Chinese notebooks. "Notes of interrogations," Jinhua explained and turned to a page of Chinese script. "The abbot of Yangkar *gompa*. 'My treasure is my eternal spirit,' he kept saying. He was beaten and lay unconscious for two days. They tried again. 'My treasure is my eternal spirit,' he repeated, never anything else until he died." Jinhua ran his finger down a list of names, each with a short paragraph of text under it. "The deputies to the abbot, then senior lamas."

"The interrogators seem to have been furious. Same thing, every one of them. 'My treasure is my eternal spirit.' They had rehearsed it. Two pages of names. Not one of the monks or lamas broke, only the layman who ran the stables for the *gompa* here in town. And all he said was that the treasure of the gods was not meant to be the treasure of men. It convinced the soldiers there was something of great value still hidden." Jinhua turned to another page. "They drew up architectural diagrams, did measurements, and identified what they thought might be false walls. They smashed open statues and found a few rods of silver and old bones.

"Then in June Lau put Yintai in charge and the team started studying caravan records. Something was discovered—perhaps a piece of intelligence from Lhasa, where other interrogations were being conducted. They began making lists of yak trains, mule trains, even trains of sheep carrying packs full of salt."

"Salt caravans would have come from the west and north."

"Right. After the first week they only focused on caravans from the south. Yangkar *gompa* was home to nearly five hundred monks and lamas, with another hundred or so up in the medical college. Caravans came and went all the time, often two or three a week." He lifted a folded *peche* leaf, with several distinct paragraphs written in Tibetan but with Chinese notes on the margins. "Tserung says each Tibetan passage describes a caravan. The Chinese counterpart accounts for the contents of each. Storehouse number one, for example, for a caravan of barley flour, or direct to the kitchens for one of fresh vegetables. Like an audit. Yintai suspected a subterfuge for some reason. There was a lot of effort to this, with references to senior officials in Religious Affairs and the military. No names given except that of Yintai. He's been Lau's front man all these years."

"Where was the Red Guard in all this?" Shan asked.

"There are early references to meetings at the Red Guard compound in the mountains, but not a word about the Hammer of Freedom after September 1966. Gone completely. No more requisitions for food for them, no record of their transport elsewhere. And there's three caravans that puzzled them, or at least three unaccounted for when everything stopped."

"Stopped?" Shan asked.

"Suddenly in October there's nothing but a report on movement of operations southward, including construction of the first roads into Yangkar and arrangements for convoys to ship inventories of religious artifacts and idolatry to Religious Affairs warehouses." Jinhua turned to the next page in the stack. "It says an order came in. Complete Rationalization of Reactionary Assets in Yangkar, it was captioned, whatever that means."

"Complete Rationalization?" Ko asked.

Shan closed his eyes a moment. "It meant total annihilation," he explained. "It was the order to destroy the *gompa*." He turned to Jinhua. "And the medical college?"

"Not a word. I think . . . it was gone by then."

"Tell us about the three caravans suspected by the government."

Jinhua pulled out a single *peche* sheet. "Tserung helped translate, like I said, but he wasn't clear on some of the old writing and usages. There was a caravan of thirty-five mules, bearing bolts of Indian cloth for robes, bundles of prayer scarves, and bows and arrows for the summer festival. The Chinese note says the army insisted the entire caravan was contraband since it included weapons. The teamsters were executed. The next is a caravan of ten yaks accompanied by three teamsters and two monks. The Tibetan report says it carried silk bags of sand from somewhere south of Lhasa. The Chinese auditors concluded this had to be a lie since no one transports sand so far and certainly not in silk bags. When they couldn't find anything, they assumed contraband must have been hidden in the bags and removed them for inspection."

"No," Shan countered. "It was special colored sand, gathered from carefully guarded deposits and blessed by senior lamas." He saw the question on his companions' faces. "For mandalas. Sand paintings of sacred images. The monks rode with it to ensure it was not contaminated."

"They executed those monks and the teamsters too. It was a pattern. Interrogate every teamster, then execute them. They were searching for a secret they wanted no one else to know."

Shan tried not to think of the carnage. "The third caravan?" he asked in a whisper.

Jinhua shrugged. "Fifty mules, twenty riders. Carrying medicines, incense, spices, and ink. The auditor said no one could find a record of the goods actually being entered into inventory at the *gompa*."

"Twenty riders? Seems like a lot."

"Tserung couldn't understand the wording. Ten teamsters for sure, and ten others. What he wrote was 'ten black feathers.' "

"Feathers," Ko said, "like that sign over the stable in the drawing."

"Suddenly there were questions about the Dalai Lama's gold," Jinhua continued. "Missing treasure from Lhasa. As if they suspected those fifty mules carried gold. Urgent messages were sent to Lau."

"When? September of 1966?"

Jinhua shrugged. "About that time, yes. There's another book Tserung hasn't examined," he added, pointing to another *peche*.

"I can read it," Ko offered.

Shan nodded. "See what you can discover. Look for—" A sharp series of taps from the hall interrupted him.

"Tserung," Jinhua explained. "Four taps to let us know it is him."

The mechanic waited on the landing. "Marpa is looking for you!" he said to Shan. "Never seen him so upset."

Shan found Marpa sitting by the door of his living quarters at the rear of the noodle shop. "Praise the Lord Buddha," the Tibetan muttered when he saw Shan, then rose and rapped on the door to his room. "He won't come out, he says only for you." Marpa futilely tried the doorknob. "Constable's here, lad."

Shan heard a click of the latch and the door slowly swung open.

By the time Shan was inside, Lodi was at the back wall of the room, kneeling beside Raj. A bloody rag and bowl of water sat beside the big dog. The hair on his head was matted with blood.

"Who did this?" Shan asked as he knelt beside Lodi.

"The one I told you about! The one you said I shouldn't fear!" the boy explained. It wasn't anger Shan heard in his voice, it was despair. "The skeleton god! I thought I could discover something to help you. The moon isn't full for another day or two, so I thought we would be safe. But there he was, jumping from behind a rock on the path to the old shed above the abandoned farmhouse. He shook his rattle at me but I didn't run, because you said I need not be scared. I said my name and he rolled his huge eyes and shook the rattle again. Then Raj wagged his tail. That really made the demon angry. He roared then picked up a stone and threw it at Raj. Raj fell senseless. I dropped to his side to see if he was still breathing, and when I looked up the demon was on a big boulder spitting fire!"

"Fire?" Shan asked. "Surely not, Lodi."

"I swear it! Streams of fire that ended in explosions of little stars! He made this terrible laugh and started aiming the fire at us. I've heard about demons that roast you alive and eat your flesh. I begged Raj to wake. I dragged him as best I could, and the demon kept belching fire toward us. I fell again and again, pulling Raj, then slipped and fell backward, and before I got up Raj was on me, licking me."

"Lodi, there is no fire-spitting god on the mountain," Shan said.

The boy looked to his uncle. "I saw it, Shan," Marpa whispered. "I went to look for the boy and saw the thing spitting fire into the sky."

"Show me where."

Marpa shook his head. "No. We are not going up there. No one should."

"Tell me where."

"I think it's always the same ridge, the one that runs from the salt shrine over to above the Demon's Den. Above the old farm. The devils stalk the hills there to make sure no one goes farther."

"Above the Taklha farm, you mean."

"No one calls it that anymore."

"An American came and spoke the name again. The Taklha farm."

"He spoke it and died."

"He spoke it," Shan said, as if correcting Marpa, "and people began to glimpse the truth about the Plain of Ghosts."

Shan had already opened the door to the cellars when he remembered the signal and rapped on the door. He rushed down the stairs, eager to hear of any new discovery, then slowed as he smelled smoke. Only one candle remained lit in the chamber where he had left Jinhua and his son. The pages that had been on the table were scattered on the stone flags, with several in a pile, smoldering where someone had tried to burn them. He stepped to the table for the candle and tripped on an outstretched leg.

Jinhua lay on the floor. The pages scattered around him were soaked with blood. He had been beaten so severely that Shan was not even certain he would find a pulse when he lifted the young officer's wrist. Jinhua groaned. A tooth lay on the floor by his bleeding mouth. A long gout of tissue lay open on his forehead. "Ko! Ko!" Shan shouted and found himself running to the rear chambers. No one was there. They had attacked and taken his son. He darted back to Jinhua and forced himself into action, lighting more candles, then gently pulling him upright against the table. As he did so the lieutenant's hand unfolded, revealing an embroidered patch of cloth. It appeared to be an image of two black feathers and had been ripped from a maroon piece of cloth, a monastic robe. Shan stuffed it into his pocket and was probing Jinhua's wounds, desperately calling his son's name, when a clamor rose from the stairway. Tserung, a bloody rag tied around his own head, darted down the stairs, followed a moment later by Ko and Jengtse.

Shan grabbed his son's arm. "Are you hurt?"

"No, no. When we heard someone at the door without the warning knocks, Jinhua made me run to the back like you said. It happened so fast. I heard him ask who was there, then there was just scuffling. After a few minutes I smelled smoke. I found him here with those burning pages. I stomped out the fire and ran outside. Tserung was knocked out by the door. I ran to the station. I wasn't sure where you were."

"Why would they do this?" Shan asked. "Is something missing?"

Jinhua studied the clutter of the room. "I don't see that wire-bound book, the book made of pages from others." His hand shot to his temple. He groaned in pain and slumped down, unconscious.

"We have to get Jinhua to the *amchi*," Shan said to his deputy.

"He's Chinese!" Jengtse protested. "I'll call an ambulance."

"Over two hours to get here and two hours back," Shan said. "He could be dead by then. Get the truck!" he ordered his deputy. "Now!"

As Jengtse darted away, Shan saw that Jinhua's hand was burnt where he had smothered the flames on the page in his hand. Much of the Chinese writing had been lost to the flames. He could only make out the last sentence. *Not one screech from the raven,* the old chronicle said.

An hour later Dorchen emerged from the back door of his makeshift clinic and approached the bench where Shan sat. "Jengtse has reminded me half a dozen times he is Public Security," the doctor declared to Shan. "I don't know if he means it to scare me or encourage me." The *amchi* shrugged, then noticed the dogs who sat staring at Shan and dispersed them with a wave of his blood-stained hand. "I have stabilized him. He can't stay. He needs X-rays, intravenous fluids, possibly surgery. He must get to a hospital."

"Which is your way of saying you won't keep a knob here."

Dorchen bent over the bucket by the hand pump and washed his face, then his hands, before replying. "Surely you understand, Shan.

Assaulting a Public Security officer is a serious crime. They may even call it an attempted murder. People are executed for such things. They will flood the town with their agents. I will have to go into the mountains with my patients. You know I have no license to run a clinic. It will be the end of all we do here."

"Public Security will know nothing about this. He is on leave. A private citizen. He will have as much difficulty as we will if he has to report to a hospital."

"Shan, I cannot. My other patients. They know who he is. They know he brought in that truck of detainees."

Shan looked inside, through the window. Nyima, whose list of Religious Affairs violations could probably fill a book, sat on the bed of Lhamo, the feral grandmother. They were already staring suspiciously at the unconscious man in the bed beside them. They might be frightened of him, but to Shan, Jinhua was seeming less and less like a knob and more like a lost boy who had wandered so far from his world he could not find his way back.

"He was in the old chapels, the archives, trying to solve the mystery of what happened here fifty years ago."

Dorchen slowly shook his head. "What mystery? The Chinese came. They took everything and destroyed our town. The Mongols once did the same. It's the cycle of history. No matter how severe the storm passing overhead, Tibet endures."

The warning in the *amchi*'s voice hurt Shan. "You saw the drawings. Constable Fen died because of them," Shan said. "It isn't history. Because it isn't over. A gang took treasure fifty years ago and they are back, looking for something they failed to find before."

The old doctor gazed at the moon. "The Chinese came," Dorchen repeated. "They took everything and destroyed our town. That is the past, dead to us now. The wheel turns. Only a fool stands in the way of destiny." He turned to Shan. "Focus your life on where you can make a difference, don't throw it away. Don't endanger all of us because of your foolish ambitions to change the world."

Shan extracted the little embroidered emblem he had removed

from Jinhua's hand. The *amchi* stiffened when Shan dropped it into his hand. "Jinhua was holding this. He found it there pressed in the pages he was reading, among the secrets."

Dorchen seemed no longer aware of Shan's presence. He stepped to the cairn at the back of the little yard, where Shan had seen incense burning. He laid the patch on the cairn, stirred the smoldering incense pot to life, and dropped to his knees. Shan inched closer. Dorchen was whispering an old death prayer. The past wasn't dead for Dorchen, despite his gruff denials.

The old doctor broke into a low mournful song as Shan sat beside him, then stayed silent for several minutes. "There were always guards for the Dalai Lama, for centuries," the *amchi* finally explained. "I used to see them on visits to Lhasa as a boy. The ones in the palace wore old uniforms from the nineteenth century and had swords in their belts. Some carried pikes. They marched in ceremonies and performed acts of daring at festivals. But there were others most never saw. Only a couple dozen at most. They were young monks who had volunteered, always monks bound by their vows because the Dalai Lama did not want them committing undue violence. They worked in the shadows, even in disguise if need be, sometimes on tasks that took them far from Lhasa. They were a secret order, a mystical order, with a long name from the old days, that meant the Sacred Messengers Who Fly in the Night, but those who knew them just called them the ravens."

Shan weighed his words. "But the Dalai Lama had gone into exile long before the Chinese came to Yangkar."

Dorchen nodded. "Several ravens went with him for the flight across the Himalayas, but not all. Things were confused in Lhasa. There were those who said the Chinese were just there to ensure India did not invade across the mountains, that they would go home when things on the border grew more settled. Then the Dalai Lama would return and all would go back to normal."

"Meanwhile," Shan suggested, "there would be things to be safeguarded. Hidden in remote places, perhaps."

"There were treasures the Chinese did not even understand." Dorchen sighed, then stood and stirred the incense pot again.

"When I was young," Shan said, "I had an old uncle who was a great follower of Confucius. He said the great sage taught us not to get too wedded to the world. Whenever my uncle took his leave of us, he would bend and put his hands on my shoulders. Don't trust the world, he would say, trust yourself."

"He would have made a good Buddhist," Dorchen observed.

"He was a merchant, taken away later for reeducation at some distant collective where many of the workers slowly starved to death. We didn't hear from him for two years, then I received a letter from him. Inside was a drawing of a small bird clutching a bamboo branch in a storm and a slip of charred paper that looked like it had been torn from the front of a burned book. *Don't trust the world,* it said. *Trust yourself.* That was all. A few months later word arrived that he had died."

Dorchen sighed. "The few ravens who stayed behind tried to keep up a subterfuge that the Dalai Lama was still in Tibet, to fool the Chinese, but that did not last long. Then they did what they could for the government in exile. Spirit away a beloved abbot in the middle of the night. Carry a message from one *gompa* to another, on fleet horses riding little-known trails. The army kept pouring in, and then the Red Guards, but the ravens knew the old trails, far from the roads the Chinese used. Some stayed in Lhasa, posing as street sweepers or beggars so they could watch the army and compile reports for Dharamsala, where the exiles lived." Dorchen glanced at Shan. "It was noble work. Hopeless but noble."

"At least one raven was in Yangkar, in 1966," Shan said.

"The Red Guard were conducting their so-called trials then. And interrogations."

A chill crept down Shan's spine. *Not one screech from the raven,* the passage in Jinhua's hand had reported. He now understood Dorchen's mourning song.

A low metallic rumble broke the silence. The beam of a solitary headlight sliced the darkness as it turned from the dry riverbed into the little shed.

"Dingri has been out tonight?" Shan asked.

"He has errands," came Dorchen's curt reply. "I think there may be some of that oolong left," he said and gestured Shan back inside.

CHAPTER TWELVE

They left after a breakfast of porridge and buttered tea, following Ati up a seldom-used path that ran parallel to the ridgeline heading west. After an hour, a rough track that led down to Yangkar came into sight. "Over the top of the ridge," the boy said. "Then a wide meadow with a dreadful structure in the center. A hall of the gods from long ago. Now the den of the demon," he added, then touched the little slip of paper that was twisted in a buttonhole.

As they reached the crest of the ridge, Ko, in front now, put up his hand and dropped onto his belly in the grass. When Shan reached him his son pointed to two distant figures coming down the far slope of the little valley before them. Shan trained his binoculars on them. "The astrologer and the American," he reported. "They've been looking for where her brother was captured. But they thought it was near the Plain of Ghosts." Now they seemed bound for the same location as Shan and his companions.

Shan studied the mound in the center of the valley. Although over a hundred feet high, it seemed almost perfectly symmetrical, as if made by the hand of man. From a distance the rock ledges and tumbles of stones at its top seemed to be natural, but as he examined it in his lenses he realized he wasn't looking at squarish ledge stones but squared blocks. Ati's hall of the gods was an ancient *dzong*, a hill fort of the type that had dotted the Tibetan landscape long before the arrival of Buddhism. The tall grasses, heather, and gorse that grew up against the rock softened the outline of the ruined fortress, and lichen grew so heavily on the lower part of the ruined walls that a casual observer might indeed consider it a natural formation.

The more remote, traditional Tibetans might call it the fortress of the protector deities, but the more worldly inhabitants of Yangkar called it the Demon's Den. Although he would say nothing of it to his companions, Jengtse had told Shan that this was where Constable Fen's body had been found.

By the time they reached the path, Jig Bartram was waiting for them. "You were right, Shan." She looked up with red-rimmed eyes. "We met them at the cave this morning and I said good-bye to my brother."

"The *ragyapa*?"

Jig nodded. "It's the way of the Taklha clan, to give our flesh to the vultures. Nyima and Shiva said it had been his destiny. Mother would have liked it. Jake would have laughed and made some joke about Tibetan bird watching." The American forced a smile, then turned toward Shiva, who had stopped a hundred paces away to sit on an outcropping. "She won't get closer," Jig explained. "But she gave me a charm—" Jig held out a little diamond-shaped frame of twigs and yarn that hung around her neck. "—and said I mustn't eat anything that grows there."

Shan glanced back at the ridge they had come down, wondering if anyone had noticed the old pilgrim path that followed the top of the ridge. Anywhere else such a path would have sent pilgrims into such a structure, a convenient and protected place to rest and pray. But there had only been a little clearing lined on its north side with a row of crumbling cairns, as if to shield pilgrims who stopped there.

"I don't understand why you're here," Jig said.

"The boy says your brother asked him about where the demons lived," Shan said.

The American's brow furrowed, and she produced the map her brother had left her of the line of sight to the distant cell tower. "I realized it just this morning. This old fort is right on the line, and the closest to the old homestead where he camped. I think this was the last place he came before he disappeared." They ventured warily into the jumble of rock at the top of the path. There had been a tower once, Shan saw, and parapets over inner chambers. The long stones of which they had been constructed had fallen, some with such force that they were embedded deep in the ground. It was indeed as if a great demon's hand had flung them down in fury.

"Stonehenge," the American observed. "It reminds me of Stonehenge." She saw Shan's uncertain expression. "Druids. Ancient wizards of England. The wizards here must have been really angry."

Shan had a vague recollection of a circle of standing stones he had seen in a book. "Just an earthquake," he said, though he would never suggest so to the traditional Tibetans. Many of them didn't believe in seismic events. They believed in angry earth gods.

He realized Jig Bartram had stopped searching the ruins and was gazing at Ko and Yara. His son was guiding the young Tibetan woman along a fallen parapet, holding her hand. "He's got it bad," she observed.

Shan glanced at his son, suddenly worried. "He seems in surprisingly good health to me."

Jig rolled her eyes. "It's always the parent who is most blind," she said.

"Up there," Ati suddenly said.

Jig and Shan turned to follow the boy's outstretched hand toward the top of one of the upturned blocks, the highest point in the ruins. A small loop of black wire extended over the edge of the rock. Jig quickly leapt from rock to rock, climbing toward the wire, followed more slowly by Shan. She waited for him, then gestured for him to give her a knee to climb up, but instead he pointed to the other side of the column, where someone had leaned a broken stone slab against the upright block, providing a step. Jig quickly leapt up the slab, grabbed the top of the tall block, and hoisted herself on top.

She sat on the edge a moment, then turned and slowly studied the peaks that lined the horizon before looking back at Shan. She lifted a compass from the rock to show him before stuffing it in her pocket, then raised a small black box from the top of the stone. "Catch," she called out a moment before dropping the box into his hands and slipping back over the side.

"I can't believe he got this into the country," Jig said.

Shan turned the box over in his hands, gauging its size. "He hid it inside a Chinese radio." He handed the box to the American, and she slid up a cleverly concealed metal door, revealing a small screen and several buttons. She then flipped it and opened a second sliding cover, exposing what might have been a lens.

"Not much different from a lot of new cameras. A remote altimeter, essentially."

"He was making maps," Shan recalled.

"Because no accurate maps of Tibet are available, other than a few put out for mountain climbers, but even those are only for certain peaks. Our mother described the size and shape of the mountains, gave us their names, and explained how they were positioned to each other from the perspective of the site of the old medical college, because I think she was beginning to worry we would find no guide. A big mountain with two glaciers to the northeast. Six humped ones in a row extending northwest that my mother called the camel caravan. The highest of all in the direction of the pole star, the next highest in the direction of Lhasa."

Jig indicated the box in her hand. "It was his fallback in case he found no one to help. The first time I spoke with him on the phone he was growing despondent, not just because no one had heard of Pure Water College but because they also had never heard of the Medicine Mountains. Jake was using this to shoot a beam to the peaks. Calibrate it with a couple known heights and distances. Then you just line up the peak you want to measure in the reticular. This was a perfect vantage point, the reason they built the fort here long ago."

Shan saw that indeed the old *dzong* was high enough—had the mound been raised to that purpose?—to take in ten or fifteen miles in every direction. Then he remembered the note in Jake Bartram's hotel room. *Potala 12523, 1.3.* He had recorded the height of the old palace in Lhasa and its distance from his hotel, as part of his calibrations.

"Why would he leave it here?" Shan asked.

"He wouldn't by choice. Way too expensive. In fact he probably borrowed it from the university. God knows what he told them at—"

A sharp whistle cut her off. Ko was waving them down, to a place where two slabs had fallen against each other, forming an inverted V.

As they approached, Yara pointed to small white feathers that had been caught by the bristles of a gorse bush, then more on weeds and heather in a line that extended from the shadow of the inverted slabs. Ko bent and pulled out a blue nylon jacket that had been repeatedly punctured, releasing its down filling, then lifted a piece of white tape that had been covered by the jacket. At its end was a heavy gauze pad that was stiff and brown. "An army field dressing saturated with blood," Shan explained. "One of the dead soldiers had a bandage on his shoulder."

"Jake had a knife, sure, but he would never—" Her words died away as Yara pointed to three bright circles of chipped stone in the lichen-covered block behind them. "Gun shots," the American stated.

Yara reached between two rocks and extracted a treacherous-looking little knife with a five-inch blade. It was, Shan saw, too narrow to be the one used to kill the soldiers, but the blade was stained with blood.

Jig knelt and lifted the jacket in one hand, then slowly looked up at the bullet marks. "It's Jake's knife. He was taking the altitudes," the American suggested, "when suddenly he realized the soldiers were approaching. He jumped down before they could see what he was doing and resisted them when they tried to arrest him. He slashed one as he scuffled"—she indicated the field dressing—"but the other pulled his pistol and fired. Then he surrendered."

Shan picked up the story. "They subdued him, then searched his belongings. They were furious. They applied one dressing to the soldier's wound, but it quickly filled with blood so they put on a second. They slashed his jacket, releasing the down, then his pack."

"They ate his energy bars," Jig added, picking up a wrapper that had blown under a bush. "Jake would never have tossed the wrapper away.

"Then they took him to the Red Guard camp. But why? And why would two soldiers torture him?" she asked in a tight voice. "They could have gone back to their base and he would have straightened things out. He would have been deported, but he would have lived."

"Back to the camp because of the old army road," Shan guessed. "I think they had a vehicle there."

Jig hesitated. "Why not use their helicopters? They could have landed right here in the valley."

"Because they were not part of Lau's unit. They were not Snow Tigers, not Lau's men."

"My brother died because Lau found out."

"Not exactly. Lau and his aides didn't arrive for two more days," Shan said. "And Snow Tigers didn't kill Constable Fen."

"It was almost like Lau and his men were on alert, ready to come when called."

"People were on watch, all these years," Shan said. "Nyima in her cave, Shiva patiently doing her charts."

"With Lhamo and Trinle," Jig suggested, "the invisible ferals going between them."

"And the skeleton demons," Shan added, "all those years waiting in Yangkar."

All a human's life revolves around perception, the varying eye on reality, Lokesh had once told Shan. It is the joy and curse of all humans. Once Shan had taken delight in the stark beauty of the mountains above Yangkar. The violence there had changed that now. The land northwest of Yangkar had new coordinates that would forever change the way he saw it. The tomb where the body of Jake Bartram had been hidden. The *dzong* where Constable Fen had been savagely killed. The camp where the Red Guard had tortured so many, and where three men had been more recently murdered. The ridge above the Taklha farm where demons kept Tibetans away.

He sat now, studying the ridge from the track above the farmhouse. In the dying light he fancied he saw other features, a dim line of shadow to the west that was the old caravan route, and another to the east that was the pilgrim path leading past the *dzong*, the Demon's Den. Shan realized that Lokesh and the other old Tibetans would not distinguish between old and new. It was always a sacred landscape, imbued with spirits who offered a healing touch, first at the old mineral springs, then at Pure Water College. It was a landscape of truth, Lokesh would say, that would eventually shrug off and shatter pretenders.

Shan stole from one outcropping to the next, pausing to study the terrain at each sheltering rock. The little shepherd's shed at the mouth of the ravine above the abandoned farm came into view. The full moon edged over the mountains. A wild goat scampered over the ridge.

He lowered himself onto a little ledge on a rock formation, watching in the direction the goat had come from. Something had frightened it. The stars slowly appeared in the darkening sky, and he found himself looking for constellations.

Suddenly the rock face above him exploded with sparks. A ball of fire blazed toward his head. He dropped to the ground, rolling as the ball burst onto the stone, followed quickly by another and another. Then abruptly they stopped and the only sound was a hollow rattling, followed by a hideous cackling laugh. He waited for the sound to stop before rising. The air had a scorched, sulfurous smell. On top of the ridge, silhouetted by the moon, a thin, otherworldly figure danced, shaking a rattle.

Shan was stealthily moving toward the demon when suddenly it stopped and turned toward the old farm. Flames were shooting out of the mouth of the ravine. The figure on the ridge darted away in the opposite direction. Shan ran toward the flames.

The little shepherd's hut was engulfed in fire. Its dry wood burned with an intense ferocity, quickly consuming the structure. Shan had begun to circle it when he spied a small figure kneeling at a nearby stump, supporting himself on what looked like a club.

Lodi didn't acknowledge Shan as he knelt beside the boy. He just kept staring at the flames, clutching the club as if he expected something to leap out of the flames. In the bright orange light Shan saw that the club was a piece of rough-hewn timber inscribed with Buddhist prayers in a child's hand.

"I was waiting," the boy said. "You told me the monsters weren't gods. I thought if I struck one and it reacted, then you were right. But then the flames reached out of the darkness. Maybe it's because I came too close."

"Did you see anyone?" Shan asked.

Lodi silently shook his head.

Shan suddenly realized Lodi was alone and began urgently scanning the ruins. "Where's Raj?"

"I tied him, left him at the stable. Last time that demon almost killed him."

"Last time," Shan recalled, "you said Raj wagged his tail just before the demon struck."

Lodi's face clouded and he did not reply.

The fire quickly extinguished its fuel. In a quarter hour the flames had died, and Shan probed the ashes with a long stick. Along one side some old fodder had dampened the flames, and he pried a smoldering object out of the embers.

Lodi groaned and leapt behind him as Shan aimed his flashlight at it. It was the head of a demon. Smoke rose from its nostrils.

"You see!" the boy gasped. "It was breathing fire. It stayed inside because I was near, and breathed on its own nest!"

"No. It's just wood, Lodi. It's smoldering where the fire touched it." But then the head rolled, and when it stopped it was staring at the boy with its big round eyes. It blinked.

The boy screamed and would have fled if Shan had not grabbed him. "It is a mask, nothing but an old mask," Shan explained, and flipped the head onto its crown, showing the boy the intricate mechanism that moved the eyes. "Monks wore such things in festivals," he explained. "It would sit on top of the monk's head and he would look through holes in the neck." He gestured for the boy to try the little rod that flipped the eyes up and down.

"So you mean I just saw a different type of demon, then," the boy solemnly observed as he calmed, working the costume's eyes. "Just a mortal demon."

Shan took the boy down to the abandoned farm. Lodi gripped his hand tightly and did not let go when Shan sat with him on a stone block in the middle of the old farmyard. They waited, listening to the crickets.

"You scared the demon," Shan finally said to the shadows.

Jig Bartram emerged into the moonlight. "At least I eliminated some of his wardrobe." The American tossed a stick that landed at Shan's feet. "I take it people around here don't see many fireworks. I pulled a box of these from the shed."

It had been many years since Shan himself had seen such an object. He lifted it and handed it to Lodi. "It's called a Roman candle. Light the fuse and balls of sparks shoot from the end."

The boy instantly dropped it. "A thing of the gods!"

"There's no gods involved," Jig explained. "Just chemicals. Here—" she buried half the stick in a small cairn and struck a match.

Lodi shrank against Shan as the first fireball shot into the sky, but by the third he was jumping up and down with excitement. When the candle was depleted, a sulfurous cloud hung about them. Lodi turned and spoke solemnly to Shan. "Now I know why you came to Yangkar, constable. You deal with those who cheat the gods."

CHAPTER THIRTEEN

"An old woman called for you," Jengtse announced when Shan arrived at the station in the morning. "Said your book is ready." The deputy shrugged. "Something you ordered in Lhasa, I guess. Don't know of a bookstore this side of the city."

Shan shrugged with careful disinterest, waited until his deputy left to patrol the town, and dialed Lhadrung. *Your book is ready.* It was one of Amah Jiejie's games. She had told him once she had always wanted to be a librarian. She answered on the first ring, reported that Colonel Tan was working late, and put him on the line.

"The two dead soldiers," Tan said, "were signalmen, telemetry experts qualifying the Snow Tigers to use new equipment. Pinpoint sensors for radio and laser signals, to be deployed along the border. They would detect a transmission device that had been concealed for training purposes, then call the coordinates in to their base for confirmation. Except that day the one that was called in had not been planted by the army. They were dispatched in a utility truck to investigate."

"The American was bouncing signals off the mountains," Shan explained. "Making a map."

"The fool. He thought no one would notice?"

"In the Ghost Mountains, with nothing but goats and yaks for miles? I doubt it occurred to him. The soldiers surprised him. They subdued him. The worst he would have expected was to be deported.

They went back to the old Red Guard camp. None of them knew death waited for them there. I found the evidence, then two helicopters destroyed it."

"They fired on you?" Shan could hear the fury igniting in Tan's voice.

"They will call it a live fire training mission."

Shan heard a whispered curse. "My driver goes out drinking with Lau's security detail. He says the two signalmen were laid out in the open, dragged from their wrecked truck."

"Someone wanted to hide the murders," Shan observed, "disguise them as deaths from an accident."

"Someone else wanted to display them," Tan rejoined. "Stay out of the mountains, Shan. That's an order. Find a big rock and crawl under it. General Lau will grow weary and soon find a game to play elsewhere."

"Shan, no!" Marpa protested, leaning out the back door of the café as if to intercept them. Shan had met Ko and Yara at the carpet factory, where she had promised to show Ko the old looms and offered to buy them dinner. Marpa urgently motioned them off his steps.

"Just a quick bite."

"The Committee of Leading Citizens is in my dining room. No!" Marpa cast a meaningful glance at Yara and lowered his voice. "They know her family. They know of the bounties. Mrs. Weng is still trying to find a way to pay for her broken windows. And she's furious with you, says you caused all the town's problems, says they are going to petition for a proper policeman."

Shan glanced at his son. He had promised his son a good meal before the long drive back to the 404th. "Then have Lodi bring our food to the garage, to Tserung. He'll know where to find us."

Jig Bartram was already in the subterranean archives, making notes and studying rough drawings of the Pure Water College grounds that Tserung had located in the old manuscripts. She was, Shan realized, trying to pinpoint the location of the old herb gardens, where her mother wanted to be buried.

They pushed the small tables together in the corridor and hung lanterns above as Ko and Yara unpacked the meal. Shan laid out the secret drawings again.

"What are we missing?" he asked in frustration. "Why won't the man who drew these show himself? Why flying horses? Why raven feathers over the stable?" He felt no closer to the murderers, and every hour his foreboding grew. The killers were growing impatient, even desperate. If they found the witness first, he would die. Shan found himself avoiding his son's gaze, for fear he would sense that his father actually wanted him back in prison, where he would at least be safe from the Yangkar killers.

"You just sit," Yara playfully chastised as Ko tried to help arrange the meal. Ati picked up the big thermos Marpa had sent but it proved too heavy, and as he tried to fill the little teacups, it slipped. As tea slopped out on the table Jig snatched up the nearest drawing, although not in time to avoid the upper corner soaking up some of the hot liquid. She paused, staring at the corner, then showed it to Shan. The tea had brought out a dim shadow of Chinese characters.

"Secret writing?" the American asked.

"I don't think so," Shan replied. "This was made by a Tibetan for Tibetans. He wouldn't record secrets in Chinese."

"A palimpsest, then," Jig declared in English.

"I'm sorry?"

"I only know the English word. Palimpsest. My father was fascinated with ancient languages. He showed me one in a museum. Ages ago, when parchment or vellum was in short supply, scribes sometimes washed or scraped away the ink on old manuscripts so they could use them again, for new writing. There's the Archimedes Palimpsest, and Roman books from Cicero and Seneca, overwritten by early Christian writings." She saw the blank stares of her companions. "These pages were recycled! Whoever drew these didn't have clean paper to work with." She cocked her head at Shan, who hesitantly dripped more tea along the top of the drawing. "'Mail,'" he read from the dim outlines. "'First day' . . . then it's blurred. I can make out the word 'penalties.'"

Ko lowered his chopsticks and snatched the paper away, studied it for a moment, and then fixed his father with a look that first showed excitement, then dismay. "Mail will be distributed on the first day of the month," he stated, "available to those who have received no penalties during the preceding month." He dripped tea along the top of the next drawing, scanned it and looked up. "Item One," he recited without reading. "Night soil not placed on the barracks steps before breakfast must be kept inside until the next morning. Item Two. Singing in the barracks brings a penalty against the entire barracks."

Jig looked in confusion from Ko to Shan. "I don't understand."

Ko dripped more tea along the top of the third drawing. "Your labor," he whispered, then his words choked away. He glanced up at Yara then looked away, speaking into the shadows. "Your labor is how you express your love for the motherland. Respect the motherland and she will shelter you. Disrespect her and you will sleep outside, whatever the weather."

Yara's face twisted with pain as she watched Ko.

Suddenly Shan grabbed a pencil, pulled out his notebook, and wrote down the numbers at the bottom corner of each page, in sequence. He felt the blood drain from his face.

"Shan?" the American asked as she saw his stricken countenance. "What is it?"

He turned the notebook toward Jig, then slowly rolled up his sleeve. "I've been such a fool. It's why the messenger fled, why the man who drew these must be anonymous. I should have seen it immediately. This," he said, and placed his uncovered forearm by the numbers he had written down. "This is what I mean." There were ten digits on the paper, just as there were on Shan's arm. "The witness who drew these is a hard-labor prisoner."

· · ·

They drove in silence for the first two hours. Ko leaned against the door, his eyes shut, but Shan knew his son was not asleep. Nothing during his parole had been as Shan had planned. He had meant to spend nearly every hour with his son, to show him he was cherished and very much part of Shan's life. Anyone can say such things, but such words meant nothing if they were not demonstrated, if they were not reflected in the hundreds of little acts and gestures that bound families together. Instead Shan had dumped him with strangers, taken him into harm's way in Lhasa, and entangled him with a family of feral Tibetans. If the prison authorities caught wind of half the things Ko had done during his time with Shan, there would be no hope of further parole.

They paused at a tiny roadhouse on the pass that led down into the plain of Lhadrung, eating bowls of mutton stew beside two truck drivers who loudly spoke of the comfort girls along the road to Szechuan, spilling beer and belching, then snickering when Shan put his tunic back on.

He turned on the radio when they cleared the last pass and put on the rock-and-roll station from Lhasa. Ko turned it off. When they reached an overlook that surveyed the plain below, Shan pulled over. The sun was low in the sky. Lights, including security spotlights, were flickering on in half a dozen prison compounds. He turned off the engine, climbed out of the car, and stepped to the guardrail along the high cliff.

"I'm sorry, Ko," he said when he heard his son's steps behind him. "I guess it was a bad idea. You and I have never had time together like this. Your mother had you in the early years. Then I was in prison. You were in prison. I never learned how to be a father."

"There are reasons I am in prison," his son replied. "Lots of reasons. Drug dealing, gang leader. Destruction of government property. More brawls than I can remember. But not you."

Shan was at a loss. "I'm sorry," he said again.

"No. You don't understand. There isn't a day when I don't think of the courage it took, and the strength, to endure it. You were in prison because you were a good man, a man of integrity, because you stood up for the truth against corrupt officials. And you made your own justice. They still talk about it in the 404th, even some of the guards. Some of them hate you, but others talk about how you got Lokesh freed, how you beat the warden. It keeps me going, keeps me alive." Ko turned to Shan. "Don't you see? You have always been the father I needed."

The mountains far to the east had been lost in a haze, but now the lowering sun struck their caps of snow. They glowed like a necklace of pearls along the purple horizon.

"I know we had talked about possible parole, but I never knew if it was going to happen," his son continued. "Some of the younger prisoners who only knew you were a constable said I would be hosed down and de-liced before entering your house, said I would probably spend my time polishing the faces of whatever Mao statues were on the streets of your town. They said I would piss myself if I had to talk with a girl, that every night I would have to call the warden to check in and report the day's activity.

"Then when the colonel came for me, I had no notion of what was to happen. I thought the parole was weeks away. No one told me. I was so damned scared I didn't want to get out of that car."

"Colonel Tan can be—" Shan searched for words. "—easily misunderstood."

Ko seemed to find amusement in his words. A small chuckle became a deep laugh. "But instead he saved me. The two of you saved me from that General Lau." Ko glanced down toward the prison camps and quickly looked away. In less than an hour he would be back in his cage. His hand went to something hanging from his neck, something he had left inside his shirt until now. It was a small frame of twigs and yarn, a demon catcher.

"You did find a girl to talk with," Shan observed, knowing who must have given him the charm.

"She said she wants to take me to the old mineral spring next time, whatever that means."

Shan grinned. "I expect you will find it thrilling. Unless her grandparents join you."

"I don't understand."

"You will."

Ko smiled and tightened his grip on the charm.

"She's a feral, Ko," Shan reminded him. "She could run tomorrow. Even against her wishes she might run, to save her grandparents and son." Shan had painfully watched as Ko and Yara had embraced each other when they departed, had seen the tears she tried to hold back. When he had turned away from her, Shan had seen something in his son's eyes that had not been there five days before, a new strength, a calm determination that hinted of a purpose in his life.

"Is this now a fatherly talk about the wiles of beautiful women?"

Shan smiled. "On all the face of the planet you would find no one less wise about such things. It's just that you're not the only one in prison. She lives in her own kind of prison."

Ko turned to the south, forcing himself to look at the razor-wired compounds now. "I told her. People like us can make no promises. She didn't reply, just put this around my neck. You are protected from demons, she said. Only the bad kind of demons, she added, because I had to remember that in Tibet there are good demons too."

Shan began unbuttoning his tunic. "In the glove box there's a little sewing kit," he told his son. Ko looked at him in confusion. "Just get it."

When his son returned with the kit, Shan had his pocketknife out. "They won't let you keep that. Too Tibetan. Too reactionary." He began slicing through the threads of his shoulder patch, an embroidered circle featuring a stylized Chinese flag. He severed half a dozen threads and then ripped away the patch. "Let me see her charm."

Ko lifted it from his neck and handed it to his father.

"Braided yak hair," Shan observed. "She must have taken hours to make it." He held up the patch to the front of the charm. It perfectly covered the twigs and yarn. "I will sew this over it. The guards will respect how you want to salute the motherland by wearing a flag and not touch it. They don't have to know that the flag is only there as a disguise."

Ko broke into a wide grin. "She said something else, at the very end, as she watched you get in the truck," he added with an awkward glance at his father. "She said you were one of the good demons."

They had no words at the gate of the 404th. The guards, rifles slung, silently opened the gate. Ko had asked Shan not to go inside.

Shan offered his hand. His son took it, then abruptly pulled his father into a tight embrace. *"Lha gyal lo,"* he whispered, then just as abruptly pushed Shan away, spun about, and marched back into his prison.

Shan parked his truck in an alley near the County Administration Center and watched as lights blinked out in the offices. The county seat had grown significantly in the years since he had first been released into the town. The nighttime streets then had been mostly dark and nearly devoid of activity. Now half a dozen streets had lights that cast a garish orange glow, and several restaurants were open for the evening meal. He got out and paced around the block, acquainting himself with the changed terrain, then entered the office building.

The surly guard at the desk, detailed from the military police, cast him a resentful glare but did not stop him from entering the elevator. Shan suspected he had known the man at the 404th, had probably known his boot on his back.

Little had changed in the offices on the top floor. The low table in the waiting area still had one of Amah Jiejie's lace doilies on it. The decoration on the walls was 1980s proletarian style, with faded posters of joyful peasant girls that somehow seemed quaint. WORK IS REDEMPTION, instructed a banner that had hung on the wall for years, one of the few political slogans that Tan had ever embraced.

Amah Jiejie was at her desk, leaning toward a computer screen.

"Xiao Shan!" she beamed. "What a coincidence! I was just on the phone with the 404th. Back safe in his barracks." She was as gruff as Tan to most outsiders, but the ever-attentive aunt to those she had taken under her wing. She saw the glance he cast toward the door behind her. "Gone, not half an hour. Talked a while with the janitor then left."

Shan was not sure he had heard correctly. Tan never even acknowledged Tibetan workers, let alone speak with them. "The janitor?"

"An old Tibetan. They've been doing it most nights for months, since he came back from his lung surgery. The colonel was out of cigarettes one night and the old man gave him one. Some nights he has me bring them beer." The gray-haired woman hesitated. "A secret, Shan. He wouldn't want anyone to know."

"Of course he wouldn't. Is he at dinner then?"

"Probably back to his quarters. He won't admit it, but he has never fully recovered from his surgery. The long dinners far into the night are a thing of the past."

"I was wondering, Amah. Do you see requests for reassignment of guards?"

"At the prisons? Usually. Elsewhere prison staff becomes a dumping ground for undesirables. In Lhadrung we are more particular." She hesitated, then nodded and dove into a stack of papers. "Here. It already happened, this afternoon. He denied the request."

Shan scanned the sheet she handed him. As always, she been able to read his mind. It was a form requesting transfer of a sergeant from the 34th Mountain Commandos to the staff of the 404th. Lau had moved fast. The general had wanted someone watching Ko.

"The general's team took over a guesthouse at the east edge of town," Amah Jiejie explained. "He's keeping a suite in a hotel in Lhasa too, using army helicopters like his personal taxi service. The colonel uttered some unpleasant words about wasting army resources, but I reminded him that at least this way we know where the gentleman is." She saw Shan look out the window toward the east side of the town. "I'll draw you a map," she offered.

Shan easily found the guesthouse, a two-story stucco structure built with red enameled posts at its corners to suggest the lacquered posts of imperial Chinese buildings. He circled it in the shadows, noting two cars with military plates, then leaned against a tree, studying it until a match flared in a sedan parked across the street.

Tan greeted him with a snarl as Shan opened the door and sat beside him.

"The idea of surveillance is to be inconspicuous," Shan said. "This car has a county insignia on it."

Tan shrugged. "I thought about taking the Red Flag, but I wasn't sure what to do with my driver. Yintai checks with him every day and is told I spend all my time at the construction site." His cigarette burned bright as he inhaled, and Shan saw a metallic reflection on the seat. Tan had a pistol beside him.

"This is a job best left for others, colonel."

"He sent a messenger with an envelope this afternoon. Private. My eyes only." Tan extracted a folded piece of paper from his pocket and extended it toward Shan.

Shan lifted the matches from the dashboard and lit one to read it. It was a scanned copy of a deposit slip for a Hong Kong bank. It showed that half a million American dollars had been deposited into an account in Tan's name.

"The bastard thinks either I'll accept it and be his puppet, or if I lift a hand against him, he will have it sent to one of those spotlight teams that prosecute corruption. It would be the end of me."

"You have friends in Beijing."

"Not many left. Most are dead or retired."

Shan motioned toward the pistol. "This is no answer."

"Or it's the answer to everything. Your ways are too subtle. You play the fox. But I was always a lion. When I die, I will die as a lion."

They watched the house in silence. There seemed to be some kind of party going on. They heard music and the laughter of women.

"Amah Jiejie found what she could on Sergeant Ma. No commando.

Just a driver, an equipment operator who had been a cab driver before the army."

"For all these years Lau assumed there was no evidence of what he had done," Shan explained. "But somehow he learned that a witness was alive, an anonymous, faceless witness. That changed everything. That's when the killing began, not just last month. First Constable Fen had to be eliminated, because he was going to share the news with Tibetans."

"A witness? How could a witness survive for all these years without Lau knowing?"

"Because he's been hiding in plain sight. Kept alive on a bowl of cold porridge and twelve ounces of rice a day."

When Tan turned to Shan, the anger in his eyes had been replaced with inquiry. Shan lifted the gun, extracted its magazine, and tossed it on the dashboard before explaining what he knew about the drawings.

"If Lau knew about this prisoner he wouldn't survive the week," Shan stated.

"So he's no use to us. He's not dumb. He must know his silence has kept him alive all these years."

"He's very old and probably dying. That's why he finally acted. We need him. You can hide him. Prisoner reassignments happen all the time. I have his registration number. Make an excuse for transferring several men from his prison to the 404th, including him. Get him back to Lhadrung. And no one is to know. If he is singled out, he's dead."

Tan seemed offended. "No one is murdered in my prisons, comrade."

Shan found himself looking away, into the shadows, swallowing his reaction. It was not the time to debate the finer points of prison culture. "Accidents happen," he said instead. "Lau wouldn't kill him, not right away. He would find a way for him to suffer an accident, then have an ambulance standing by to whisk him away."

"I'm not sure I follow. You said the man would be killed."

"First Lau will interrogate him, torture him. The general isn't so worried about someone publicizing what happened in the Ghost Mountains. He has people to take care of such things. This is China, where even reports of bad weather get censored. The story would never get out. Even if there was some leak on the Internet there would be a counter story issued, probably saying it is just the Tibetan resistance issuing false stories to embarrass the government. No, when Lau heard that secret drawings had surfaced in Yangkar, he assumed they were about the lost treasure, or that at least the one who made them would know about it."

"Chasing a myth," Tan said.

"I think he knows what I know now. In 1966 fifty mules arrived from Lhasa carrying secret cargo from the palace. Twenty of them were unloaded at the old medical college. Lau knows those twenty carried gold bars and gems because he took them all. Thirty mules of the treasure caravan were never accounted for. Say the missing mules carried only gold. Each mule could carry at least two hundred pounds. Lau's done the math, probably runs the calculation every day based on the market. At least six thousand pounds. Three tons of gold. Ninety-six thousand ounces."

Tan was silent long enough to light another cigarette and exhale out the window. "And he gave me a mere five hundred thousand? I should be insulted."

Shan knew the money was of no more interest to Tan than it was to Shan himself. What mattered to Tan more than anything was the integrity of his precious army. "It's why he won't leave," Shan said. "Returning Sergeant Ma was a distraction, not a finishing blow. It kept him from Ko but raised the stakes. And made us his enemy."

Tan stared at the house. "I could have a team of my men here in a quarter hour, arrest the lot of them inside. I want that prick Yintai in a military prison. Shoveling phosphorus."

"No. The killers I want aren't in that house, they are in Yangkar. If they find the treasure for Lau, they win new lives, a new incarnation with wealth and power in Hong Kong. They can smell it. They are getting sloppy. Don't make them shy away."

"So what do you need?"

"Find that prisoner. And keep Lau interested. Don't let him go back to Hong Kong just yet. I want his agents in Yangkar to know he's waiting on them, impatiently standing by for them to take him to the Dalai Lama's treasure."

CHAPTER FOURTEEN

Shan, sipping his tea, was watching dawn wash over the western range when a long wail split the quiet of the café. He heard Marpa's muffled voice trying to comfort a weeping child. Shan rose, then halted in the doorway to the kitchen. Lodi was clinging to his uncle, talking through long sobs as Marpa seemed to argue with him. Shan watched as the frustrated uncle took the boy by his shoulders and turned him toward the dining room.

Lodi cried out and frantically slipped behind his uncle.

Marpa looked at Shan with wide, frightened eyes. "I'm sorry," he said as Shan approached. "I don't know what he . . . The boy says Constable Shan is dead." As he spoke, Lodi took a tentative step from behind his uncle. Shan stood motionless as the boy, his face drained of color, reached out and poked Shan with a finger. He backed away, his eyes still wide, then darted out the door. A moment later he reappeared, Raj the mastiff at his side.

Lodi halted a few feet away, still fearfully gazing at Shan. The dog approached, probing Shan with its nose as it circled, then wagged its tail and sat at Shan's feet.

A joyful cry escaped the boy's throat and he leapt forward to embrace Shan. "Some old ghost played a trick up on the mountain!" he exclaimed.

. . .

The trick played by the ghost had attracted a crowd of frightened on-lookers by the time Lodi guided their two borrowed horses over the ridge toward the salt caravan shrine. Shan could see his own truck, which had been missing when he ran to the station, at the little flat where the caravan trail met the road, along with half a dozen other vehicles, including Jinhua's sedan. At the sharp bend in the trail where Shan often coasted on his bike after visiting the shrine, a crowd stared mournfully over the cliff.

No one saw him descending the trail until he was a hundred feet away. Someone shouted and others began pointing at him. Half the assembly fled, running toward the road. Jinhua grinned at him. Jengtse stared in confusion. He stepped back and pointed below.

The uniformed body had tumbled off the curving cliff trail on a bicycle.

Jinhua stepped to Shan's side. "It does look like a constable's tunic," the officer observed.

"Not mine. Not Jengtse's," Shan said. "No one has bothered to go down there?"

"The death of a policeman is a matter for Public Security, they said. I arrived only minutes ago."

"Get some ropes," Shan ordered Jengtse, then made an impatient gesture for Jinhua to follow him up the track to where the cliff faded into a less steep descent.

Ten minutes later the two men stood over the body, whose head was obscured under a thick growth of heather. A few feet away lay the twisted remains of a bicycle.

"Who else would be assigned to this area?" Jinhua asked as he bent to pull back the bush. "Do you know the constable from the nearest—" He turned away and vomited.

Mrs. Weng's lips were curled up in an expression of surprised rage. She was still angry in her death.

"Where would she get a tunic?" Jinhua asked as he recovered, glancing nervously toward the expectant Tibetans above. Jengtse and Tserung were tying a rope to a boulder.

Shan looked more closely at what the dead woman was wearing. The tunic had none of the insignia common to a uniform and only plain black buttons. "Secondhand," Shan observed. "The fool, always pretending to be an official." A blue cap, devoid of markings but very similar to Shan's uniform cap, lay beside the body.

"It worked," Jinhua said as he straightened the body. Weng's lifeless arm, which had been covering her neck, dropped onto the gravelly, blood-soaked soil. "Good enough to fool the killer."

Shan, studying the cliff face as he worked out the plunge of the bicycle, turned. "What do you mean?"

"You go up there sometimes, on your bike."

"Yes, but I wasn't—"

"A lot of work to go up," Jinhua interrupted, "and you probably have to walk your bike up that last steep section. But then you can coast down."

"Yes, but—"

"On a bike she would sit much the way you do. Neck at the same height. Short hair covered by a blue cap. The killer was watching from a distance and went to work after she went up the ridge."

Shan stepped closer to the corpse. "I don't understand why you . . ." His words choked away as he followed Jinhua's extended hand.

Weng's head lay at an unnatural angle. Half the neck had been severed. A length of thin silver wire extended from one side of the sliced flesh.

"A sloppy job," Jinhua said. "The wire was strung across the path at the right height, but it came undone at one end. Otherwise we'd be searching for her head."

A cold fist seemed to grip Shan's chest.

"They all said you were dead," Jinhua continued. "You were supposed to be dead. This trap was laid for you. But the bitch couldn't stop interfering. She came into the station when Jengtse and I were there. She asked for my card, wanted to see my badge. She asked what you were investigating, and I told her that was for official law enforcement only. Then she wanted to know what it was that you found so interesting at that old salt shrine. She said—her words— that you were a secret revisionist and the town had to be warned."

A whistle from above broke Shan's stunned silence. Jengtse was waving the end of a rope.

Shan stepped away from the body and cupped his hands to his mouth. "It's Mrs. Weng! She had a biking accident. Send down a blanket!"

It was nearly an hour before the grisly recovery task was completed and the little convoy of vehicles departed for Yangkar, leaving Jinhua standing with Shan by the constable's truck, with Mrs. Weng's blanket-wrapped body lying in the cargo bed. The lieutenant seemed to understand Shan's intentions and was the first back up the trail.

The thin wire had been strung in the perfect location, at the base of the steepest part of the trail and just before the sharp curve at the cliff. It had sprung back on itself and was tangled against a root that extended from a split in a ledge rock. Opposite the root, growing at the lip of the cliff, was a gnarled juniper with one limb that leaked sap where the wire had scraped away bark. Jinhua gauged the height by putting a flattened hand on his chest. "Unlucky for her that she was the same height as you. A bigger person might have just received a nasty cut in the shoulder."

Shan pulled the wire free and coiled it around his hand before stuffing it in his pocket and ascending farther up the trail, a grousing Jinhua a few steps behind.

Mrs. Weng had indeed visited the salt shrine. The first three of the saints were toppled over, one of them broken in half. The fourth, the constable saint, still stood but had a stick embedded where one of its eyes should have been.

Jinhua sensed Shan's despair and stood silently with him before the eroded sculpture. "They're old," he finally offered.

"Centuries," Shan replied. He had not anticipated the deep sense of grief he felt at seeing the toppled statues. "The caravans came this way for centuries. Some would have two or three hundred sheep wearing special packs filled with salt, some with yaks carrying much bigger loads. It was a way of life, traveling hundreds of miles, sometimes all the way to Nepal or even India. Some sort of miracle probably occurred here that caused the shrine to be built, though it's lost in time. They all had faces once, careful representations of old saints, and offerings would have been left here for a safe return to loved ones. Centuries," he repeated. "But they didn't have a chance against the Committee of Leading Citizens." Shan extracted the stick out of the saint's eye and patted the top of his head.

"Surely you're not going to let her win," Jinhua said from behind him. Shan turned to see that the lieutenant had his tunic off and was walking back to the toppled statues. "We can do this, comrade," he called out and rolled up his sleeves.

Using tree limbs for levers they were able to right the two unbroken statues. They raised the base of the other, then Jinhua sank a limb in the ground along its back. As Shan held the broken top in place, Jinhua used the wire from Shan's pocket to fasten it to the supporting limb.

Shan was so touched by the lieutenant's satisfied smile that he waited until they were back at their vehicles before he told him his next task.

"Not possible!" Jinhua protested. "Never!" He backed away, staring wide-eyed at Weng's shrouded body.

"You must," Shan said as he pulled down the tailgate. "Her body cannot be examined." He stepped to Jinhua's car and opened the trunk. "The crematorium is outside of Lhasa, just past the first big bridge."

"I can't just show up in the middle of the night with an obviously murdered corpse and tell them to cremate it."

"You can if you show them your Public Security badge. Buy one of those cartons for shipping. She had a sister in Nanjing."

Dorchen steadfastly followed the old Tibetan custom of dismounting and walking beside his horse when ascending steep slopes, making their progress into the mountains slow and laborious. Time was short, Shan knew, and Pure Water College still had not given up its secrets. The *amchi* had reluctantly agreed to take Shan to the vantage point of the drawings, but only if they would go by way of the old *dzong*.

When they reached the ridge overlooking the ruined fortress, the *amchi* halted and studied the landscape in silence. "My father brought us this way when we brought my mother for healing that first time. We slept there"—he gestured to the little flat with cairns Shan had spied on his prior visit—"because my father wanted to reach the gate of the Pure Water College at dawn, the most propitious hour. A pilgrim was camped there too and warned us that powerful earth gods lived in the old *dzong*. There were prayer scarves tied to the bushes all around the mound, to pay homage to them. They had grown weary of men always crawling on their backs, so one day they rose up and threw all the stones down. The tale terrified me, but later, when we were staying in the college while my mother received treatment, I realized that the pilgrim hadn't said evil gods, he just said powerful gods. There were days when my father spent hours in one of the chapels and I would escape and come back over here."

Dorchen began leading his horse toward the *dzong*. "At first I just crept up that far ridge on my belly and stayed flattened at the top so the gods would not see me. But after a few days I ventured into the ruins. I was intensely curious but also intensely frightened, and when one of the rocks inside rose up I fell onto my knees and begged for forgiveness. The god laughed and I threw myself prostrate at his feet."

The dry chuckle from the *amchi* was the first time Shan had ever heard Dorchen laugh. "He was one of the monks, who preferred to wear a dark brown robe because he was a forager, who went into the wilds to gather medicines and didn't like to frighten the animals. He was a jovial soul who became one of my favorite teachers. It was from him that I first learned the traditional name for this area. Before it was the Ghost Mountains, it was the Medicine Mountains. He was the one who raised the leopard who lived at the college, had discovered him as an injured cub and healed him. He insisted that any herb that had been touched by one of the great beasts of the wild always had more power, and he was constantly looking for places where they slept."

Dorchen tethered his horse to a small spruce and sprang up the earthen ramp with surprising energy, disappearing behind the great blocks of the ruins. Shan found him by following the sound of muffled laughter from inside what was the largest pile of fallen slabs. He had to crawl on all fours down a short passage and found himself in a small, dim chamber. Dorchen was standing before a stuccoed wall with a faded painting of a white elephant carrying a jovial Buddha. "Always my favorite. Those who built this place did not shrink from the joys of life." He paused, then with boyish energy reached into a wide crack in the wall that ran up into the elephant's mouth. With a gleeful cry he pulled out a leather-wrapped bundle. "My first master always said when I did this, be careful or the elephant will bite you!" He shook the dust from the bundle, laid it on a fallen slab and unwrapped it, revealing the dried wing of a bird, its yellow feathers fading to brown, a little crystalline stone, and a scrap of paper with Tibetan script written in a crude, child's hand. *Gem medicine, stone medicine, soil medicine, fire medicine,* it said.

Dorchen flushed. "I was just a boy, learning the classifications of medicines," he murmured, then seemed to lose himself in memories. Shan silently retreated. It was another ten minutes before Dorchen climbed out of the low tunnel. He was much more somber now and seemed not to notice Shan as he paced around the ruins, pausing every few moments to place his fingers on the ruined walls, as if taking their pulse.

Shan worried that his tide of memories was pulling the old man too far away. *"Amchi?"*

Dorchen turned to him with a sad smile. "I have never been back here, Shan, never since . . . since then. I used to worry about what I would do if I had a patient up here. But no one ever comes here, no one lives up here. Only Nyima. And she is beloved of the gods."

They spoke no more until they had mounted and ridden out of the little valley, and only then when Dorchen exclaimed over sightings of birds and the small mammals of the high altitudes. At a small verdant shelf the *amchi* dismounted, saying the horses would rest there, then he led Shan up a goat path, so steep they often had to grab onto the exposed roots of wind-beaten shrubs to pull themselves up.

By the time they reached the cave high up the mountain a dozen questions were on Shan's lips, but as he stepped over the low wall at its entry he found himself strangely mute. If indeed, as the traditional Tibetans insisted, there were spiritual power places in Tibet, then surely this was one. The low wall across the eight-foot-wide entrance had been built so long ago that its surface was encased in lichen, giving it the appearance of a natural formation. The walls inside had been shaped by the hand of man, not to give them crisp angles, but to highlight their subtle features. What the Tibetans called a self-manifesting Buddha smiled down from a fold in the rock, a series of naturally occurring curves and hollows unmistakably forming his face and even his bald temples. The living rock below had been carved in the shape of a robe, including a necklace bearing a stone *gau* amulet that seemed styled after that of the Pure Water abbot. On the wall opposite, Buddhist symbols had been painted in some distant century. Most were so faded as to be impossible to identify, but Shan saw the hint of a bat, a conch, and a lotus. Above them, where wall and ceiling met, a long seam of reddish rock had been subtly worked to suggest a dragon. In the back of the cave, which was only twenty feet deep, was a pile of rotting cloth that may have been a pallet. On it were bits of bluish wool where wild goats had slept.

Somewhere over their heads the wind was caught in a fissure, creating a very low humming sound, the pitch of which rose and fell with the wind. It was as if the mountain were offering up the great harmonizing syllable *om*. It was a chamber of stone and spirit, where nature, men, and gods were as one.

"We were taught that once this had been the place of lifelong hermits," Dorchen explained. "The front wall had been all the way to the top then, with little holes for small buckets of grain and water to be passed through once a week to the hermit inside. When I was at the college, coming here involved a somber duty. The abbot had to approve each person who came, and no one was allowed who did not vow to stay seven days, in absolute silence except for his recitations of scriptures and mantras. Failure to do so would disrespect the countless generations of devout souls who had used the cave. Only once did I know of a monk who violated that rule. The abbot called for an assembly, then ripped the robe off the man's back and sent him away with an alms bowl."

Dorchen approached the self-manifesting Buddha and dipped his head, then rubbed the stone *gau*, shiny from centuries of such gestures. "It was always deemed good luck to rub his *gau*," he said with a melancholy smile, then stepped to the entrance. His face was so twisted by emotion that Shan was beginning to regret bringing the old man to the place.

As Dorchen stared down at the empty plain of the old medical college, less than a mile away, Shan laid the drawings out on the half wall, anchoring them with stones. The cave was, unquestionably, the viewpoint from the drawings.

"Who would come here," Shan asked, "amid the chaos of the Red Guard being at the college?"

"I don't know. I was gone. The abbot would have tried to keep everything as normal as possible. He might have sent a monk up here to calm him, to keep him focused in adversity. A test of his spirit."

"If someone was up here, wouldn't they have run down when they saw the distress at the college?"

"I told you. One week. It was a sacred rule. There were no exceptions."

"Seven days," Shan said. "He drew the feathers over the stable. That means he knew the ravens were there and had been at the college to hide the treasure."

"Only the most senior of lamas would have known such secrets."

"I think our witness was a senior lama. Maybe he wasn't sent here to meditate, he was sent here for his protection, to save one life at least, to save his life. Now at the end of his life he's trying to pass on those secrets with these drawings."

Dorchen, clearly in torment, said nothing.

"The Red Guard came. Then the army. You were away the entire time?"

"There used to be trees," Dorchen said in a hollow voice, pointing to the north side of the plain, around the well. "Tall junipers, even an oak or two."

"Why weren't there trees in the drawing?" Shan asked, then answered his own question. "Because they were taken down while the Chinese were there. He drew what he saw. Instead of trees he drew a small circle, a circle of smaller circles really."

Dorchen bent over the first drawing. "The circle of stones around the old well, disused since the big earthquake in the prior century." He indicated a little structure outside the oval of *chortens* at the opposite end of the plain. "The new well. That's what we called it, though it had been used for many decades by then."

Shan pointed to the last drawing. "I still don't understand this one. Monks and birds and horses dancing in the air. "

"Monks and ravens," Dorchen corrected. "And we never had horses. Mules."

The *amchi* went very still. He stared at a large black bird circling high over the plain of the old college.

"The sign of the raven was over the last building," Shan stated.

Dorchen glanced uneasily at Shan, then back at the solitary raven that seemed to be keeping watch over the plain. Or was it watching them? The *amchi* sighed and put a hand on the wall as if he suddenly needed support. "Forgive me, Shan, for the truths I have not told you."

The *amchi* went back to the Buddha and bowed his head to gather strength before continuing. "I have told you no lies," he declared in a pained voice, his head still bowed. "But I have not given you the full truth." He seemed much older and careworn when he turned back to Shan.

"I did first come to Pure Water with my ailing mother. What I did not say was that my father then was a minor official in Lhasa, one of those who communicated with *gompas* all over central Tibet to coordinate food and other supplies. If one *gompa* had a poor harvest, he would see that those who had not suffered shared their bounty. In the time we spent here at the college he grew very attached to the abbots of Yangkar *gompa* and the college. Over the years while I studied, he rose in rank and entered the inner circles of government. He was entrusted with other duties, taking care of more than supplies. Protecting holy assets, he would sometimes say."

"You mean secret assets," Shan suggested.

"Not only those, but yes. The office of the Dalai Lama had set aside reserves and other treasures for hard times. There was much gold, though most of the gold was held for use in making statues of deities or gilding temple roofs to honor the gods. My father felt honor bound to protect such things, and he stayed behind when the Dalai Lama left." Dorchen stared out at the empty plain of the college. "They urged him to go, to leave the treasures, because there would be many new *gompas* to be built and managed in India and Nepal, but he would not hear of it. He said the treasures were a link between Tibetans and their gods."

"So he stayed behind and worked with the ravens."

Dorchen nodded. "I did go to Chokpori, the medical college in Lhasa to study, but not just to study, and I did not always stay there during the time I was assigned there. I carried messages back and forth, because I knew so many of the officials and the ravens. The treasure had been well concealed in Lhasa, but as the Red Guard advanced we knew it would not be safe. Pure Water College seemed the perfect place. So remote. So difficult to get to. My father saw to it that the records were altered, so that the college did not even appear on any official lists of *gompas*, then he hid the lists, but not too well, for he wanted the Chinese to find them and think them authentic.

"First the ravens moved everything to Chokpori, on the outskirts of Lhasa, hiding everything in normal deliveries. When all was ready, I helped my father and the ravens load the mules. Fifty mules."

"The Chinese who took over Yangkar studied the caravan records," Shan explained. "There was one they couldn't account for. Fifty mules, with ten teamsters and ten others. The others were ravens."

"Yes. By then most of them carried weapons, mostly pistols that had been dropped from the sky in the packages sent by the Americans. Squads of the resistance were assigned to meet the caravan at intervals and escort it. Someone from the college who knew of the old secret trails was sent to meet it when it approached Yangkar."

"The gold was in the last of the buildings standing, the final one destroyed," Shan ventured.

"We were always so innocent. No one ever thought about thieves or nonbelievers like those Chinese. The ravens probably thought it clever to conceal gold in the stables, probably under fodder or at the bottom of the big jars of grain fed to the animals."

"It took three days to destroy it," Shan stated. "The other buildings were demolished by then. The raven sign over the building must mean they defended it. A last stand."

"The Chinese were probably frightened of damaging the gold," Dorchen continued, "so they used no fire, no explosives. The defenders probably only had the bullets in their guns. I doubt they even aimed to kill their attackers, just wound them. They were monks, not soldiers." Dorchen wiped at an eye. "I've never told anyone this, not all these years."

"There was more, *amchi*, thirty mules unaccounted for. I think it was more valuable than the gold. By putting the gold in the stable and defending it there, they let the Chinese believe they had found the Dalai Lama's fortune. They were monks, but warrior monks. They could have found a way to flee. They knew they had to die there, to complete the ruse."

Dorchen gave a ragged sigh and stared again at the raven.

"Did you ever encounter the Red Guard?" Shan asked.

"By the time they reached Lhasa, we had heard horrible stories. We fled into the mountains, stayed in camps the resistance set up for a while, until the food ran out. I met a young boy in one of those camps, only ten years old, who months earlier had been sent by his family to work at Yangkar *gompa*, where his parents thought he would be safe. He sometimes ran messages between the *gompa* in town and the college. The Red Guard had been at Yangkar for weeks already, had built their base and had begun to hold their trials. He had still been able to go back and forth, in the night, between Yangkar and the college. The boy had delivered a message for the abbot of the college saying that all those there should hide in the mountains, but then a big company of Red Guard arrived. He was trapped there because no one was permitted to leave.

"The first day they put those dunce hats on the abbot and the senior lamas, then tore off their robes and made them parade around the circuit of *chortens* in their underwear. The Chinese hit them with switches if they went too slow and made them chant slogans about Mao. After a few hours they arranged them in two lines and made them throw stones at each other, and no one was allowed to stop until they had drawn blood from another. The boy kept asking me, where were the parents of those young Chinese, that their parents should have been told what they were doing. They were just teenagers, but they carried army guns. Those teenagers had their own parade, he said, shooting guns in the air and shouting '*Zaofan! Zaofan!*' It meant 'rebellion,' of course, but no one in the college would have known. The next day they hung their red flags from the eaves of the buildings and began their trials. They made the monks open the base of a *chorten* and they took out the mummified lama inside to the courtyard where they tried him for oppression of the peasants and cut off his head." Dorchen's voice trailed off as he watched the raven swoop low over the plain.

"On the second day after their arrival, they forced everyone inside the main assembly hall and stood guard while others searched the grounds, destroying many old things as they did so. The next day the army arrived. The abbot was relieved at first because the officer in charge seemed more responsible, even offended by what the Red Guard had done. The leader of the Red Guard shouted at the officer, saying they were in charge, and the officer slapped him like a spoiled child. I think everyone expected the army to be more respectful."

Dorchen's voice became a hoarse whisper. "The soldiers sent the Red Guard back to their base and then ordered all the young Tibetans to leave. The boy fled into the mountains. After that I don't know exactly what happened. I should have gone back," he added after a moment.

"There was nothing you could have done."

"I spent months trying to find my father, praying all the time that he had had the sense to finally flee across the border. I took my robe off and posed as a beggar in Lhasa, then later in Shigatse, looking for him or anyone who might have seen him. Finally I found one of the palace cooks, in a line of workers hauling night soil out of an army base. He said my father had never fled Lhasa and had been one of the first the Red Guards put on trial, in the courtyard of the Norbulingka, the old summer palace in Lhasa. He threw off the dunce cap they put on him and kicked down the stool where he was supposed to sit. He had memorized enough Chinese to say one thing, to be sure his accusers understood. 'May the Dalai Lama live ten thousand years!' he shouted, again and again. They shot him in the head and threw his body in the river." His voice faded as he watched the raven again, tracing its path with a finger in the air.

"I made my way back to Lhasa on old pilgrim trails, out of sight of any Chinese. When I finally arrived I sat by the river and recited the Bardo rites for the soul of my father. I prayed for five days and nights. It should have been longer, but I was tired and hungry and soldiers began taking shots at me from across the river. I think they had decided I was a spy. I didn't move. I laughed. I wanted them to kill me. But the fools were bad shots.

"The next morning I put on my robe. I knew more Chinese than my father. I was filled with rage. I was going to the army barracks and make a speech. I had rehearsed all night. You can't kill Tibet, I was going to say, for Tibet lived in the Dalai Lama, who was an eternal spirit. Their Mao, I was going to say, was a lowly beetle who would burst into flame when he felt the heat of the Dalai Lama."

"Your body would soon have been in the river with your father's."

Dorchen gave a bitter grin. "There was an old woman sweeping the street outside the army base. She saw the defiance in my eyes. I blessed her as I passed, and she promptly knocked me unconscious. I woke up in beggar's clothes, packed into a truck with other Tibetans, on the way to a labor camp."

"She saved your life."

"And many were the days when I cursed her for it." The *amchi* sighed. "But the gods look after tormented souls. I was imprisoned with a dozen medical professors from Chokpori. We worked on Chinese roads all day but for half the night they secretly taught us. A lot of good doctors came out of that prison. Especially adept at treating malnutrition, frostbite, and broken bones."

They silently watched a wild goat wander across the slope below, grazing on cinquefoil blossoms.

The *amchi*'s gaze drifted back to the circling raven. "They say ravens live for long decades. Maybe that one was there."

"A bird didn't make those drawings. Who could have been sent here by the abbot?"

"Monks and nuns were sent here for many reasons. Sometimes as punishment, sometimes as a reward. Sometimes as penance, to reflect on sinful acts or sinful thought."

"But why then, when the Red Guard was there? Why would they allow him to leave the college?"

Dorchen shrugged and looked down at the drawings. "We will never know."

"You said a guide was sent from Pure Water to lead the ravens here. A perilous job—a job involving great secrets, which must mean it was a senior lama."

"Whomever it was," Dorchen said, "he had the courage to give the drawings to the old constable but not the courage to stay."

"The one who brought the drawings was only a messenger."

Dorchen's brow furrowed. "Those drawings could have been made years ago. Decades even. The one who drew them is probably long dead."

"No. The paper is new. It was salvaged, you could say, the original words scraped off. It had been recently taken from a prison bulletin board."

Dorchen stared at Shan in disbelief. He took several long breaths before he could find his tongue. "Impossible. A monk from Pure Water? No. We would have known. He would have reached out. There would have been messages years ago. And why would they keep one monk alive after killing all the others?"

"I don't think they knew about him. I think he was sent up here just before the violence started, maybe because the abbot wanted to protect him, maybe as a reward for helping the ravens. I think he kept the rules about his stay here, then left after his seven days here and was arrested elsewhere, so he was never connected to Pure Water College. And I believe he had good reason to keep his existence a secret. To protect lives, and perhaps something greater."

"Something greater?"

"There is still treasure there, unaccounted for. Those missing thirty mules were carrying it. It's why the general is here, why he kept his agents here for years. The man who drew these has the secret those agents have been killing for. I think somewhere in these drawings there is a clue to it."

Dorchen's countenance clenched with pain. "I don't want to believe it. Do you grasp the agony he must have lived with?"

"Fifty years and more in prison. He glimpses the end of his life. He decided to finally reach out, in his own way, a way that would be understood by only a few, so the secret could be passed on."

Dorchen gazed at Shan, his face desolate. Then he looked up at the circling raven, down at the empty plain, and wept.

CHAPTER FIFTEEN

Dorchen was so withdrawn as they rode down the mountain that he only acknowledged Shan with a weary wave of his hand when Shan announced he was taking a track that veered off from the Yangkar path. He watched the forlorn old Tibetan, worried that he had ripped open a wound that would now never heal, then nudged his mount forward.

He approached the plain of the old college slowly, studying it as if seeing it for the first time. Everything in the secret drawings had had a meaning, an intention of the witness. Dorchen had finally interpreted the signs Shan could not understand. Everything had played a role. Pistols, pick axes, mules, ravens, drinking skulls, and what Dorchen had described as sleeping gods had been drawn beside the sacred signs. Guiding his horse down onto the plain, he let it free to graze as he walked the oval of the ruined *chortens*. The Tibetans would never have used the sacred tombs as hiding places, but their locations had been carefully noted on the drawings, as though they were reference points. He stood by one of the slabs he and Jinhua had exposed, then slowly began pacing the ground beyond it. In the first drawing there had been a small circle of stones on this northwest side of the plain, where trees had once grown. Heather and wind-beaten rhododendron prevented him from clearly seeing the surface, and it was nearly a quarter hour before he found the old structure. A shiver ran up his spine, and he realized the air over the circle of stones was noticeably cooler. He leaned over the empty well. The air in the well was very still and very cold. He cleared away one side of the ring, then went back to the borrowed horse and to his relief found in the saddle bag one of the coils of thick cord that farmers and herders often carried with them in the high meadows, ready to tether an animal or even make a temporary corral.

At one end of the cord he fashioned a harness for his plastic water bottle and lowered it. Over thirty feet had uncoiled when the cord went slack. He tied the cord, then rose and stepped to the edge of the steep, fifty-foot embankment that ended in the wide ledge where the caves opened. He had seen many underground springs emerge from the side of Tibetan mountains, but here, though the spring of the well would logically have run downward, there was no stream, no waterfall. He studied the gravelly slope below him and saw now the little eroded swale where indeed water had once flowed.

Suddenly he remembered the passage from the 1897 manuscript that been stored with the final records in 1966. *The earth deities woke briefly last week. We lost a temple wall, three chorten steeples, and the well. We bid good slumber to the beloved gods.* The old well had been lost in the great earthquake at the end of the nineteenth century. The words of the old manuscript echoed in his mind as he returned to the well and retrieved the bottle. A half-inch of ice had formed on its bottom.

Ten minutes later he stood by the ice cave. He paced along its entrance, studying its irregular mouth, then the jumble of rocks that blocked further passage along the ledge that led toward the chasm at the north edge of the Plain of Ghosts. Below, on the embankment that led to the parking area, hundreds of rocks had been dumped. He slid a few feet down the embankment to lift some of the rocks. They were all small and sharp edged, nothing like the weathered boulders elsewhere on the slope.

Lighting one of the lanterns that had been left at the entry, he stepped inside the now-empty cave, first rubbing his hand along the rough ice along the back wall and then turning, lantern raised, to study the demons on the front wall, the way Lokesh would have done. The deities Begtse and Brahma flanked the entry. Above them were Palden Lhamo, Vaisravana, and Yama. They were known as fierce protectors of the faith and numbered among the eight *dharmapalas*, the Eight Defenders. Shan had had a vague sense that something about the *gonkang* chapel was incomplete, and now he understood. The three most fierce drinkers of blood—Yamantaka, Hayagriva, and Mahakala—were missing. Sleeping gods. The drawings held images of sleeping gods. *We bid good slumber to the beloved gods,* a monk had written after the earthquake of 1897.

Back on the Plain of Ghosts he studied the drawings again and visualized where the stable must have stood. He kicked at the dirt with his heel until he found a line of set stone that had been a foundation, exposing it until he reached a corner. Then he lowered himself onto the sparse grass that grew out of what must have been the earthen floor of the structure, tucking his legs under him in meditation position and arranging his fingers in a steeple, the Diamond of the Mind *mudra*.

Once again he weighed each of the pieces of his puzzle, satisfied finally that at least now he understood what had happened during the last days of the college and how Nyima had spent her years in the land where no other human walked. He lost all track of time as fragments of the horror appeared in his mind's eye, and he did not stir until the horse, more mindful of the lowering sun, nuzzled his shoulder.

The outcroppings above town that marked his house had come into sight when an old yak lumbered across the track in front of him to reach a patch of sweetgrass, trailing a splash of color from the thick hair of its neck. Shan hesitated, then dismounted. He tied the reins to the saddle and slapped the rump of the sturdy little horse, which gladly trotted off toward its home.

He circled the yak, speaking low comforting words. The massive creature recognized him, perhaps even recalled that Shan, mired up to his knees himself, had once helped free him from a muddy ford.

The old bull, the lama yak, was part of Lhamo and Trinle little's herd, and probably their most valuable animal, but now lengths of bright red yarn had been tied into the hair of the yak. The animal had been ransomed.

He congratulated the yak, stroking its broad head for a few minutes, then took a few steps toward his house before slowly turning as he realized the gravity of his discovery. The bounty to keep such an animal from suffering would have been huge, a life-changing sacrifice for anyone from Yangkar. The yak fixed him with a soulful stare, and Shan understood he was looking at an ending, an act of contrition by someone in personal anguish. The red yarn was a confession of sorts, if only to the gods.

There had indeed been terrible acts committed in Yangkar, and the one who now repudiated them would know the final secrets that had eluded Shan. But the ransomed yak didn't provide an answer, only another secret. The one who paid such a penance would never reveal himself to Shan, and the feral family that owned the yak was itself deeply secretive. They had been paid to never slay the great creature, to never harm it, to preserve it to the best of their ability, and they were unlikely to speak of it, partly out of fear of revealing the windfall they would have received, and partly because the gods always had a hand in ransoming.

Shan suspected the family had slipped away, back to their hidden life in the high ranges. But as he approached his house, he heard an unfamiliar rumble and saw a cloud of dust. Yara, standing by his door, was waving excitedly toward the track that led up to his house from town. Racing up the track was her grandfather, with Ati, laughing, clutched to his back. The old man was driving an orange motorcycle.

Jengtse was asleep in a cell when Shan returned to the station. He closed the door to the cell block, then rummaged in the back of a desk drawer and found a narrow strip of plastic, as thin as a credit card, which they had confiscated from a young burglar two months earlier. He stuffed it in a pocket and left the station.

More than once Shan had waited outside the building where Jengtse lived while Jengtse ran inside for something, but never had he ventured into the little second-floor apartment. He did not hesitate when he reached the landing, just inserted the strip between the door and the frame and swept it down, a skill he had not used since leaving Beijing. He heard a metallic click, turned the knob, and stepped inside.

The little tenement smelled faintly of garlic and beer. A surprisingly expensive television and sound system lay on a cabinet along one wall. A government-issued calendar was on a second wall, a poster of a military parade on another. With a self-loathing shudder, Shan began opening drawers and cabinets. In the only closet, the clothes he found were plain and simple, the kind a deputy might afford, but on a shelf above the hanging clothes a shoebox held a pair of shiny black loafers with tassels. Vanity, a forensic mentor once told him, started with shoes. Look for the shoes to find an edge of corruption.

Minutes later, in the back of a drawer of clothing, he pulled out what seemed to be a little bronze obelisk. Then he saw it was a souvenir, a replica of a clock tower. He held it under the light and stared at it for several long breaths. Along the bottom it said BIG BEN, LONDON.

Shan walked back to his office slowly, reconsidering every piece of the puzzle he thought he had solved. At the square he hesitated, then climbed up the old tower, where Lodi kept his vigil on the road. "That day the general came to town," he said to the boy. "You took something from his aide. The bully with the scarred neck."

"And didn't Uncle Marpa yell at me! But they weren't going to hurt a boy, not there, not then. I had to shout those words for my parents, to let them know I don't forget. They need to know I am not afraid, not even of a Chinese general."

"Yangkar, not Buzhou," Shan said, repeating what the boy had said to Yintai.

Lodi shrugged. "People say it all the time. I mean . . ." He seemed embarrassed.

"You mean when Tibetans here see Chinese."

Lodi gave a hesitant nod. "Kind of like a mantra."

"You took something from Yintai," Shan reminded the boy.

"I didn't expect that. Uncle Kapo was pleased."

"I don't understand," Shan admitted.

"Whenever I find a shiny object on the ground I snatch it up for him. He loves shiny things, buries them in his sand."

"But you had a beetle."

"In my other hand, yes. I was saving it to show Ati," the boy replied with a mischievous grin. "For a moment I thought that Chinese believed in Tibetan magic."

"What was it, your present to Uncle Kapo?"

"That? Just one of those tin discs the inn down the road passes out. You can exchange one for a free pot of tea. I've given Kapo four already, but he still buried it with joy."

The little inn ten miles south of Yangkar was called the Long Wheels, for the long-haul trucks that made its existence possible. The plump owner, a retired Chinese teacher, always tried to ingratiate himself to Shan, who suspected him of paying bribes for his various permits, and offered a free meal as soon as Shan stepped into the cramped, dusty lobby.

"A much smaller favor, comrade," Shan suggested. "A room number."

The man behind the plastic desk stiffened, then tilted his head to look out toward Shan's truck. "You need a bed for an hour or two, constable?" he asked with an uncertain grin.

"A man named Yintai has a room here."

The man's breath caught in his throat. "No! No one by that name, no."

"A big man with a long scar across his neck. A soldier, though maybe not always in uniform. Sometimes comes with one or two other men."

A tiny groan escaped the innkeeper's throat. His smile vanished. "No, no. Not that one." He took a step backward and glanced at the door as if thinking of fleeing his own establishment.

Shan reached behind the counter and turned off the electric OPEN sign. "Get a jacket. Maybe a pillow. You're coming with me for interrogation. I won't have time to bring you back tonight, but I have a vacant cell."

The man pushed the switch back on. "You don't know him. His eyes are like ice. My chambermaid got in his way and he kicked her to the floor."

"Just the number and the passkey. Or should I try every door?"

"If he knew . . ."

"Does he keep his window open?"

The innkeeper nodded.

"If he complains about someone intruding, say it must have been through the window. His own fault. You're just going to save me the trouble of climbing in and out the window."

"Number ten, at the back," the innkeeper fearfully whispered.

"Does he have visitors often?"

"Three men have a key. They come and go."

"Do you know the others?"

The man winced. "They come and go," he repeated.

"How do they get here?"

"I don't know," the man whined.

Shan switched the sign off again.

The innkeeper groaned and switched it back on. "A truck painted olive. An orange motorcycle. Once a helicopter brought men in military fatigues."

The room was surprisingly spacious, with a table in the center and two beds along opposite walls. The beds showed no sign of being slept in. One had military maps laid across it, depicting Yangkar Township and the land to the north, including the secret military base in the adjoining county. The table held maps of Tibet and glossy brochures of a seaside club in Hong Kong. On top of them was the death chart Shiva had prepared for Jake Bartram.

He parked his truck out of sight of the *amchi*'s house, downwind from the mastiffs, and made his way across the field to the dry riverbed, a lantern in one hand and a tire iron in the other. He found himself dodging puddles from the recent rain, and might have missed the little shed below the house, obscured as it was between two outcroppings, were it not for the rut of tire tracks that so plainly led up from the river. It was a compact, sturdy building, with a modern padlock on its heavy door. He edged the iron behind the hasp and with a single heave pulled it out of the wood.

The air inside was heavy with oil and gas fumes. Although the motorcycle was gone, cans of fuel and lubricant were on a mechanic's workbench along the rear wall, as was a small case of Roman candles. The shed was otherwise empty except for four chests covered with a tattered piece of canvas. He opened the first and for an instant recoiled. An angry deity bared its teeth at him. The papier-mâché mask was intricately worked, so vivid and detailed that he knew it must have been another authentic festival mask taken out of a Religious Affairs warehouse. There were four masks in the first two chests, made for the Tibetan rituals in which monks wearing such disguises would dance around *gompa* courtyards until chased away by protector gods. In the remaining chests were the colorful robes that would have been worn below the masks. As he lifted one of the masks, a floor plank creaked behind him. He had begun to swing around just as something hard slammed into his skull.

. . .

He woke surrounded by flames. The shed and its contents were on fire. Oily rags had been piled by the door and cans of oil upended on the workbench. The old robes heaped on his chest had been soaked with gas, the masks scattered around the shed. He leapt up, knocking the robes aside, and desperately pushed at the door. It would not yield. One of the old masks burst into fire, its papier-mâché flames joined by real ones. Roman candles starting exploding, shooting balls of fire into the ceiling, the walls, the floor. He grabbed one of the robes out of an open chest and threw it over the box of fireworks, then used another to futilely beat at the fire, giving up a moment later to slam his shoulder against the door, again and again. He grew dizzy, short of breath, and realized he was on his knees now, pounding helplessly against the blocked door. Then his arms grew leaden and he could barely raise them.

He heard a trembling shout. "Ko! I'm sorry, Ko!" Shan recognized his own feeble voice, and the words seemed to come of their own accord. He collapsed against the door, returning the stare of the nearest demon, a smoldering tiger mask. Death was coming for him out of a particularly Tibetan hell, surrounded by demons.

Suddenly the door fell away behind him. As the fresh air added a new ferocity to the flames, someone roughly dragged him out by his collar and dropped him on the ground. He gulped the fresh air, then crawled away from the inferno until he reached a little pool in the river bed. He thrust his face into the water and then, with what seemed like a great effort, propped himself up against a boulder.

His rescuer sat on another boulder, a few feet away, two of his mastiffs with him.

"It's not easy, saving someone you hate," Shan observed. His throat stung as he spoke. "It shows character."

Dingri spat in his direction.

"I've had to do it myself more than once," Shan said. "An old lama once said it was my karma, the price I pay for the hatred I have pushed deep inside."

"*Cao ni ma!*" Dingri muttered under his breath. *Fuck your mother.* The big dog at his foot looked up at Shan and showed his teeth.

"At least you had already disposed of your motorcycle," Shan pointed out. His breaths were short, as if his lungs were clogged.

"I should have told the old fool just to use it up in the mountains."

"How long were you in the Snow Tigers?"

In the movement of the flames Dingri's wrathful face danced like one of the demons. "Only eight years. I fractured my leg jumping out of a helicopter. They were going to put me on some desk job in Manchuria. It would have been the end of me."

"But General Lau had a different idea."

"Yintai came first, said I was one of the few Tibetans who had served in the Tigers. He wanted to confirm I could still speak Tibetan, then said he had an offer. The next day the general appeared, the famous man whose photographs were always on the wall of our barracks. He said he could arrange for me to go out on full disability. He needed a special kind of man in Tibet. Only occasional work, just make reports about any strangers in town and keep the taboo alive. There would be prospects for great wealth, Yintai said. Only catch was that I had to live in Yangkar."

"It must have been amusing, turning into a demon every few weeks."

"The night festival. That's what we would call it. Time for another night festival. Should we be a skeleton or a blue bull?"

"One thing I never understood. Why leave the phone with the dead lama?"

"Not me. He's always the damned joker. I told him he shouldn't mock old saints, dead or alive. Who would have thought anyone would call before the battery died? Or that anyone would hear it?"

"Nyima never would have heard if you had put the stone all the way back." Shan saw the anguish in Dingri's eyes. Shan could walk away and the Tibetan would still pay a terrible price. His life revolved around Dorchen, and once the truth was known, Dorchen may never forgive him.

"I know where the rest of the treasure is," Shan said.

Dingri stared at his dogs for several breaths. "I don't want to know. I'm done."

"I'm going to tell you. And you're going to see they are there at noon the day after tomorrow."

"Why?"

"I want the killing to stop."

"Why would I help you?"

"Because although you work for killers you are not one yourself. I saw you that day with Nyima, helping her. Dorchen thought you were acting like a dutiful son, but it was guilt. You knew who attacked her, and you felt guilty because he was your partner. Now Yintai and the others are here. They mean to kill again."

"Red work, they call it." Dingri sighed. "Those two soldiers. The American. I never signed on for that. Just watch and send reports, they said, and keep the taboo alive."

"Until today I never would have believed you," Shan said. "But today you sacrificed your prize possession to ransom a yak."

Dingri grimaced. "They'll kill you, Shan. By the time they're done, you're going to wish I left you in the fire. You never should have meddled. None of your concern."

"And you—" a fit of coughing choked off Shan's words. He held his head, suddenly dizzy. "And you," he said when he had recovered, "still have a chance at the fat life in Hong Kong. You will be Lau's hero when you tell him where those thirty mules went."

"They won't believe me."

"Of course they will," Shan said, then tossed a gleaming object to Dingri's feet. "You'll give them a sample."

Dingri picked up the little golden Buddha and stared at it.

"But first," Shan said, "help me up to the *amchi*. Tell him some oily rags caught fire. Spontaneous combustion. I saw the flames from the road and foolishly tried to extinguish it. You pulled me out just in time."

"Sometimes," Dingri observed in a hopeful tone, "people die hours after a fire, just from breathing in the smoke."

CHAPTER SIXTEEN

He reached the gate of the 404th just after breakfast, having endured several coughing fits that had been so severe he had had to pull his truck over. The heavily guarded prison crews were dispatched to their work sites. The two guards at the entrance were old veterans who recognized him, and despite their sour gazes they silently opened the gate for him. The deputy warden waited on the steps of the administrative building, hands on hips, resentment on his face.

"I called," Shan observed.

"Do I care?" the officer snapped. "You of all people, comrade, know that we do not bend the rules."

Shan nodded toward the line of heavy cargo trucks, where trustee prisoners were watching a mule cart approach with crates of the midday meals that would be eaten in the field. Somewhere another mule brayed. The teams that worked at the road building sites were being loaded into a truck at the end of the line. "I know better than most that if the meal crates and mules aren't yet loaded, the prisoners won't be boarded for at least a quarter hour."

"I can't spare guards to help some pathetic village constable."

"Just five minutes in the exercise yard, in plain sight of the towers. If we get within ten feet of the wire you can shoot us."

The officer seemed encouraged by the suggestion. "What do you suppose happens to your son, Comrade Shan, when the old man dies? I hear he's been sick."

"I pray daily for Colonel Tan's long life."

He heard the officer's mocking laugh long after he had disappeared back inside the building.

Shan was in the exercise yard when Ko appeared five minutes later. His son understood they had very little time. "Seven new prisoners arrived," he reported, "three from some camp in Qinghai and four from one of those damned camps in the Xinjiang desert."

Shan had not dared ask Tan to separate the man whose registration was recorded on the drawings and therefore had no way to give the man a face.

"Surely Colonel Tan has a file that will reveal the name based on his number," Ko suggested.

"It's coming in the mail. Could be weeks. We can't risk special treatment for him." The prison service, well aware that Tibetans often refused to acknowledge the Chinese names officially assigned to them, dealt with numbers, not names. "How many are Tibetan?"

"Most, as usual. But there's a Chinese murderer from Fujian with his death sentence commuted to life. And a rapist from Chungking. So five Tibetans." Ko anticipated his father's question. "Two of those are under fifty. Three oldsters, who might be the right age." He shrugged. "They're not in my barracks, so not much chance to speak with them. There's a tall one, really old and thin as a stick, who mutters to himself a lot and eats weeds. A short, feisty one who has one of those long rectangular scars on his forehead." Years earlier there had been an outbreak of Tibetans tattooing the Dalai Lama's name on their foreheads. Public Security had rounded them up and sliced off the tattoos. "And one with a wispy beard who shouts out names to every beetle and butterfly he sees, like he knew them in another life. My money's on him."

Shan smiled, trying not to show his disappointment. He still had no proof that his theory was right. Glancing at the guards, he reached into his pocket and with a furtive motion dropped something into his son's hand. Ko stared uncertainly at the little carved bird in his cupped hand. "I told her it was too dangerous, that a mere constable could never protect her if prison guards asked for her papers."

Ko's head jerked up and he stared over Shan's shoulder. The joy that suddenly lit his face made the hours of driving worthwhile. Yara was a hundred yards away, sitting in a patch of wild flowers on the slope above the prison.

Ko dared not acknowledge her, for it was not a visitor's day, but for a moment he and the outlawed Tibetan woman gazed silently at each other. A whistle blew and Ko turned away, tightly clutching the little bird. He halted after two steps and spoke over his shoulder. "There is that one thing. Even the guards laugh at him. The damnedest thing."

"One of the new prisoners?"

"That really old, stick-thin one. He speaks to the mules and they seem to understand everything he asks them to do. No one has to touch them to get them to work anymore since he offered to handle them. Everywhere he goes at the work site all their ears are turned toward him."

Shan raced over the mountain roads to Yangkar. He had stared dumbfounded as his son had walked away, had even trotted back to the gate to watch the trucks being loaded, against the impossible chance of seeing a tall, aged prisoner who spoke to mules.

Life in Tibet brought too many unexpected disappointments for him to accept what his heart so desperately wanted to believe. But just the possibility would change everything for Nyima and Jig, would give the American a way to quench her burning need for revenge, to let her focus on hope, not death, to pry her from her obsession with confronting Lau's men. Before leaving for his meeting with Ko, he had gone to her camp at the old Taklha homestead to warn her that the killers might seek her out for the same reason they had taken her brother, but she had laughed. "I already took one of their hands," she had quipped. "What other body parts do they want to lose?"

He almost forgot Yara was in the truck with him until the last hour, for she had just stared out the window, looking up at the mountain wilds above them.

"What is it like?" she suddenly asked. "I mean day to day, what is the routine?"

It took him a moment to understand. "Every prison is different," he replied. "Some aim for rehabilitation and give the prisoners light work between reeducation sessions. But the 404th is just about punishment. Sometimes on Sundays they are herded onto the exercise ground and made to stand in ranks while Party scriptures are read to them. One time when I was there such a session went on for three months, with a chapter of one of Mao's biographies read each week. Otherwise each day is much the same as the other. Breakfast of porridge. Off to work, usually making new roads in the mountains. A cold lunch at the site, then more work and back around sunset."

"Not so bad, then," she said.

Images flooded his mind's eye, of prisoners choking on porridge composed mostly of sawdust, gentle old sages disappearing under avalanches, prisoners fighting over worms to eat, and the blood of defiant monks spattering him as they were shot in the head. He swallowed hard. "Not so bad," he echoed.

"Sometimes visitors are allowed," she suggested.

"Usually only to stand at the inner fence to talk. On special days like May Day or the New Year visitors are sometimes allowed to go inside the fence, into the exercise yard." He glanced at the woman, so wise and savvy about the ways of their world but now seeming like an innocent teenager. "But I told you, Yara. You have to show papers, you have to sign in at the gate, with an identity card. They wouldn't just turn you away, they would arrest you. It would destroy your family. It would devastate Ko."

Yara's deep eyes flared. "I told you! I will never register with a government that has raped my country!"

"Then write him letters. I can send them with mine, less chance of being opened. I wouldn't read them," he added with an awkward glance.

She answered only with a sad smile, then turned and looked out the window for several minutes. "It's what we do," she declared toward the mountains. "Live life at a distance."

The sun was slipping behind the peaks as he hurried up the worn track that led up to the Taklha homestead. He saw with relief the smoke that rose from the other side of a ruined wall and slowed his pace. What would he tell Nyima and Jig? He could not promise they had found an old family member, but he had to at least offer them the encouragement that the survivor of Pure Water College had been located.

But as he rounded the ruined wall all thoughts of hope vanished. The little cooking fire in front of the lean-to shed where the women slept had been scattered across the ruins, its embers smoldering in the dry weeds. Nyima sat against the old stone wall, her arms crossed on her knees, her head buried as she wept, the young nun Rikyu at her side, trying to comfort her.

Shan kicked the embers back into the fire and looked for Jig Bartram. The American was gone. He lifted the tin cup from the water bucket and knelt by the nuns.

Nyima shrank back as she saw him, then accepted the cup with a nod and drank, pressing a rib as she swallowed. She had, as Dorchen expected, left his care too soon.

"She's gone, Shan," Nyima groaned. "They're both gone now. Will this season of death never end?"

Shan grabbed Rikyu's arm. "Where is she?" he demanded.

"Saving her mother," the nun answered in a frightened whisper.

"We thought Pema would be safe, hidden there with all those charms around her," Nyima scrubbed at tears as she spoke. "But they captured her, brought her here. Just an hour ago. They shouted out from the little hill above the house and held up the carved box."

"Pema? What do you mean, *Pema*?" Shan shook Rikyu, fighting a desperate fear. "Who? Who shouted out?" He leapt up onto a pile of rubble to look in the direction the nun pointed.

"Two men in black clothes," Rikyu explained. "There was someone else behind them. They said they were going to flush her down a Chinese sewer, where she belonged. Jig begged them to stop, asked what they wanted. They said they would trade her mother's ashes for the location of the second treasure."

"But she doesn't know," Shan said.

"That's what she told them. The man with the box opened it up and lifted some ashes out in his fingers, letting them fly away in the wind. Jig took out that big knife of hers. I begged her not to use it."

"But she doesn't know," Shan repeated as he surveyed the slope above the house.

"They will do it, Shan!" Nyima sobbed. "You don't know their black hearts! But I do! I saw those demons carrying the bodies, poor Jake and those soldiers."

Shan paused. She was speaking about the day of the murders. "You saw," he suggested, "and then you told Jig. It's why Shiva was working on the death chart even before we found her brother's body. You took Jig to Shiva after you told her Jake was dead."

Nyima seemed not to hear him. "She was going to do something terrible, Shan," the old nun said. "I told her to let her mother go, just let the wind carry Pema's ashes over the fields where she ran as a girl. But she was too angry." A sob wracked the old nun's body, and her hand went to her still-healing ribs.

Shan grew still. He knelt by Nyima again.

"She had to have her mother back, don't you see?" Nyima cried. "Blessed Pema. She was the best of us. I made Jig promise to leave the knife here."

Shan gently put a hand on the old nun's damp cheek and eased her head toward him. "You knew, Nyima, because you have been protecting the secret all these years. It's why you live in that cave and pay homage to the protector gods. You knew, and you told her."

"They would have killed her. They have guns."

"So she went up to them to trade the secret," Shan said, "but they still didn't give up the ashes."

Nyima sobbed, then looked up and nodded. "They hit my niece, knocked her down, then took away Jig and the ashes too. They are going to kill her anyway, Shan!"

CHAPTER SEVENTEEN

"Jengtse! Where is Jengtse?" he demanded of Jinhua when he returned to the station. Jinhua, a bandage on his head, had settled into the station for his rehabilitation, sleeping in a cell.

"I don't know," the young officer said. "There was a phone call. Half an hour later he said he was going out to walk a patrol. But I watched him. He got into a truck that waited for him on the far side of the square."

"Can you walk?" Shan asked.

"Of course." Jinhua seemed to sense danger in Shan's eyes. "And I can still hold a pistol."

Shan gazed in frustration into the shadows outside. There was no point in going into the mountains at night. They could have taken the American to any number of places, and once she told them where to search they would have to collect equipment.

"Get some sleep," he said. "Be ready at dawn. Wear your uniform. Bring your gun and manacles."

A grim smile rose on Jinhua's face. "Sounds like one of those old movies. When the lawman finally comes for justice. Except there's usually soldiers and natives tangled in the mess, and in the end you're never entirely sure who to root for."

"This is Tibet. We bypass the melodrama and go straight to the reckoning."

"So more like a karmic event," Jinhua said and saw Shan's surprise. He shrugged. "I've been spending time with Marpa in the noodle shop. He talks about immortal souls the way other people talk about the weather. It's when destinies collide and souls get reconciled."

It wasn't Jinhua's words that filled Shan with foreboding as he walked across the square, it was the resigned, almost melancholy way he spoke them. There had been a reckless glint in his eyes. Jinhua had recognized long ago that his vow to revenge his partner jeopardized his life, but Shan had seen the fear that kept him cautious. Now that fear was gone.

A crescent moon slipped out of high clouds as he reached the top of the old tower. He whispered Lodi's name and was answered by a quick bark as Raj sprang from the shadows.

"How long have you been up here?" Shan asked as the boy reached his dog's side.

"Since midafternoon, constable. My uncle gave me a new book, and I can read up here without the wind grabbing the pages. I wasn't watching all the time," he said with apology in his voice.

"Did you spot a helicopter nearby?"

Lodi nodded. "One landed a few miles to the south. I think they met one of those little army trucks. Because not long after there was a cloud of dust and the truck drove into town and stopped in an alley off the square."

"Who got in?"

"Deputy Jengtse. Sometimes the army has trouble on the road. You know, they need someone to direct traffic so a convoy can pass. Or tend to stray animals on the highway. They drove back out to the highway and turned to the south, toward the helicopter. Later, at sunset, that helicopter lifted off, going farther south." Lodi pointed toward Lhadrung, where Lau's men had taken over a guesthouse.

"Lodi," he said to the boy, "I think Shiva may need help. Get your uncle. I'll meet you at her house."

He descended the tower with the boy then watched him run, Raj at his heels, toward the café before turning to the phone in the square.

"The colonel left here and has no phone," Amah Jiejie reported. "I can put you through to one of his aides who might be with him."

Shan waited, then heard orders being given by what sounded like a drill instructor before Tan took the phone. Shan quickly explained what had happened to the American.

"If they brought her here I can have the house surrounded in minutes," Tan offered.

"No. This has to reach an ending. Lau is probably in Lhasa, waiting to collect what he has been waiting for all these years. Just make a presence, keep them off guard. Yintai won't hurt her if he knows you are watching."

Tan's voice became muffled as he spoke to someone else. "Our officers' association is going to take an impromptu dinner to the representatives of the famed Snow Tigers," the colonel announced. "Beer and cards afterward, far into the night. My men will be insistent."

"They will want to leave early in the morning," Shan said. "Just let them go."

"I will send men up to you tonight."

"No. No one."

"He'll kill you."

Suddenly a chamber seemed to open in Shan's mind, and he was with Lokesh, standing by the salt saints at the ancient shrine. "The gods will decide that," Shan replied.

"I'm sorry?"

"Nothing. The only chance we have is if Lau thinks he has already won."

"Dammit, Shan," Tan said, then went silent for so long Shan was about to hang up. "If you get killed it will mean the fourth constable in as many years. It's going to make me look negligent."

Shiva's house was never particularly orderly, but now the astrologer's home looked like a storm had blown through. Furniture was upended.

Her precious bottles of ink had been smashed against the walls. The little easel where she worked was in splinters.

In the center of the chaos the old woman sat in a chair, holding a bloody rag to her mouth with one hand as Marpa bandaged the other.

Shan righted a stool and sat before her. "Grandmother, I am sorry."

Shiva's effort at a smile turned into a grimace. "The signs were all of evil. Something bad was going to happen." The astrologer fingered a loose tooth, then looked down at the bloody rag in her hand. "I don't know what I will tell the poor American girl. Jig trusted me. The family relied on me to keep Pema safe." She dabbed at her eyes.

"It's not your fault." Shan surveyed the room. "Tell me what happened. Who did this?"

"Someone opened the door and called my name, a Tibetan. As I rose from my easel these two Chinese men came rushing down the hall. One had a huge scar across his throat. He demanded to know where the mother's box of ashes was. That's what he said, the mother's box of ashes. I told him someone should finish cutting his throat and said I would be glad to do his death chart. He hit me. I told him he was going to the *avichi* hell, where those who harm the faith are endlessly tortured. He hit me again. Then they tore everything apart. They wouldn't have found it except that I glanced over to make sure Kapo was alright."

With a shudder Shan saw that the old aquarium that housed her gerbil was shattered. "You hid the box in the sand?"

Shiva smiled through her bloody, swollen lips. "Uncle Kapo bit him when he reached in, bit him real good. That's when he pulled his gun. He shot the glass. He was furious."

Shan dreaded to ask the question, then to his relief he saw two black eyes watching him from a pocket of Shiva's apron. "My uncle's too fast for some fool soldier," she boasted and made little jumping motions with her hand.

"How did they know, Shiva?" Shan asked. "How did they know the box was here?"

The old woman shook her head and held the bloody rag to her lips. "The chart," she murmured.

Shan gently pulled away her hand. "What about the chart?"

"Someone stole it, a few days ago."

He straightened, then whispered to Lodi, asking him to bring the big envelope in the top drawer of his desk. The boy was back, breathless, in the time it took Shan and Marpa to straighten the chamber.

"Yintai, the general's aide, had your chart," Shan explained as he opened the envelope and extracted the chart. "But why would it matter, Shiva?"

"Because I am a fool. Because I wanted it for Jig to take to her American family."

For the first time Shan read the fine lines of script that had been completed along the bottom, inscribed so elegantly it looked like a passage of scripture. It began with the traditional death poem that Shan expected, but ended with Shiva's own words. *Cherished brother and cousin,* it simply said, *we of the Taklha clan embrace you.* The chart hadn't simply told Yintai and his local conspirators that the dead American had been in the Taklha clan, it had also told them that Shiva was of the same clan.

"I am the only one of the clan with a house," the astrologer explained, "the safest place for Pema, we thought." She looked up with pleading eyes. "What those men do to our Pema!" she blurted, her voice cracking. "It will be like she died twice!"

CHAPTER EIGHTEEN

Shan drove as far as he could up the ridge that led to the Demon's Den and then set out on foot up the old pilgrim trail, apologizing to Jinhua for the two miles they would have to walk to reach the Plain of Ghosts to avoid being seen from the road. The young knob looked ready for a parade. He had ironed his uniform, polished the badge that Public Security officers wore on holidays, even rubbed a sheen into his shoes. Shan had tried to sleep in a cell, then, giving up, had found Jinhua solemnly cleaning his gun at Jengtse's desk.

"You should get your pistol," Jinhua had said. "Clean it, make it ready."

"I don't carry guns," Shan had replied, then brushed his uniform and cleaned his *gau* instead.

They walked in silence, each man lost in his own thoughts. The night before Shan had written two letters that he had left on his table, knowing that Yara or Trinle would eventually find them. *If you get this, know that I have been freed of all cares,* he had penned to Lokesh. He had lit his brazier and thrown in the registration card he had secretly, illegally obtained for his friend, watching until it was reduced to ashes. Then he had apologized to the old man for ever opposing his efforts to become a feral Tibetan in the service of the Dalai Lama. *One of the greatest blessings of my life,* he wrote, *has been to call you my friend. You are the bravest, wisest human I have ever known. If I have to throw off this face then I pray we meet again. I have a recurring dream of you and I as farmers in a high mountain valley with a white yak looking down on us. I know you would tell me it is a sign of future incarnation. Now I embrace the joy of that knowledge.*

He had torn up four letters to Ko before finally writing just *You are all that is left of me on this earth, son—and I rejoice in that thought.*

He resisted the temptation to look back toward Yangkar. In his short time there, he had developed an unexpected affection for the unkempt little town. He paused and shut his eyes, pushing back the premonition that he would not see it again, fighting the recurring sensation of a cold blade driving down into his neck.

When Jinhua, clearly still feeling the pain of his injuries, dropped onto a boulder at the top of the ridge, Shan admonished him. "You must stay here. I will be back later," he added without conviction.

"It was *my* partner who was murdered," Jinhua replied and touched the two pairs of manacles that hung from his belt. "One of these was issued to him, one to me, when we were first assigned as partners. I am going to put them to use today." With obvious effort he stood and set out along the trail, Shan a step behind. The constable from nowhere and the fugitive Public Security officer were marching to do battle with the Hero of the Motherland and his Snow Tiger protectors. Shan stopped only once, to straighten a line of *mani* stones.

An hour later they looked down on the Plain of Ghosts. Jinhua had begun to descend the final slope when a loud, threatening snort stopped him. His hand went to his pistol as a yak appeared from behind an outcropping.

Shan could not help but smile when he saw the red yarn on the animal's neck. "It's the lama yak," he said, as if the name explained the animal's presence. The old bull, far from its usual pastures, stared at Shan for a moment, then appeared to nod at him before slowly turning to gaze at the distant snowcapped peaks. The yak seemed to have grown more contemplative since being ransomed.

They crossed the grounds of the old college and paused at the path down the embankment as they saw the black helicopter sitting idle on the flat below. Shan pushed Jinhua into the shadow of the entrance to Nyima's cave and they briefly watched to be sure there were no soldiers stationed below. At the entrance to the ice cave they halted once more, hearing the sound of machinery inside, then straightened their uniforms and stepped inside.

Yintai and a man in a ski mask were burrowing into the ice wall, using battery-powered impact hammers and drills. General Lau was kicking away the chunks of ice as they fell. Jig Bartram was sitting in a corner, her arms tied against her chest and a gag in her mouth. Lau turned at her muffled cry, then followed her gaze to Shan and Jinhua.

"Comrades!" the general exclaimed. "How convenient that you would arrive now! It's your destiny! You can witness our final triumph!" The general made a gesture that swept in both men and the American. "And then we can deal with all our problems at once!"

The tools, making short work of the thick ice, had already penetrated two feet, following a passage between rock walls that had been chipped smooth and plastered. Shan leaned close and peered through the thin layer of ice that remained on one side. The golden eye of a *garuda*, messenger of the gods, stared back at him.

"If you had told us about this, Shan," Lau said with a shrug, "things would have gone so differently." Yintai lowered his hammer and fixed Shan with an expectant gaze.

"I didn't know," Shan replied. "The evidence was there for all to find, but no one knew how to look. The manuscript describing the 1897 earthquake was with the later records for a reason. It explained how a new well had to be dug because springs shifted and the glacier spread its roots. Lamas who came into this chamber would have known it was incomplete, that it is missing its most important gods. There had to have been an inner chamber that had been sealed by the ice. The ravens chipped away the ice like you are now and blew up the entrance when their task was complete. Over years, as the ice grew back, Nyima cleared away the blockage of rubble to open the outer chamber so she could pray here.

"Simple, really. But you killed everyone who knew the secret. Almost everyone."

Lau smiled. "Tons of gold. Just waiting for us all these years. Even more valuable today. Our investment has appreciated, you might say."

"I've learned something about this land, general," Shan observed. "Tibet doesn't give you what you want. It gives you what you need."

"Perfect! I need that gold! I need to buy companies in America!" Lau pointed to the ice chunks at their feet. "Now help with the work."

"I came to make arrests."

The man in the mask lowered his tool to listen.

"You never cease to amaze me, Shan," Lau continued, his silver hair shining in the lantern light. "How can a man who has been punished so severely by the world still have such a poor grip on its reality?"

Shan looked past the general. "The time for masks has passed, deputy."

"Buddha's breath!" came the familiar epithet. Jengtse peeled off the mask and sneered at Shan. "Constables come and constables go."

"But General Lau's spy endures," Shan continued. "Never complaining about the lack of a promotion, just offering to help each new constable while sharpening his knife in the dark. Constable Bao was lucky to have survived you. I never checked earlier records. How many constables have you killed?"

"The first one, before Bao, he tried to transfer me. Didn't know I had seen the papers. Stopped him before they reached the mailbox. He fell off a cliff, scared by a walking skeleton. Then Fen. Counting you, it will be three by the end of today. I will take you to the vultures. In a few days no one will know who the bones belonged to."

"How did you know about Constable Fen's secret? How did you know where to intercept him?"

"He laid out the drawings on his desk, even asked me what I made of them. Then he went to see the astrologer. He came back all excited, told me to find some canned food to take to the old nun, and asked if I knew how to find her. I said she had been staying with some feral herders in a winter camp, but I could find them."

"You took him to the Demon's Den," Shan said.

"He did me the favor of walking right behind me all the way from the road, just to be killed. Saved me the trouble of hauling his body all that way in the snow. Then I went back and eased the truck off the road."

"To insert the blade with such precision, you must knock out your victims first."

"I had a good teacher," Jengtse said with a glance at Yintai, who fixed Shan with the stare of a hungry predator. "To obtain the right killing angle the subject is best immobilized."

"One of those Snow Tiger traditions," Shan suggested. "Fifty years and counting." He turned to Yintai. "Of course, if a knife isn't practical, a dump truck will do. And if you do use the knife near a city, try to find a pile of lime to hide the victim."

Yintai's grin was as cold as the ice. He touched the big sheath knife on his belt. "They go limp as a rag doll if you do it right. Severs all the nerves connecting the limbs to the brain. Usually they live a few more minutes, not able to move anything but their eyes. More entertaining when they stay conscious. Oh, those eyes! It always makes me laugh."

Jinhua made a growling sound and stepped toward Lau's aide, his hand on his pistol.

"Enough!" Lau snapped. "Lieutenant, your gun."

Jinhua didn't seem to understand as Jengtse extended his hand, until Jinhua turned and saw that Lau's own pistol, his old Russian weapon, was aimed at his head. Jengtse took Jinhua's gun, and Lau motioned him toward the debris. "Clear the damned path!" the general ordered. "You too, Shan!"

For a moment Shan wondered why Lau had not brought more men, then realized that the general expected to uncover secrets he did not want shared. Knowing that they would never reach the final act of their drama until the last secret of the Plain of Ghosts was revealed, he bent to the ice on the floor. "Better if three of us helped," he said, nodding toward Jig Bartram.

"Not a chance," Yintai growled. "The bitch kicked me in the balls." He drove his drill into the ice again, and the blockage began to fall away in great shards, in places exposing the plaster surface of the passage wall.

Lau's impatient anger was quickly replaced by excited anticipation, and he repeatedly pushed Yintai and Jengtse out of the way to swing a hammer himself at the thick ice. He hesitated as a small sheet fell away. "What the hell is this?" he demanded of Shan. He was pointing at another painted figure.

"One of the wrathful protectors who inhabit this place. I think you are waking them up, general."

Lau laughed and smashed his hammer into the eye of the god. "Not that one!" he crowed.

Shan and Jinhua labored in silence, picking up the ice shards to deposit along the walls of the outer chamber. No one noticed that Shan's trips to the walls gradually took him closer to Jig. At last, balancing a load in one arm, he dropped his opened pocketknife into one of her hands.

Minutes later Lau hammered loose a jagged sheet of ice that had nothing behind it but black, empty space. The general took a step forward, then hesitated. He thrust a flashlight at Jinhua. "You go in," he ordered.

As Jinhua stared fearfully into the darkness, Shan stepped forward and grabbed the light. He aimed the beam directly in front of him as he entered the chamber. Two huge yellow eyes stared back at him.

Someone gasped behind him. A pistol cracked, and a bullet ricocheted somewhere ahead of Shan.

"It's a painting, Jengtse," Shan stated without turning around. "And those ricochets could hit one of you as easily as me." He aimed the light at the rear wall, revealing a huge black leopard god on the rear wall. Yintai laughed, saying they had found a friend.

The chamber certainly had been the inner chapel of the *gonkang*. Shan's light illuminated one painting after another on the upper panels of the plastered walls. Above old altars, the remaining protectors waited. Hayagriva, the horse-headed demon, extended a blood-filled skull beside Yamantaka, Conqueror of Death, draped in the skins of humans. Then came the three-eyed Mahakala in his black, savage form, riding a tiger. Arrayed around them were their escorts and demon guards, including an especially disturbing image of a grinning skeleton deity that held a human head in one clawed hand and extended its other hand outward as if in invitation. It had been a long time since any had heard a prayer.

Jengtse took one step inside and halted. He stared uneasily at the skeleton. "This is where he lives," Shan said to his deputy. "The god you've been mocking all these years."

Jengtse seemed to try to sneer, but his mouth twisted into a grimace. "Bag of bones in a cold, dark hell. Can't be too powerful." He picked up a piece of ice and threw it at the demon.

"Find it!" Lau barked. He had entered with a bright gas lantern in his hand and was clearly displeased at not being greeted by stacks of ingots. Yintai and Jengtse hurried along the walls, pulling out and emptying crates from under the old altars, spilling out old rolled *thangka* paintings and empty copper altar bowls. The bowls had been on the altars, which themselves had each been turned into the base of makeshift shelves of planks and blocks. The shelves were packed with *peche*.

"What is this?" Lau shrieked. He kicked an altar bowl across the chamber.

"The treasure of the Dalai Lama," Shan said. "He had gold, yes, but it was only used to honor the deities and maintain the *gompas*." He surveyed the precious manuscripts and realized he felt no surprise. "The real treasures were the collected teachings of lamas over the past thousand years."

"You stole all the gold already, general." The thin, carefully controlled voice came from the ice-framed entry. Colonel Tan was alone and clad in fatigues, wearing a full equipment belt as if ready for battle. His face was haggard but set with a determined glint. As he took a step inside, Jig Bartram appeared beside him.

General Lau seemed confused for a moment, but then nodded, gesturing Tan forward. "At last you see the sense of my proposal. Bring the American in. As good a place as any. Her family has caused enough trouble." He turned to Yintai. "When we finish, blow it all up with the bodies inside."

Tan didn't move. "I suppose things were too disorganized back then to worry about those missing in action," he observed. "A few dozen Tibetans." He shrugged. "Liabilities to the state. A company of Red Guard punks. God knows I wanted to shoot a few of the little pricks myself."

Lau gave a distracted nod. "Yintai! Sergeant Jengtse! Empty those boxes and shelves. There has to be more hidden here. They were devilishly clever, those ravens. Pull down the altars. Look for false bottoms in the bottoms of those boxes. No one would go to all this trouble over heaps of crumbling paper! It could be gemstones. Rubies and emeralds, secreted in the wood panels!"

As if to help, Tan went to the nearest of the shelves and pulled out one of the ancient volumes, contained in an ornate box. He carefully lifted the top page of elegant script inscribed on palm leaf paper. Lau shoved Tan aside and grabbed the book. The general had decided Tan had become another servant, bought and paid for with money in a Hong Kong account.

"You were ever the efficient officer, Lau," Tan continued in the same level voice. "You had soldiers and heavy equipment drivers here. No one could be spared, of course. I think you locked the Red Guard and the Tibetans in the buildings and then shoved them off the cliff with your bulldozer. Driven by Sergeant Ma. Is that why he got a place of honor? The hero of your battle for Pure Water College?"

Lau hesitated. "We had orders to destroy all facilities of the reactionaries. You know that."

"You wouldn't have locked your soldiers inside. You still needed them. They had dealt with the ravens in the stable but all that gold had to be loaded and everything else pushed over the side. There were mules and the one bulldozer. I suppose you used the mules to haul debris to the edge of the ravine as well. It must be damned deep, one of those chasms where you can't see the bottom. Nothing but shadows. Tibetans say such places can reach all the way to bottom of the world."

Yintai tossed a manuscript cover made of gold brocade to Lau, who brightened as he examined it.

"But after a day or two the work was done," Tan continued. He handed the manuscript page he had been holding to Shan. Its margins held images of birds flying among clouds.

"Colonel, look for more of the gold cloths," Lau ordered.

Tan, still ignoring him, paced along the shelves, touching dusty manuscript covers. "I've heard books like this could take a year or more to produce," he said. Jig Bartram inched along the wall. Jengtse cast her an uncertain glance and crossed to the opposite side.

"You were done," Tan continued, "but still had a company of soldiers who knew too much."

Lau eyed Shan, then frowned at the colonel. "This is getting tedious, Tan. Get to work! Clean things up in Yangkar and you can come visit me in Hong Kong."

"They would have been blindly obedient. Your men always adored you. You would have done it in stages, probably picked one squad to take care of the others." He turned to Yintai. "What did you tell them? The others were advocating treason, siding with the Tibetans?"

Yintai seemed amused at the suggestion. "Just a victory photograph. Lined them up at the edge of the ravine so we could get the snow peaks in the image, we said. All lined up like targets."

"Ah," Tan said. "A hidden machine gun."

"In the back of a truck," Yintai confirmed.

"The few left would have been no problem," Tan said in a passionless voice. "Separate them, send some out on guard duty. Is that when you learned to use your knife, Yintai?"

"That was a trick from one of those Red Guards, a zoology student. He had demonstrated it on a captured Tibetan rebel. The funni-
est thing, how he still kept blinking his eyes. As an experiment we
broke his legs with a sledgehammer and he didn't feel a thing." Yintai
picked up another manuscript box, glanced at it, and tossed it on
the floor before glancing up at Tan. "First we got rid of the mules.
Rounded them up, shooting guns in the air, and drove them right off
the cliff."

Shan closed his eyes. The mules, the monks, and the ravens in the
last drawing. They had not been flying. They had been falling.

"Sergeant Ma must have been the last. You needed the bulldozer
until the end."

Yintai shot Tan one of his lightless grins. "The general told him to
drive the bulldozer over the edge," the captain explained. "We had
already reported it lost in a sabotage incident, so we did not have to
account for it. The general said just leap out at the last minute. The
fool hit his head when he jumped. Never regained consciousness."

"Why put him in the tomb?" Shan asked.

"The slab had been knocked open by the bulldozer the day before.
If any Tibetan came back, that would be the one they opened since the
seal had already been broken. Tibetans are terrified of ghosts. One look
at the dead sergeant and they would never come back."

Lau had paid no attention to the conversation. He was busy ripping open manuscript cases.

"It's true, then," Tan said to the general. "You killed a company of
your own men. Loyal Chinese soldiers."

Lau threw him an impatient frown. "We can salvage this catastro-
phe, Tan. We will call it in together, say that our joint investigation
team discovered the biggest cache of illegal Buddhist artifacts found
in years, hidden by spies working for the Dalai Lama gang. That's the
line! Front page in Beijing! Clandestine enemies of the motherland
subvert the—"

The gunshot ripped the still, cold air. Lau sagged. He gazed with a
curious expression at Tan's smoking pistol, then became aware of the

blood pouring onto his chest from his throat. He raised a hand toward the wound as he slowly collapsed. The bullet had gone through his neck, ripping apart an artery.

Shan bent to check Lau's pulse, then saw the rapidly expanding pool of blood and knew there was no point. Jig Bartram grabbed his flashlight and aimed it at the opposite wall. The little white circle of shattered plaster made it clear where the bullet had struck. It was precisely in the center of the outstretched, clawed hand of the skeleton god, as if the demon had directed the shot.

There was motion at Shan's feet—Jinhua was checking the body—then at the entry, where Jig Bartram and Tan were blocking the flight of Yintai. The general's aide, ever the warrior, swung his heavy knife at Tan's belly. The blow was blocked by a broken plank from a manuscript box thrown by Jinhua, who then kicked Yintai's leg, knocking him to his knees.

"You killed my partner!" Jinhua growled, then leapt back as the knife slashed at his thigh.

"He was nothing but dirt under my fingernails," Yintai snarled. He crawled backward to Lau's body, shaking the general's lifeless shoulder, then reached for Lau's pistol.

"You killed my partner," Jinhua repeated as Yintai looked up in surprise. The holster was empty. Jinhua held the general's gun. As Yintai flung back his arm to hurl his knife Jinhua fired a single shot into his chest. Yintai collapsed onto the general and Jinhua flung the gun on the bodies.

"Jengtse!" Jig cried. The deputy was gone. She darted down the passageway.

Shan was about to follow when he saw Tan's face. The colonel was still staring at the skeleton demon. He seemed to have aged years in the last few minutes. "Colonel!" Shan said, tugging at his arm. Tan took no notice of him.

"I have him!" Jinhua shouted to Shan. He was tightening a belt around his bleeding thigh. "I will get the colonel outside. Jengtse still has my gun. Go!"

As Shan emerged into the brilliant sunlight, Jig Bartram was running frantically along the lip of the steep embankment. Jengtse was already halfway down the path to the flat parking area, where Lau's helicopter had landed.

Suddenly his deputy halted. The American too slowed her pace. Both were staring downward. Shan ran past the outcroppings by Nyima's cave, where at last he had an unobstructed view of the flat below. A second helicopter was there, no doubt flown by Tan, but so too were Tserung's old Red Flag sedan, Trinle's orange motorcycle, and one of the battered trucks from the garage. Spread out in a line, blocking Jengtse's flight, were a dozen Tibetans. Shan saw Yara, Dorchen, Dingri, Lodi and his dog, Marpa, Shiva, and several farmers. They were holding spades, pitchforks, lengths of pipe, and other makeshift weapons. Dingri raised a club over his head and charged at Jengtse.

Shan's heart sank as Jengtse lifted his pistol and fired. The bullet ricocheted off a rock beside Dingri, who kept running up the path. Jengtse fired another shot and Dingri staggered, clutching at his shoulder, but then extended his makeshift weapon and took an unsteady step forward. The others slowly advanced behind him.

Jengtse did not have enough bullets to stop them all. He turned and ran back up the trail, keeping Jig at bay with his gun as he passed her.

Shan and the American reached the top of the path to the Plain of Ghosts together. The plain was empty except for the big lama yak, grazing above the ravine. It paused and looked up, first at them, then at the outcroppings near the old well. Shan remembered the little niche in the rocks Jengtse had found the day he and Jinhua had explored the plain.

"Go around," Shan said to Jig, pointing to the outcroppings. "I will flush him out. He will run up the trail along the edge. You can surprise him in the rocks there." He extended a set of manacles to her. She pushed his hand down. "He killed my brother," she reminded him and darted away.

"Jengtse!" Shan called as he approached the short tower of boulders. "You'll get a trial. You can tell your story. You were forced to kill by your former officers."

As Shan gazed up at the little niche in the rocks, Jengtse appeared from around a boulder in front of him, his gun aimed at Shan's heart.

"You deserve to die just for being such a fool." There was nothing of the subordinate officer in his voice. "People like you are ruining the future of Tibet, helping them live in the past. I'd be doing the motherland a favor."

"I'm a fool, yes," Shan said, "for not checking your background at the start. How did you like serving Lau in London?"

Jengtse grinned. "I drove the general's Mercedes. What a place! Last week he said he was thinking about buying a house there, said I could be the caretaker if I was successful here."

"That's gone now."

"I can still disappear in Hong Kong. He had companies there. They'll give me a job."

"Why did the American have to die? He just wanted to bury his mother."

"Who comes from the far side of the world to bury some ashes? No, he was after the treasure too. He had to be. I was sure he knew more. But the bastard was silent as a stone."

"Did Dingri help you kill him?"

"That weakling? All bark and no bite. He had no stomach for that kind of work. He thought I was bluffing when I said I would nail that American's hands to the table, so he helped me hold the first one down. When I pounded in the first nail he shouted, louder than the American. Said I had to stop. I told him he would never get a new life by playing the coward. But with both the American's hands nailed down I didn't need him for the rest. He ran."

"And Nyima?"

"She started sending messages to the herders. It had to stop. I didn't kill her. She was supposed to say a demon attacked her, to scare away the others. But the old goat never said a word."

The gun was still aimed at Shan's chest. "The others will be here any moment, Jengtse. Are you going to kill them all? Nyima? Lhamo? Old Trinle? And Colonel Tan is made of iron. Bullets bounce off him."

At the mention of Tan, Jengtse lowered the gun, glanced over Shan's shoulder, and disappeared around the rocks. Shan warily followed. By the time he emerged onto the open plain, Tan and the Tibetans were indeed at the head of the path, working their way toward the ravine. Jengtse, running along the edge, suddenly halted. Jig Bartram had appeared in front of him.

"I'll shoot you, I swear!" Jengtse shouted at the woman, then retreated a step as the old yak appeared behind the American, still grazing.

"You're going to have to, deputy," the American said as she slowly advanced. She was only half a dozen steps from Jengtse when she halted. Her knife was in her hand and she slightly bent, as if coiling for a leap.

"Why the hell did you come?" Jengtse spat. "You ruined everything."

"My mother wanted me to understand Tibet," was all Jig said. She took a step forward. Jengtse fired.

She jerked as the bullet grazed her arm, then took another step. Jengtse glanced at the approaching Tibetans and fired at her again. The shot ripped away fabric at her shoulder. She kept walking. She was reciting a mantra.

Jengtse took his time now, steadying the pistol in both hands, aiming at her head. She stared back at the gun. Her only reaction was to chant the mantra more loudly.

The angry bellow seemed to come out of the earth itself. There was a blur of something heavy in motion, as if a boulder were rolling. Jengtse took his eyes off the pistol an instant before the yak was on him. The great beast had him in its horns and with a deep bellow it swung its mighty neck. Jengtse was thrown impossibly high over the abyss. For a moment Jengtse clawed the air just as the figures in the drawing had done. Then he was gone.

The bellow still echoed off the side of the mountain.

No one moved. Jig slowly dropped to her knees. The lama yak went back to its grazing. Shan stared at the animal so long he did not even see Tan until the colonel himself was at the edge of the bottomless ravine.

At first Shan thought he was looking for Jengtse's body, but then the colonel turned and Shan saw the desolation on his face. He could not understand what Tan was saying, then he realized Tan was speaking to the yak. "No!" Shan shouted as Tan unbuttoned his gun belt and let it drop to the ground. Shan tried to run forward, to pull Tan away, but his feet were leaden.

Tan spread his arms wide. The yak raised its head and stepped closer, studying the colonel. It stopped a dozen feet away and cocked its head. Tan, arms still outstretched, gazed up at the sky as if in prayer, then stared into the yak's eyes with a pleading expression.

Time stood still. The old soldier, ravaged by time and his heartbreaking country, and the weather-beaten yak seemed aware of nothing but each other. Then the yak gave a shuddering sigh, turned its back on Tan and began to graze again. Shan walked slowly forward and pulled Tan from the edge.

A quarter hour later they watched as the motley caravan from Yangkar drove away. Tan, still wearing a glazed expression, had collapsed onto a rock, then weakly pointed to the American, who now stood herself at the edge of the cliff. Shan realized he had never told her what he had learned from Ko.

"I have an idea," Shan had said as he approached Jig. "A theory about who drew this place as it became the Plain of Ghosts. A hope."

The American turned. She ignored the blood seeping down her sleeve.

"I can't be sure, Jig. We couldn't do anything more than move him to the 404th, not while Lau still lived. Prisoners get assigned Chinese names. Sometimes they themselves forget who they were."

She looked up at him with dull eyes, then back into the abyss. "All these years, my mother kept writing to the dead."

"All but the one we found, the one who sent the drawings. He speaks with mules."

The words took several moments to sink in. She slowly turned back to Shan, then sobbed and embraced him.

By the time the Tibetans were gone, Tan had revived. A familiar guile had returned to his countenance, and Shan asked no questions as he directed Shan, Jig, and Jinhua to carry the bodies of Lau and Yintai out of the cave. He examined Yintai carefully, confirming that Jinhua's bullet had passed through his body, then took Lau's lifeless arms and helped carry him down to the general's helicopter.

"I need cord," the colonel said to Shan. "Something that will burn."

"We could have just thrown them off the edge," Jig suggested when she and Shan finished a fruitless search of the gear compartment of the helicopter.

"No." Tan had the voice of command back. "If the famous general disappears there will be inquiries, search parties dispatched all over the mountains. He must die like a hero." Tan turned to Shan, who shrugged. "Your boot laces, then," Tan said, then motioned to the cockpit. "After I start the engine, belt Lau into the pilot's seat, then Yintai beside him."

The colonel climbed into the cockpit, and with a low whine the rotor started moving. He climbed out to help them with the bodies, then took the laces from Shan. He tied a loop in each, then leaned into the cockpit, adjusting controls and securing them in position with the laces.

The helicopter was already off the ground when he leapt out. It climbed slowly but steadily. When it was several hundred feet high, the wind caught it and it gradually veered north.

"Good," Tan said. "By the time it crashes they will be far away from my county." He watched the receding helicopter with a satisfied gaze. "I'll wait a few hours then call his quarters to see if he is free for dinner. When they can't account for him I will order an urgent inquiry. I will report that I agreed to let him take one of the new helicopters out for a test flight with Yintai this morning. The brave general, ever a friend of the common soldier, took time out of his retirement to make sure new equipment was safe for his beloved Snow Tigers. There will be great pageantry in Beijing, and he will be laid in a hero's tomb." Tan cast a mock salute toward the north. "May you rot in eternal hell, general," he added.

They waited in silence until the black speck of the helicopter disappeared behind the first range of snowcapped peaks. "What's that the old ones say, Shan?" Tan asked with a new light in his eyes, then remembered. "Ah, yes. *Lha gyal lo*. It means victory to the gods."

EPILOGUE

It was a skittish, self-conscious audience that waited at the benches outside the gate of the 404th People's Construction Brigade. Colonel Tan and Amah Jiejie had been inside for nearly an hour, and Shan had watched anxiously as the ever-surly deputy warden ran across the compound into the offices when they arrived. Jig Bartram nervously looked at her watch.

Yara glanced back and forth from the guards to the hills above, as if thinking of bolting. Shan stood beside her and rested a calming hand on her shoulder. The afternoon before, she had arrived in his office to deliver an official form. "It's for replacement of a lost registration card," she had awkwardly announced. "I know the circumstances are a bit ambiguous, but I was a teacher once and with a new card I can be one again. There's an opening right here in Yangkar. Maybe someone who is savvy about the ways of government could fill in the gaps," she had suggested to Shan. The card meant she was acknowledging Chinese citizenship, but with a card she could visit Ko and not be fearful of sending letters. With a card her son could be enrolled in her school.

Shan had accepted the form with a smile. "You are exactly the kind of teacher Yangkar needs," he said.

Lhamo and Nyima were watching the prison barracks. Shan had tried to discourage them from coming, but they had insisted, saying that they understood no one knew for certain who the man was, but whomever he was he deserved help from those of Yangkar.

Jinhua, his bag packed, watched by his car before starting the long drive home. The young officer was going back to fight corruption in Beijing, with a protective charm now inside his shirt. Shan had tried to talk him out of returning, suggesting there might be a place for him in Tibet, but Jinhua had insisted he had a duty to his dead partner. He had taken Shan's hand and gripped it hard. "Someday you might need a friend in low places in Beijing," he had said with a self-mocking smile.

As Shan watched the office door, Trinle warily approached with still another question about the paper Shan had translated for them. It had been one of Amah Jiejie's most resourceful creations. The money Lau had deposited in Tan's name had been transferred, over Tan's signature, to a newly formed charity using Amah Jiejie's address in Lhadrung. A quarter of the money, the note signed by Tan said, would be used to repair and improve Yangkar, and the rest would be used to restore the *chortens* and construct a modest complex of buildings on the Plain of Ghosts, to launch a new medical college under the leadership of Dorchen.

When the time was right, during the quiet days of winter, Lokesh and other secret representatives of the exiled government would come and take away the ancient books in the ice cave. Those under the streets of Yangkar would become the library of the new college.

Yara suddenly stood as a whistle blew and prisoners began to stream out of the barracks into the exercise yard. Emaciated monks and lamas began shuffling along a rutted track, their fingers working at makeshift *malas*. A figure broke out of the line and hurried to the inner fence, where a guard barked at him. Ko dutifully stepped back a few feet, then raised his hand. They could not exchange words, for this was not an official visitation day. Yara raised her own in reply, then pressed her hands together, her thumbs extended back, the next two fingers folded down, the next pointing forward. It was called the *mudra* of the Precious Horse. Ko smiled as he recognized it, then folded his own hands, making the *mudra* called Lady of the Diamond Laughter. He had been practicing. They smiled at each other for several heartbeats, then Ko pointed toward the administration building.

Colonel Tan was marching to his limousine, answering the salutes of the guards he passed. Amah Jiejie emerged from the building, supporting an aged man in ill-fitting civilian clothes. At the bottom of the stairs he shrugged off her help and straightened, then proceeded at a slow, limping gait. The tall man had a determined, somehow graceful air about him despite his weakness and advanced age. The stubble of hair on his balding head was all gray. His cheap denim clothes hung on him as if arranged over sticks. But his eyes, though betraying the fear of every newly released prisoner, burned with a deep intelligence. His lean, weathered face turned toward the men in the exercise yard, who quieted and stared as they realized what was happening. Few of the old ones ever walked out of the camp.

The officer of the guard snapped a command and the high gates creaked open. The old man hesitated, looking at the guards as if for permission. He was leaving the only world he had known for over fifty years. The nearest guard nodded, and he slowly limped through the gate, gazing warily at the small group on the bench.

A low shuddering cry escaped Lhamo's throat. She collapsed onto the bench, weeping. Nyima took a halting step forward, tears streaming down her face. "Kolsang!" she cried and took another step, repeating the name. Jig suddenly gripped Shan's arm. "He has my mother's eyes!" she whispered, her voice gone hoarse. Her uncle had returned to the living.

AUTHOR'S NOTE

From time to time readers comment on what they perceive as threads of fantasy woven into my Shan novels, citing the role of demons, sorcerers, astrologers, fanciful costumes, and medieval-style structures. I remind them that while these are works of fiction, they are not fantasies. Until it was overwhelmed in the 1950s, Tibet was a world unto itself, so unique in every facet of its material and spiritual culture—including its routine use of symbolic demons, exotic rituals, and ancient buildings—that to outside observers it did indeed often seem mystical. It was a society that did not view economic and technological advancement as the primary goal of civilization—for centuries Tibetans' main use of the wheel, for example, was for mechanical praying devices—but instead focused on exploration of the human spirit. The characteristics that reflected such profound differences with our world may have an aspect of fantasy to some outsiders, but they were vital realities in traditional Tibetan life, and their vestiges can still be found today.

The main elements that appear in the backdrop of this novel are rooted in the Tibetan experience, past and present. Salt caravans that traveled over some of the most difficult terrain on the planet were a common feature of life in Tibet for centuries, as were the shrines that offered spiritual nourishment to those intrepid trekkers. For hundreds of years treasures, nearly always spiritual in nature, were deliberately hidden by lamas to surprise and benefit future generations, acts that for me have always reflected both the whimsy and the eternal hope that are ingrained in the Tibetan DNA. This same selfless, spiritual character meant that precious metals and gems were used primarily to honor deities, not as signs of wealth. Astrologers were esteemed members of many Tibetan communities, providing both death charts and horoscopes, and demon costumes were frequently utilized in Buddhist festivals.

Tibet was famed throughout central Asia and China for its doctors and medical colleges, which practiced diagnosis and treatment based on principles unknown in the West. Tibetan medical colleges developed the richest natural pharmacopeia ever known, made possible by expeditions of monks and doctors who harvested rare medicinal plants on high alpine slopes. Tibetan *amchis* considered both the empirical and the spiritual roots of illness in treating their patients, and they were diagnosing some diseases centuries before their European counterparts. The *amchis'* sophisticated techniques for diagnosis by pulse reading—including even use of subtle pulses in the earlobe—have never been matched in the West, where medicine has always been a purely scientific pursuit.

The 1897 earthquake referred to in these pages wracked Tibet and the entire eastern Himalayan region. In an area of more than a hundred thousand square miles, nearly all masonry structures were destroyed. Temples collapsed, villages were wiped out, waterways shifted, and the earth's crust rose more than fifty feet in some places. It is safe to assume that more than a few underground chapels, like the *gonkang* described herein, were never the same.

That natural devastation, however, pales in comparison to the seismic ruin caused when Mao Tse-tung unleashed his Red Guard revolutionaries. The dismantling of Tibetan institutions by the Chinese army during the previous decade was escalated on a massive scale by the Red Guard during the mid-1960s. Mayhem was inflicted not only on the million-plus Tibetans who were killed or maimed; it extended to the very foundations of their ancient culture. Ninety percent of Tibet's temples and monasteries were annihilated. Tibetan medical colleges, including the world-renowned school at Chokpori, near Lhasa, were blasted to rubble, with no attempt to preserve their unique, centuries-old learnings about the mysteries of the human body.

While the destruction was particularly widespread in Tibet, it was not confined to that land. Those teenage cadres, equipped with military weapons, not only attacked fixtures of traditional life and those who embraced it, they actually devised ways to assault the past itself. In China, Mao's zealots dug up the body of the seventy-sixth-generation direct descendant of Confucius and hanged it, then ripped apart an ancient Ming dynasty tomb and burned the bodies of the emperor and empress resting inside. The wounds inflicted by the Red Guard are still so raw that very few who endured the era will openly speak of those dark years.

The shadow that settled over Tibet decades ago sometimes makes writing novels set in that land feel like searching for jewels in a dim cave. It is tempting for Western observers to write off Tibet as an abject example of an entire culture that was wiped out as a result of global geopolitics. But Tibet is not destroyed. Rather, for me it has always been an example of how a people with deep spiritual and cultural foundations can endure sustained adversity. The shadow may exist, but dig a little deeper and brilliance can still shine through.

Eliot Pattison